Also by .

Carter's Return

By

Peter Phillips

New Generation Publishing

Karl thanks for all your patients

And to Carol for giving him all the time

Love D.C.

Carter's return

Carter recently promoted to the rank of, Deputy Commander CID, had on receipt of his new rank, asked to be allowed a twelve month sabbatical on personal grounds. His immediate boss, Commander Tony Frost CID, although knowing how much he'd be missed, consented.

The main reason for Carter's sabbatical was due mainly to the tragic death of his wife, Helen and their two children, murdered on the orders of a psychopath, in an effort to slow Carter, and his team down on their investigations.

It had been four years since the loss of Helen. During his time off from the force, he visited and spent two months with Helens parents, making frequent visits to the grave of both Helen, and their children. He found it a wrench having to say good bye to her parents, but realised that he had to head home to his own place.

Carter returns home after two month, he was greeted by Mrs Murphy, his housekeeper. Carter is left mulling about his flat constantly recalling the happy times that he had spent with Helen.

He saw Helen as a true friend, partner, and wife. He strongly believed that police officers who spend so much time delving into the cesspit of life, which seems to manifest itself when dealing with high end crime, should have a bolt hole such as a warm, and tender home life. Both Carter and Helen found a perfect life.

He unpacks his belongings. The following morning he attends at Tom's deli, for a full English breakfast.

It's whilst he is eating that he notices an attractive lady, who shows an equal interest.

Unbeknown to Carter, the attractive lady works for Sam, Lloydie's partner. Carter is invited to a dinner party at, Sam and Lloydie's flat. He there meets Penny, the very same lady from, 'Tom's deli.' A relationship evolves.

One morning Penny tells Carter, that his phone has g.

Carter is sent for, by his boss, Commander Frost.
And so it begins.

Chapter One

Carter awoke on the first morning of his sabbatical, for a split second he thought better get ready for work. That thought quickly diffused from his mind, for he lay back in bed smiling to himself, 'Well son, this is the beginning of a totally new concept in your life' for you can slob around, and act in whichever way you like.

He decided that if all else fails there was always *'Tom's'* his mainstay, and provider for the reasonably priced full English breakfast. He showered, shaved, and for once not having to indulge in his usual working garb, he smiled as he stood and picked out some casual clothes.

On arrival at Tom's they all made their usual fuss. Tom, lead the way to a table on the raised area of his deli. As Carter walked towards his table he plucked from the newspaper holder, one of the daily's.

Tom brought Carter's usual mug of black coffee, he then took his order. All the staff knew to leave Carter with his thoughts. It was whilst he waited for his meal that he decided to call, Diane and Martin Helens parents, to invite himself down to their farm.

Carter received a warm invite over the phone. On completion he replaced his phone on the table. As if by magic Tom ghosted over with his breakfast. He began his meal with gusto only stopping to hold up his mug, to gain Tom's attention for; it was never taken as him being rude, but a sign for a refill. Tom never took exception. He rested his newspaper on the menu holder, only again pausing to turn the page of the paper.

He was fully aware of the interest being shown by a very attractive lady, sat at one of the nearby tables. Carter tried to act nonchalantly, hoping not to portray any of his inner feelings.

The lady remained very discreet managing to sneak the odd look in his direction whilst gainfully eating her *club* sandwich.

On completion of his meal, Carter got up replacing the paper in the paper rack he walked up to the desk, and paid his bill. Tom said, "Thanks Carter, and hope to see you soon we hope?" He smiled saying, "Sorry Tom, it's your breakfast I crave, you I like, but I can't eat you." Both laughing, Carter turned and left.

Carter had no sooner left when the attractive lady walked up to pay her bill. Looking at Tom she said, "Did I hear correctly, was your last customer called, Carter? And is he a frequent diner?"

Tom looked at the lady, "The man comes here because it's quiet, and we respect his privacy. I'm sorry I am not at liberty to answer your questions, good day."

The attractive lady returned to her office at the 'John Moors University' building. On parking her car she walked over to her building, in the corridor she bumped into Sam, her American boss, and director of the criminal psychology department.

Sam dressed as usual in her very casual type clothes said, "Hello Penny, what's up? You look upset, come and have a coffee."

The two ladies entered Sam's office, Penny headed for one of the comfortable arm chairs. After letting her settle, Sam walked over offering Penny her mug of coffee. Sam then went and sat behind her desk.

After five minutes Sam said, "Shoot" Penny replied, "Well, I was minding my own business, eating my sandwich during my early lunch break, when I happened to look up to my left, and wham! This great looking guy came in and ordered a full English breakfast. He went over and picked up a newspaper from the rack, he was no stranger to the place, seated, he then immersed himself in it."

"I managed to snatch a quick peep at him when he turned the page of his paper. Eventually he paid for his meal and left, I caught the name, Carter! And I asked the manager a couple of questions about him. To which I got a very curt reply."

Sam's eyes lit up, "Hey Penny, were you eating in a small deli on Allerton Road, called, *'The Auberge'* known affectionately as, *'Tom's deli'?"* Penny replied, "Yes, why, do you know the place it was recommended to me?" Sam replied, "Yes, Penny it's a famous watering hole of a great friend of ours, who just happens to be called, Carter."

Penny was euphoric, "Sam, Sam how the hell do you know him?" Sam with a wry smile on her face replied, "He's my partner's boss..." Penny interrupted, "But Sam! Isn't your partner a police officer?" To which Sam replied, "Yep."

Penny's coffee time with Sam, lasted for about an hour, as Sam painstakingly brought her up to date about Carter. When Sam had finished Penny sat back in her chair, totally speechless.

Sam looked at Penny, "Now you know the whole story, I have to say that Carter is a very introvert type of person when off duty, and asks for people who know him, to give him space. He never chases the limelight, and yet as the leader of the 'Major Crime Unit' on successful detections and arrests, it's always his name that is so prominent."

"Now on his own, he will on his return from his 12 months sabbatical drive the team from the front as usual. Although as recently promoted, Assistant Commander CID he will relinquish some of the reigns to his very capable deputy, WDC Sue Ford, and in there somewhere, my Jim and Ian his two DI's who would walk on broken glass for him."

"Working full bore he demands full loyalty to himself, as well as total loyalty to his team colleagues. He derives such comfort from the team. In his personal life his team will always come first, second, and third. He explained to Helen his wife, that he had two mistresses in his life, his wife, and his team. Although Helen, became the closest, during their life together they split up on three occasions. Are you still interested?"

Penny said, "Sam I'm your Director of research for your department, with a shy look on her face she said, "Do they ever hold parties?" Sam said, "Well not as frequent since the death of his wife." Smiling she continued, "But perhaps we may think of something."

Chapter Two

On Carter's return to his flat he quickly pulled from the wardrobe a brown canvas hold all. He quickly packed thinking he would spend some welcomed R and R down on the farm.

When ready he phoned Mrs Murphy, the wife and widow of his first uniform sergeant. He had asked her if she would keep house for him, which was beneficial to them both. He informed her that he'd be away for a time, and will contact her when he returns.

He locked up, leaving for his car, in the foyer he told the doorman that he'd be away for a few weeks, he said his goodbye's and left.

The journey to his in-laws farm took about 40 minutes he eventually left Whitchurch, heading for the beautiful village of, Calverhall.

Carter never failed to appreciate the absolute beauty of the countryside, which enhanced the area. He thought the best was when leaving the hamlet of, Ash it was but a cock's stride to Calverhall. He often thought back to the first time he ever came to Helens parents.

His mind remembered the arrival into the hamlet was heralded by a left hand bend, and with the high hedges it was as if you were suddenly deposited into one of the most picturesque hamlets in the country.

To top it all, it only consisted of a shop come post office, a pub, a smattering of houses, and the beautiful Norman parish church carved out of local stone, which stood regally, surrounded by some of the oldest headstones, in the graveyard.

As Carter passed the church he turned right into the farm entrance, going over the cattle grid, and headed for the farmhouse. On either side of the road the fields were full of Hereford cattle, the signature bread of the Sinclair's.

On arrival at the farmhouse the door opened, and as

usual Pippa and Bruce Helen's two faithful Labrador dogs ran to greet him. Opening the car door Carter, alighted bending down to greet them. They were of course followed by Martin and Diane, Helen's parents. Greeting Carter, with their ceremonial hugs, they ushered him into the welcoming kitchen.

Diane made hot drinks, Carter sat and the two dogs took up station, lying at his feet. Carter looked up at Martin and with tears in his eyes said, "My God Martin after all this time, they never ever seem to forget." Martin just smiled, "Why of course." Carter asked if he could put his things in Helens room. Diane exploded, "Carter! You don't have to ask, yes of course, and let that be the end to it."

As he walked passed Diane he lent down and kissed her on the top of her head, she raised a hand and stroked the side of his face.

As Carter left for the car to recover his bag, he was closely followed by the two dogs. He collected his bag, and made for Helens room, together with his escorts. On entering the room the two dogs rushed forward and jumping on the bed, Pippa, laid with her head resting on the shoulder of Bruce, who lay with his head resting on his two front paws, which were crossed.

Carter unpacked his few things he quickly opened the door to Helens wardrobe, and while doing so, inhaled with large gulps, all of the scented smells, reminding him of Helen. Carter looked at the two dogs that suddenly looked up, "How about a walk?"

There was an almighty noise of the dogs pours attempting to gain traction on the wooden landing floor, although always beating Carter to the front door. He smiled, "Just going out, or being taken for a walk?"

Outside in the yard he met the stockman, Jimmy who on seeing Carter, and the dogs removed his cap saying, "Good afternoon Mr Carter, sir, it's so good to see you, unfortunately Amy, and Doris, are all grown up, having calves of their own, in fact they are in this top field, would you like to see them?"

Carter's face beamed, "I'd love to Jimmy, and will it be okay to bring the dogs?" Jimmy roared, "Why yes, Mr Carter, sir, all the cows are used to the dogs, they are well trained they never worry the cows, or calves."

Jimmy led the way and followed by the dogs they headed off for the field. On arrival he saw two calves lying in the grass, closely attended by their mothers. As Carter walked over a wonderful thing happened, both the mothers walked over towards him, they stood off for a couple of seconds, and then walked over to him and nudged him one after the other.

Carter, sat on the grass field crossed legged, and stroked the heads of the two mothers, who had both lowered their heads allowing him to do so. Whilst this was happening, Jimmy returned with a bucket of young calves cattle feed. Handing it to Carter he said, "There you go sir, see if you still have the knack.

Carter slowly walked towards the two calves, he crouched and kneeling waited for the two young calves to get up and trot over. He looked up at Jimmy and with tears in his eyes he said, "My God, Jimmy if only...Jimmy interrupted, "Yes, I know Mr Carter, sir."

After that wonderful experience he thanked Jimmy and continued on his walk.

Chapter Three

During his stay with Helens parents, Carter had endless walks in the country with his two friends, plus feeding the calves belonging to Amy, and Doris.

One Saturday evening, Carter and Helens, parents had a lovely meal in the *'Olde Jack'* the local pub in the village. To say a lovely meal, it was sumptuous, and set in a lovely extension built onto the side of the pub, they were all impressed. It was the same place that Diane and Martin, with pride introduced them both to announce their engagement.

After a wonderful month, one morning after breakfast Carter, told Diane and Martin, he needed to leave for home, as he had things to attend to. Outside in the yard Carter, said his goodbyes he lent down also saying goodbye, to Pippa and Bruce.

He got into his car and as he drove off the two dogs ran after him for about 30 yards, they both stopped turned and slowly trotted back towards Diane and Martin.

On leaving the farm's drive he turned left and pulled up at the church. Leaving his car he went to Helen and the children's grave. He stood for about 10 minutes all their thoughts came flooding back. He stood with tears rolling down his face. He asked ask Helen to understand, that if he should meet another... He turned and wiping his eyes, left for the car.

Chapter Four

On his return he had contacted Mrs Murphy, telling her he was on his way home. On arrival he shouted. "Good morning" to the doorman, and walked up to his flat. Opening the door he was met by Mr Murphy. "Morning Carter, welcome home, I've put all the mail on the centre island in the kitchen, coffee in ten?"

He smiled as he walked to the bedroom to unpack his bag. Looking inside he lifted his clothes from the bag, perfectly ironed and packed by Diane, prior to leaving.

Entering the kitchen he sat while Mrs Murphy poured out his coffee. He looked through his mail separating all the junk mail, while he was doing it he said, "Mrs Murphy, isn't it time that I called you by your Christian name, you do have one?" "Carter don't be so bloody cheeky." They both fell about laughing.

He looked at her and smiling he said, "Well?" She spluttered, "What would Tom, say?" Carter said, "Well he'd kick my arse for asking, but as he's not here, just go ahead." Blushing she said, "Kate." He looked at her, "Kate it is then."

Carter took his coffee and the remnants of his post and walked through to the lounge. He sat on the settee and began to sift through the letters. One jumped out from all of the others.

He took a sip of coffee, and replaced his mug down on the coffee table, and began to open the silver engraved envelope, having a design in each of the coroners. On opening the envelope he saw an equally lavished designed invitation card.

Carter read that he had been invited to an evening '*Soiree*' being organised by Sam and Lloydie, at their flat, on Saturday 14th June, 7pm for 7.30pm. RSPV Carter picked up his mobile and called Sam via his speed dial facility.

"Morning Sam, what a lovely surprise, I've just this

very instant returned from Helens parents. I realise that your invite is for this very Saturday. Christ, Sam, a *'Soiree'?* Sam laughing said, "Well Carter, I sent out the invites two weeks ago, not realising that you've been away on leave."

"Will you be joining us?" Only if you tell me whom will be there, then I'll give you my reply." Sam replied, "Sue and Peter, Ian and Wendy, and Lloydie and me." Carter laughed, "I'm in."

The following morning Penny, found a white envelope under her office door, picking it up, she walked over to her desk, as she walked she read the note inside... *'He's in'* Penny, screamed with delight.

Chapter Five

On Saturday the day of the dinner party, he spent most of the day relaxing watching sport on, TV in between deciding what he was going to wear, for the evening *'Soiree'*

Carter went into the bathroom to shower and shave. On completion he wrapped a large towel around his waist, he then sat on a chair in the bedroom enabling him to cool down prior to dressing, as he stood, and walked over to his wardrobe, looking for something to wear. He thought if only...his thoughts immediately recalled how Helen always seemed to know.

He sighed, Oh well. Carter selected a blue Ben Sherman shirt, a pair of grey trousers, a blue blazer, and a black pair of loafers, and socks.

Prior to dressing, and only in a pair of boxer shorts, he went into the kitchen. Opening the fridge door, were he took out a can of larger. Relaxing he drank the lager, whilst looking forward to the evening.

Dressed, and then when ready, on leaving he pulled the flat door locked. He then walked, stepping down into the foyer. On arrival he got into the awaiting cab. After a 20 minute ride he arrived outside of Sam, and Lloydie's flat. Alighting from the cab, he climbed up the three steps and knocked on the door to their flat. The door was answered by Lloydie.

Lloydie said, "Evening sir, please come on in." Carter shook hands with Lloydie, "Hello Jim, how are things?" He quickly followed with. "As Eric once said, never, ever answer to that question, as you're likely to be covered in a load of shit."

As they both laughed, and talked in the hall, they were joined by Sam, "Precious, are you both staying out here all night? Carter looked at Jim and mouthed 'Precious' Jim blushed, "Boss can that be our secret?" Carter replied in a sarcastic dulcet voice, "Why, yes of course Jim" He thought I'm fucked.

He brought Carter through. Jim stood to one side saying, "Please sir do come in." Carter immediately turned and whispered, "Before we go any further, Jim no titles okay."

In the lounge Carter said hello to Sue, Peter, Wendy, and Ian. Sam turned, "Carter this is Penny Wilkinson, who works in my department, and volunteered in assisting me, tonight.

When they all had said their, 'Hello's' whilst Sam, and Penny, were gainfully engaged in the kitchen, Jim whilst refreshing their drinks, joined with Carter as he talked with Sue, and Ian, who brought him up to date on a few things, not wishing to talk too much shop, cutting their partners out.

Eventually Jim said, "Dinner is served." They all walked through to the kitchen to take up their seating arrangements around their large kitchen table. Sam sat next to Lloydie, Ian next to Wendy, Sue next to Peter, with Carter, left sitting next to Penny.

Sam, nodded to Penny, and they both got up and walked over to the two large ovens, when opened they took out trays of assorted hot meats, tureens' filled with roast potatoes, and vegetables. All the meats for serving were on large oval size platters, which were placed down the middle of the table, together with three bottles of red, and three bottles of white wine.

When sorted they all helped themselves to the sumptuous food. There was the usual throng of conversations all going on at the same time.

After polite conversation, Penny said to Carter, "And where do you fit in with the assembled company?" Carter, who had been bowled over with her beauty replied with a smile on his face, "Oh! I work with Jim, Ian, and Sue." As Penny said it, Wendy, coughed almost choking on her drink. Ian gently kicked her under the table.

As the meal continued and they were all chatting. Carter looked at Penny, and in a quiet voice whispered, "I meant to ask you, Miss Wilkinson, did you enjoy your chicken sandwich in Tom's the other day?" Penny looked Carter in the eyes, please call me Penny, and without skipping a heartbeat said, "Oh! Why?"

Carter smiled, "Well, I happened to come top in my surveillance lecture, on my CID course, and immediately recognised you when I first arrived."

Penny leant over saying, "It's a fair cop guv are you going to put the cuffs on me? And with a wicked look in her eyes she said, "Please say you will."

Carter stood up, and Penny thought, Oh! Shit, although the more disappointed, for she noticed that Carter asked if he could have some more roasters. He smiled down at Penny, "Did that shock you, and did you think I was going to nick you?"

For the rest of the evening they were deep in conversation, Sam looked over in Penny's direction, whilst she was talking with Carter, and winked.

The meal completed, Jim brought in two coffee pots, and a pot of hot milk, whilst Sam put a selection of liqueurs on to the table.

On leaving Carter thanked Jim and Sam, for the lovely evening, for he had called a cab, while the rest were busy talking Carter looked at Penny, could I offer you a lift? Penny smiled, "Yes please, one should always be safe in the company of a police officer." He laughed, "You'd think?" They again laughed.

In the cab and away from prying eyes they exchanged phone numbers... Minutes later the cab pulled up outside of her apartment. He opened the door as she leant forward to get out she kissed Carter, "Will you call me?" He said, "How about tomorrow?" With a radiant smile she replied, "That would be lovely."

Chapter Six

The next morning Carter awoke at about 8.30am, he realised his first thought was to ring Penny. He dressed in sweats and walked through to the kitchen, he turned on the coffee percolator. Minutes later while sat at the kitchen's island, he poured himself a mug of coffee.

He picked up his phone and called Penny, it was answered on the second ring. *'Hello'* It's Carter; sorry I forgot it was Sunday, perhaps I should have rung later?" Penny replied, *'No Carter that's fine.'* Carter thought he could detect a note of excitement.

"Wondered if you had any plans for today?" Penny replied, *'Washing my hair, doing the cleaning, and ironing, whilst waiting for this gorgeous chap, who promised to ring me"* Carter said, "Well I'd better get off the phone." Penny shouted down the phone, *'Carter, and no, I have no plans for today.'*

Carter said, "Well how about I pick you up in about an hour?" She screamed, *'An hour, see ya.'* and replaced the receiver. Penny picked up the phone, and rang Sam, after two rings, Sam answered Penny shouted down the phone, *'Carter's asked me out'* and replaced the receiver.

At about 11am Carter pulled up outside of her apartment. Penny was waiting in the foyer. Carter got out of his car and stood next to it. Penny walked towards him. She certainly looked lovely. Her dark shoulder length hair was still damp, evident of a recent shower.

Penny wore a fawn polo neck sweater, a brown leather jacket, over washed out jeans, and brown loafers, she was carrying a brown shoulder bag, clasped in her hand.

Walking up to Carter she kissed him gently on the mouth. They both got into the car and as Carer drove away he said, "Are you hungry?" Penny replied, "Starved" Carter said that's good, as I know this place that makes great breakfasts." They both burst out laughing.

On arrival at Tom's they both walked in and was

greeted warmly by Tom. He looked at Penny. "Madam you seem to have had your questions answered. He invited them both to follow him to the top end of the deli, sitting them at Carter's usual table.

During breakfast they both chatted, Carter spent a brief time explaining to Penny his career to date, most of which Sam had already mentioned. Penny never for one moment gave any indication of her knowledge of his personal life.

After breakfast, ad after Carter had settled the bill, they said their good buys and left for his car, when inside Carter said, "I see you have walking shoes on, fancy a walk around *'Colderstone's Park'*? Penny agreed. Carter said, "I've a surprise for you."

On the outset of their walk, Carter noticed that Penny had linked his arm, he immediately felt at home. After about an hour and a half and several meetings with excited dogs getting under their feet, Carter steered them both towards the ice cream parlour, where they both selected large cornets filled with delicious flavours.

They both sat at a nearby table, which overlooked nearby building which had once been stables, but now had been converted into garages for the park personnel's vehicles.

Whilst they both watched the various children jumping up and down with excitement, pulling on the hands of their parents, whilst waiting in line anxious to see the assorted flavours of the ice cream on offer. As they got closer to the shop their voices increased in pitch.

One of the many families had a dog with them that sat more patiently than their children, obviously anxious to impress.

Chapter Seven

Carter and Penny's relationship started to flourish, a situation that they both encouraged, they were in Carters flat, and on one occasion after making love, Penny collapsed on top of him, saying, "My God Carter, it gets better each time." Carter pushed the duvet back and invited Penny to join him in the shower.

He turned on the shower, as Penny entered he began to soap her body with a soap glove. Her body was covered in soap she turned and began to rub herself up against Carter, Penny then used the glove to soap Carter all over.

Penny with a wicked look in her eyes said, "Oh! Carter I see you're ready for seconds. They both washed the soap from off their bodies. Carter wrapped Penny in a large bath sheet, and lifted her carrying her through to their bed.

He gently laid her on the bed, and Carter kneeled on the floor, and gently removed the towel while he started to kiss Penny all over her body. Penny responded with little noises of pleasure, whilst he rested his head on her lap, she gently opened her legs and he started pleasuring her in the most wonderful way.

Penny had to resort to stuffing the corner of the towel in mouth to stop her from screaming. Carter straightened Penny around and realising that they were both ready he entered her, she shouted, "Please God Carter I hope you are ready I can't wait much longer, with that they both began to feel an electrifying shudder pass between their bodies.

The following morning as Carter awoke he kissed Penny good morning, he then got up and went into the shower, as Penny was about to join him, she heard the sound of his phone activating. Penny put on his dressing gown, on entering the bathroom she said, "Carter it's your phone?"

Carter wrapped a towel around his waist, and as he walked through to the lounge, and with a second towel he busily rubbed his hair, to stop the excess water dripping onto the floor.

He walked over to the breakfast bar, and picking up the phone he identified the number of the force control number. He rang 709-6010 a voice said, *"Duty Inspector how may I help you?"*

Carter said, "This is Carter." The Inspector suddenly identified the voice, realising who it was said, *"Yes sir, will you please contact Commander Frost, at your earliest."*

On returning to the bedroom he noticed that Penny had laid out some clothes for him. Carter walked into the bathroom, just as Penny was getting out of the shower. He immediately took in the image of her beautiful body, and her pert breasts. Carter intuitively thought, down boy.

"Penny said, "Is it work?" He replied, "I don't know, I've just been told to contact Tony Frost?" Penny returned to the bedroom.

He dressed, and after which he thanked Penny for placing out his clothes. When he walked through to the lounge he said, "I wonder what he wants?" Penny replied, "Well you won't know unless you call him." After two rings the phone was answered, *"Frost"* "Sir it's Carter, did you want me?" *"Yes Carter we have a problem...* Carter interrupted him, "But Sir, what about my sabbatical?"

Tony Frost blasted, *"Carter you are my deputy, I've sorted an office out at HQ."* He replied, "If I'm coming back early, He said, "Now sir you know where my office, and team are, I do hope you haven't changed things."

"Alright Carter, make Derby Lane at your earliest, we have a problem." The phone went dead.

Penny, who had dressed passed Carter a mug of black coffee, after thanking her Penny said, "Carter is everything okay." He replied, "He's recalling me back to work, "On my return he wants me to work out of HQ?"I won't have it, my team and I work from Derby Lane police station."

Carter looked at Penny, "Can I call you later, to tell you if I'll be late, will you come here after work, and we can have a meal together?" Penny smiled, "Carter I'll be wherever you need me." Carter turned and kissed Penny on the lips, as he left for his car.

Chapter Eight

Whilst on his way to the office, Carter thought of all the similarities experienced, knowing full well it had all been started between him and Helen. He thought of the conversations that he'd had with Sam, and felt less guilty.

He then contacted Eric. The phone was answered in seconds, *"Morning sir the coffee is on, and we're all waiting to greet you."*

Carter interrupted, "Eric, I thought they were putting you out to grass?" Eric replied, *"Well, sir it was considered, as we all thought you'd be working from HQ on your return, in an office next to TF, with Jane as your new secretary?"* Carter said, "No bloody chance." Carter heard Eric roaring down the phone.

He said, "I will be with you shortly, will you kindly summon all personnel, and I mean all personnel."

On arrival in the police yard, he met Eric, and Sue waiting for him. He shook hands with Eric, and gave Sue a big hug. He then followed them both up to the general office.

He signed on duty, after which he looked around the office, where are your young ladies?" Eric coughed, "They've been moved to other offices." Carter shouted, "What!" He continued, "After our chat get on to the admin department and get them back, any problems refer them to me."

En route to the conference room he noticed the smirks on their faces. Sue said, "Welcome back boss." Carter smiled at them both.

On entering, all the attending personnel stood to attention. Carter said, "As you were." Carter went and stood next to Sue, at the head of the room. He said, "Before we get started, I want to mention two matters. 1. I get the feeling that senior management thought that I'd relocate to HQ, 'Rubbish'

There was a raw of laughter. He put up his hand, "And

2. They thought that they could re-gig the set up, 'Rubbish' Again another ring of laughter went around the room.

Carter looking around the room said, "I have not altered my stance on when we're all in this room, that I will not welcome any stuff shirted greetings. Outside DCS Ford will be known as 'Boss' and I'll be 'Sir' But around here, I will be called, 'Guv' Now allow me to get up to speed with my senior officers, do I still have an office?"

Eric when on their own said, "Carter you don't know how proud I am on your promotion, and in my book, I will always refer to you as 'Sir' Carter went over and gently banged his head on the office wall. He then took the welcome cup of coffee from him, and left for his office.

As he opened the door, all his team stood to attention. He looked at them saying, 'What,' were you not listening to what I said back in the conference room?" Sue said, "Please guv allow us on this occasion to show our respect."

There was a knock on his door he said, "Come in" They all looked up to see one of Eric's young ladies, grinning from ear to ear, carrying a tray of hot drinks. Placing it on his meeting table she looked up at Carter saying, "Thank you sir." She turned and left.

Carter laughing said, "Well has the shit hit the fan?" Sue placed a file in front of him. Opening it he saw picture of an Asian girl lying on the side of the road. He recognised that his team, and Mr Chambers the pathologist, were in attendance, as seen in some of the photos.

After looking through them he looked up at Sue, saying, "What do we have?" Sue replied, "Well guv we got a call yesterday from the control room, reporting the incident, that she had been found with a gunshot wound to the side of her head." Carter replied, "What is her condition?" Sue replied, "The girl was whisked away to the Royal A and E, Lloydie followed it up."

He looked at Jim Lloyd, "Lloydie, does this young lady

realise that you only follow the dead?" There was a raw of laughter. Looking at Carter he said, "Guv the trauma team removed a 9mm bullet from just above her right ear; shot aimed at her head, the bullets tangentially took it under her scalp, lodging above her right ear, she is at present under protection in 'Major obs.' to the rear of A and E."

Looking around the table he said, "I realise that the boss informed TF, who panicked and recalled me. Now, I do not want any folk to realise that senior management have flipped on receipt of the call. Now your boss and I will get together and chat over this."

"In the meantime let's be all over this." Sue, looked over, "Peter and Philip and some of the team are there as we speak, and will update us later."

Carter said, "Right, DCS Ford and I are off to the hospital to see the victim."

They all stood and left. In the general office Sue informed Eric, "We're off to the hospital to see the victim, and we'll be in touch." Eric smiling looking at Carter and said, "Perhaps guv, you may start with a call to TF at your earliest convenience." Looking at Eric he said, "You think you're so bloody funny."

As they both walked along the corridor they could hear Eric laughing. In the yard Carter said, "Sue do you mind if we go in your car?" Sue smiling said, "Carter, sir, do you happen to have five pennies for a shilling?" Carter looking at her laughing face said, "Oh! Now there it is? The Penny joke, you want to get in on the act as well, just drive please, Chief Superintendent."

En route to the hospital, Carter, explained to Sue, how he felt being called back off his sabbatical. While she brought him up to date on things both happening in, and out of the office. In the mean time they arrived at the hospital, and leaving the car, both walked into the A and E. They both showed their id's and were summoned through.

Chapter Nine

As Carter, together with Sue walked through what seemed to be the aftermath of a major incident in the A and E unit, they came across the delightful, Sister Chris Atkinson, on seeing Carter, all her staff stood to attention. Carter said, "And yes, there it is, even with your mob." Chris Atkinson, walked over and kissing him on the cheek saying, "Well done Carter, it's well deserved."

Sue, asked Chris for the gunshot victim's personal effects, and clothing. Chris went into her office, and returned with a large yellow coloured hospital patient's belongings bag.

Chris, said, "In my opinion your victim will be admitted into hospital, as in her condition it would result in approximately one weeks stay in hospital. Chris looking at them said, "You realise that your victim not only presents with a gunshot wound, but is showing signs of severe malnutrition. Her attending doctor states, it will be some time before you can speak with her."

Carter looked at Chris, "Could we both share your office to take a quick peep at the victim's property before we haul them off to Forensics. Chris smiled, "Yes, Carter help yourself, and I'll send in some hot drinks."

Sue offered Carter a pair of forensic gloves she then placed a large piece of paper onto the top of the desk. Sue slowly emptied the contents out. They then started to spread them out, before they methodically went through the victim's clothes and property.

Sue whilst she was examining the victim's trousers paused, for inside one of the pockets, she took out what appeared to be a crumpled piece of paper. When flattened on the desk, they both stood back with foreboding, as they both saw what appeared to part of a delivery note.

Carter said, "Sue will you call for SOCO to attend here at their earliest, we need blood samples for analysis, and in the meantime I'll take a photo of the delivery note, with my camera for our benefit. When finished we must go and have a word with the victim, to see what she can tell us?"

"Can you please contact the lads at the scene to look for a possible blood trail however faint; we need sniffer dogs down there, for the girl must have lost a lot of blood?"

Carter looked at his watch, it was 2.00pm, Carter said, "I won't be long, be back in a minute, and if you're a good girl will treat you to lunch." As he left the room Sue said, "Are you going to look for some change, as I have some pennies?" Carter said, "DCS Ford lunch is cancelled." Sue burst out laughing.

Out in the corridor Carter took out his phone, and dialled Penny's number. On the second ring Penny said, *"Hello Carter, I thought you'd forgotten all about me, I've been at my desk looking at my watch every five minutes."* Carter said, "Sorry, Pen, Oh Knickers you didn't mind me calling you, Pen did you Penny?" Penny laughed, *"Carter, that would be lovely,"* (Laughing to herself for her name was always reduced to, 'Pen' since a child)

Penny said, *"Would it be okay if I went round to yours, as I could prepare a meal for us?"* Carter said, "Look forward to it if I should be late, I'll call you."

Carter returned to Chris's office. He opened the door, and Sue said, "Guv, could SOCO meet us at Derby Lane, with the evidence?" Carter replied, "Call them back and let them know we need to see the victim first, and will be back at the ranch in, say an hour?"

They both walked to the back of A and E and in 'Major obs.' they were met by the uniformed officer as requested. On seeing Carter he stood to attention, "All correct Sir." Carter smiled saying, "As you were."

One of the duty nurses who took them both to a curtained area. Pulling the curtain back, their eyes fell on the victim lying in bed with her head swathed in bandages; she looked very pale, with a drip in her arm. Her eyes were closed and although her breathing was stable, it was clear to them both that any questioning would be futile.

As they were about to leave, Carter walked up to Chris,

asking could they inform his team should she come round. Chris agreed, Sue said, "We have an officer *'on call'* contactable via our control room we need to interview her as soon as possible."

In the car as they drove back to the office, Carter called Tony Frost, the phoned answered immediately, *"Frost"* Sir, it's Carter, just to let you know we may have a problem."

"The victim was found on the dock road, close to one of the gates. Members of the team together with SOCO, and police search dogs are all checking out the scene. We feel there could be a blood trail leading back onto the dock estate."

"The victim received a head wound, and we need to find the site of the shooting."

"The victim was whisked away by the paramedic's; Mr Chambers was on site, so I may have a preliminary medical report shortly." Frost said, *"Carter, keep me informed."* And the line went dead.

Back at Derby Lane, Sue, and Carter both booked back in, and went through to the conference room giving the victim's property to a SOCO officer.

Carter ordered sandwiches for their promised lunch; in the meantime, Sue and Carter returned to his office, they were both sat chatting, whilst having their lunch, whilst talking about the incident when there was a knock on his door. He shouted 'Come in' the door opened and the SOCO officer entered.

"Sir, I will have a more detailed report for you later, but off the bat, it would seem that the victims clothes are of Asian, or of Middle Eastern origin, there are a couple of makers names for us to check up on. There is heavy blood staining to her blouse particularly to the right side of her garments. I'm now off to the office, is there anything else?"

Carter looked at him saying "No thanks." The officer picked up the bag and left. Sue stood and said, "Guv I'm going to check on how things are doing, why don't you go home and I'll call you if anything develops, by being 'Sir' there is a privilege of rank." Carter smiling looked round, "Why not."

After Sue had left he picked up the phone and dialled Penny, after one ring it was answered, *"Carter how wonderful, is it good smiley news or bad crying news?* Laughing he said, "Well that's a new way of putting it, it's good smiley news. I should be home in half an hour, I could eat a horse." Penny replied, *"A horse it is then."* And burst out laughing.

Chapter Ten

Carter arrived home, and as he strolled through the foyer towards his flat, saying good evening to the doorman Paul, he was suddenly hit by a fusion of aromas, tantalising his nostrils' all adding to the anticipation of his expected evening meal.

As he opened the door to his flat he was met by Penny standing in the hall wearing just a halter necked apron. Penny walked up to Carter, and placing her arms about his neck, kissed him fully on his lips.

Penny guided Carter to the bedroom. He said, "But tea smells as if it's ready?" Penny smiled as she began to undress Carter saying, "Oh! That's, *'seconds'* you are about to have, *'first's'*

On completion yet again of another sexual experience, they both managed to accomplish a formidable level of lovemaking. Falling back in bed exhausted, Penny raised herself on one elbow, she looked down at Carter, and noticing a thin vale of perspiration covering his face, she realised something wonderful had just happened."

Penny said, "Carter, our love making is like music made, together we can play in perfect time and rhythm, and yet we both have our different needs, you have your desires, and I have mine. If we are both in sync, then we will both attain total satisfaction. We of course can tweak our level of music to increase our needs and satisfaction..." Smiling down at him she said, "Of course beware of the bum notes?"

After experiencing another of their exotic showers, they both dried off and dressing in sweats walked through to the kitchen. The smell was divine. Penny had already set the table as she reached down to remove the large glass casserole dish, and the tray of garlic bread, Carter smiled, "I see you had all this planned, and timed to perfection?"

The meal was delicious, Carter could not stop complimenting Penny, he said, "It's been years since I'd had a beef stew, with cobblers, I love the way they absorb a degree of the gravy."

"Penny threw her head back laughing said, "Well seeing as it started out as, spaghetti bolognaise, not bad, hey!" They both roared with laughter.

During their meal they both enjoyed a glass of red Merlot wine, and in between slurps talked about their day.

Penny leaned over and poured them a second glass of wine... It was at that point that Carters phone activated, looking at Penny with a look of anticipation, "Sorry love."

He walked through to the lounge and picking up his phone, Penny could not help hearing, "Yes, will you ask one of the lads to pick me up?"

Carter walked through to the bedroom after dressing; he walked back into the lounge where he met Penny. Looking at Carter she smiled saying, "On nights such as this, well at least I got the best of the deal?" Smiling she walked over to Carter, "Your second mistress is calling? Now remember, no matter how late wake me, or you'll be sorry."

After kissing Carter, they both heard the activation of the door inter com. Carter pocked up the handset and said, "I'll be down in s second." He kissed Penny and left.

In the hall he was met by Peter, looking at Carter he said, "Sorry guv, but it's all hands on deck." Entering the car he said, "Where are we off to?"

Peter replied, "To the docks guv, some of the team who dealt with the crime scene earlier had with the help of the dog section, they traced a blood trail into one of the large HGV parking areas." Carter sensed the air of trepidation in his voice.

Chapter Eleven

Peter set off with the blues and two's activated they sped off in the direction of the city centre, Peter decided to take the festival road, he joined Sefton Street, and headed towards the Strand, driving parallel with the Mersey, he joined Regent Road. It was whilst they headed along Regent Road that Carter got the full view of all the activity.

Peter on seeing the police road block cancelled the siren, it was set up at the junction of Regent Road, and Sandhill's Lane. All traffic wishing to complete their journey out of the City was directed up Sandhill's Lane, towards Derby Road.

A traffic officer wearing his cap, with a white cover and a high viz vest, walked towards their car. Both Carter and Peter produced their ID's, the officer who recognised Carter said, "All correct sir, I was warned of your arrival." And he walked over to remove the temporary barrier, allowing them access.

Peter continued their journey following the high dock wall on their left, known to have been built by the Napoleonic prisoners of war, until they arrived at, The Huskisson dock entrance. From some distance away Carter could see the bright halogen lights and the blue lights which emblazoned the night sky.

At the entrance to the dock estate they were met by a uniformed officer, who had been pre warned of their arrival. Peter stopped the car. He put down his window and showed his ID. The officer leaned in and looking at Carter said, "Sir, DCS Ford has set up a temp HQ by the dock warehouse straight ahead of you. Carter thanked him.

Carer could see some of his team walking in and out of the warehouse. He thanked Pete, and getting out of the car he walked towards the warehouse entrance. The warehouse was huge, further along the dock site some had been converted into flats.

As he entered he was met by Sue, dressed in her forensic suit. She walked towards him with a sullen face, which showed signs that she had been crying, evident by her red eyes, and smudged makeup.

Carter looking at Sue said, "What on earth is the matter?" She looked up at Carter, "Sir... Carter interrupted her, "Sue we're on our own." She gulped, "Sorry, Carter, it's a blood bath." Carter could see the strain on Sue's face, a typical trade mark when dealing with horrendous cases. As they began to walk Sue said, "You'd better take this." And she produced the usual forensic suit for him, Carter, dressed within minutes, as they walked she said,

"You can see all the fucking HGV's parked up, there are hundreds of them. As requested we gained the help of the dog section, your old friend *'Prince'* and his handler. He and Prince, followed a scent trail leading from where the girl was found by the dock gate, into the estate."

Due to all the amount of HGV's, and trailer units, parked up, you can imagine how difficult it must have been. *'Prince'* eventually led his handler, and our team members to the rear of one such trailer unit, Prince barked as he looked up making attempts to jump up at the two rear doors.

Carter tried to comfort Sue as she led him to their operational set up. On arrival he saw team members, and SOCO officers looking through a load of material, which he thought may have been removed from the initial vehicle.

Sue looking at Carter said, "Guv please follow me, but be prepared for the terrible sight inside of the trailer."

After a 5 minute walk between all the vehicles, he noticed the start of the usual blue and white police plastic tape, offering a narrow corridor that they needed to follow.

He stopped in his tracks, because as they came round a corner, he saw the bright arc lights of SOCO illuminating the area. Carter noticed the metal trays on which to stand left by SOCO, at the foot of some wooden erected steps allowing access through the two rear doors of the trailer.

He slowly walked up the steps, on reaching the top he stopped in sheer disbelief. As he looked around his eyes fell on Mr Chambers, the pathologist, who was bent over one of the victims. He saw eight other such bodies covered with yellow coloured plastic sheets.

He noticed blood splatter and lots of it, and brain particles everywhere along the walls of the trailer. He also noticed pools of blood seeping from under the sheets, and in places they made a large pool in the middle of the trailer.

Mr Chambers stood up, and with his usual booming voice said, "Carter, I see your back? Pleased to see you, sorry it's in such awful circumstances. What!"

He walked over to where Carter stood, with a look of utter shock and disbelief on his face. On this occasion there was no friendly banter between Carter and his close friend, the pathologist, who held Carter in great esteem. Both he and Carter realised that they were on the cusp of yet another major happening. Gordon Chambers said, "Carter this is a bad one, a sheer blood bath."

Gordon Chambers walked Carter over to each of the bodies, in order and he pulled back the yellow plastic cover from each of the victims in turn. At the first victim Carter noticed that it was a young Asian girl, with long black hair, her hair was matted with blood, Carter noticed a single gunshot wound to her head.

He noticed black soot, or powder burns to the side of her head it must have been at point blank range. The right hand side of her head was a mash of hair, brain, and blood.

Carter followed Gordon Chambers around each of the bodies, noticing that each victim showed similar signs of attack, but not all the victims were Asian.

The pathologist on completion of his gruesome task, looked at Carter and said, "This has been like the proverbial, shooting fish in a barrel. This trailer is your usual GHV length, that the killer or killers pulled the doors closed, and only had to turn to shoot each girl, at close range, the poor creatures had nowhere to hide, or to take any evasion action.

Sue spoke up to Carter, "Guv we think that another of the girls got away, as one young girl stopped a passing motorist having a gun shoot wound to the side of her head."

When all the girls had been examined, Gordon Chamber's, and Carter left to walk down the steps of the trailer back onto the floor.

Outside Carter said, "Have we done a PNC check of the registration to this bloody vehicle?" Sue replied "Yes, it's a Joey."

Back in the warehouse, all three managed a hot drink of coffee, Mr Chamber's walked over to his nearby medical bag, and taking out a bottle of scotch made sure each present took a nip of scotch in their drinks. Carter looked at the pathologist, "It's no wonder I like you? You always not only have the medical answers, but the answer to our immediate needs to hand."

Under other circumstances Carter's comment would have raised a laugh.

Gordon Chamber's looking at Carter said, "Do you think we can remove the girl's home? As I need to make a start on a more detail examination, of the victims.

Carter looked at Sue, "Well DCS Ford, don't look at me, it's your unfortunate case, which needs your decision." Sue smiled, and looking at the pathologist nodded. Looking back at Carter, Sue said, "There's no point in keeping obsie's on the trailer, as with all the activities of the last several hours, the offenders will realise there's been a police presence all over it."

Lloydie walked over to them both, "Boss do you want me to follow the girls? Sue was as ever grateful for it was a point she had picked up from Carter, nodded and thanked him.

As she turned Sue said, "Are you sure Lloydie, do you not need a hand?" He smiled, "No boss it's oaky I will manage. He turned and left for his car.

Carter looked at his watch it was 11.30pm. He looked

at Sue, "Let's go to the hospital, I think DI Baxter, together with Peter, and Phil can manage here." Sue said, "See if you can lock and secure the trailer, and this place, and arrange police cover of the site, and we'll continue tomorrow, good night." They both got the usual reply, "Good night Sir's." They both sniggered.

Chapter Twelve

En route to the hospital Carter was in with Sue, he took out his phone looking at Sue, "I'll put it on speaker. I'm calling TF and you can give him an update." Sue replied, "It's okay Carter, you go ahead."

The phone was answered on the second ring, "Sir it's Carter, together with DCS Ford, we're en route to the Royal." TF said, *"Why what's happened?"* Carter replied, "You know of the young girl found on Regent Road close to The Huskisson dock, with gunshot wounds to her head?"

"Well, DCS Ford, called me out tonight, as a search of the blood trail left by the victim, was picked up by the police dog, he found a HGV trailer inside of the dock estate, amongst a load of others, the dog went mad at the rear of one such trailer."

"Members of our team broke the seal, and found the bodies of nine girls all with gunshot wounds to their heads...TF shouted, *"What! You are fucking joking, sorry DCS Ford, I didn't mean the outburst but you do understand."* Sue said, "What outburst?" TF gave a weak laugh.

"Carter ring me when you have more information from the medical team." "Sir, DCS Ford will do the calling." TF said, *"Yes right."* And the phone went dead.

As they reached A and E Carter said, "Sue, I'll follow on." She smiled, "Yes Carter do you need some change...?" Carter smiled it was pointless.

After a few rings Carter heard Penny's voice, *"Hello stranger, "If you're not home shortly, I'll be closing up shop, but I may just warm up your side of the bed."* Carter replied, "Won't be long, see you shortly, have to go."

As Carter walked over to the entrance of A and E he smiled to himself, *'Now where have I heard that remark before?'*

In A and E Carter met up with Sue, who was talking

with Chris, turning Sue said, "There you are guv, the second girl who made it out of that bloody trailer, and I mean that in every sense of the word. Has been placed in, 'Major obs. and, in the same condition, only she has a deep gunshot wound to her head."

The difference being that the bullet in her case, grazed the side head, but equally caused a great loss of blood. The victim also presented, suffering from signs of malnutrition.

Sue dropped Carter off outside of his block of flats. He looked at his watch, "It's 1.30pm, I suppose it's the sofa for me?" Sue burst out laughing, "And the band played. *'Believe it if you like'* "See you later guv?"

Carter turned, "Sue let's sign on in the office and get any updates, before going down to the docks, we can also chat with the team."

On entering his block he acknowledged the doorman, and continued to his flat. He entered and went into the spare room, where he undressed. He walked through to their bedroom he gently lifted the duvet and got into bed.

Penny turned, "Carter your freezing, remain on your own side until you warm up." Penny snuggled up to him, "Or I suppose I could help out?" Carter turned into her saying, "Pen do you mind if we both go to sleep? This evening was a disaster; the wheels had truly fallen off."

Chapter Thirteen

The following morning Carter awoke and went through to the shower on his own. He stood and as on so many other occasions, he just let the water cascade over him. His sleep was punctuated by the sights that he had witnessed in that awful trailer.

On completion he dried, it was whilst he was shaving that the apparition of that, that was Penny, stood naked scratching her head. Looking at Carter she said, "Morning" Standing there completely naked on any other occasion would have resulted in a totally different reaction, but under the circumstances, it took him all his time to acknowledge her.

He turned thinking, 'Carter it's not Penny's fault?' He walked over to her and buried his head in the nape of her neck, with a muffled voice he said, "Morning, sorry about last night, the least I can do is to thank you for responding to my arrival in bed, however cold I presented."

Penny hugged him, "Carter please realise that I'm a willing listener, and were possible, not wishing to pry, will help in sharing the load. I do however realise that some matters are taboo, and as I haven't signed, *'The official secret act'* cannot always be privy to such matters."

She sat him down on the loo, with only a towel around him, and her in the nude, she knelt before him.

"Carter you do realise that I work with Sam, and although not a professor am qualified in such matters. It was then that he started to laugh, "Please tell me that you don't conduct your business this way with all your clients?" Penny looked up at him, "Why would you mind?" With that they both burst out laughing.

Carter dressed, and after Penny had completed her shower and dressed they both sat in the kitchen with their mugs of hot coffee. Penny said, "Was it terrible Carter?" With a pained look he said, "When I left after tea one of the team took me to the docks."

"Earlier in the day a young girl was found with a gunshot wound to her head, as a result of that the team together with the dog section made a search of the" "area, and *'Prince'* a favourite of mine from the dog section, found that the blood trail, and sent led to a HGV trailer.

Sue and the team gained access to the trailer which resulted in one of the most horrifying of crime scenes. For in the trailer, their torches scanned backwards, and forwards, revealing the bodies of nine young girls. It was a blood bath."

On my arrival, the bodies had been covered, yet as per protocol I together with the pathologist examined each of the bodies." Penny, who had begun to cry, sat back and covered her mouth with her hand to stifle a cry. "Oh! God Carter it must have been terrible?"

He looked at Penny, "I'm sorry but I must leave, I have a meeting first thing." Penny walked over to where he was standing, and kissed him, saying, "Remember Carter, however late, I'll be waiting up." He kissed her and left.

Penny, left about 15 minutes after Carter, on entering her office there was a knock at her, she called, and "Come in" The door opened and as Penny looked up from her desk, and saw Sam. Standing dressed in her usual garb of T Shirt and jeans. "Morning Sam, what can I do for you?"

Sam walked in and sat, making herself comfortable in an armchair opposite Penny's desk. Looking around her office she said, "How are things?"

Penny looking at Sam thought; well that's definitely a rhetorical question, for Penny realised that both of their loved ones, worked together, and probably engaged on the same case, as Carter, is Lloydie's boss.

Penny was the first to speak, "Sam, Carter came home late last night, as I suppose Lloydie did. Although late, I always feel that I should welcome him, after being called out, I thought it must have been something serious. As you must know it was?"

"He snuggled up to me, and although he put his arm

about me, never indicated any sign of a romantic endeavour, stating that he'd had a terrible night, through work. It was this morning that he told me how terrible."

Sam looked at her, "Penny, you would expect the same if things were reversed, but they're not. Now you'll remember the long talk we had, when you first told me of your thoughts regarding Carter?"

"You'll also be aware of the examples of the relationship he had with his wife, Helen? And how many breakups they went through, not only with the job, but the stress it put in their lives."

Sam looking at Penny said, "Men who have jobs such as theirs, need a place to chill. Call it a den, bolthole, or more conservatively, a mere home. But chill they must, it's no use storing things up, and even worse, not having a safety valve to release, and even more important a love one, partner, or wife with good listening skills."

As Sam stood to leave she turned saying, "One good thing about Carter he has the utter respect for his team, and knowing that they may be stretched, he always finds an occasion to let off steam, and I mean the whole team, and partners."

Carter is an excellent boss, the team all love him, one of his famous mantras... *'The whole is only as good as the sum of all its parts.'*

After Sam had left, Penny sat back and smiled to herself, well it won't be without a good input from me. She returned to the file on her desk.

Chapter Fourteen

Carter had just booked on duty, and was sat talking with Sue and Eric over their usual mug of coffees. Eric informed Carter that he had the enlargement required from his phone, and had pinned it up on the white boards, together with the terrible photos from SOCO of the scene.

The phone went on Eric's desk, he answered it in his usual way, "Morton MCU how can I help you?" After what appeared to be a longish silence both Sue and Carter looked round at Eric to see that the paler and intensity had left his face.

He stared at them both saying, "Yes will do, message timed at 09.15 hrs" And he replaced the receiver.

Carter looked at him, "Eric what on earth is the matter?" He coughed, and looking at them both said, "They have just found that one of the Asian victims in 'Major obs.' she has been found dead, shot in the head.

Staff made a search for the uniformed officer on security detail, and found his dead body in a store cupboard in 'Major obs.' Shot twice in the back of his head."

Sue shouted, "What!" Eric just sat and quietly nodded, units are attending from 'A' division." Carter stood up, "Eric will you show both myself and Sue en route to the Royal, I will contact TF on the way."

Looking at Sue he said, "We will go in your car, now let's go." As they left he turned saying, "Eric, will you page Ian, Lloydie, Peter and Philip, for them to meet us there, and have some of the team on standby here as we may need them."

In the car Carter called, TF he answered immediately, "I know Carter I'm en route as we speak. I want you there, together with DCS Ford, in assistance; the Chief is aware, and issued direct orders."

Sue had put on the blues and two's and gunning the car they cut through the traffic like a knife through butter. On arrival the traffic division had taken charge of the main entrance to the hospital, in Prescot street.

They had a temporary 'no entry' sign in place, and were re directing ambulances, visitors, and out patients through another second convenient entrance.

It was mayhem, but due to the major incident all personnel had to realise that a crime scene had to be preserved.

Sue and Carter entered the A and E by the original entrance, the reception desk had been re allocated to police personnel, on seeing Carter officer's stood to attention. Carter said, "As you were, who are present." A sergeant answered saying, "CID from 'A' division, Mr Frost warned us of your arrival, together with DCS Ford."

Carter and Sue met up with Chris Atkinson, amongst all the chaos. Looking at him she said, "At last Carter can you get this lot sorted?" Carter said, "Chris do you have a boardroom, type room that may accommodate our circus." She smiled, "Of course Carter, there is one such place behind the x-ray department."

Carter said, "Chris will you show Sue for me?" He continued, "Sue, will you then herd everyone up even, TF whilst I go through to the crime scenes.

He walked through to the 'Major Obs.' unit on arrival he noticed that all the patients had been moved apart from the dead Asian girl, whose body he could see, it had been covered with a sheet, with a faint blood stain which had seeped through the sheet.

As he looked passed the cubicle he could see the back of Mr Gordon Chambers, the pathologist, knelt next to the body of the uniformed officer. On hearing a noise he turned.

"Ah, there you are Carter I was informed of your arrival. We all of us, are aware that death one way or another is inevitable, but death of a colleague, particularly one so young is unpalatable. I feel that all of this is connected?"

"He smiled, now come over here, the two men were on

their own, although SOCO officers were in an out, but far too busy to pay them any heed. Gordon chambers whispered, "It's not a pleasant sight old chap, so let me get it over and done with."

Carter who was already dressed in his forensic suit, walked very reluctantly towards him. Mr Chambers moved to one side to reveal the officer with two gunshot wounds the back of his head that he must have knelt prior to his death, as he was sloped over to his right. Carter took a step back, he to whispered, "It's execution style?" Gordon Chambers in a loud voice said, "Exactly" "We must also realise that the culprit had a silencer, or suppresser fitted to his pistol.

"You can see that the bullets must be still in his head, but one can clearly see gunshot residue to the rear of the victim's head, I think they may well be 9mm's and so yes, our friends are leaving a message." Carter whispered, "I'll give them a fucking message."

At that moment Lloydie walked in, Carter looked up, "Hello Jim, can I leave it in your capable hands?" Jim smiled, "Yes guv, will meet up later, with a resume of Mr Chambers reports."

Chapter Fifteen

Carter walked down the busy corridor, following people walking on either side, and patients in wheelchairs or laying on gurneys. The corridor had the usual hospital protocol coloured walls in white and green, with a hand rail along the middle.

He arrived at x-ray, looking up he saw a corridor that went to the rear. At the end he saw a door with a wooden name plate, 'Conference room'

He opened the door, and his eyes fell on a large white board on one of the walls, displaying medical practices, and training times. His eyes also fell on a full length skeleton on display in the corner. He smiled saying, "Is that a cold case?" There was a raw of laughter.

His eyes then fell on a sea of faces, sitting around the board table. Looking round the room he saw TF, Wendy Fields, DCS Smith 'A' division CID, Bill Wallace senior SOCO officer, and Joe Purcell, the hospital security manager, and a collection of other high ranking officers.

Tony Frost stood up, "Well Carter what have we got?"
"Sir, on speaking with the pathologist, Gordon Chambers, and making an examination of the bodies, we both feel that this is all related to the incident on the docks."

Tony Frost who could not help himself said, "What the fuck? Is this open season on police officers and witnesses, in all the related matters?"

By this time Sue had come and stood next to Carter, he looked at her. Sue said, "Sir whilst you were with Mr Chambers in 'Major Obs. I went and examined the surviving witness, she is still out of it, but alive none the less."

Tony Frost who was still agitated looked around the room, "It would seem that anyone can just fucking walk in and shoot who they want?" He blushed, looking at Wendy as well as Sue he said, "Please excuse my language DCS Ford, and Miss field's, but as you can see we have the

43

making of a shit storm."

"Sue smiled, "Sir, I think I speak for the both of us, no problem."

Carter looked out at them all, "Commander Frost, you and your colleagues from the top floor at HQ must realise that a hospital is a private building that the public have access to 24/7."

"Not everyone in a white coat is a doctor? Hospital staff leaves discarded uniform items all over the place, and one can walk into any A and E on any day of the week and pick up a stethoscope, a staff ID and hang it from their waistband, and you are off to the races."

"Mr Chambers and I think that PC Clark, suffered an execution style killing, receiving two, of what we both think are 9mm shots to the rear of his head. The officer must have been made to kneel down in front of the assassin. On death he slumped to his right, one can see that his two legs are tucked back.

The other Asian witness was killed, also by means of a 9mm bullet, just to keep her from becoming a potential witness."

He continued, "Of course Mr Chambers will complete the PM's and issue the results in the near future, or liaise with DI Lloyd.

It so happens that the other witness was off the ward when this was being committed, and our friend could not risk any further time, as his arse was already sticking out far more than he wanted."

"We all realise that a hospital can't be secured one hundred percent of the time. Staff, contractors, out patients, and a host of others pass through their doors, and when we have need for a witness to be secured it's hopeless."

"I feel when all investigating personnel have finished we can hand Major Obs. back to the hospital, as medical matters, and patients are already backing up."

"In closing I recommend that MCU continue with the investigation, and that orders be issued that all relevant officers to be armed. Carter looked round and found a seat next to Sue. He sat down, not before he received a round of applause.

The room was filled with a buzzing of chatter. Tony Frost walked over to Carter, "When you have a minute I need a chat with both you and, Wendy Field's. We need to prepare a press release as the press will be all over this like shit on a blanket, say my office on an hour?"

Chapter Sixteen

Well within the hour, Carter arrived at TF's office. He was met by Jane, his secretary, who on seeing Carter, was about to enter into her typical sexual teasing, until she saw Sue following behind him.

He smiled, "Morning Jane, how are things?" He burst out laughing when he saw the look on her face. Looking at her he said, "Jane do we have a problem?" She replied, "I'd rather that you'd been on your own, blushing she said, "I just love our sexual banter..." He laughed out loud, "You mean all of yours."

Minutes later Wendy arrived and Jane after talking with TF sent them in. Carter stood back allowing Sue and Wendy to enter first. He suddenly heard a childish voice whispered, "Oh! Carter you still have a lovely arse?" Carter turned; "Jane" He could hear her sniggering.

In the office they were offered a seat. When settled TF said, "Well, how do we handle this?" Wendy said, "I always feel that honesty is the best policy?" TF smiled, "Spoken by a true newspaper Wallah?"

Carter, smiled, "Sir, You must have realised, that by inviting Wendy to this meeting, knowing of her famous quote, "It's founded on, if we say nothing it will come back to bite us on the arse."

"At present we have the second witness, who is totally unknown to us, via the PNC. We also have the second witness, also unknown to us. It could all fall apart if when she comes out of her coma that we find that they are related, and to whom? One never knows they may be from an important family?"

"The other important matter is the death of PC Clark, so there it is. We also need to go and see his wife, partner, or parents."

Wendy interrupted, "He is single with a girlfriend." TF said, "Carter I feel that we let the acknowledging of the death of the young PC with 'A' division senior officers."

He looked at Wendy, "Will you prepare a press release, and show me your copy before we go to press. Do you feel that you release it to a favourite newshound, or should we have a press conference?"

Carter looked at TF "Sir! We need to discuss the arming of my team? Tony Frost said, "Carter it goes without saying it's come from the top, the jobs yours please issue the order for fire arms, be careful, and now be off with you."

Outside of Tony Frost's office, whilst talking with Sue, and Wend the phone rang on Jane's desk, Carter looking at the two colleagues said, "I wonder what he's forgotten now." Jane said, "No Lloydie he's still here."

Jane looked up and smiled at Carter, "Carter it's for you, and it's DI Lloyd." Carter walked over to her desk she looked up and smiled, "Would you like to take the call on this side of my desk?" Carter smiled, "No Jane just give me the bloody phone." Jane looked down crested, "Oh! Carter, you've spoilt my day." Both Sue and Wendy, together with Jane, started to laugh.

He took hold of the receiver, saying "Carter, hello Lloydie, do we have a problem?" Lloydie replied no guv it's just that Mr Chambers is asking for you, and with respect, ASAP." He replied, "I'll see you shortly." And he put down the phone.

He looked at Sue, "Can we make the mortuary post haste?" Sue replied smiling at Jane, "Oh! Yes guv that means we will spend all day together." Jane let out a muffled laugh, "Some people get all the luck."

Carter leaned over to Jane, "Will you please fax over to Eric Morton, a copy of the order raised by the Chief Con. a copy of the order for designated officers in the MCU team to carry firearms, and will you ask Eric, to mark it for the attention of DI Baxter." He then leaned over and kissed her on the head.

Jane looked at him smiling, "What was wrong with the last target?" As he was walking away with his arm around Sue he said, "Sorry I'm in company." Sue burst out laughing.

When in the car Sue pressed the blues and two's, as they sped off back to the LRI (The Liverpool Royal Infirmary). On arrival at the mortuary Sue pressed the doorbell. A voice from the inter com. Said, "Yes" Sue said, "It's DCS Ford, together with Assistant Commander Carter CID." The door release operated and the voice said, "Pull the door."

As they walked in, and after showing the technician their ID's, Carter said, "What bloody else could we do with the door?" The technician just had a blank look on his face. Carter made the sigh of passing his hand over his head. Sue nodded as they both walked through to Gordon Chamber's office.

Carter knocked on the door, Gordon Chamber's immediately stood up, "Hello Carter, I see you have brought with you your trusty deputy, Miss Ford." In the office they noticed Lloydie sat in the corner.

Chamber's said, "Will you both follow me; and Carter looked at Sue, with a look of, *'Do we have too?'* Gordon Chambers, who is very astute, burst out laughing with his, James Robinson Justice laugh, "Oh! It's alright you two; there is nothing grizzly to see."

He was still laughing when they entered the PM room. Carter looked back and caught Lloydie with a smile on his face. Carter said, "Just you dare." Lloydie said, "What me guv?"

Chapter Seventeen

Inside the room they both noticed the usual PM equipment, with the three large lights, one over each of the PM tables all brightly lit. There were several of the usual trolleys. They both noticed that all the equipment had been discreetly covered and push to one side. It was for two reasons; Gordon Chamber's knew that both Carter and Sue had a dreadful foreboding of the room.

Secondly to make room for 7 gurneys, each of which had the bodies of the young girls all covered with the yellow coloured plastic sheets? The remaining three tables had a body on each, making a total of 10 girls in all.

Both Carter and Sue realised that the young girl from A and E was included, but the body of PC Clark was elsewhere.

Gordon Chambers turned and said, "The reason for my request Carter is something of an interesting, and unusual matter. Pointing he said, "This is the body of our Jane Doe, who was shot at the same time as PC Clark. He walked over to the nearest table, and he discreetly raised the sheet. He revealed a portion of the victims head, her left shoulder and left arm, of the young Asian girl.

Carter walked over and immediately saw the alabaster coloured face of the girl. Her eyes were closed, looking as if she was asleep, but Carter noticed that his staff had placed a green cotton cap over her head.

Gordon Chambers said, "The cap covers the wound to her head, but notice a small birth mark on her left cheek under her left eye. But it is this that I wish to show you." He walked to the side of the table and he reached down and brought up her left arm. There was no sign of rigor mortis.

He said smiling, "Carter if you lean over you will see a small criss-cross sign drawn in black indelible ink, on the back of her left hand, plus a needle mark in another wise clean arm, found in the inside crease of her arm." Gordon

Chambers confirmed it was the same on each of the girls.

When they were all sat in Gordon Chamber's office, he reached down into one of his desk draws, and retrieved a bottle of Scotch. He then turned to Lloydie who rose and without any instruction went and retrieved four plastic drinking cups, from the water cooler.

Gordon Chambers poured a nip of Scotch into each of the drinking containers. He looked at Carter and Sue, "I believe congratulations are in order, "Well done" he then raised his plastic cup saying, "All the very best to you both."

Prior to leaving Carter shook hands with Gordon Chambers and said, "It's a privilege to have a man of your honour to work with." Gordon Chamber's replied, "No Carter, It's an honour having to work with a person such as you."

Whilst chatting in his office, Carter received a call from Chris Atkinson, in A and E. "Carter, its Chris, your young witness is coming round, I thought you may well want to come and have a chat?" Carter just said, "Thanks Chris, see you shortly." And he closed the call.

Whilst driving back to A and E, Sue said, "Carter, you have a lot of respect for Gordon Chamber's?" Carter, with his eyes closed, replied, "He is the one person who knows of my feelings when met by horrible sights, such as we see, and are meant to endure, and take in our stride."

"He realised early on in my service, and never uttered a word, but just allowed me to never have to indulge in rooting through dead corps."

"You realise that he dealt with the three young girls in the Carla Davenport case, in Rad's suicide, and latterly, Helen and the children's deaths all of which needed PM's."

"Me as senior officer should, no protocol demanded at times, that I be present. Yet he allowed me to use Lloydie as a go between. He could have got himself in a load of shit if the, Home Office were to find out."

"No he has my vote all hands down." Sue said, "Carter

you do know that the whole of the team know, and Lloydie most of all, but they have total respect for you and never mention it. Now I on the other hand have told everyone." They both burst out laughing.

Chapter Eighteen

On arrival at A and E they both could see that matters were getting back to normal. After showing their ID's they met up with Chris who took them to a small annex room, at the rear of the department.

As they walked up to the door they both saw an armed uniform officer stationed outside of the door. On arrival they both showed their ID's the officer looked down and said, "All is correct." He then opened the door to let them in.

The room had concealed lighting, but they could see the young Asian girl sat up in bed, they noticed that she still had a drip in her arm, but looked decidedly better than the last time they both saw her.

Sue did the honours, "I'm Detective Chief Superintendent Sue Ford CID, and this is my boss, Assistant Commander Carter CID, we are both of, The Major Crime Unit." As Sue did the introduction they both showed the young girl their ID's

Sue said, "Can we begin by you telling us of your name, and date of birth, and your home address. The young girl said in a quiet voice, "My name is Alisha, Patel. I'm 18, and my birthday is 17.07.68. I was born in Liverpool. I live with my sister and our parents at 16, Lancaster Street, in Walton.

Sue turned, "We can see that you are tired and need rest, will it be alright to return tomorrow, she looked at her watched and smiled, I mean later today."

On leaving Alisha suddenly said, "Did you find my sister, for I was with her in that terrible trailer, she also managed to escape, but we separated, when we got away."

Carter with a look of dread on his face said, "Can you give us her name and details?"

Alisha replied, "Yes, her name is Neysa, she is 16 and her date of birth is 6.4.70. She has a birthmark under her left eye." Carter froze, he quickly gained his poise. "Alisha we will make some enquiries and get back to you later today." She lay back on her pillow; it was obvious that she was still very weak.

They both left, outside of the room they met Chris, and gave her the girl's details for their records. Carter said, "I just couldn't tell her of her sister's death. Sue looked at him, "It's okay guv, I'll break the news to her tomorrow, why don't you get off home."

Carer said, "But Sue you are my lift?" A voice he immediately recognised said, "Not anymore." He turned to see Charlie standing there, with a broad smile on his face.

Before leaving Carter looked at Chris, "Could I possibly trouble you, and your nurses to look after our friend?" He looked in the direction of the armed officer. Chris smiled, "But of course Carter, now get from under my feet." He leant over and kissed her on the cheek, smiling he then left.

After he had gone Chris said to Sue, "That man thinks he can charm the birds out of the trees?" Sue also as she left said, "He seems to have your measure." Chris blushed, and burst out laughing.

Outside in the hospital car park, used by the emergency crews, Carter looked at Sue. "It seems that I've been allocated my minder, so I'll see you in the morning can you arrange for a full scrum down, please include Eric and his team." Sue smiled up at him from her car, "See ya guv" and drove off.

Whilst en route home Carter, discussed the case with Charlie, although the news of PC Clarks, murder had spread within the ranks of the police like wild fire.

Charlie informed Carter that it was the God's in the marble halls that reinstated his protection, plus added input from TF. On arrival home Carter looked at Charlie, "See you in the morning? Say 8.30am." Charlie smiled, "Yes sir." Carter pulled a face; "Please, do we have to go through the same rig ma role?" Charlie smiled and drove off.

When Carter entered the flat he knew it was late, but

noticed that there was a light on in the lounge. It wasn't bright he thought that Penny, must have left one of the table lamps on.

He entered the lounge to find Penny, curled up on one of the armchairs. Penny had a blanket draped over her. He walked over and gave her a kiss on the cheek. In a sleepy voice she said, "And what time do you call this to be coming home? Hope you are not looking for your tea, as it's in the dog."

Carter instantly thought this is Déjà vu, matters in which he had previously encountered with, Helen. He immediately thought that being so; within seconds the deliberation was lovingly placed back in the compartment in his mind, where it belonged.

Carter bent down and picking up Penny, gently wrapped her in the blanket, and walked through to their bedroom. He gently placed her on the bed, and in seconds had completely undressed her.

They mutually experienced their usual sexual delights, after which, he leant forward and pulling up the duvet covered themselves up, within seconds they were both asleep.

Chapter Nineteen

The following morning they both took part in one of their exotic showers. Carter, felt that he needed the warmth, and closeness of Penny. He placed his head on her shoulder, allowing the water to cascade over them both.

Penny moved to leave the shower. "Carter, I'll leave you with your thoughts, I realise that yesterday seemed to have caused some upset to you, as borne out by your pattern of sleep. You tossed and turned for an inexhaustible amount of time?"

On leaving the shower he dried off and shaved. On completion he went through to the bedroom to find that Penny had laid out his clothes. He dressed then before he put on his jacket he went into the wardrobe and from the safe collected his firearm and holster.

After putting on his jacket he went through to the kitchen to receive his usual mug of coffee from Penny. They both sat on the kitchen bar stools. Carter turned to Penny. "There is something I need to tell you? The case, in which we are dealing, is quite horrific."

"When called out last evening, I was collected by one of the team and taken to the docks, where as a result of good work carried out by the dog section, we identified a HGV trailer in which we found the bodies of nine girls, all who had received gunshot wounds to the head."

"Two of the girls managed to escape, both ending up in major obs. in the Royal, at the rear of A and E. Both had been shot but only received head wounds. They were both in comas. Whilst in hospital and under the protection of an unarmed police officer, a culprit gained access to the area."

"He shot one of the girls and the police officer, fortunately the second girl was off the ward receiving treatment." When Carter looked at Penny she could see the look of horror on her face."

"Penny I'm telling you all of this in the uttermost

confidence, and that due to the seriousness of the incident myself, and my team, who are engaged in this major incident are to carry firearms."

We have placed a 24 hour armed detail on the remaining young girl." Penny walked over to Carter, and hugged him, no sooner did she hug him, than she suddenly pulled away.

"Carter looked at her, yes, and I've also been given a protection detail, and there will be one stationed in the doorman's office. In matters such as these my bosses have even protected my loved ones? It is all due to events that have occurred in the past."

With that the intercom sounded by the front door to his flat. He walked over and picking up the handset said, "Is that you Charlie? Please come in, and come through to the flat."

Carter opened the door. "Penny let me introduce you to my minder, detective sergeant, Charlie Watson, of the armed protection detail. Charlie smiled, "Good morning guv, and Miss Wilkinson it's nice to meet you." Penny smiled, Charlie nice to meet you as well, but my name is Penny."

Carter kissed Penny goodbye, he smiled and said, "Will call you later." In the hall Charlie introduced D/C Andrews, who was on morning duty." Carter smiled, "Morning son." And he and Charlie left for the car.

Whilst driving to the office Carter called Eric. "Morning guv we are all waiting for you, see you shortly." The phone went dead.

Chapter Twenty

On arrival at the office all personnel stood to attention and in unison said, "Morning guv." Carter looked at them, "It must take an awful long time for information to seep through to you lot." He smiled, as went over to the diary to sign on duty.

As Carter walked passed, Eric handed him his usual morning mug of coffee, he opened the office door saying, "I'll see you all in the conference room, and I mean all." as he looked at, Eric.

As he entered there was the usual rumble of feet, Carter smiled, and said, "As you were."

He walked to the front of the room and noticed that the photos of all the victims had been placed on the white boards, even the photo of PC Clark, and photos of the HGV trailer inside and out. Carter sat next to Sue on either side of a nearby desk. He looked at Sue, she smiled.

"Carter stood up I hope that all operational officers are armed, as I see that yet again we may be dealing with top draw criminals, please do not under estimate them."

"Before we start I need to make sure that you all know that DCS Ford is the senior investigation officer, in this matter. We are a team, and ever will be so. I am here purely in a consultative role. I may carry the title, but I never see us any way as I did on day one, when MCU was first launched."

"Well, it doesn't take rocket science to know that we have landed an awful case, not only do we have a killing sight, but we also have the bodies of the victims, but also the body of a colleague. Now you all know that there is a survivor, who is under armed protection 24/7."

"Now we have a load of work, which will mean a division of labour. We need to continue with enquiries on the docks, see if we can ascertain; any CCTV of the lorry park, and of any of the surrounding roads."

"We have a reg to the HGV but we know it's a Joey,

but that vehicle prior to being parked up, must, or could have been driven through the Tunnel, and through the streets of Liverpool. Make a call to the Liverpool City Council Traffic control look through any CCTV for about the same period.

We have a witness in hospital, she happens to be the sister of the girl that was killed whilst in hospital, together with PC Clark. The witness may know something. As a survivor, let's be gentle with her, and try to first of all see why they were there, how did they come to be there? And we have a home address let's interview the parents."

"I have no need to tell you that this witness is of an Asian background, now their whole lifestyle is different to ours in so many ways, especially in relation to morals, I'd bet the mortgage that they know jack shit about their children's lives and behaviour?"

"I need someone to contact Lloydie if you haven't noticed all the victims have a needle puncture mark on the crease of their left arms, 'Why'? What on earth could it be for, ask if there are any signs of drug misuse?"

"I also want to see the police press report before we go to press, could I suggest someone, he smiled I think, DI Baxter could manage that." A snigger went around the room.

"Whilst, we all receive our various tasks re this enquiry, I will need to see you all, and to have a scrum down this evening last thing, we need to collate any information that may take us forward in this case."

"Last but not least, we need to make sure that the surviving witness receives full protection.

As Carer got up to leave Sue said, "Guv did you get much sleep last night??? There was a hail of laughter... With a straight face Carter looked around the room. "I slept like a baby." On leaving Carter turned, "Will someone please call, Lloydie to see if he has an update for us?"

Carter left and walked through to the office to chat with Eric, who had returned to his desk after all the important issues had been dealt with. Carter walked over and sat next to him, one of the young ladies brought him his usual mug of coffee.

Eric turned, "Guv you'll be careful, as I have an awful feeling over this one, it's funny that the bastards made no effort to remove the crime scene, and to top it all went into the bowels of a hospital without detection, and shot, the witness, and worst still shot one of our own."

Chapter Twenty One

Whilst they were talking the phone rang on Eric's desk. He answered it, holding up the receiver offering it to Carter, "It's Lloydie for you?"

Carter said, "Hi Lloydie what can I do for you?" Lloydie said, "Guv, Mr Chambers was wondering if you could spare him a minute?" Carter said, "I'll be with you, and him in about 15 minutes."

He looked at the young secretary, "Could I trouble you to go and fetch Charlie, for me, he's in the conference room, could you also ask DCS Ford to spare me a second?" The young lady smiled and she was off.

Seconds later both Sue and Charlie arrived in the office. Carter looked at Charlie, "We may be going down to the mortuary, but I need to run something past DCS Ford first." Looking at Sue he said, "Will you please come through to my office?"

On arrival he said, "Sue, I didn't want to speak in front of the others. Sue, Lloydie has just called, Mr Chambers, wants a word with me, now I must tell him that you are the SIO in this matter?"

Sue laughed out loud. "Guv when will you accept the matter that you are not just the boss, but you are the team, and all in sundry know that. Now I have enough on my plate, go and see Mr Chambers."

He walked over and said as he gave her a hug, and kiss on the cheek, "I fail to see why I was brought back off my sabbatical, I have no doubt that you and the team are quite capable of dealing with this case." Sue looked up at him, "Guv you must be joking, let's not mention it again, we fit round you like a glove, she turned and left.

Whilst en route to the mortuary, Carter called Penny, *"Hello Carter, how are things?"* Carter said, "Will you be over tonight?" Penny replied, *"Yes"* And he could hear a snigger in her voice, *"Why, was there something you wanted?"* He replied, "Yes, I'll let you know if I'm going to be late, see you later." He closed the call.

The journey continued without any further comments. On arrival at the mortuary Charlie did the honours, and the introductions. They entered Mr Chamber's office, and received his usual warm and hearty greeting. When Carter looked through to the PM room he could see Lloydie busily dealing with some of the victims properties.

Mr Chambers looked at Carter, "Would you mind joining me in the PM room, before you say anything it will all be discreet." Carter coughed, "Lead the way."

The pathologist walked over to one of the PM tables, Lloydie turned and greeted his boss. Whilst he had a brief chat with Lloydie, Mr Chambers, walked over to the table and pulled back the bottom of the sheet that was covering the victim.

He revealed the naked feet of the victim, he said, "Carter, have a look see, can you notice anything unusual?" Carter discreetly walked over, and leaned forward to have a look. He said, "Yes, I presume it's the ink mark under her left foot you are interested in, I believe it could be, or is the victim's blood group?"

The pathologist roared, "Correct, but what is most unusual, this is not the only example, all of the girls have the same tattoo, or mark."

Carter took a step back and, looking at all present, "What on earth are we talking about? Are you saying, as he scratched the top of his head, that the culprits were carrying out a type of censes, whilst looking for something?"

Mr Chambers, let out another roar, "Well, AC Carter, I may be able to help in this matter. You know that we found a single needle mark in the crease of each of their arms? Well, what do you think? That the criminals, may have been pre selecting victims for and, I say this as if I'm thinking outside of the box. Is it to find possible *'Transplant victims?'*

Carter stood totally bemused, he looked at Gordon Chamber's, "Please don't think I'm rude, but could we

61

please all retire to your office? And take part in one of your tots of Whiskey?" The pathologist without his usual characteristic roar, simply motioned with his hand, and all four walked off towards his office.

As Lloydie poured the drinks as requested by, Mr Chambers, they all sat in total silence. The pathologist was the first to break the silence. "DC Carter..." Carter suddenly interrupted the man that he held in total respect. "Mr Chambers, by now I feel that you can call me Carter."

"Gordon Chambers replied, "So be it Carter, you must realise that by now your team will have received all the mortuary pictures of all the Jane Does, including that of Neysa, sister of the surviving witness."

"Lloydie has been very busy, tagging and bagging of all their property taken from each of the victims. Soil samples, scrapings from under their fingernails of each victim. All bodily fluids, drug toxin levels in relation to each victim, and hair samples to attain DNA, for help in possible identification measures. All have been preserved and sent off to forensics."

Carter looked over at Jim Lloyd, "Thanks Jim, it must have been an immense task." Jim replied thanks guv."

Gordon Chamber's looked at each of them. "Gentlemen if we consider each of the victims have a tattoo of a star, made by a Chris cross design on the rear of each hand."

"That they have also a puncture mark in the crease of each arm? I presume that the samples of blood were recorded, and the category of their blood groups tattooed under each foot for easy recognition."

He continued, "Blood groups vary between A, A-, B+, B-, AB+, AB-, O+, and 0-, the most common being 0+, and the most rare is 0-.

Carter looked over to Charlie. "Charlie, could I ask you to contact Sue Ford, asking that the officers on the docks dealing with that aspect of the job to seal off the area, putting a hold on the area where the terrible trailer was found."

"I want a team of dog handlers, and their charges to

make a full sweep of all the remaining trailers. I want to make sure that there are no other vehicles, trailers whatever."

"If there is any chance that the dogs may detect anything what so ever, I want warrant's drawn up and sworn. I then want owners details obtained from PNC checks, and for them to be brought to their vehicles to open them up? Charlie replied, "Yes Guv, he left to use a phone in the outer office."

"Lloydie, I know you have a lot on your plate, but could you contact the CPS asking that we may have need of urgent warrants to be sworn, any problems mention Commander Frost's name." Lloydie just smiled and went about his business.

Gordon Chambers looked at Carter, "Do you feel, or realise that we may have an organ transplant type of serial crimes, going on?"

Carter looked at the pathologist, "Well Gordon, I'll know a lot more after I've spoken with the surviving witness. We need to see how the perpetrators managed to attract the victims, in such numbers.

Gordon Chambers looked at Carter, "The harvesting of body parts is another way of saying, organ transplant. But if you have willing recipients' who turns a blind eye to how the organs are obtained."

"One can honestly say that the full body organ's, can fetch upwards of £200.000, and if the perpetrators' have a ready supply of fit victims, all they need is to ascertain the blood group, as victims who need a transplant who have a rare blood group, one can name their own price."

"This outfit will need a trained medical Doctor, to carry out the transplant, because if just ripping out the organ, is all that is needed then anyone could do it. But in this case it must be done properly, as damaged goods will be of no use."

"The organs would have to be put in ice whilst delivering to the recipient, or bent Doctors who have use for the parts. It would be like how the legal organs are transferred."

Chapter Twenty Two

After thanking Gordon Chambers for his help, Carter stood with both Lloydie, and Charlie. Charlie said, "Guv, Message passed to DCS Ford, who stated that she'd see you later at the scrum down." He looked at Lloydie, Jim said, "The CPS will act on any information when supplied, in the preparation of warrants."

Carter looked at Jim. "Jim, when your work here is done, ring Eric, asking for you to be shown 'off duty' from here, the mortuary. There is no need for you to attend the scrum down, you have done more than enough, and I need to stay on the right side of, Sam."

Jim laughing looked at him saying, "If you are sure guv?" Carter nodded. Lloydie said as he got into his car, "See you in the morning guv." As he drove off.

Carter looked at Charlie, "The Royal please." En route, he called Tony Frost, the phone was answered immediately. *"Frost"* "Sir it's Carter, thought I'd fill you in on the enquiries to date? We seem to have stumbled across some sort of donor transplant ring? Before he could finish TF shouted, *"What! Carter, in all that is Holy, what the fuck do you mean?"*

"Well sir it's like this, I'm on my way to speak with the surviving witness, I'll know more shortly." *"Where will you be later?"* "I'm returning to Derby Lane for a scrum down." Tony Frost said, *"I'll see you there."* And the phone went dead.

Carter and Charlie returned to Derby Lane, Carter looked at his watch it was 7.30pm. He called Penny, the phone answered immediately, *"Hi, I don't suppose you're on your way home?"* No, sorry Pen, this will be a late one, I have to return to Derby Lane before I can come home, but will you please wait up? I have something important to say?" Penny replied, *"Yes, of course Carter, see you later,* and the phone went dead.

Prior to going through to the conference room he went

into the general office and signed back in. He noticed that TF had hit the book, arriving earlier.

He entered the conference room and the team began to stand, Carter caught a smile on TF's face. Carter said, "As you were."

"Now let's cut to the chase. Mr Chambers, informed me that we are dealing with a team of *'Organ Harvesters'* He explained to me that all the Jane Does, have a needle mark in the crease of their left arms, it could mean that a blood sample was taken from each victim. Their blood group was then tattooed on the bottom of their feet."

"The tattoo marks on the heels of the victims, who portray a popular blood group, may be used in more frequent cases, bringing in a regular income. The victims that portray rare blood groups although, not in any great numbers, will fetch the big bucks."

"Now whilst talking to Mr Chambers, he informed me that if they take all the perfect organs from a body it could return upwards of £500.000." There was a gasp in the room.

He continued, "They must have a setup which includes someone with medical experience, perhaps a struck off doctor? You see that only organs removed with care and attention, a known surgeon, even one struck off will then follow the correct procedure in the protection of the attained organs be placed in ice bags as per the genuine cases, will then be transported to the recipients".

Carter explained his interview with the surviving witness, Alisha. He explained how she went into detail of her, and her sister's traditional upbringing, and how they would find an excuse to change from their traditional Asian 'saris' into more western type clothing.

They both loved modern records, and loved the popular singers. They wore jeans, T shirts like that of their school friends. On one occasion they happened to receive a flier being given out by a young man in the City centre.

The flier said, 'Do you want to be a model' Carter pointing to the white board, showing the enlarged photo of a scrap of paper said, "I believe that the piece of paper found in the property of one of the girls may relate to the flier."

Carter continued, "I didn't want to hassle the witness, but she mentioned phoning the number and here, and her sister made an appointment. Now I want one of our female officers to attend at the Royal tomorrow and continue the interview."

Sue Ford stood up, "Guv we attended at the parents address to give the death message relating to, Neysa. We also mentioned that Alisha survived the attack and was in the Royal. I've told a white lie, I've said that she can't have visitor's even parents, as she is still under severe medical attention. I thought it would give us time to interview Alisha in greater detail." Carter smiling looked at her, "DCS Ford, naughty, naughty."

Carter looking at Tony Frost said, "Sir, I wish to involve Wendy, as I wish to mention about the attack in the Royal, as I have a plan?"

Carter said, "Sir, it's getting late can we reconvene tomorrow, say 9.30am?" Tony Frost smiled as he got up, "See you all in the morning. The whole of the team stood as he left the room.

After he left he said, "Sue will you give me 10 minutes before you leave for home?" In his office Carter said, "Look Sue I want Wendy to get a story in one of the papers about the attack, playing up that we have a survivor who was away receiving treatment when the attack was in process."

Sue with a smile on her face said, "Carter what are you up to?" He replied, "See you tomorrow, now let's get home it's late.

Charlie dropped Carter off as usual. He entered the flat tip toeing into the bedroom. He started to undress when he heard Penny say, "It's alright Carter I'm awake."

Carter got into bed and pulled up the duvet, he turned and cuddled into Pennies gorgeous warm naked body. He yarned as he said, "Good night love." Penny said, "Carter, what was so bloody important that you wished for me to be awake for when you returned home?"

He replied in a tired voice, "Oh! Yes, as he remembered, and in the midst of a tried mind he said, "Penny, it was just would you like to move in permanently?" Penny, turned and taking hold of him in her arms, "Carter what a wonderful idea, can we talk later as I'm about to make love to you." Carter said, "You'll have to help yourself." And she did.

Chapter Twenty Three

Carter awoke the next morning to find Penny already in the shower, he walked through to the bathroom saying, "Madam if you are about to take up residence in this household, then you invite the man of the house to join you."

Penny burst out laughing, "Carter you must have been very tired last night so I just thought I'd leave you to have a sleep in?" Carter rushed into the shower saying, "My God it's 8.15am Charlie is picking my up in half an hour."

Penny responded with, "Well Carter show me what you can do in say fifteen minutes?"

After a short exotic shower he shaved and dressed, and walked through to the kitchen. Penny offered him his coffee saying, "Will we be able to sort things out at the week-end, and what do I do with my place?"

Carter's mind flooded with Helen's comments on the same subject, he recited exactly what he said to Helen. "If truly committed, then either put your place up for sale, or rent, both are a win, win situation."

Carter looking at Penny said, "I have an operation in mind for the team, and if given the green light, it may mean a late one, but I'll call you if it's very late so you can be off to bed instead of waiting up." As he kissed Penny goodbye Penny whispered, "I'll want to say good night..." Carter kissed her back and left.

He got in with Charlie, and left for Derby Lane, en route he called Eric, "Morning Eric, has Sue managed to get hold of Wendy?" He replied, "Yes all are here waiting your arrival."

Carter closed the call when his phone activated, he saw the caller, "Penny" He said, "And yes madam, what can I do for you?" Penny replied, "Putting that to one side for now, were you serious in what you were saying, as I'm totally committed." Carter said, "That's great Pen, but I can see it being a late one?" After which he closed the call.

On arrival at Derby Lane, he signed on duty, and received his traditional mug of coffee from Eric. Eric said, "They are all in your office awaiting your presence."

He walked through to his office and found Sue, and Wendy sat waiting for him. He sat in his usual seat and looked at them both. "Now you will both feel that my scheme could be classed as insane." Sue laughed, "Why Guv would we have it any other way?" They all burst out laughing.

Carter eventually said, "Now we have a surviving witness, in a room, in the Royal? What I want to run pass you is this, Wendy, could I have your thoughts in preparing a press release to that fact. 'The Police have a surviving witness to the atrocities' that occurred in the hospital, and has a description of the offender, and it is only a matter of time blare, blare, and blare."

Wendy, who was very astute said, "Carter are you going where I think you are going?" He replied, "Yes, I'm setting up the witness as bait, to lure the murderer out. He may, and could return to silence anyone who may well identify him, via his actions on his last visit."

Sue, before Wendy, could answer burst out, "Guv what on earth are you thinking?" Carter smiled, "Now let's get our blood pressure back to normal. If we have a positive press release, it may lure the killer back to the ward. We of course will remove Alisha, putting her in a different ward, or room."

"We replace Alisha with one of the female members of our team, we will make it look authentic with a drip en all, we will have armed members of the team deposited in the en suit in the room, together with armed members of the team one as a domestic, and a couple as nurses', sat at the nurse's station at the head of the ward."

Both Sue's and Wendy's faces were a picture, for they both in unison, exhaled a large bellow of air, Wendy said, "Carter have you gone truly mad?" Sue said, "What about permission for such an idea, not only from TF, but the Hospital Trust etc?"

He said, "We replace Alisha, with an exact replica, a hospital drip, sleep apparel and all. I know we don't have an Asian female officer in the team, but please assure me that we could lay our hands on a bottle of tanning oil etc. The officer, playing the part of Alisha, will of course be armed. All other personnel chosen for this operation will be armed."

Carter leant back in his chair, he raised his arms in the air shouting, "Ole" Well guv it's alright saying 'Ole' What about TF, Carter said, "I'll call Chris Atkinson, first before I explain everything. I just want to tie up the loose ends with hospital uniforms etc for the team."

He looked at Wendy, "What do you think?" With bulging eyes she said, "Well Carter, if I prepare a press release we'll have to give warts and all, it would seem that you want to entice the shooter back to the hospital." He shouted, "Exactly" Sue remained stoic, not saying a word.

Carter looked at Wendy, looking at his watch he said, "It's 10.30am what time will you need the information for the matter to be put to the press?" Wendy said, "For the afternoon edition, about 12pm, but what about TF."

He looked at Sue, "Could I ask for you to contact Chris Atkinson, and explain our needs, see who we need to speak with in the Trust. We need to relocate Alisha, and for us to take over the room, for it has as I remember an en suit."

Carter got up Sue, looked at him, "Guv where are you going?" He replied, "To see TF."

He left his office as he did so he said, "Right you have your tasks see you both at about 12.30pm if I haven't been sacked." He burst out laughing as he walked off in the direction of the general office.

In the general office he looked at Eric, "Could I trouble you to ring TF's secretary, Jane, telling her I'm on my way down and will need about 15 minutes of his time." Carter signed out, writing now going to HQ to see TF.

Whilst en route he received a message via Jane, "The Commander will see you as soon as you arrive, but be alone ha, ha."

Both Charlie, and Carter arrived at police HQ; they both wondered out of the lift at the appropriate floor. As he walked up to Jane's desk she noticed Charlie, was accompanying him, the large smile quickly disappeared from her face.

Carter always thought her a very attractive woman, but married. She welcomed Carter, with her usual sexual risqué attitude and verbal fore play. Carter, laughing was about to reply when the phone rang on her desk.

With a blushing face she said, "Carter, both you and Charlie, can go in, what a pity we didn't have time for a chat, perhaps when you come out?"

Carter knocked and entered, Tony Frost was as immaculate as ever. He looked up at Carter saying, "Well what can I do for you?" It took a matter of seconds for TF to start resorting to type, with his usual rant and rave. "Carter, are you fucking insane?" He got up from his desk, and walked over to the large window overlooking, The Mersey.

"You do realise it's a fucking hospital, in which you choose to run round with armed personnel, for Christ sake."

Carter looked at Charlie, before they both looked towards the back of TF. He seemed to be looking out on the Mersey for solace. Carter raised his eyebrows whilst he awaited for yet another salvo from TF.

He jumped in first, "Sir, I have a mortuary full of young ladies bodies, plus the body of PC Clark. I have explained the MO of these bastards, who are using the victims to harvest bodily parts; in fear of getting caught, they have no compulsion but to shoot the victims, for fear of being caught."

"I wish to lay a trap, that with the help of the hospital, and Wendy Fields, we may entice the shooter back, thinking that he can kill the remaining witness."

Tony Frost, inhaled a large intake of breath, and there was a short delay before he said, "Put together a plan, include Wendy Field, and forward it to me I will run it passed the Chief, he may well contact the Chairman of the hospital trust, to get permission to carry out such an audacious plan."

Carter said, "There will be no staff, or patients at risk. I will ensure that all patients, in beds, but not in rooms, who are unable to be moved will each have an armed guard, and all the ward duties, will be overseen by a member of my team."

Tony Frost looked at Carter, "Let's say you have the orange light." He smiled, "Now be off with you."

Carter and Charlie left the office, Jane looked up, "Carter have you got my good bye kiss?" Carter smiled at Jane, "In your dreams." Jane whispered, "Carter if only you knew."

Chapter Twenty Four

Whilst on their return to Derby Lane, Sue contacted Carter, "Carter, I've spoken with Chris Atkinson, TF of the Chief must have contacted the powers that be, at the Royal. It's all been agreed that you may put your plan into action. Can you meet her at her office ASAP? Wendy, will have the press release for you shortly."

Carter rubbed his hands together, "Charlie, can we make the Royal ASAP? I need to speak with Chris Atkinson. On arrival they both showed their ID's and were let into the A and E.

They both recognised Chris, amongst the mala of people, with her staff dealing with both the sick, the local drunks, and addicts. Chris waved and gestured them to her office. On arrival she flopped down in her chair behind her desk.

She looked at Carter saying, "What on earth is this audacious plan you wish to conceive?" Carter using his entire mannish charisma, looked at Chris, perhaps you could take me, and my sergeant here to the area where Alisha, was being treated?"

Chris stood up saying, "Follow me gentlemen, she led the way to the rear of A and E following the signs for the, 'High dependency unit' on arrival both, Carter and Charlie, saw the name over the two doors to the unit.

Chris, using her ID pass gained entry, she pulled open the door, and they both immediately noticed that there was a key card entry system allowing access to the ward. They also noticed that each staff member is shown on the TV screen, viewed on the nurses' station.

Walking into the ward they immediately noticed the nurse's station. There was a long desk, with three a chairs, several filing cabinets, telephones, and a desk top computer, and screen, for medical information, and x-ray results. They noticed a metal trolley, used in ward rounds by the medical staff, which contained patient's files.

The ward had two side room's, for individual patients, each situated at the top of the ward on the left, and right. The rest of the ward had eight beds, each with the facility to allow screens to be pulled round for privacy. Half way down the ward was access to washing, and toilet facilities.

Chris beckoned the two men to follow her back to her office. On arrival she looked at Carter, "Alisha Gupta was in the first room on the left, which is fortunate. You could have either one of your team in the bed, or we can mould it like a person being in the bed, with a drip, and drip stand in position. With subdued lighting, you may get away with it?"

As you are well aware there is an en suit facility within the room in which other team members may hide.

Carter stood up walked over to Chris and leaning over kissed her on each of her cheeks saying, "Chris I know you have always had a soft spot with the police, but if you feel that we are pushing it, please say, as I'd never put you or any of your staff at risk."

She looked up at Carter, she smiled, "Carter, not wishing to embarrass you in front of one of your junior officers, but you must realise that I had to fight off a lot of my young nurses when I had to undress you after one of your many escapades." They both burst out laughing.

En route back to their car Charlie looking at Carter, "Guv is there a past?" Carter laughed, "No Charlie, only that we both have the utter respect for each other." Charlie just smiled as he looked over at Carter.

When they both returned to Derby Lane, and after they had both signed back in, Eric offered them both a mug of coffee. Whilst Carter took his place of preference next to Eric, his old boss gave him an envelope.

Carter opened in and pulled out a full 'A' size piece of paper. Looking down he read: **Press release - The Liverpool Echo, afternoon and late edition...**

'Officers from the elite 'Major Crime Unit' are making intensive enquiries following the recovery of six bodies found in the rear of an HGV trailer located on

The Liverpool dock estate.

As a result of information received, officers attended at a site in, The Liverpool docks, were they recovered the bodies of six young girls. It is believed that two young girls although severely injured, managed to escape the carnage.

One young girl was found at the entrance to the dock estate, and the trail of blood from her injuries led officers, with the help of the dog section, to follow the trail, which led to the dreadful location.

The young girl with the help of The Liverpool paramedics was taken to, The Liverpool Royal Infirmary. Where, she received attention to a gunshot wound to the side of her head.

The second victim managed to flag down a driver in a car, and he phoned for the police and the ambulance service.

The two victims were placed in medical comas, whilst they received treatment for their wounds. A police uniform presence was placed on the ward.

It is thought that the criminals knew that they had initially had captured eight girls. The perpetrators knowing that two of their victims had escaped, and may hold vital evidence, to share with the police. The criminals carried out an audacious plan.

They sent an armed criminal who perpetrated the hospital ward, shooting the uniformed police officer and one of the surviving victims. This happened as the second victim, was receiving treatment for her wounds.

Deputy Commander Carter, of 'The Major Crime Unit' stated that whilst deeply shocked as to how the perpetrators, managed to gain access to the specialist area within the hospital, that all endeavours are being taken to protect the surviving victim.

The second victim, is receiving treatment in 'The High Dependency Unit, and is able to help police with their enquiries...so on, and so forth'

On completion Carter asked Eric, "Is Sue was in her

office?" He replied, "Yes and she had read the release, and awaits your opinion." If you agree then copies of your plan of action, together with the report can be emailed to TF for his comments."

Chapter Twenty Five

Carter went down to Sue's office he knocked and walked in. She looked up, Carter said, "Do you have a minute?" She replied, "Yes of course guv." He sat down in a huff, but before he could say anything, Sue said, "Ops, sorry of course, Carter. He sat opposite her, and taking a deep breath he said, "Have you a list of chosen officers, for our honey trap?"

Sue sat upright, "Why yes, Carter I haven't mentioned it as yet, but I was thinking of, Julie Niki, and Kate, for the nurse's station. Peter and Phil, to take up positions in the en suit, Alex as a cleaner, and me, in bed with the bottled tan?"

Carter said, "No Sue, no arguments, pick another female from the team, or we make an outline of the patient in the bed." Sue stood up, "Off the record Carter, it's alright for you to lead from the front, why not me." Carter looked at her, "No"

He sat down, "Now I want earwig comm.'s for all personnel, I want one for Chris Atkinson, I need her to recognise any Doctors name given, and why the visit?

Sue looked at her watch it was 12.30pm she picked up her phone, and dialled Eric. "Would you please get in touch with the following officers, Peter, Philip, Julie, Kate, Niki and Alex asking that they attend at the guv's office ASAP?"

Sue before he left looked at him, "Why the knock back Carter?" He looked at her, "Not only do I wish no harm to befall you, or any other officer in the team, but you Sue are my future replacement, as leader of MCU, with a promotion to my rank." He turned and walked away. Sue sat in her office mouth dropped open.

In Carter's office with all present and all, he extended an invite to, Chris Atkinson; Charlie on Carter's orders had gone to fetch her.

Carter said, "DCS Ford, and I have chosen you for this

detail. Niki and Julie will take up positions behind the nurses' station. Peter and Philip will hide in the en suit, whilst Kate will take up a position in an empty curtained cubical close to the private patient's room. Alex you will pose as a cleaner in the corridor outside of the ward."

Carter looked at Christ Atkinson, she blushed, "You all realise that the ward has a key card entry system, which is controlled by personnel ID codes. All staff even Doctors, need to gain access via a staff card. If they fail, they may try and blag their way in, that they are new and awaiting delivery of an ID."

She looked at Carter, "I'll be sat in a room behind the nurses' station, and will hear anyone trying to gain entry. Officers in the nurses' station must ask for details, name etc and reason for access to the ward."

"We have no urgent cases, or a patient in the ward, all patients have been moved for safety reasons. So should a doctor, nurse or anyone wishing to gain access, they will need an ID card. Now I understand after being briefed by Charlie, it is imperative to let him or her in. I will of course recognise any genuine medical staff, as no one knows of this situation.

Chris Atkinson opened a bag in her possession, looking around she said, "Here are some scrubs that will act as temp uniforms for your team." Charlie took hold of the bag and said, "I'll need to whisk this off to Derby Lane, to have them issued." Chris said, "I've given larger than usual sizes, as it's easier to reduce the size, rather than having to increase."

Back at Derby Lane, all the nurses' uniforms were issued, Peter Phil, remained in their usual civvies as they will be hidden out of the way.

Carter and Sue looked at the officers, Carter said, "Remember not all Doctors wear white coats? And can we now play, Doctors and Nurses' before you leave...just to practice?" They all burst out laughing. Sue said, "Right the press release will be in this afternoons paper, so be off with you all, report to Chris Atkinson in A and E...And good luck to you all."

On arrival at A and E, they met up with Chris, who took them to her office, were they all got changed. Peter looked at Kate, "Kate where are you hiding your gun?" She turned laughing, "Never you mind." Chris said the dummy is in the bed with the drip and stand in position. Phil gave Chris, her earwig which had a two way reception. They all left for the ward.

When in position, Peter said, "DS Wallis to control, all personnel in position." Carter said, "Roger." Carter and Sue, had set up a position in an office further down the corridor, allowing then to send and receive all messages.

Chapter Twenty Six

Unbeknown to Carter, and his colleagues, there was yet another meeting taking place on the other side of the City. A smartly dressed man was sat behind a desk looking out on the three men sat in front of him.

The three men could see he was annoyed. He stood up, and as he walked towards the front of his desk he slammed down what seemed to be a curled up newspaper onto his desk, shouting.

"Have any of you idiots seen this article in the afternoon edition of the, Echo?" As he said it, he hit the nearest man, by thrusting the paper onto his chest.

The man opening the paper immediately saw an article released by the Merseyside Police, press office... 'Officers from the elite 'Major Crime Unit' are making intensive enquiries following the recovery of six bodies, found in the rear of an HGV trailer located on The Liverpool dock estate...'

The man looked out at the three men he was apoplectic with rage, "If one of you bastards would care to read on aloud, you will notice a certain fact, a fucking very important fact, which could result in all of our arrest, and land us all in the shit, with the bastard in charge of the project?"

One of the men took it up and began to read, he suddenly stopped... "Oh! Fuck, one of the bitches is still alive! And may well be able to identify her assailant?

"The other two men said, "What the fuck do you mean?" The man reading the article continued, "It would seem there were two bitches that got away from that trailer, the one we killed, with that bloody policeman, but the other one survived, she was off the ward getting treatment when we did the job."

The man reading the article said, "But it's alright, they have put the name of the ward, were she is being treated, only in the fucking article. She's in, The High Dependency

Unit, the ward where we already got into."

The business man got their attention by banging on his desk with his fist. "Now it doesn't take fucking rocket science, we have to get rid of her, like the other one. Now if you've done it before, you can do it again."

The three men began to argue between themselves, they all realised that to return to the scene, was pushing their luck. Two of the men, John Jackson, and Billy Collins, both looked at Tommy Parsons the third member of the team.

John said, "Look Tommy, you were missing, 'off sick' with a bug, when we did the others in that fucking trailer, I don't see why you don't do this one?" Tommy said, "Look, you're asking me to go back, into the bloody hospital, and do the job? You all know that's always the time you get caught."

One of the men said, "Look Tommy, we will all go back with you, to help out. We can all pretend to be doctors." there was a roar of laughter. Tommy looked at them all, "It's no joke, the first time you were lucky, and do you think that I could be so lucky?"

John, one of the gang said, "Tommy, hospitals are like colanders, and can't hold fuck all. They have literally, fuck all in a way of security. Their security is totally none existent they're all like chocolate soldiers."

The man now sat behind his desk said, "So are we going to sort this out or what?" Tommy, took in a deep breath, okay I'll do it. Is the ward, the one on the ground floor, behind A and E, so it's an easy in and out? But, and it's a big, But! They may have extra security on board."

Bill the remaining member of the team, said, "Don't worry, Tommy you can do it. So the quicker we do it the better, the police, and the fucking hospital will never expect another attack so soon after..."

Chapter Twenty Seven

All of the operational officers were now in place. Niki and Julie were in place at the nurses' station, with Kate, in the body of the ward, in one of the bed areas, with the curtains drawn around.

Chris had placed some drips, and drip stands around some beds, feigning authenticity with low lighting, pillows had been put in most of the beds to forge the presence of patients, the curtains had been drawn around the first two beds, left and right at the head of the ward, to detract from the presence of original patients.

Peter and Phil, were about to take their places, in the side room, Chris whispered from her location, "Peter or Phil, will one of you please remove the light bulb in the en suit, as it comes on automatically when you open the door."

Phil, did the honours and removed the bulb, after which, Peter and Phil, were beginning to argue about who sat on the loo, and or who sat on the floor. The next voice they heard through their earwigs was Sue, "Gentlemen! We can all hear your, 'Tate a tote' just get on with it." There was a short burst of laughter.

The next voice they heard was Alex, "One, in corridor, he has just walked past me towards the ward. He is white, about 6'2" wearing a three quarter length coat dark trousers', and brown shoes. The important thing, he has a stethoscope draped around his shoulders, and what appears to be an ID hanging from a lanyard, which was around his neck.

Alex said, "I'm pushing my cleaning cart behind him. I'll deal should he try to run." Sue suddenly said, "Alex take care, the guv is on his was to assist you."

The tall look alike Doctor, pressed the ward admission button, a voice came through the speaker, *yes?* The man said, "Sorry, this is Doctor Elliott, one of the medical house officers on Mr Williams medical team, he has asked for me to call, and take a blood sample, sorry it's late, but the results are needed for his medical round tomorrow?" Chris from the back office whispered, "Bull shit."

Niki's voice said, *"Okay Doctor, just pull the door."* At that point all the team were suddenly on alert.

The man entered the ward and walked up to the nurses' station. He smiled at Julie? "Nurse, sorry but I need a blood sample from the patient in the side ward, Niki, deliberately said, Alisha Gupta?" The man replied, "Yes that's right."

Christ Atkinson, unseen in the back office, pushed a trolley forward. It was loaded with a cardboard tray, with syringes in sterile packages, for the removal of blood, with a thin length of rubber, for a tourniquet, all the necessary equipment. Niki stood up, the man pretending to be the Doctor said, "It's alright nurse I can do it." Niki replied, "Okay Doctor, it's the room on the left" He thanked her, and took hold of the trolley, pushing it towards the side room.

As he entered he noticed the patient, and what appeared to be a drip on a stand, in the bed. He thought all was in order as he took hold of the patients file from the holder at the foot of the bed. He opened it, making sure he had the correct victim.

He said, "Miss Gupta, I'm Doctor Elliott, sorry to disturb you but I need...He suddenly took out a revolver, with a fitted silencer, and smiling said, "I'm here to finish the fucking job." He then without any remorse, discharged two bullets into the dummy of the body shape, "Thud, thud."

With that Peter and Philip, rushed out of the en suit, Peter shouted, "Armed police drop the gun?" The assailant shouted, "What the fuck?" Philip said in a calm voice, "We are armed police officers drop the weapon, and get down on the floor, I won't ask you twice."

The man dropped the gun and fell to the floor, Philip kicked the gun from his reach, and then took station over the predator firmly holding his revolver in a two handed clasp standing over him whilst Peter, brought his arms behind his back, and attached handcuffs to his wrists.

When the prisoner had been restrained, Philip with gloved hands leaned down to pick up the gun, and removed the clip from the handle. As a qualified gun and small arms expert, he pulled back the slider which ejected a single bullet, making the pistol safe, and secure. He then placed the weapon, and it's parts into a police evidence bag.

Peter and Philip raised the man to his feet, and Peter said, "All is secure" Both with the prisoner detained between them, walked out from the room into the ward.

Carter and Sue, walked up to Peter and Phil, and congratulated them. Sue turned to Julie and Niki, "Could you both liaise with SOCO, I want the bullets recovered from the dummy, and photographs taken of the ward, and the room. The recovered bullets are to be taken to forensics ASAP for comparison." They both replied, "Yes boss."

Carter looked at Sue, "DCS Ford, why don't you caution your prisoner, whilst I inform, the Chairman of, The Hospital Trust that they can have their hospital back after SOCO, have finished."

Whilst Sue cautioned the prisoner, Carter walked to the office at the rear of the nurses' station and looking at Chris he said, "I don't quite know how to thank you Chris, it was due to your co-operation in this matter, which made it go so smoothly. He lent forward and kissed her on both cheeks.

Sue turned, "Right, let's get this piece of scum back to Derby Lane, and a well-deserved working lunch? Carter jumped in, "My treat."

Outside the main entrance to the hospital, whilst standing, loitering amongst the thong of the public, and visitors, in the day to day business of a hospital, stood the two colleagues of the assailant, both wondering where the hell he was?

Chapter Twenty Eight

Peter and Phil put the prisoner into a waiting police van, for transport to Derby Lane. They then walked over to their car. Sue turned to the members of the team, "See you all back at the ranch." She then got into the car with Charlie and Carter.

On their way back to Derby Lane, both Carter and Sue, brought Charlie, up to speed over the operation, although he was part of the armed protection detail, he had remained in the background, to be included if needed.

Whilst travelling back to Derby Lane, Carter noticed that Sue, was rather pensive, and reserved, he thought that it was the culmination of the latest operation, with the adrenaline rush subsiding.

On arrival at Derby Lane, they all booked back in returning to the office, with the prisoner. Whilst in the general office Carter sat talking with Eric, over a mug of coffee, telling him of the arrest and how it all went.

Sue walked into the general office, after having booked the prisoner in the Bridewell, downstairs.

Sue sat and enjoyed a well-earned mug of coffee after which she looked at Carter, guv have you a minute, he realised by the look on her face, it must be personal, "Yes? Come through to my office."

On arrival they both sat around his meeting desk, he smiled, "How can I help?" Sue, replied, "Guv, whilst you have inferred that one day I may have responsibility for the team, would you take it as no disrespect, or any negative vibes on my part, but would you object if I relinquished control of the team, and for you to be the lead investigator in this operation."

Sue continued, "I feel that the team respond better with you at the helm?" Carter smiled as he looked at her. He said, "Sue you know how TF sent for me, to tell me that MCU's were to be formed in all police forces, and that I had to go away and set up the one for Merseyside?"

"Sue, I'd hate for you, or anyone to have to go through such an ordeal. My instructions was to go away and form a team, with orders that I could ask for any CID officer, to be detached from present duties, to join the new team."

He continued, "Well you could imagine all the jibes being said behind my back, and for the divisional CID bosses panting with excitement, to see this new project, and team to fall on it's arse at the first hurdle, well it didn't."

"That was mainly due to the team I picked, which included you, and the others. Eric, for although retired I recalled him for his wealth of experience, and the support that I would need. Now one day you must realise that I will put in my ticket, and I feel that the team in your hands will continued on the right lines."

Sue got up, "Guv whilst you call TF, I'll go and organise the meal for the team, and we'll see you later for the scrum down." Carter smiled, "Okay Sue, I'll be through in a minute."

Carter made the call; it was answered immediately, *"Frost"* "Sir, it's Carter just informing you of the one arrest, from the hospital operation, all went well no problems." TF said, *"Carter, that's great news well done, congratulations to all who took part, I will let the Chief know, as you can well imagine, the Chief loves to hear how your hair brain ideas pan out, yet they always seem to work, he laughed aloud, well done son."* And he closed the call.

Carter rang through to Eric, "Have you got a minute?" He replied, "Yes" "Well, will you come through, but please make sure you bring the coffees' through." There was a knock at his door, Carter said, "Come in"

He looked up at Eric, "Please take a seat, I need a chat with you, and this is off the record. I've just had a chat with Sue, who wishes for me to take over as SIO, now as you well know I've been trying to hand matters over to her, prior to the day I put my ticket in and retire."

Eric said, "Well?" Carter looked at him, "Is that all you

have to say?" Eric replied, "Look Carter, Sue will always be like that whilst she has you as a safety net. The only way to get her to take over is for you to retire, and for her to get her hands dirty."

Carter looked at him, Eric quickly jumped in, "No, when you go I go, but I will make sure she gets a good clerk." He smiled and left.

With all the team enjoying their working lunch, Carter returned to the conference room, the team tried to come to attention, before he shouted, "As you were." He winked at Sue. "The prisoner has been placed in a holding cell, awaiting interview?" Sue replied, "Yes guv" he walked over and sat with a sandwich and coffee from a nearby table.

"DCS Ford and I will carry out the initial interviews, so when we've finished our scoff *(Police term for a meal break)* I would like you to deal with the following; the bullets from the ward room to be compared to the bullets recovered from the bodies in the back of the HGV?" He looked at Jim, who smiled, "Yes guv."

"I also want enquiries to be made from the information gained from the witness; we need to track down the source of these flyer's and the photographer. I want an interview with Alisha's parents, and lastly, the biggest job of all, continued efforts to identify the victims from the shooting in the rear of the HGV."

He looked at Ian Baxter, "Ian, could I ask you to pass a message onto Wendy. There is to be no press involvement until tomorrow, please will you ask for her to attend my office first thing." He smiled, "Say 10ish?" Ian smiled, "Yes guv."

Later in the day Carter looked at his watch, he shouted, "Christ it's 10.30pm! Sue we will interview the prisoner first thing tomorrow? Now let's all pack up and go home, see you all in the morning." There was a loud, "Yes guv."

Sue, smiled with relief, as she left for home.

Chapter Twenty Nine

Charlie dropped Carter off at his flat, it was about 10.45pm, and he waved Charlie away as he entered the front entrance. The night protection officer wished him, "Good evening sir, all is correct."

He walked over to his flat door, and he placed the key in the door, to open it when suddenly he was met by Penny, she walked over to him placing a kiss firmly on his lips saying, "I've missed you, how has your day been?"

Carter said, "I'm sorry Pen, but we've been engaged on an operation since early. I was given the green light to an operational plan, and it meant all hands to the pump, hence no communication by officers involved."

Penny looked worried he put an arm around her as he led the way to the lounge. "Carter looked at Penny, "Can you give me a minute?" Fifteen minutes later he returned with wet hair, dressed in grey track suit bottoms, and a blue T shirt, he walked through in bare feet.

He said, that's better, she looked at him, "What on your own?" Penny laughed, "Perhaps later. I have some gastronomic delights for you; I've made a cold meal. Cold meats and salad stuff. I have a French stick, which can be broken up and smothered in butter."

During the meal, accompanied by a delicious glass of French, Cabinet Blanc, Carter explained what had taken place at the hospital. Penny said, "Carter I'm glad you never called prior to events." He said, "With the help of our press officer, I thought we may pry the offender to return to the scene of his previous crime."

"I believe that we will have him and his cohorts, for a total of eight murders, so we'll be rather busy in the next few weeks, as I see this leading to a bigger picture."

Penny after taking a sip of wine said, "Well Carter, will it all mean enquiries at base, or will you be ferreting around with the team?" As Carter took a sip of wine from his glass he said, "Well Pen that is something I need to run pass you."

Penny looked rather pensive leaning back in her chair. Carter went on to explain the Sue situation, her reluctance to lead the team, whilst she had Carter as a safety net. After which he looked at Penny.

"Penny, I've been here before. The fate Gods, played their dirtiest trick, snatching Helen and the kids away from me, but the fate Gods, atoned for their dirtiest trick, in allowing me to meet somebody else."

I realise that I asked the question the other day about you moving in with me, to which you agreed? She let out a long, "Yesssss, should I feel like there is a *'but'* coming?" Carter burst out laughing, "No Pen, just replenish our glasses and I'll explain matters to you."

Penny sat down and smiled, "Ready" Carter said, "Well I was the one, and only recipient of my parent's estate. That made me, The Chairman of the, 'Chapman Empire' my parents happened to have been, Sir and Lady Chapman."

"I was Christened Carter, the main reasons being that my father wanted me to stand on my own two feet, and my mum loved the name. My father, never wanted for me to be supported by their, name and fortune."

Carter quickly went on to explain the situation when joining the police force; I had to explain the situation. They approached the Home office, who gave permission for a man with a single name to join the force.

He continued, "I'm Chairman of Chapman enterprises in name only. It's all a formality, and above board. I receive a Director's remuneration which is paid into a separate account from my police salary."

"Now the reason for all this explanation is that, I love you, and would like us to spend the rest of our lives together." Carter hadn't realised that just as he said his closing statement, Penny, had just taken a slug of wine, which happened to de camp down her nose, with total shock.

When Penny had gathered herself, Carter said, "My

reason for telling you this is not to show off, but that I could retire from the job, and that I have a potential partner who could be in it for the long haul, I thought I'd tell you."

"You see Penny, I could put my ticket in now *(Police jargon for resign, or retire)* But I keep on telling Sue, that she is more than capable of running the team, but she keeps on asking that I take the helm, I think that she always want to have the team as it was in the beginning. Eric seems to think that if I was to go, then she'd have to take over."

Carter continued, "Penny, the team has dealt with matters that have taken the lives of two police officers one, my best friend, and the other one of my team, and lastly, my wife and children."

"I see that it was my entire fault, as I was the common denominator. It was all done in an effort to stop me, and the team?"

"Now I would only be willing to hand over the team to a likeminded person, although I could pack up tomorrow, and retire somewhere in the sun. My problem is I have officers who look to me for direction, yet I would hate to put another person in the firing line, should this operation become serious."

Penny topped up his glass, "Carter, I see it as you vocation, now I feel that there are other officers could breeze through their service without as much as a scratch.

"Yet the likes of you, have officers who look up to you, willing to hang on your every whim, which enables them to work in such a specialist unit. I would say that there is a line around the block of personnel who would give their right arms to join your team."

"Penny said, "Now take me to bed and please explain the art of CID work in the community?" They both burst out laughing.

Chapter Thirty

The following morning Penny, knowing that Carter, was feigning sleep, got out from under the duvet, and totally naked stretched, and yawned as she was stood facing Carter, who was under the duvet pretending to be asleep.

He suddenly threw the duvet back and jumped out of bed, also fully naked. Penny said, "Morning Carter, you look as if you are clearing the decks ready for action?" He ran over to her, and catching hold of her took her into the shower.

Penny let out a scream, as for the first 5 to 10 seconds of any shower the water runs cold, until heated to the correct temperature.

After their exotic shower, whilst Penny dried herself, Carter had his usual shave. He dressed and walked through to the kitchen as he was adjusting his holster. He quickly put on his suit jacket.

He sat and enjoyed the coffee that Penny, had prepared. But as usual he left half, as Charlie was waiting outside with his lift. He kissed Penny goodbye saying, "I'll call you later." He left, leaving for the office.

After he booked on duty, Carter took hold of the mug of coffee offered by Eric it always seemed the one he best enjoyed. As unlike the others he always tried to make a point of finishing it. They both sat chatting when Sue walked in.

"Guv I've had the prisoner brought up from the holding cell." Carter said, "Morning Sue, I think he can stew a bit whilst I enjoy my best coffee of the day?" They both burst out laughing.

Carter eventually stood up, "Eric, before we leave do you happen to have one, a morning newspaper, and two, can one of your young ladies come in with a tray of coffee's, and three bottles of water?"

Eric reached over and handed him his newspaper, I will also send one of the girls in as asked." Carter said, "Let battle commence." They both walked out of the office, Carter was carrying the paper, and the arrest file, Sue looked at him with amazement. They arrived at the interview room. The uniform officer stationed outside said, "Good morning" as he opened the door for them both.

Inside they both saw the prisoner, Sue who still looked shocked at Carters request sat down next to him. Carter looked at her, "Sue will you please do the honours." Sue still amazed at carters request for the newspaper, suddenly spluttered, "Yes guv."

Sue, looking at Parsons said, "You do realise that you are still under caution?" He just nodded. Sue leant forward and placed two unopened tapes into the recording machine.

Sue said, "Interview commencing. 10.30 am Friday 17th October2012. "We met on your arrest, and later, on arrival at this police station. For the purposes of the tape I would just like to introduce the presence of, Deputy Commander Carter CID. After a short pause, the machine bleeped, and Carter commenced the interrogation.

Sue, on the introduction of Carter, noticed that the prisoner sat upright, as for on their arrival he was lounging around on the table.

Carter said, "I believe when in the charge office you refused to give your details?" He smirked, "Yes you'll get fuck all out of me."

At that precise moment there was a gentle knock on the door, Carter turned, "Come in" The door opened and walked in with all the requested items. Carter said, "For the purposes of the tape, drinks have been brought in for both me, and my colleague, and for the prisoner if required." The tray was placed on the table.

Carter looking at the prisoner said, "Help yourself?" Both he and Sue took their coffees. The prisoner leaned forward, and lazily took hold of the bottle of iced water. Carter said, "The prisoner has taken a bottle of water."

The prisoner said, with a sardonic smile on his face, "For the purposes of the tape, 'cheers', but you are still getting fuck all." He then opened the bottle, and holding it firmly took a hearty swig of water.

The interview had lasted two hours, after all the questions, and denials, Carter said, "I think we'll take a break, this is beginning to get monotonous." The prisoner said, "I fucking agree." With that he stood up, and basketball style, made a jump shot. He threw his bottle several yards into a wastepaper bin, on the other side of the room. He excitedly exclaimed with a smile on his face, "Yes"

Carter called in the uniform officer who opened the door, "Yes sir." Carter said, "Will you please take the prisoner back to his cell?" He then said, "For the purposes of the tape, the prisoner has now been removed." Sue said prior to switching off the tape, "This interview terminated at 12.30pm Friday 17th October 2008.

Carter, after making sure the tape had been switched off, raced across the room. On arrival at the waste bin, he bent down and started to rummage through the rubbish until he found what he was looking for, the only empty plastic bottle amid the litter.

He placed two fingers inside the neck of the bottle, he looked at Sue, and "Will you please place the bottle into an evidence bag, and send it off to SOCO for urgent fingerprinting, if any problems mention my name."

He looked at Sue, and he could tell that the penny had just dropped; she walked over and kissed him on the cheek. "You see guv that's why you're the boss." And she walked out the office to set his request in motion.

Chapter Thirty One

Carter was sat talking with Eric, over a quiet after lunch coffee, when suddenly the office door abruptly swung open, heralding the entrance of Sue. She dashed over and kissed both Eric, and Carter on the top of their heads, whilst she danced around the room shouting, "We've only just bloody gone and got him?" Whilst she kept flashing a piece of paper, that she held in her hand.

Carter with a look of utter surprise on his face, smiled at Eric, "I wonder who we've only bloody gone, and got?" Sue shouted in a melodic tone, "Tommy Parsons, 26yrs, 10.01.1978 of 42, Red Rock Street, West Derby, Liverpool." Parsons, having previous convictions for, Aggravated burglary, GBH, and numerous assaults. Sue continued dancing around.

Sue, eventually sat in one of the chairs laughed saying, "I feel quite drunk with the adrenalin rushing around my poor weak and frail body." Sue looked directly at Carter saying, "And it's partly down to you, guv."

Carter smiled, "Well DCS Susan Ford, we'd better send for Mr Parsons, and give him the shock of his life perhaps we could tell him that we're all clairvoyants, what do you think?"

Sue stood up, and skipped over to the phone close to Eric, and after dialling a number, issued orders for Parsons' production.

As they both left, Carter reached over as he asked Eric, "Mind if I have a loan of your paper?" Eric passed it to him. "Why yes, certainly guv."

In the interview room Sue, said, "You realise that you are still under caution, Parsons the prisoner just grunted, "Yes" Sue, took out two fresh tapes and removed the packaging, and did the honours.

Sue began the interrogation. Parsons looked at Sue, saying, "What the fuck is he doing?" Whilst he nodded in Carter's direction?"

Carter was sat doing the crossword in the newspaper on his knee. Carter looked up, "I do hope you don't mind, Tommy? By the way it is, Tommy?" He immediately stood up and with an apoplectic look to his face said, "What the fuck, what's going on?"

Carter looked up from over the top of newspaper, please sit down Tommy, or else we'll have to restrain you. Now you are Tommy Parsons? The same Tommy Parsons, 26yrs date of birth, 10th May 1978, and that you reside at 42, Rock Street, West Derby, Liverpool. He again stood up and shouted, "How the fuck do you know that?" Carter said, "Well you left your calling card."

Parsons flopped down in his chair, as it began to dawn on him. Carter said, "Tommy, I seem to be stuck on a clue in my cross word...It's maximum sentence, two words 4 and 8.

Whilst Parsons sat in utter amazement as he looked at Carter, he failed to see the utter look of respect Sue, showed for Carter it was all over her face.

Carter suddenly sat upright, "I've got it, yes, I must be thick, and it seemed to take me ages." With that he stared at the prisoner, "Why, yes of course, 'Life Sentence' how does that grab you Tommy?"

The prisoner suddenly stood up, "You, can't fucking put it all on me?" Carter shouted for the officer, who came in at the rush, being a tall and fit looking officer he said, "Yes sir, what can I do for you?" Carter said, "After repeated warnings, will you please restrain this prisoner?"

With that the officer took hold of Parsons, he handcuffed the prisoner to a nearby rail, close to the table, which allowed him to sit on the recovered chair.

Carter said, "For the purposes of the tape, after repeated threats, we've now had to restrain the prisoner. After the officer left, Carter looked at Parsons, "It's at this point of the proceedings that Parsons is asked if he needs the help of a Solicitor."

Parsons looked at Carter, "It's true what they say, you are straight." Sue, looked at Carter; interview terminated, allowing the prisoner to attain legal assistance, at 1.30pm on Thursday 17th October2012." Sue then said, "Officer" He came in. "Will you please remove the prisoner to his cell downstairs."

After he was removed, Sue, and Carter returned to the general office, where Carter returned the newspaper to Eric, thanking him.

Sue said, "Eric, you should have seen what took place during the interview of Parsons." Carter suddenly interrupted... "Where do you think I got the newspaper idea from?" Sue, looked directly at Eric, he just slowly nodded.

Carter looked at Sue, "Will you come through to my office?" Eric looked at her, "Who's in the sh...? You have to report to the headmasters study...ha, ha. Sue looked down at him, "Please get on with your work, Mr Morton." She laughed, as she walked out, following Carter.

In his office Carter said, "Sue, please take a seat, the reason I asked for you to come through, is purely that I'm off home, and could you please keep the team delving into the ongoing enquiry from the site of the HGV, to keep the surviving witness under surveillance."

"And will you please let me know of the situation re the Solicitor for Parsons, when organised?"

After Sue left, he picked up the phone and dialled Penny's number, Penny answered immediately, *"Carter how's your day?"* Carter said, I'm just leaving for home, how's things with you?" Penny replied, *"I'm putting on my coat, and I'm half way out of the door, see ya."* And the phone went dead.

Carter walked through to the general office, and signed off duty. He looked at Sue, he smiled, "See you tomorrow."

Chapter Thirty Two

After being dropped off by Charlie, Carter walked through the foyer of his flats he greeted the doorman, and the evening protection detail.

He opened the door to his flat, to be met Penny in the hall, and she was wearing a see through dressing gown. Penny, wondered through to their bedroom, she looked at Carter, "You are to take me to bed, and pleasure me."

Carter began to walk towards their bedroom in little steps, and undressed as he walked, matters were under control until he tried to take his trousers off. He ended up with his trousers around his ankles. He tripped close to the bed, and dived, it was like a tree being felled.

Penny, who was crying with laughter, whilst looking at his antics said, "Carter will you please remove your pants, and get into bed, but will you please excuse me for a couple of minutes, as I've need of the loo, before I wet myself.

Penny, returned and, joined Carter under their duvet. Penny looked at him saying, "Carter will you please let me pleasure you? There have been many occasions in which you have done the same for me."

She then gently passed her hand down his chest, and took hold of him. Carter immediately laid back, letting out a low whisper; "Wow" Penny then moved down and gently took him in her mouth.

Carter turned, and after kissing Penny, he repaid her actions with spades, ending with Penny, having to bite on the edge of the duvet to stem her screams.

After their sexual delights Carter took hold of Penny, and carried her through to the wet room, and shower.

On completion of their shower, they both dried, and dressing in casual sweats, they both went through to the kitchen, and both sat on the kitchen bar stools.

Whilst they both sat each with a glass of red Chilean Cabernet Sauvignon, Carter said. "I'm waiting to hear from Sue, as I've told the prisoner Parsons he needs to arrange legal representation, for today, what's left of it, or for first thing in the morning."

After consuming the prepared Spaghetti Bolognese, with grated parmesan cheese, they retired to the lounge, were they both enjoyed coffee, and liqueurs.

Penny looked at Carter, "Do you feel that you may be dealing with a domino effect in relation to this matter, as it's plainly obvious that this man is not on his own, and may well be part of a team?"

Carter smiled at her, "You never know, I might well have to call on your boss, for some psychological profiling, or she may lend me you as an assistant." Penny burst out laughing, "Well, if that be the case, not much work would get done." And they both burst out laughing.

Chapter Thirty Three

The following morning after kissing Penny good bye, Carter left to meet up with Charlie, who was waiting by his car. After their usual greetings, Carter phoned the office, his call was answered by Eric.

Carter said, "How are things, Eric said, "Well your prisoner a waits, and Sue is in her office, as we speak chomping at the bit."

On arrival at the office and whilst booking on duty, Sue, entered the office, "Morning guv" Carter, slowly looked around the office, there were only the four of them, and Sue said, "Op's"

Carter said, "Well, DCS Susan Martha Ford, how would you feel if the team were to suddenly find out your middle name?" Sue blushed, "Carter, it's the respect for your rank."

They could both hear Eric, and Charlie laughing. Eric was hidden behind his newspaper. As they both left for the interview room Eric, looked at Sue, and silently mouthed the word, 'Martha' and burst out laughing.

The uniform officer on duty outside of the office said, "Morning, Parsons is present with his Solicitor." He opened the door for them. Carter said, "Thank you, as they both entered the room.

They sat down, and looking at each other, they both recognised Parsons' brief. He was a Barrister by the name of, William Silverman, Carter looked at him and smiled saying, "Good morning Mr Silverman, we meet again? He smiled, "Well, Carter I believe congratulations are in order since the last time we met."

Carter looked at him, "Please may I introduce you to my colleague, Woman Detective Chief Superintendent, Susan Ford. He just nodded.

Carter looked at Parson's, you do realise that you are still under caution, he nodded. Sue lent forward and placed two unopened tapes, placing them both into the recording machine.

After the machine bleeped, Sue did all the necessary introductions, stating the time, day, and date, also naming all the assembled personnel.

Prior to the start of the interview, Mr Silverman suddenly stated, "I wish to state here, and now, that all the evidence gathered from the drinking bottle is inadmissible, due to the way it was obtained."

Carter smiled at Parsons, "Tommy, you don't mind if I call you Tommy?" He replied, "Fucking get on with it." Carter said, "I'll take that as a no."

"Parson's, will you just state for the purposes of the tape, were you at any time coursed, or that any action, or series of actions, took place in which you were forced to take the drink?" Parson's replied, "No"

Carter again smiling at Parsons, "Tommy, were you offered a drink of coffees, tea, or a cold drink, presented by my secretary, after I suggested a break in the proceedings, and did you not choose the bottled water?" He replied, "Yes"

Carter looked at Mr Silverman, "May we proceed to a more serious matter?" He just nodded. Sue said, "For the purposes of the tape the prisoner's Solicitor, Mr Silverman just nodded."

Carter proceeded with the interrogation, "Parsons is it true that you were detained by members of the Major Crime Unit, posing as a Doctor, to gain access into the High Dependency Unit, At the Liverpool Royal Infirmary?"

Parsons, through gritted teeth, replied, "Yes"

Carter continued, "Parsons is it not true that prior to your arrest, you withdrew a pistol, with a silencer fitted, and discharged it twice into a mock up figure in the bed?"

"Mr Silverman suddenly interrupted, "Carter, none of this is in doubt?" Carter, looked at him and said, "When addressing you, I have used the curtsey of calling you Mr Silverman, I trust that you may show me the same curtsey by calling me Deputy Commander Carter, after all Mr

Silverman, you did congratulate me at the beginning of these proceedings."

Mr Silverman, said, "Whatever? Now DC Carter, I hope that, that will suffice; my client accepts the circumstances of his arrest, now can we not move on? You may formally charge him with the offence, or offences, and let's stop wasting time."

Carter sat back in his seat and looked at Sue, "DCS Ford, I wonder why Mr Silverman, is in such a hurry to see this matter closed, and that his client is dealt with in due process?"

He continued, "Why, we need to speak to his client about the other eight murders, and one attempted?" With that Parsons jumped up, "You can fuck off, you can't pin those on me." His brief pulled at his jacket sleeve saying, "Sit down Tommy, and let me handle this."

With that the officer opened the door and stood inside, "Is everything alright, sir?" Carter replied, "I think so officer."

Sue then said, "For the purposes of the tape, the uniform security officer entered the room, that if needed he would restrain the prisoner."

When all was back under control, Carter again looked at Sue, "DCS Ford, and "I have several problems with all of these proceedings?" Sue replied, "Do you sir?"

Carter said, "Yes, firstly we have the prisoner, Tommy Parsons, from Red Rock Street, West Derby. Now how do you think he manages to secure the services of one of Liverpool's top Barristers?"

"Secondly, did he act alone? Why, on one morning did he suddenly choose to enter the High Dependency Ward to carry out such a mission?"

"Thirdly, could it be in response to an article in 'The Liverpool Echo' Finding, that there was a possible witness to all the slaying of the victims?"

"Fourthly, forensic evidence reveals that the bullets recovered from the dummy patient, in the hospital room, match the bullets recovered from the victims, found in the rear of the HGV?"

The prisoner looked totally dumbfounded, at that point Mr Silverman, interrupted Carter. "DC Carter, I think that this would be a goodtime to take a break?"

Carter looked at Sue, "Before we break we must remind the prisoner that he is still under caution, and that when he returns with his legal counsel, we will require the answers to all of my questions?"

Sue, lent forward; "Interview terminated at 11.30am on Friday 18th October2012." At that point Carter called in the officer, he opened the door, "Sir" "Yes, will you please remove the prisoner to his cell, and will you kindly show Mr Silverman the way out."

The officer took hold of Parsons, whilst Mr Silverman followed on.

After they had both left, Carter started to rub both of his hands together, "Well, what odds will you give me that we will parlay on their return?" Sue said, "I'll put my mortgage on it." And they both laughed as they walked back towards the general office.

Carter looked at Sue, "I'll see you in a minute, just going to make a call." Sue laughing, "Do you need any change Carter?" He just turned away for as usual he knew dam well what she meant.

Sue continued into the general office, when she went in some of the team were present. Eric said, "So what was all the laughing about?" Sue looked at Eric, with a look of sheer respect in her eyes when she said, "That man clearly stands on the shoulders of giants."

Whilst having a coffee, she recounted the interview, to all the captivated party, after which Sue said, "I feel that we have a deal coming on?" After the team members left, leaving Eric, and Sue, alone in the office. Sue said, "Was it ever so obvious in Carter, from the beginning?"

Eric, holding his coffee mug said, "The chances of a person like Carter, not only joining the job, but getting into the 'Jacks' *(Liverpool police jargon for a CID)* and become such a great boss, it's a thousand to one chance?"

Sue looked at him, "Did you not have any input in the matter?"

He smiled as he looked at Sue, "First you are given the clay..." "Now Susan Martha Ford, be off with you." As he just finished, the office door opened, and Carter walked in with a huge grin on his face, "Anyone for *Tom's?* Lunch is on me."

They all signed out, enquiries West Derby Road...on their way out Sue, said to Ian, "We have our phones and bleeps if needed, we're also taking, Methuselah with us."

Chapter Thirty Four

Carter received a call from Ian Baxter, informing him that their prisoner, together with his brief had returned, and were placed in the interview room awaiting their return.

He closed the call with Ian, and he immediately called, Tony Frost the phone was answered on the second ring, *"Frost"* "Sir it's Carter, as you know DCS Ford, and myself have been interviewing the prisoner, Parsons, arrested by members of the team at the Royal."

TF replied, *"Well what do you have?"* Carter replied, "I Feel that Parsons, is in a bit of a dilemma, it appears that persons, at present unknown has secured the services of a top draw Barrister, Mr William Silverman?"

TF said, *"Oh, Yes he is a big fish."* Carter said, "Sir, I feel that the person paying the bill is throwing both of them to the wolves."

"I feel that Silverman, thinks he is only there to get Parsons dealt with in relation to his current arrest, and subsequent charges, I don't think he knows of all the other charges, because when I mentioned the matter, both of their faced turned to boiled shit."

Tony Frost paused, and then said, *"What are you saying, Carter?"* He replied, "I feel a deal coming on, what if Parsons flips over on the organisation, we could get Silverman to represent him, yet I feel that the crew may well fell that he turned as well, as he knows who is paying for all of this."

Carter continued, "I feel that the person paying the cheques, must be the same person who recruited the ground team involving Parsons and a few mates."

Tony Frost said, *"Be very careful Carter, if handled correctly we could have another Davenport, and others, I know you are well versed with all of this, but when you know what they have to offer, give me a ring, and we can go and meet with the CPS."*

Carter said, "Will do sir" And the phone went dead.

Back in the office, and having signed back in, Carter looked at Sue, are you ready, She nodded, "We'll let battle commence, *'Let right prevail'* He collected the file, and together with Sue left for the interview room. The same officer was stood outside he smiled as he opened the door. Carter thanked him and entered.

On entering the interview room, they both saw Parsons sat with his Barrister. After the introductions both he and Sue, sat opposite them.

Carter looked at Parsons, "You do realise that you are still under caution?" He just nodded. Sue lent forward, and placed two unopened tapes, into the recording machine.

With Silverman knowing what was coming next he said, "Officers before you start the recorder, could we have a word with you both, off the record?" Carter looked at Sue, and smiled, "Why, yes of course, how can we help?"

It was Silverman who coughed before he spoke, "I have spoken with my client at great length, over lunch, and on hearing your summation, my client feels that he has been used as a scapegoat, he was asked to finish a job, and during the commission got caught."

Carter laughing looked at Sue, "DCS Ford, I feel that your mortgage is safe." Parsons had a blank look to his face, but not so our Barrister. He looked at Parsons, "Both officers realised that after lunch we will want to make a deal? It was painfully obvious."

Carter said, "I've no reason to explain matters to you, Mr Silverman but I feel that you, or we, may need to explain the legal matters to our friend, Parsons."

"The problem with doing *'Deals'* is that each party wants to come away with something of value. For my part, I want enough evidence to put you and all your mates away."

Carter looked at Silverman, Parson's Barrister. "Your client, of course will wish to diminish the courts authority, wanting them to look favourably upon him, for his part in all of this?"

I have to point out that when the defence find the word

'Deal' has been mentioned; they automatically look for the incentive. Parson's, I am aware that you are a person of bad character, and in the eyes of the law, Mr Silverman, should warn you that the Judge, will caution the jury, of the validity contained in your evidence, and your reason for it."

Silverman quickly explained matters to Parsons re the ramifications of such an issue, the net result being that both parties need to come away with something of value.

Parsons looked at his Barrister and nodded, "Well Deputy Commander Carter, my client has some crucial evidence, which if he turns 'Queens evidence' will put the gang away for a very long time."

Carter looked at Sue, "Mr Silverman, we'd better listen to what your client has to say?"

Sue lent forward and placed two unopened tapes into the machine, after a short time it bleeped. Sue then mentioned the time, day, and date together with all that were present.

Carter looked at Parsons, "You realise that you are still under caution?" He replied, "Yes"

Carter said, "Well what do you have to say?" Parsons, fidgeted in his seat, he looked at his Barrister, Silverman. Who pointed with his chin in the direction of Sue, and Carter and the recording machine?"

Parsons began, "Well, you caught me in that bloody hospital room, with the gun, which I was given to finish the job, getting rid of any witnesses."

Carter looked at him, "Well Parsons, we caught you on your own in the bowels of a major hospital someone put you up to it?

Parsons, you must also realise, that you were caught with the same gun that some person, or persons, used it in the killing on eight other victims?"

Again Parsons jumped up from his seat, "You can all fuck off, there're not all down to me."

Carter looked at Parsons, "Well, you want to do a deal, now I can only lay out in front of you, and your Barrister, the full extent of this case? It is more than being caught in the room?"

"I, together with my team am investigating, the deaths of seven young girls, and one police officer, the evidence shows, all shot with the same gun, and bullets that you were found in possession of."

"Your fingerprints were on the gun, the bullets in the clip, together with the one in the barrel, ready for discharge." Parsons screamed, "They made me load the bloody thing."

Carter looked at William Silverman, "I Feel that this evidence puts you both in a rather precarious position?" Silverman looked very shocked. "What on earth do you mean officer?"

He replied, "Well we have Parsons, bang to rights for the offence that he was arrested for. Whilst our part of the deal, is of a somewhat larger case."

"Mr Wilkinson, are you prepared to tell me the name of the person, or persons who asked you to represent your client? For let's face it, Parsons, does not have the wherewithal to afford your legal fees?"

Silversmith looked directly at Carter and said, "No comment."

Chapter Thirty Five

Carter looked at Sue, "For the purposes of the tape, you Parsons, will be taken down to the charge office were you will be formally cautioned and charged with the following offences;

1. Conspiracy that you, whilst acting with others, did conspire to endanger life. 2. Trespassing, having been found on private property, namely in an enclosed room in the Liverpool Royal infirmary, without permission. 2. Being found in possession of a fire arm. 3. That you did discharge the said fire arm twice, endangering the lives of the nurses, and patients of the said hospital. 4. Being found in possession of bullets for the said fire arm."

Parsons looked at his Barrister with a face as white as a sheet, Silversmith said, "Sorry Tommy." Parsons said, "What the fuck do you mean sorry?" Silversmith just remained silent.

Carter called the officer into the interview office, he then said, "For the purposes of the tape, I'm asking for the prisoner to be removed to the charge office, in this station, until he be charged. The prisoner is now being removed."

After Parsons had been removed, Carter, looked at William Silversmith, "Continuing with my investigation, Mr Silversmith, you remember I asked you who was paying for Parsons' legal fees, and you chose to answer, "No comment."

Silversmith replied, "Yes, that's correct officer." Carter then cautioned Silversmith with the usual caution." He again replied, "No comment."

Carter said, "William Silversmith, you too will be taken down to the charge office in this station, were you will be charged with, the wasting of Police time."

Sue half coughed and spluttered on hearing Carter's action, in the meantime, Silversmith suddenly jumped up out of his seat, "You can't, do you know who I am?" Carter looked at Sue who was still getting over the shock.

"Why, yes I do believe I do."

Carter looked at him, "Silversmith, please sit down. It's funny isn't it, for you now know how Parsons felt?"

Carter looked at Silversmith who was spitting mad with rage.

"Councillor, I have asked you three times the same question, 'Who engaged you' to act on behalf of Parsons?" He again replied, "No comment."

Carter said, "You leave me no option but to charge you with the said offence.

Carter looked at Sue, interview terminated, he stated the time, day, and date. Sue leaned over and switched off the tape.

Silversmith, who by now had regained his composure, looked at Carter, "I do apologise, DCS Ford, but Carter, what are you fucking playing at?"

Carter looked at him, "Silversmith, if you want to take the gloves off, and get down, and dirty. It's known by all of the criminal fraternity, that you are known as the *'Go to man'* when they fall in the shit, both Sue Ford, and I are not fucking stupid, some bastard has put you up to this, and you must realise that you yourself are now in the same shit."

Silversmith said, "What the fuck do you mean?" Carter started to laugh; you, or they, have dropped a fucking big clanger, why on earth did they not obtain the services of a middle, or lower rate brief? You stick out a fucking mile, saying class all over."

Silversmith looked down at the table, "This was set up by my, Clerk of Chambers, he gave me the case, and off I ran with it. I realised it was too late when I arrived at the station."

Carter looked at him, "Could your Clerk of Chambers be bent?" Carter realised that by the delay in his answer, that it was self-evident? Well William, what are we going to do?"

Carter looked at him, "Could you not recusal yourself from this matter, say you've been taken ill, telling your

Clerk of Chambers, to send say a junior brief? Also for your Clerk of Chambers, to come to the station, to see you, as you need to discuss the ramifications of this matter, prior to handing it over to another brief. It is essential that he doesn't smell a rat."

Silverman looked at Carter, "We've had our run inns particularly, when we were both young in our service. I owe you Carter? He said no you don't we all make mistakes." Silverman, said, "If I remember correctly you worked with that old fox DS Morton?" Carter and Sue, both burst out laughing, he said, "Have I said something funny?"

Carter replied, "Why, yes that old fox is my civilian clerk, in my general office." Silverman stood and smirked, "You could not have a better ally." Carter just nodded his head.

Chapter thirty Six

Carter said to the Barrister, "Come with me to my office, and let's get out of this infernal room." En route, Carter stopped, and opened the door to the general office. Eric looked up. Carter said, "Look who I have with me?"

The Barrister filled the doorway. Eric said, "Well I never, I heard that you were here, and up to your old tricks? But you must admit that my boy has blossomed."

Carter said, "Eric, could you ask one of your young ladies to bring some drinks through to my office, there will be four of us." Eric smiled, "Four?" Carter said, "Yes, you are to come through as well." "Yes of course guv?"

Later in Carters office, when they had all received their hot drinks, he picked up his phone and immediately rang Tony Frost. The phone was answered on the second ring, *"Frost"*

Carter very succinctly set about telling his boss of the events leading up to the present. Tony Frost said, *"Well Carter, what are you after?"* Carter replied, "Sir, I believe that Parsons is the tip of the proverbial iceberg, and that he unfortunately knows nothing, and for the time being he is the *'patsy'* in all of this, the one caught in our honey trap."

He continued, "I thought that by offering him to turn on his pal's, would reveal the whole caboodle, in all of this. But I now realise that perhaps, all of this is like, *'Matryoshka dolls'* although they all fit into one another, they do not know what is stored in each segment?"

"Someone at the very top is quietly, filling his pants. TF, burst out laughing, *"Carter, say shit when you mean shit, I am a man of the world? Sorry please continue."*

"I therefore feel that that is why our friend, Mr Silverman, was instructed in these matters. I really believe that they didn't think we'd connect the dots. Parsons, wouldn't, and couldn't have a hope in hell of acquiring such a brief as Mr Silverman, a Barrister in the top echelon, of the most expensive law practice in the whole of, Liverpool."

Tony frost said, *"So Carter, what are your intentions?"* Carter replied, "Well sir, they are three fold, 1.Whilst we have Parsons, he is technically, safe in police protection? 2. Hopefully by Mr Silversmith dropping the case, he may remain safe? And, then the last matter, 3. When the Clark of Chambers arrives we interview him as to his actions in this matter."

Tony Frost said, *"Keep me informed."* Carter replaced the receiver, he leaned back in his chair, letting out a gasp of air, TF is going along with things, or should I say he didn't say, "No"

Silversmith looked at Carter, "If you don't need me any longer, I'll get off, as I'd hate that shit, Chris Rotherham, to see me."

Carter looked at Silversmith, "You may need another Clerk of Chambers, and I suppose that the news will filter through when he fails to turn up for work on Monday. Do you have such a man?"

Carter looked at him, "William, keep safe and please be very careful these people play for keeps." He stood up, and shook hands with him, as he did so he said, "Thank you Carter, you have this day, saved my career, and my reputation. I'll be eternally grateful." He then left, at Carter's request, one of the team showing him out.

Carter looked around the table saying, "Well you can both close your mouths, and let's get on.

"Right Sue, will you get two teams, one headed by Ian, and the second headed by Lloydie. I want for warrants to be sworn out, one for John Jackson, and the second for, Bill Collins, you know what to put?" I wish for you Sue, to remain here while we deal with, Chris Rotherham.

He looked at Eric, "Can you organise some scoff, for both Sue and I, Sue, will be in her office while I use my own phone." They both burst out laughing, whilst they went on their merry way, he could hear Eric, saying to Sue, "Have you any pennies for the phone?" They heard Carter shout, "Bugger off."

Minutes later Penny answered her phone, *"Hi Carter, have missed you it must be 5.30 ish, are we going to be late?"* Carter said, "It's beginning to look that way, I wanted to make sure that whatever you may be preparing for tea, won't spoil."

Penny started to laugh, *"Well now Mr, what would you like? You can have a take away, that's straight into bed, and a rather designer menu...Or you can have the standard meal of the day, a curry, Pizza, chicken salad. Now what would be your culinary desires?"* Carter could not hold back his laughter, "What about a beacon butty, I love them when I come in late from work, with loads of HP sauce." Penny said, *"Oh! Carter, sorry but, I've only prepared the first option, it's the only meal that never spoils, the rest I only made up."*

Carter said, "I tell you what, you choose, sorry have to go."

With that there was a knock at the door, he shouted "Come in" The door opened and in walked Sue. She looked at Carter, "Both teams dispatched, and low and behold, Rotherham is here, he's in the interview room."

Carter said, "Let's get to it."

Chapter Thirty Seven

On arrival at the room, the duty uniform officer opened the door. They both thanked him and walked it. Their bottoms had hardly touched their chairs when Rotherham said, "Is that completely necessary?"

Carter said, "What?" Rotherham said, "The police officer stood outside of the door, as I've just come to see Mr Silverman. Carter said, "Well! Mr Rotherham, any civilian personnel entering this part of the police station, must be escorted, and for an officer to be posted outside of any office door."

Rotherham looked rather blank when he said, "Anyway when can I see Mr Silverman, who wishes to see me." Carter stared right at him, "Oh! Sorry but he's just left. But you see it's you, Mr Rotherham that we want to see."

He suddenly sat bolt upright, "And why me?" Carter said, "Firstly let me introduce you to, WDCS Susan Ford, and I'm, Assistant Commander Carter, of the Major Crime Unit."

Sarcastically Rotherham said, "Well, again why me?" Carter suddenly said, "Mr Christopher Rotherham, I must caution you, are not obliged to say anything, but what you do say...Blardy, blardy, blarr." He looked shell shocked.

Sue leaned over and taking two unopened tapes placed them into the machine. She then said, "It's Friday 18th October 2012, she then mentioned all persons present, when completed the machine bleeped.

Carter began the interrogation. "Mr Rotherham is it true that you are, Clark of Chambers, for messes, "Harris, Gordon and Jones, Barrister's in Dale Street, Liverpool?" He replied, "Yes, you know very well I am."

Carter said, "Do you happen to know of a client by the name of, Thomas Parsons, of 42, Rock Street, West Derby, Liverpool?" Rotherham suddenly began to slowly sit up, "Why yes, what's happened?"

Carter said, "I'd like to ask you, how does a person

like, Thomas Parsons, manage to secure the services of, Harris, Gordon and Jones a very expensive firm of barristers?"

Rotherham said, "Well! I got a phone call asking for me to send, Silverman to Derby Lane police station, were Parsons had been arrested, and taken to."

Carter said, "So you as, Clerk of Chambers for your firm, act on a phone call? Who was the caller?" Rotherham just started to shuffle his feet, on the floor, under the table. Carter shouted, "Who?"

Rotherham, jumped up, "It was just a call." Carter said, "Did you go to your immediate boss, or perhaps one of the partners, putting to them the situation, and the request of the caller."

Rotherham said, "No"

Carter said, well! Mr Rotherham, I have asked you several times, to inform me of these matters, your answers I have to say are somewhat limp?"

"I have to tell you that officers from my team, are as we speak, arresting and searching the homes of John Jackson, and Bill Collins, the two men who accompanied Parsons, which as you know, lead to his arrest."

Carter looked at Sue; "Interview terminated at 6.30pm, on Friday 18th October 2012."

He looked at Rotherham and continued, "Now, you have been given every opportunity to answer the questions asked, yet you failed to give adequate and, helpful information? We will then see what you have to say after our interrogations with Jackson, and Collins."

"Now when they both arrive at, Derby Lane police station, they will both be interviewed, and one of the questions asked; "Do you know a 'Chris Rotherham' now what do you think their reply will be?"

Both Sue and Carter, stood up, and began to leave the interview room. He cried, "Alright, alright, I'll tell you what you want to know?"

Carter turned, and returned to the table, and stood opposite him. "Well Mr Rotherham, before you decide to

116

sprout forth, with the supposed answers to my questions, I have to tell you that at this very moment, the charges against you are, at the very least, 'Wasting police time' and at worst, 'Conspiracy'

He screamed, "What?" Carter interrupted, "Oh! Yes, I see that the penny has finely dropped, you must have realised that you could be out of a job. Now, if you don't wish to go to prison, tell me what I want to know?"

Chapter Thirty Eight

At that moment, Sue walked back into the office, and stood next to Carter. Looking at Rotherham, Carter said, "Now the tape isn't on, as we will give you the opportunity to discuss matters, before we take legal steps in dealing with your evidence."

"Rotherham looked at them both, "You see, I happen to like a bet; and although I'm not addicted, and insist not over my head in debt. The bookie has always allowed me a line of credit for my bets. On the other hand, has never chased me at times, over monies owed."

Carter looked at Sue for she knew what was coming. Rotherham had a watery smile to his face, "I see that you both know what I'm going to say next?" Carter looked at him, "I'm afraid so, there is no such thing as a free lunch?"

He immediately thought of his best friend Rad, but the thought passed as quickly as it came.

Sue looked at Carter who nodded, Sue said, "Rotherham, does this bookie happen to know what you do for a job? He replied, "Yes"

Sue continued, "So if such an opportunity arose, he'd know where to come for a favour, particularly one as urgent as this?" He made no answer he just looked at the floor.

"Sue continued, "It's funny that the bookie just happened to know who to contact? Let's say you were approached for this special favour?"

"Now this could put your job in jeopardy, you must have said, "No chance." Rotherham replied, "That's correct."

Sue looked at him, "Well say the bookie said, Chris, if you were to do this favour for me, then I'll wipe your debt clean?"

Sue showed a degree of apathy towards him, "Rotherham what sort of money are we talking about?" Rotherham replied, "Ten grand."

"He expanded, "I know £10k seems a lot of money to most people, and yes, it is, but as a Clerk of Chambers, my job is not salaried. I earn ten percent of any of the business brought over my desk."

Sue said, "Well Mr Rotherham, please lead us through what went on?"

He started to cough, and had a rattle in his throat, when cleared he started, "I was in my office, when my phone rang. The person said, "Hello Chris, I immediately identified the voice,"

"I thought that he may have wanted me to settle my account? Which if so, would cause a bit of a problem, but none the less I could manage it."

"But no, he asked, who is the best criminal Barrister in your chambers, and does he happen to be available?" I obviously complained stating, "It's impossible to act on what you seem to need."

He suddenly said, "Well Chris, how would you like it if I was to contact one of the partners, informing them that they have a senior member of staff, with a gambling problem?"

The caller turned the screw, "The partners may before dispensing with your services, may look into the petty cash, and client's accounts, to see if you have been illegally tapping into funds or resources, to aid your addiction?"

Rotherham went on to say how he was pressurised by the caller. He eventually admitted that he recommended, and engaged the services of, Mr Silverman, to attend at Derby Lane, to interview Parson, and prepare a brief.

Mr Silverman was to also attend, and assist Parsons in any of the police investigations. He knew that the Barrister was very busy, and would only 'speed read' the instructions, that I prepared, leaving him to prepare the rest."

Carter looked at Rotherham, "Well Chris, I need the name of the bookie?" He just nodded. "Chris, you must also realise that for you to have engage the services of

Silverman, this in no minor event."

"Did your bookie friend explain to you the circumstances of this case?" Rotherham said, "He mentioned that, Parsons was found in a hospital room, with a gun?"

Sue suddenly dropped the apathetic look, and turned on Rotherham, she sarcastically said, "Well Chris, we happen to have a mortuary filled with eight bodies, one of which is a police officer."

Sue went on to say, "The reason why you were asked to engage the services of Mr Silverman was to smooth the way for Parsons, through all of this. Now I have to say, Parsons is a member of a gang."

"Someone from that gang insisted that he had to go into the Royal Infirmary, and act as a Doctor, allowing him access into a ward, and a room in which he thought contained the surviving witness."

"Unknown to Parsons, we had the ward, and room under surveillance. In that room he thought that he was killing a surviving witness. He discharged a gun twice into what he thought was the witness, where in fact it was a dummy."

"He was arrested and taken to, Derby Lane." On completion Rotherham said, "He didn't mention the whole story, he under sold the issue."

Carter said, "Right Chris, we will now interview you under caution and your conversation taped." He just nodded.

Chapter Thirty Nine

On completion of their interview, Carter said, "Rotherham, you are still under caution?" He nodded, Carter said, "For the purposes of the tape, the accused just nodded.

Carter looked at the accused, "Rotherham, you will be taken down to the charge office, were WDC Ford, will formally caution and charge you with, Deception, and Conspiracy. You will be detained in custody, and produced in the Magistrates court tomorrow, for a plea."

"The prosecution will ask that you be refused bail, due to the severity of the offence." Rotherham burst out crying.

Carter called the officer from outside in the hall, he opened the door saying, "Yes sir" Carter said, "Yes officer, will you please keep our friend company until DCS Ford, comes to collect him." He replied, "Yes sir"

As they both passed the general office, Carter opened the door. He saw what he was looking for. He walked over to the two large hot drink flasks; he looked over his shoulder at Sue, he said, "Can I interest you in a mug of coffee, or tea "My treat."

Sue burst out laughing, "Well guv you know how to treat a woman...Make mine a coffee, with milk, and two sugars." As they both walked to Carters office armed with their drinks.

Carter burst out laughing, "You'd have thought by now that, I'd know your tipple."

Sitting comfortably, he looked at her, "Sue, can you after coffee go, and over see how things are getting on with Jackson, and Collins, make sure their resumes are ready for court in the morning. Now with it being late will you ask Peter, and Philip to bring in the bookie on Saturday, Rotherham will give them his details?"

"I want resumes prepared for the four accused, please call the 'on call' CPS and, make sure they are up in court tomorrow. If you have any problems give me a call, I'm playing the 'boss card' and going home."

Sue looked at him and said, "Why not Carter, you were starting to look tired, see you on Monday."

There was a knock at his door he looked at Sue, he then said, "Come In" He looked at the door to see Charlie standing there, Carter said, "What the fu..." Sue said "It's alright Carter, I called him when I went to the loo." He looked at Sue, he smiled singing..." "Ah! Yes you know me so well." And burst out laughing.

En route Carter made two calls, the first to Penny, informing her that he was now on the way home. His second call was to TF.

Frost answered the phone immediately, *"Frost"* Carter said, "Sir, it's Carter, I really feel that we are going to unravel, yet another major crime, in which I feel there is a skeletal thread, running throughout."

Frost said, *"Well!"* Carter explained all the issues to date, that they had in fact made three arrests, added together with the perpetrator found in the hospital room, making four in all. Each victim is being processed as we speak."

Frost said, *"What are your thoughts in all of this?"* Carter said, "Well as you know we have the seven bodies of the young girls, and our PC. I feel that this is just a forerunner."

"What stunk in all of this, we have a prisoner with the rags battering his arse, so to say, somehow he manages to secure the services of a top draw Barrister. Why, and How? The barrister, William Silverman, suddenly appears at Derby Lane, as his brief."

He continued, "Sir, when the question was asked, how you managed to secure the services of such a Barrister? The prisoner replied to all questions, 'No comment'

"After a while we removed the prisoner, and we had a quiet word with Silverman, threatening him with, 'Conspiracy' He then informed us that the job was farmed out via the clerk in his chambers."

"Prior to letting Silverman go, we asked the clerk to attend at Derby Lane, to speak with Mr Silverman. He attended, and after interrogation, he rolled over on a local bookie, who, telephoned him, threatening to tell his employees, of his gambling addiction, should he not send a top Barrister."

Tony Frost said, *"Well, all seems under control, any problems, call me."* The phone went dead.

Carter sat back he looked over to Charlie, "I'm sorry Sue called you out, to do the home run?" Charlie smiled, "No probes."

On arrival home, he thanked him, and walked off towards his flat. On arrival he walked into the lounge, and after taking off his jacket, loosened his tie as he flopped down into one of the armchairs.

He had been there a matter of seconds when Penny, materialised wearing her dressing gown. Looking down at him she said, "Long day I know what you need?"

Carter was just about to speak when Penny said, "A nice warm showers, when in your PJ's, then jump under the duvet and sleep?"

He gave a weak smile, walked through to their bedroom, where he undressed, and took the lovely awaiting shower.

After towelling himself down, he walked through to their bedroom in a clean pair of boxers, and jumped into bed. He was a sleep in seconds. Penny leaned over kissing him good night, as she kissed him on his cheek.

It only seemed like seconds, when his phone rang on his bedside table, he heard the ringing of his phone, through his fog of sleep, and he put an arm out from under their duvet, grabbing his phone. In a tired voice he said, "Carter."

An apologetic voice said, "Sorry Carter, to disturb you, it's Sue. I've just received a call from, Phil who is 'on call' this week; he told me that a body had been found in the 'Sports ground' Thomas Lane. I've dispatched Charlie, to pick you up."

Carter still in a sleepy voice said, "See you shortly."

Penny after being disturbed said, "Carter, you go and

take a quick shower, and I'll get some clothes together." As he meandered into the bathroom he shouted, "What time is it?" Penny replied, "3.30am." Carter replied, "The death hours."

After showering, and a quick shave, he dressed in the awaiting clothes. When dressed he walked through to the kitchen were Penny, had made a mug of black coffee. On handing it to Carter she said, "I've added some cold water so you don't scald yourself."

Chapter Forty

They had no sooner stopped speaking when the front door intercom sounded. Penny said, "I'll go, while you at least have a couple of sips of your coffee, before you rush off." He then heard, "Morning Charlie, he's on his way down."

Penny said, "How about I make a large flask of coffee, with milk and some mugs." Carter went over to her, "It's a lovely thought, but the team will think I'm a wimp." Penny laughing said, "They wouldn't dare, you're their guv."

He smiled at her and gave her a big kiss on the mouth, as he left to meet Charlie.

"Penny, in a soft voice, whispered, "Will you be home for seconds?" Laughing he said, "Get in woman, before you awaken all our neighbours."

Carter got into Charlie's waiting car, "Off we go! Not wishing to disturb his neighbours, Charlie refrained from putting on the blues and two's, when a couple of streets away, he leant forward switching them on.

Charlie at speed made for the location, he turned right at the junction of Edge Lane and Queens drive, at this time of the morning it allowed him to make great speed. He turned right onto, East Prescot Road. At a roundabout, he went round it until reaching, Brookside Avenue, which led into Thomas Lane.

It was there that they noticed all the other emergency vehicles, with their blue lights illuminating the night's sky.

They came to a halt, on alighting from the car, they were both met by Sue, who wearing a dark coloured heavy coat to keep out the early morning cold, was waiting.

Uniform officers had cordoned off the crime area, with the typical blue and white plastic tape, showing 'Police line do not cross.' Sue quickly handed Carter his forensic suit. Charlie had also quickly changed.

The three began to walk over the 'Sports ground' after a matter of yards they came across an officer with a clip board. They all showed their ID's the officer raised the tape for them to gain access.

They continued along the metal trays all placed by the SOCCO officers. Whilst they walked Sue said, "Sorry Carter, I've got bad news for you, the body is that of, William Silverman."

Carter suddenly came to a halt he looked at Sue, "Please tell me that you are fucking joking, after apologising to her for his choice words, he looked down at the floor, please, and it's only a matters of hours since we last saw him."

Sue, who had been also looking down at the ground, looked up at Carter, her face draw with shock. They continued on the metal path which lead to a large tent, erected to protect the crime scene. On arrival they all heard the booming voice of Gordon Chambers.

One of the SOCO officers opened the tent for them, Carter nodded his thanks. They found the pathologist kneeling at the side of the body, he looked up, "Carter it's been a while, many congratulations on your promotion, it's well deserved." Carter thanked him.

Mr Chambers, struggled in getting to his feet, but with a degree of empathy said, "I believe you know the victim?"

In a low voice Carter replied, "Yes, he is an eminent Barrister, employed by the best Chambers in the City, and to my great regret, we released him from our enquiries some hours ago."

Mr Chambers stood dressed in his forensic garb, and with his hood up, Carter thought he looked as if he had been shrink wrapped. None the less a more competent pathologist would be hard to find.

The pathologist let out a loud deflated noise, for one moment Carter thought he was deflating like a large balloon. Carter had the greatest deference for the man, and there was mutual esteem shown on both sides.

He looked at Carter and taking a great breath he said, "Well our friend was not killed here, there is very little blood. He was shot twice to the left side of the head, and at close range."

"We found a small residue of blood, and brain matter, but again insufficient amounts to make this the killing site. This is also borne out by the total lack of blood and, blood splatter."

"The victim as you can well see is lying with the right side of his head to the ground. If you look closely," He winked at Carter as he said the words, for he always knew of Carters reluctance for sordid crime scenes.

He again continued, "One can see the black powder burns to the surface of the skin, I think he was shot with a 9mm gun, but will be able to tell you more when I get him home."

Carter looked at the pathologist, "Sir, Gordon Chambers interrupted him, "Sir, sir! Have we not agreed after all this time, and our many cases we can agree on first name terms, can we not agree?"

Unbeknown to Carter both Sue and Charlie stood behind him, and both smiled realising the respect that each man had for one another.

Carter said, "Okay Gordon, can you now please give us a TOD? *(Time of death)* He smiled, "Well Carter, I carried out a thorough examination of the victim, and found the body was cold, due to the location, an open field. Rigor mortis is still prevalent in the body.

The victim is not over weight, I derive that it's been present for about 1-6 hours. A rectal liver temp reveals he has been dead about 4 hours.

Carter thanked him, and left. Outside Carter saw Lloydie, Peter and Phil. Carter looked at Lloydie he just smiled, and began to enter the tent. Carter patted him on the shoulder, he said, "Thanks Lloydie."

Stood outside he noticed that dawn was beginning to break. Looking at Sue, he said, "I want Ian, and a team, to do door to door, along the houses on either side of Thomas Lane. Will you organise a dog unit to attend the field, to see if they can find anything?"

Carter looked at his watch; it was 4.15am He sighed, then looking at Sue said, "Well we need to regroup at Derby Lane, in order for us to set up a battle plan, and to get warm drinks into us."

Chapter Forty One

En route, back to the police station, Carter contacted Toney Frost, the phone was answered with the usual bark, *"Frost"* "Sir, it's Carter, sorry for the early call, but we have a body found in, Thomas Lane, Sports ground."

"The victim is William Silversmith, the eminent Barrister of, Harris, Gordon and Jones, of Dale Street."

Frost said, *"What! Wasn't he just at Derby Lane, yesterday, representing your prisoner, Thomas Parsons?"* Carter replied, "Yes, when he left, he was fit and well, now whether I should have warned him of the severity of this case, I felt that if offered protection, he would laugh at us."

"Never the less, it would seem that someone must have thought that he, and Parsons, may have leaked information to us."

Tony Frost replied, *"Well, Carter that is the risk they take being a Defence lawyer, or Barrister. When, we talk about risk in the job, what about you, and the members of your team. I rest my case."* He closed the call. Carter then looked at the phone receiver. "Yes and a bye sir to you."

As he got out of his car Carter, making a shivering noise, had his arms bound around him saying, "Coffee, coffee my kingdom for a mug of coffee. Charlie said, "I'll get it sorted guv."

He ran ahead up the metal staircase, which lead up to the rear entrance to the CID office.

As Carter made his way into the general office, Charlie greeted him with a mug of black coffee. Looking at Carter he said, "Carter they are waiting for you in your office." Carter thanked him saying, "Do you have yours?" He replied, "Yes." Carter looked at him, "Well come along." And he walked off to his office.

He opened the door, and there was a shuffle of chairs, he called out, "As you were. Do we all have drinks?" They all said, "Yes" "Now I have quickly made a list, of what we need to do?" He started to pace backwards, and forwards.

"Right, Sue I want you to get things organised? I want Ian, to gather a group of the team, and do door to door enquiries along Thomas Drive. I also want

Jill, and Kate, to go and interview Mrs Silverman; we need a full statement as to what happened. I also want SOCO, all over her road there may be tyre tread,

If they left skid marks from there get away, with their victim. Also drive, and hall; the abductors may have left some vital evidence."

"Sue, can you liaise with Lloydie? I, what forensics all over Silverman's, clothes. They may find hair follicles, from out of the abductors car, for comparison when found.

Carter continued, "Peter and Phil, do you have the Bookies details?" Phil replied, "Yes guv, it's Bernie Ford, and the betting shop is in Castle Street."

Carter looked at Sue, "Chris Rotherham, didn't have too far to go to place his bets, Sue just smiled, "Very convenient." Carter said, "Boys, I want you to prepare an arrest warrant for our friend Ford, for, Bribery and Conspiracy. I want him lifted, no questions asked. It's still early, act before the news gets out." They both replied, "Yes guv" and left.

It wasn't long before they heard the distinct noise of the team starting to come in. Carter looked at Sue, "Can we arrange a quick meeting in the conference room for say 9.00am.We need to get a handle on this, I know it's Saturday, can we make sure that Parsons, Jackson, and Collins are set for the Magistrates court, she replied, "Yes guv."

After they left Carter, sat and picked up the phone. Penny answered in seconds. He said, "Did you manage to get back to sleep after I'd left? Penny spluttered, "Me get some sleep? I'm okay it's Saturday, what about you." He replied, "I'll just tuck up all the loose ends, and slip of early."

He'd no sooner finished when there was a knock at his

door. He said, "Sorry, I'll have to go, speak soon." He called, "Come in" It was Sue, and "We're all ready." He got up and followed her to the conference room.

He stood at the top of the room next to Sue. He looked out at their faces, "Yes! I know we all have better places to be on this lovely Saturday morning? For all that don't know which I know is no one! We have a murder!"

"The boss, will go into detail about the victim, and the location of the body, and draw up your duties for today."

At that very moment Phil entered the conference room, he said, "Guv we have the Bookie in an interview room, with an officer standing by." Carter turned to Sue, "When finished come to the general office, and we'll interview, Ford together." Sue replied, "Yes guv."

Whilst Carter sat enjoying a mug of coffee, the door opened, looking up he saw Sue. He said get yourself a drink and let's have a chat re Ford."

Carter said, "As you well know this is all inter-connected, we have Parsons, who gets Silversmith, who allows us to get Rotherham, who gives us Ford. Now I know it sounds like the Bible, with the, *'Begot and the Begets'* He looked at Sue and immediately saw the confused look on her face.

He burst out laughing, "It's alright Sue, I'm not asking for religious studies. But the way this is shaping up, there is this interconnection throughout all of this. It's similar to pyramid selling." Carter scribbled on a piece of paper.

Ford
Silverman - Rotherham
Parsons - Collins - Jackson

"Now we need to know if there is a Mr Big, on top of Ford, who is issuing orders, or are there other layers still to be revealed. So let's take our drinks, interview Ford, and find out."

Chapter Forty Two

They both left the general office, and walked down towards the interview rooms. At the nearest one they saw a uniform officer stood at the door. On seeing them he opened the door and stood to one side.

Carter thanked him and walked in. He there saw a very indignant looking Ford. Carter and Sue sat opposite him. Carter said, "Mr Ford, I'm Assistant Commander Carter CID, and this is my esteem colleague, Woman Detective Chief Superintendent CID, funny enough also *'Ford'*

They both looked at him, Carter looked at Sue, WDC Ford, I thought that was rather funny, but our guest showed not a flicker?" Carter said, "Sue will you please do the honours."

Sue lent forward and placed two unopened tapes into the recording machine, after a couple of seconds, the machine bleeped. Sue said, "This interview conducted on 9.30am on Saturday 19th October 2012, Sue went on to introduce, all the assembled personnel.

She looked at Carter, and with a sullen face. He said, "Mr Bernard Ford, "You do not have to say anything. But, it may harm your defence if you do not mention when questioned something which you later rely on in court. Anything you do say may be given in evidence."

Ford looked totally dumbfounded saying, "What on earth is this all about?" Carter said, "Mr Ford, my officers attended at your place of work, and served you with an arrest warrant, which resulted in you being arrested and, brought here to Derby Lane police station."

"Do you think that you've been brought her for us to place a bet?" Sue let out a splutter. After about a minute he shouted well! Ford said, "Sorry but I don't know what you mean?"

Carter said, "Well Mr Ford, I've plenty of evidence that you're good at your job? In some cases you allow, some punters to amass a debt, whether or not they can pay it off.

Can I also please tell you that I'm good at my job as well?"

He continued, "What odds would you think Ford, would offer on us winning this matter, and the odds on him walking free? DCS Ford, I told you he'd have given us *short odds,* I'd have to give him *'100/1 on,* if he felt lucky?"

Ford shouted, "What the fuck are you going on about?"

Carer said, "Well Mr Ford, and I only call you by your official name for the opening of my investigation to this matter. You realise that you are still under caution?" He just remained blank. Carter said, "For the purposes of the tape, the accused made no reply."

Ford said, "The accused! What, on earth have I done, and why the accused?" Carter said, "You are Bernard Ford, who owns the betting shop in Dale Street? He replied, "Yes."

Carter continued, "You are the Bernard Ford, who made a phone call to a Christopher Rotherham?" Ford replied, "Who is Christopher Rotherham?"

Carter looked at Sue, and then at Ford, "Why Mr Ford, Rotherham, is one of your punters." Ford laughed out loud, "I have fucking thousands of punters who do business in my shop."

Carter said, "How many with the name Rotherham? And how many who happen to be 'Clerk of Chamber' for a firm of Barristers in Dale Street, the street very close to Castle Street, where you happen to own a betting shop?" Ford remained tight lipped.

Cater said, "For the purposes of the tape the accused made no reply."

Carter then said, "Ford, we have two ways of dealing with this. 1, I can tell you that a man who we have in custody, clearly states that he received a phone call whilst in work, employed as a Clerk of Chambers."

"Our witness, clearly states that the call was from you Ford, you asked our witness to supply the best Barrister to help a friend arrested, and being held at Derby Lane, police station."

"He of course said no; telling you, the caller, that it was more than his jobs worth. You then went on to mention about, what would his bosses think of a man that they employ, has a gambling problem."

"But in the meantime, you the bookie would consider writing off his debt, of approximately 10 grand."

Carter said, "Now Ford, before you say anything, just listen to point number, 2. That we produce our witness, and you take part in an ID parade, now you must know what they are?"

Ford was as white as a sheet, after a couple of seconds he shouted, "Alright, alright, I'll tell you what you want to know, and all that I know, it's not much?"

Carter looked at him, "Ford why make me go all round the houses to end up with you, coughing your part in all of this." Carter looked at him, "Do you want a glass of water, and I don't want you fainting on me." He replied, "Yes please."

Carter looked at Sue; interview terminated at 11.30am on Saturday 19th October 2012, to allow the accused to have a drink of water. Sue called, "Officer could you get the accused a glass of water?"

He said, "Certainly Mom!! He suddenly stopped as he remembered the last time he called Sue 'Mom' the officer said, "Certainly boss." Sue smiling, said, "Carry on officer."

Ford was left alone to take his drink of water. Outside in the corridor, Carter said to Sue, "Send one of the team to check on calls made on his mobile, the mobile in his property, and others to search calls made 'in or out' of his shop, dates, and times."

He continued, the information may take a load of investigating, so I intend after this interview to arrest and bail him, to return say in two weeks to answer to our enquiries." Sue said, "I'll get to it."

Minutes later and feeling somewhat fortified, if one was to ask, Ford, for his definition of being somewhat fortified, he'd say that he would wish to be anywhere other than in Derby Lane, police station, being interrogated by such a hardnosed police officer.

Carter with Sue, returned from her task, looked at Ford saying, "Alright if we push on? Oh! Sorry Ford that would give the impression that I care."

Carter looked at Sue, and nodded, Sue leaned over and started the tape, after it beeped Carter looked at Ford, saying "You do realise that you are still under caution?" He just nodded. Carter said, "For the purposes of the tape, the accused just nodded his head."

He continued, "Well, Ford, what have you got to say, after your outburst?"

Ford, who seemed to have aged in the period of the pause, took in a deep breath, "Well I received a phone call." He looked at them both and said, "Yes I know what you're going to say, what a very apt excuse?"

Carter said, "Ford, do you now admit that you know, Christopher Rotherham, and that you asked for him to supply, a Barrister, to attend at Derby Lane, police station?" He replied, "Yes."

Carter said, "Was all this done as a result of a phone call made to you?" He again answered, "Yes"

Carter said, "How did you receive this call? Was it to your mobile phone or to the phone in your shop? He began to shuffle on his chair he looked very sheepish, "My mobile?"

Carter said, "Right Ford, as I previously stated, this will all go round in circles, so for that reason, you will be taken to the charge office were you will be charged with, 'Bribery, and Conspiracy' You will be bailed, to re appear at Derby Lane, police station."

"When you were arrested, officers confiscated, and removed your passport to, stop your flight, from the UK."

Chapter Forty Three

After his interview with Ford, and while he awaited for Sue's return from the charge office. He called, Tony Frost bringing him up to date with recent events.

He said, "Sir, it's Carter, the investigation is proceeding re the murder, and together with DCS Ford, have sat, and interviewed a man, and I use the word revise ably, who is also called, Ford."

"Ford, who is a bookie, admits ringing, Rotherham he states that he called him to engage the services of, Silverman. The team are at present checking calls made from his shop, and calls made on his mobile."

Carter said, "Sir, I wish for your permission to hold a press conference. We are fighting fires on approximately 9 sides...Frost interrupted, *"What's the list?"*

Carter replied, 1. The girls found in the rear of the HGV trailer, 2.The young Asian girls from the outside of the docks, 3.The killing of one of the surviving witness and the PC, 4. The attempted murder of the remaining witness's catching Parsons. For Parsons gave us Jackson, and Collins. 5. Silversmith. 6. Rotherham, the Clerk of Chambers, and 7. Ford the bookie."

He continued, "Nine murders, one attempted murder, and four for Conspiracy, and perhaps, bribery. 'A big bag of shit' Now if we get it out there via a press conference, and or a news release, even a statement, we may rattle a few cages."

At present apart from Silversmith, all the others are cannon fodder, there has to be the one at the top, the one who is controlling everything?"

"Now Gordon Chamber's, thinks there is a large market for body parts that a body, systematically harvested, could fetch in the region of £200K, and this gang have taken it upon themselves to illegally supply the necessary parts."

"First, they have a person who acts as a photographer, who swans around a place such as Liverpool 1. He approaches girls telling them how beautiful they are? Have they ever thought of becoming a model, and could be the next, Kate Moss."

"This bloke tells them that he will produce a portfolio for them, and suggest he make arrangement to see modelling agents...?"

"Gordon Chamber's, believes that from the evidence obtained from our seven victims, they each show a tattoo, on their wrists. Which he feels in our case, that they must have the many common types of blood?"

"Should they find a victim, or victims with rarer blood types, a different design of tattoo will depict this fact? They go on to harvest their body parts, and farm them out to the awaiting recipients."

He went on to say, "It doesn't matter all victims will be murdered, as they can't afford any trace of evidence revealed which may lead back to the perpetrators. It is the main rule of the job. They all end up the same."

"Now how do they go about identifying possible victims? Gordon Chambers, believes, that the six victims found in the back of the HGV all showed puncture marks on the inside of their arms, stating blood samples extracted are quickly identified, to determine victims with rare blood."

Carter realised that there was a pause at the other end of the phone, eventually Tony Frost whispered, *"Carter, this sounds like wholesale slaughter for parts."*

"Frost continued, *"Clients, who have the money, and wherewithal, who are able to afford such costs, haven't got the time to wait for the normal NHS practice."*

"I'll clear my schedule; see you Monday, my office, 9.00am will you please inform Wendy Field, and Sam Watson, to join us. Carter, as to use your famous quote, 'It could all turn into a ball of shit.' The phone went dead.

There was a knock on his door, he shouted 'Cone in' Looking up he saw Sue, stood framed by the door, carrying two mugs of coffee. He smiled, "Now there's my favourite girl." Sue said, "It's only that I come bearing gifts." They both burst out laughing.

Carter said, "How was Ford, when he was bailed?" Sue said, "He flew out like shit off a shovel, there was no stopping him." They both laughed.

As she sat down, he said, "Sue before I forget, please make sure that we are both at TF's office, 9.00am Monday, will you please call, Wendy and Sam, he wants' for them to be there as well?"

"As a favour will you ask Sam, to bring Penny, as I want her to get an insight as to how we do the job?"

"It's 7.00pm I'm leaving for home, see you Monday? He got up and left for the general office. On his arrival he signed off duty turned and left. Charlie quickly did the same and followed him down the corridor.

Carter thanked Charlie, as usual for the lift. He walked to his flat entrance saying, "Hello" To both the doorman, and to the duty APD, as he walked towards his flat.

Chapter Forty Four

As he entered their flat he was welcomed by Penny, in a delirious state, she ran towards him with arms opened wide, nearly knocking him over, as she gave him a bear hug shouting, "Carter, Carter you'll never guess what's happened?"

Keeping a serious face he said, "Penny, what on earth's the matter?" Penny, in an elated voice said, "It's Sam, she's attending a meeting on Monday, in your bosses office, and she wants me to attend. I do believe you'll be there as well?"

Carter fighting to remain serious said, "I know of the meeting, and I know Sam, is on the guest list, but why on earth should she bring you?" Penny shouted, "Carter, Carter, what is the matter with you? I'm her, *'Research Director'* and as such, will assist were necessary."

He turned and walked towards the kitchen to grab two beers saying, "Well I suppose it may give you an insight into my job, and the team?" As he said it he, nearly burst out laughing. He could hear Penny, running after him, profusely shouting statements that justify her job, and career.

As he turned with two beers in hand, he could hold matters no longer, he burst out laughing saying, "Oh! Penny you are a funny fish?" Penny screamed, Fish! I'll give you fish?"

She suddenly came to a halt. Carter, why are you bloody laughing?" Carter, said, "Because I set it all up, I honestly felt it would give you an opportunity to get an insight of my job, because you have a legitimate reason to be there."

As he gave her, her beer he said, "Penny, I realise how difficult it must have been for Helen, or any other wife, or partner of a CID line officer, who on a whim, goes out in the middle of the night, who on occasions, gets called out after only been home a matter of hours.

After all the excitement they both sat down to relish their beers, on completion Carter said, "What's for tea? It smells delicious." Penny said, "Lancashire hot pot" Penny took hold of his hand, and walked him towards the bedroom saying, "It's in a 'slow cooker' it won't spoil."

The very words immediately reminded him of Helen, but the thought in seconds had gone.

In bed, they both took part in their high as ever standard of love making. Yet as ever, it began with them both taking great pains to explore each other's bodies, eventually dwelling on each of their favourite erogenous zones.

On completion they both laid back in total satisfaction, Penny laid with her head on Carter's chest, listening to his heart beating in his chest, gradually returning to it's usual rhythm, whilst he twisted trisell's of her hair, in his fingers.

In harmony, thy both got up out of bed, and leaving for the bathroom, knowing full well that they'd take part in yet another prolific exercise, their gorgeous exotic shower, again relishing it's full format.

On completion, whilst laughing and joking, they excitedly towel dried each other, and dressed in dressing gowns they both left for the kitchen, to enjoy their sumptuous meal. During which they both enjoyed two glasses of red wine.

Penny said, "Carter let's leave the dishes until the morning, I felt like some small animal who on completing their meal, just wants to curl up and go to sleep."

Penny hoped that her comment was excepted by Carter, as for nothing would give her greater pleasure than to return to their beautiful lair, and make mad passionate love.

But Penny had detected tiredness in his eyes, and although he was one who would not refuse such a proposition, on this occasion she hoped her animal example would be excepted.

In bed they took up a position as if spoons in a draw

140

and after passionately kissing each other good night, they both drifted off into blissful sleep.

It was again that in the early hours of the morning, his sleep was interrupted by the melodic sound of his phone. As if on auto pilot, he extended his arm from under the duvet, and in unison took hold of the infernal contraption, and answered, "Carter."

The voice at the other end of the phone in an apologetic voice said, "Sorry Carter, it's Sue, we have another, and it's Ford."

Carter as if hit by a vast electrical surge, suddenly sat upright in bed and said, "What the fuck?" Sue replied, "Charlie is on his way." Carter recovered from his foggy sleepy haze, and said, "Sorry Sue, please...before he could finish, she said, "It's alright boss" and closed the call.

He could hear Penny from under the duvet, "Carter what on earth...?" He said, "Sorry to disturb you Penny, try and go back to sleep, I'm afraid, I've been called out."

Fighting with her over her abundance share of the duvet, a frequent argument made by Carter, she sat up saying, "Go get a quick shower, while I put some clothes out for you?"

Whilst showering he began to smile, he thought, why is it that woman seem to think that men are totally devoid of making simple decisions, such as take a shower, go to the kitchen with dirty plates, and giving directions, as if we, men are lacking in the concept of considering possible choices.

After kissing Penny, good bye he left to join Charlie who was patiently waiting for him.

Chapter Forty Five

After Carter settled himself in the car, he looked at Charlie, saying, "Where to?" Charlie said, "Carter, this is a bad one, we're off to Sandstone Park, off the Drive. *(Locals often use the word Drive, as a shortened version for Queens Drive.)*

Out of sight of Carters address, Carter leaned forward putting on the blues, leaving off the siren, due to the hour, he realised there was no traffic to combat. Charlie drove along Ullet Road, turning left onto Smithdown Road, through The Old Swan, along Derby Lane, onto the Drive, were he turned left until he arrived at Sandfield Park.

He turned right along Central Drive, as he turned left onto North Drive; they both saw the evidence for themselves, of all the mustered troops. They were difficult to miss with all the blue incandescent lights, illuminating the night sky.

On arrival as Carter left the car, the personnel who were present, all stood, and parted, dividing allowing Carter, the view of what appeared to be the drunken figure of a man on the floor, hugging the lamp post.

Sue, walking towards him, already dressed in her forensic suit. It was very apparent that she had been crying, with the evidential tears in her eyes. She looked at Carter saying, "We only bailed him about 8 hours ago?"

He suddenly thought to himself, Oh! Fuck, at the same time he clocked the road sign, Bracken Way. Fords address. The look on her face, answered his questions. He looked at her, "I'm in the shit?" Sue said, "No guv we're both in it."

He also caught sight of Gordon Chambers, crouched examining the victim, and the lamppost.

As Carter showed his ID to the officer with the clip board, he took the forensic suit from Sue. In a matter of minutes, he was dressed and ready to go. He looked at Sue whispering, "Do you want to take ten? You can take a seat in our car."

Sue, just looked at him, so he took it as a 'No'

Gordon Chambers came over as members of his team were beginning to construct a tent, covering the victim.

The two men stood together, Gordon looked at Carter, "This is a bad one Carter? Nothing but pure evil, not happy in just killing the poor man, we found the victim bound to the lamp post, by means of, tie wraps to his hands and ankles, with his tongue missing."

Carter gasped, he looked around to find Lloydie, and members of his team, by this time he had noticed a patrol vehicle, a short distance along the way. It was obviously a bereavement officer.

Gordon Chambers walked over to join them, looking at Carter he said, "The victim was killed elsewhere? And brought here, to be displayed in this manner, there would be a severe loss of blood, due to his wounds."

"Although, we have the severing of the tongue, one should realise that death, was due to the two gun wounds to the victims left temple. Death was instantaneous."

Carter looked at the pathologist, "Before you take the victim away, will you walk me through your findings?" Gordon Chambers looked at him, and whispered, "Are you sure Carter, for it's rather gruesome, your deputy, and Lloydie, were present during my examination of the victim?"

He looked at Gordon Chambers, he nodded saying, "Gordon, thanks all the same." Looking in the direction of Lloydie, he said, "I'd be obliged, Lloydie?" He smiled, "Yes, guv no problem."

The two men returned to the tent, they entered, the pathologist, with a weak smile said, "Carter, over here." Carter walked up to where Gordon Chambers stood. He took out a metal retractable pointer from outside of his forensic suit.

He extended it and pointed it to the head of the victim; his head was leaning on the concrete, lamp post, with the light originally illuminating the victim. Giving the impression that he had either fallen, or ending up hugging the lamp post, as per a drunken man?"

"But Carter, you can see that half of his head is missing as a result of being shot, and that his mouth is wide open, due to the severing of the victims tongue."

"On arrival I found that, rigor mortis, was apparent and together with his rectal temp, calculated that he'd been dead for some seven to eight hours. I've taken blood samples to see if he'd been drugged prior to death."

As you can see there are large black powder burns to the side of his temple, I feel he must have been shot with a 9mm hand gun at point blank range, and his tongue removed by the use of a, 'Stanley knife'

"Carter, if all is connected, the girls in the HGV trailer, the remaining witnesses, and the PC in hospital, and the barrister found murdered in the playing field, and now this man called Ford. You are clearly dealing with pure psychopathic killers.

Carter looked at him, well Gordon, this latest victim, was interviewed by Sue and myself and bailed to re-appear at, Derby Lane police station. Allowing, us to investigate a myriad of telephone calls, made to him personally on his mobile, and to his shop."

"We both felt that they contained information that may have led us up the food chain, in our efforts to uncover other members of the gang."

Gordon Chambers said, "Well?" Carter, burst out laughing, "Oh! Gordon, do you not see that potentially we could both be investigated for allowing Ford, to walk free, and pro tem, to walk into the hands of his colleagues, who obviously felt that he had talked, or passed on names and details to us, hence there action."

Chapter Forty Six

Tony Frost was seated behind his desk, immaculate as ever, being the main focal point of the proceeding meeting. In front of him in a semi-circle were seated Carter, Sue Ford, Sam Watson, Wendy Field, and Penny.

They were all sat nursing hot drinks. TF said, "Well, welcome to you all, but I feel that Carter, and Sue may fall off to sleep before long?" They all started to laugh.

TF said, "Well all of last night's matters have been investigated, and now in the hands of Gordon Chambers, the pathologist. But we must all realise that this latest matter, is not the conclusion in all of this?"

Tony Frost had no sooner stopped talking when there was the sound of a disturbance, sounding outside of his office. He said, "Excuse me" He pressed a button on his intercom. "Jane, what on earth is going on out there?"

"Sir, I have two gentlemen, and I use the term loosely. Carter laughed inside thinking, *'That's our Jane'* They claim to be two officers from IA (Internal Affairs) and having attended at Derby Lane, to interview Deputy Commander Carter, and Detective Chief Superintendent Ford., were both told that they were attending at a meeting at your office."

Tony Frost shouted, "What the f?" He stopped in mid word, as he looked up in the direction of Sam, Wendy, and Penny. He smiled, "Sorry"

He gazed back at the intercom, "Jane, tell your friends, that they can either wait until we are finished, but will have me to deal with, or leave a contact number so that another appointment can be made. But tell them rest assured it will involve me at all times." He closed the intercom.

Tony Frost jokingly raised a hand to cup his ear, and stood for several seconds and then said, "Where were we?"

Carter said, "I feel that we have to look at this matter

like a pyramid, we have a possible 'Mr Big' at the top, who on the one hand, is funding all of this, with a team, of villains who are made up of foot soldiers, who carry out the basic murders were needed, such as the silencing of potential witnesses who they feel will help our cause."

"He also has medical help, where they can identify victims, who may help in the supply of transplant organs. They have a dedicated team, from a sleaze bag, which walks about shopping centres, where he lures young girls to be photographed as potential models."

Although we know that happens for we have a surviving witness. It would appear that they are taken to a studio, after they are photographed, the man says that becoming models may result in them having to go abroad, it all helps to generate potential jobs."

"He goes on to say that they need to give a blood sample, to be used for a passport, although we now know it is to blood type them. The victims receive a tattoo which relates the value of their blood group. Not forgetting the value of transplant body parts, to unscrupulous benefactors. "

Carter looked at Tony Frost, "Sir, all I ask is that you don't bring in outsiders to handle this case. I want MCU to continue, I ask that we remain contained, and that we don't deal with anything else." Tony Frost said, "Granted."

Tony Frost looked at Wendy Field, "I don't have to say that I know what is going on in your mind at this very moment, and that is, 'WOW' Wendy looked around the room saying, "From a police PR aspect, it's dynamite, I personally feel that we have two options. Do we sit on it, or do we release it by drip feeding it to the public?"

He then looked at Sam, he smiled, Yes, it's your turn?" She drew in a large breath. "Well, we are dealing with a business type of criminal that is in it for the money. He may have been approached, or tumbled across a business plan that can earn a phenomenal amount of money."

"Together, we have dealt with criminals who have murdered, or killed for their own reasons; money, drugs, sex, or revenge. Money is the common denominator in most of our examples."

Sam continued, "Our business man, who I think may not show any signs of your typical psychotic behaviours, he seems to have no underlining reason for doing what he's doing, although at present we have no evidence as to who he is?"

"Somewhere along the way he has developed a business model. He has his own money backing it, but he wants more. He may well have found a disgraced Doctor, he uses for identifying the victims by their blood groups, the medic may well have him behavioural problems, either disgraced for his use of drugs, or alcohol, or both?"

"He may have lost his standing in the community, lost property, and family because of his needs.

Sam, turned saying, "This is purely an off the cuff impression, formulated by my colleague, Penny Wilkinson, who is my, Director of research."

There was a sudden knock on the office door, TF shouted, "Come in" Jane, entered carrying a fresh tray of drinks. After all the thanks, and after Jane had left, TF sat behind his desk said, "Well what next?"

It was Sue who spoke first, "What if I was to contact IA see who, and what we are dealing with? And most importantly are we going to have a shit explosion, of such a magnitude that we'll be unable to control?"

Looking at Tony frost, Sue said, "With respect sir, we can talk all we like about keeping this matter under wraps, but if say the, IPCC (Independent Police complaints commission) are involved, or get involved, it will be out there for all to see. Worst of all our gang will just shut up shop, disappearing into the either."

Chapter Forty Seven

As Sue left closing the office door behind her, TF looked at Carter saying, "Right son, how are things really doing?"

Carter looked at all present, "Well, my DCS Sue Ford, is more than capable of dealing with this ball of shit, as she was involved in all of the other shit we have dealt with, in the past."

"Like most second in commands they all know that at the very least, there is always a safety net? *"The Governor"* They are always there. No doubt if the question was asked to me my past CID office. In my own case it was a certain, DS Morton."

"Now there are umpteen stories, too many to mention. But as a young sprog, he moulded, kicked, and cajoled me into what you see today?" So I want no mention of Sue, being either out of her depth, and needing support in this matter." Tony Frost interrupted, "Yes, she has you?"

He continued "Well, you all know it was I, who called for Carter to return back early from his sabbatical, to assist in this matter. Most feel that I was a bit hasty, but in my defence, I didn't want to be the person who ruined an officer's illustrious career."

Carter whispered, "What the fuck did you do to me?" TF said, "I heard that?" They all burst out laughing, after which he continued, "Carter we need to clone you, now let's get on with it."

Penny felt a glow of pride flow over her.

Tony Frost got up from behind his desk, and started to pace backwards and forwards across his office floor. Looking at Carter he said, "Well, 'Sonny Jim' when do I get your input in all of this?"

Carter looked to his right, and noticed a wry smile on the face of Penny. He said, "Well IA is a possible problem? At present all is tight with our enquiries, the three defendants, who we have in custody, have been mainly charged with conspiracy."

"Except for the man, Parsons who was charged with 4 major charges, all four are remanded in custody, and being kept safe. The same can't be said for Silverman and Ford it is thought that the same gun was used on both victims. Except in the case of Ford, they also cut out his tongue, a classical warning sign. I feel that the deaths of Silverman and Ford have instigated a lot of questions, asked by their loved ones, wanting answers?"

He continued, "Here is our investigation to date. Reports, lead us to investigate, the reported gunshot injuries to two young girls, one found with head injuries at a dock gate. The second young girl, with a severe head injury ran out into the traffic, and stopping a passing car, managed to get help. The young girls were taken to the royal and the trauma unit, where they received attention to their injuries."

"DCS Ford and members of our team started to investigate, they realised that there was a large blood trail leading back into the dock estate. With the help of the dog section, and our land sharks, *'Prince'* he picked up the scent, where he led us back into the estate, and out of the hundreds of HGV vehicles, found the rear of that horrendous vehicle."

"Now not wishing to dwell on the circumstances of what was found, I'm going to deal with numbers; eight young girls, six found dead, with shots to their heads, and two found severely injured after escaping from that dreaded trailer."

"The offenders knowing there were two survivors, sent a gun man back into the hospital to silence them. He or they killed one of the survivors, as the other young girl had been sent off the ward for treatment. Whilst carrying out this attack, they killed a young PC, who was the unarmed protection detail. We have the remaining survivor in a safe place."

"The offenders realising that we had a survivor, thanks to Wendy, we set up a honey trap. That resulted in the gang sending a man back to kill the young girl. We caught him and he is now in custody."

"From him we now have the names of other gang members involved, although on the bottom rung of the ladder. Unfortunately we have two murder victims, we feel that the gang thought they may have talked to us?"

"Further enquiries reveal that the six victims found in the rear of the HGV posed a serious problem, as we were unable to trace them, in our 'missing from home' records. This led us to look further afield, and we found them products of the 'In care' system?"

"Enquiries with other forces, and photographs of identification sent out, have revealed their identifications. Carter looked at the floor, and made a sudden gasp, if only we could find their parents, so they can at least be kissed whilst asleep!"

Penny went to sand, but Sam placed a gentle hand on her knee, and whispered, "Penny give him a minute."

He looked at Tony Frost, "Sir, I have no doubt there is a place were the victims are taken to, and after taking blood samples, their medic will proceed in removing the organs the rare blood types, to be shipped off to waiting clients."

"I also feel that we may well be dealing with the supply of young girls to be shipped abroad; they also will be given the bull shit of blood samples being needed prior to leaving these shores for abroad.

"But in their case they will wake up on the high seas. Call it a coppers nose, as yet to be proved. We are waiting for this case to unravel; there is little doubt that this is not the end. Rest assured I have the team hell bent making enquiries in both fields."

Tony Frost said, "Carter, please be aware, these bastards may well see you as a target, you're getting protection 24/7. I'm getting in touch with the APT's boss. No arguments. While we're at it all officers to carry firearms, be off with you."

Chapter Forty Eight

After his goodbyes, and outside of TF's office Carter, found Charlie waiting, he mentioned TF's request.

He also could see that Jane, was about to open up into her usual sexual rant. She looked at him, "Carter don't worry it's enough for me to see you, to remember your last kiss."

He looked at her, "Behave yourself woman." She burst out laughing as they both walked away.

Carter looking at Charlie, "You do realise that her behaviour has been constant with me, because when asked to attend at TF's office at the creation of the MCU. I asked her why she hadn't given me, *'The heads up'* A warning in advance and the reason for the special appointment?"

"Can you believe her answer, *'Well Carter, it's like this, if you'd asked me out for the odd meal, I might have thought of it.'* I like a fool answered, *'Jane you're a married woman for Christ sake.'*

"Now every time I attend at TF's office, I have to run the gauntlet. If the people in my life and you know who I mean, were to hear her drooling over such matters, I'd be killed."

As they walked away towards the lift, Charlie and Carter both heard, "Goodbyeeeee, Carter." Charlie found it hard to stifle his sudden bout of laughter, letting it out when in the lift.

He said, "Sorry boss, you can trust me." Carter looked at him, "That's the problem."

Back at Derby Lane, Carter entered the general office, followed by Charlie, to find the two suits sat drinking mugs of coffee. He walked over to the duty book, and as he was about to sign back in the office, he looked at Sue, who was sat talking to Eric.

"Erm, Detective Chief Superintendent Ford, is it not customary for junior officers to stand in the presence of a senior officer?" Sue trying hard not to laugh said a smart,

"Yes sir."

Carter knew the two officers, one a DI, and the other a DS. They both jumped up nearly spilling their coffees. They both shouted, 'Sir'

Carter looking at one of the secretaries winked, "Could I trouble you for two coffees for my office, one for DCS Ford, and one for me, the young lady smiled, "Of course sir."

As he walked out of the office, the two suits went to follow. He looked at them, "I'm sorry gents, but I can never get my head around, Bobbies doing Bobbies, it leaves a nasty taste in one's mouth. I'll tell you what, after I've had a chat with my DCS Ford, I'll send for you. They both replied, "Yes sir."

Sue followed Carter into his office and they both burst out laughing, "Carter you put them in their place?" He said, "Well" "Anyway what were they talking about before I entered the office?" Sue said, "A load of shit."

The young lady entered with their coffees, he thanked her and she left with a smile on her face.

He looked at Sue, "We don't have much time so after you'd left TF asked how things were going, now he meant with the job! Now I've told him I feel that we have these bastards dealing with the harvesting of vital organs, and the possibility of girls being drugged and sent abroad?"

Carter said, "TF on my advice feels that we are dealing with personnel that have no compulsion but to kill their way out of trouble. They have committed so many murders, that they could turn on members of the team investigating them. So the team are to carry firearms, and that unfortunately I'm back on protection 24/7."

Sue looked at him, "You will take care boss, I agree with TF, these bastards may well feel cutting the head off the snake, may derail the investigation."

Carter said, "Let's have the, Blues brothers in." He picked up the phone. "Eric, will you show them in?"

152

Chapter Forty Nine

There was a knock on the door, he shouted, "Come in" The door opened and they both walked in. Carter invited them both to take a seat. He looked at them, "Okay let's have it?"

"Sir, I'm DI David Jones, and this is my colleague, DS Bill Phillips, we are both with IA, It is rather obvious for our visit, that matters have been escalated by the Solicitors acting on behalf of the relatives of Silversmith, and Ford, to the IPCC."

He continued, "I feel that we have got off on the wrong foot...? Carter interrupted him, "Well DI Jones the person who you need to worry about, and who I feel that you definitely got off on the wrong foot with is, Commander Frost. I assure you that he is not a man that you need to upset."

Carter noticed that Sue had a smirk on her face. DI Jones said, "Well DC Carter, I feel that we may be able to circumnavigate matters without involving Commander Frost."

"We are here to prepare a report for the IPCC so that they can go back to the Solicitors acting for the respective parties, and inform them of the situation to date. Can you please inform us the situations around the two victims Silversmith, and Ford?"

Carter said, "Well, they are two very different matters. Silversmith, the eminent Barrister, attended at Derby Lane, to represent a client by the name of Parsons, now Parsons, is involved up to his neck in this matter, but never in a million year able to afford a Barrister such as Silversmith, and in particular his fees."

"Our enquiries found that Silversmith was engaged by his Clerk of Chambers, Christopher Rotherham, a person of interest. I felt that Silversmith should recuse himself from this matter."

"Now due to the intensity of this case, I felt that

someone high up on the criminal food chain thought that by engaging the services of Silverman, it would be a slam dunk."

"That Parsons would be up for a quick plea in the *'Maggie's* (Short for The Magistrates court) and whilst out on bail, facing a remand to a possible trial date, does a runner, home in time for tea?"

"I now feel that the protagonists' believe he became privy to information that resulted in his early downfall and death. I more than anyone grieved in his demise. I dearly wished that I could have forewarned him."

"Now, Ford is a different kettle of fish. He is also up to his neck in these matters, being a link in a small chain. Ford, being a bookmaker, with a shop in Castle Street, contacts a regular punter by the name of, Christopher Rotherham, who he knows to be the Clerk of Chambers for, 'Messrs Harris, Gordon, and Jones' a firm of eminent firm of Barristers in Dale Street."

Bernie Ford asks Rotherham for a top draw Barrister, to deal with Parsons. We have interviewed Ford, who admits his involvement in all of this, someone who he won't mention must have called him, putting the Parsons problem to him."

"He eventually admits, that he knew of Rotherham, he twisted his arm with threats, after which Rotherham, ultimately directs Silverman, to attend at Derby Lane, to act for Parsons."

"We charged, and bailed Ford to return to Derby Lane, in two weeks, which would allow members of my team to investigate all of his received calls on his mobile. We believe that it would lead to the other piece of the puzzle."

"Now it would seem that Fords involvement, and having been arrested, caused panic, hence his murder, in such a terrible way. Apart from our current enquiries, my team are all over this. That covers the whole on my dealings with this matter to date."

Carter said, "Now, DI Ford, I will prepare a report for IA, a copy of which will go to Commander Frost.

Unfortunately no one could have predicted what would happen to both Silverman, and Ford."

The two men stood up said their, "Goodbyes" and left.

Carter let out a long breath, looking at Sue, "Why do those people have an all-encompassing effect on us, they give me the bloody creeps." Sue with a serious look on her face said, "Carter why on earth did you use 'I' and not 'We' in all of your dealings and relating the situation to those two goons?" Carter started to laugh, "Why Sue, it comes with the territory."

They both walked through to the general office, as they arrived Carter looked at Sue, "Now you have the territory." They both burst out laughing.

Carter looked at Eric, "Well Mr Morton where is my minder?" Eric said, "He's just popped out to go through to the conference room, will be back in a sec."

He was correct, the office door opened and Charlie, walked in, he felt all their eyes locking on him. Carter said, "Well my fair friend, will you take me home, I have another life." He walked over to the diary, and signed off duty. He turned saying, "Good night all, see you all in the morrow."

Chapter Fifty

En route home Carter phoned Penny, informing her that he was on his way home. Penny said, *"Carter are you on the speaker?"* He replied, "No" Penny replied, *"Good, now do you want me to start running the shower? Just ring when you are five minutes away."*

He replied, "Penny, you know how we keep the cutlery, she replied, *"Why, yes I understand, a bad day?"* He closed the call without any further comment.

He looked over at Charlie, "I feel that I'll be increasing your work load, please explain to that lovely wife of yours, offering my apologies." Charlie smiled as he replied, "No need guv."

On arrival outside the entrance to his flat, he got out of the car saying good night to Charlie, he smiled and drove off. Carter looked at the rear of the car as it disappeared out of sight. He took in a deep breath, and walked towards the entrance and foyer to his flat.

Carter hadn't realised how tired he was, for on walking through the foyer, he failed to acknowledge the, 'Evening sir' from the doorman, plus the, 'All correct sir' from the new APO.

He entered his flat and was welcomed home by Penny holding a can of beer ready, and waiting. Penny suddenly pulled up and said, "Carter you look awful, come through to the lounge and relax."

He immediately turned, "Sorry Penny, give me a minute?" He opened the front door to the flat, and left for the foyer. He stood in front of the two men present behind the reception desk.

He looked at Mike, the doorman, and apologised for his inept behaviour, explaining, "Sorry Mike, how are you, is all quiet on the western front?" He replied, "Yes Mr Carter sir, all is well."

Carter then turned looking at the other smart man looking at him. Carter said, "Evening, I realise you are the new APO set up by, DS Charlie Watkins?" He replied, "Yes sir, but it's now DI Watkins, it was in Chief Cons order's this afternoon. I'm DC Smith."

Carter smiled, "Well at mid-night the block is locked, access to residents is by a security fob only, so if all is quiet, get your head down, but please sleep with one ear open." He burst out laughing as he walked off.

In the flat he returned to the perturbed looking Penny, he smiled weakly, "You know that bugger Charlie, has been promoted to DI and he never mentioned it, you wait till I see him."

Penny said, "Carter we have some more important issues, at present. A shower, on your own, some tea, and bed in that order." He smiled to himself 'Now where did I hear that last' he walked towards their bedroom, and the welcoming shower.

Fifteen minutes had gone by, and still no sign of Carter? Penny as she walked towards their bedroom could not hear the shower, as he walked into the bedroom she immediately noticed that Carter was fast asleep under the duvet.

Penny smiled as she walked into the bathroom picking up the towels, it would appear he was so tired that he'd just left items were they fell.

After finishing some work that she had brought home, Penny stretched and went off to bed. She undressed and climbed into sliding under the duvet. Carter didn't even flinch; all she heard was a light breathing noise, looking down on him she thought, relaxed at last?"

Fifty One

Somewhere in the dark recesses of her sleep pattern, Sue began to hear the sound of bells. Mike, her partner, in a sleepy voice said, "Sue, your phone is going off?" Sue replied, "Yes, I know I just thought, it's only a dream, until you spoilt it for me."

When fully awake, Sue, leaned out and picked up her phone from her night stand, through sleepy eyes she concentrated on the green shaped phone motive pressing it saying, "Ford"

A calm voice, with an anxious under tone at the other end of the phone said, *"Is that DCS Ford?"*

Sue, immediately recognising the voice through her still sleepy haze said, "Yes, Mr Chambers?"

"Sue, is it that obvious? I hope you don't mind but the night duty Inspector gave me your number." Sue replied, "Why, no Mr Chambers, what on earth is the matter."

Gordon Chambers replied, *"The mortuary alarm activated, and the 'on call' technician, who also acts as 'keeper of keys' whilst on call, attended at the mortuary, to find the premises insecure and that... he paused. All the bodies have gone?"*

Sue immediately sat up in bed, "What bodies?" He replied, *"The six from out of that dreaded HGV. The surviving witness and the poor PC shot in the hospital...What the hell am I going to do?"*

Although shocked on receipt of the news, Sue had begun to get her head together, Sue said, "Christ, Mr Chambers, who the hell could possibly remove eight bodies, one would need a large transit type vehicle?"

Sue said, "Are you at the mortuary as we speak?" He replied, *"Yes"*

Sue continued, "When you asked the control room for my number, did you happen to tell them why?" He replied, *"Not as yet."*

Sue said, "Good, I'll contact Lloydie, and ask him to

attend to assist you. He replied, *"Thanks, do you think we need to involve your boss?"*

Sue replied with a lighter tone to her voice, "Carter or TF?"

Gordon Chambers screamed, *"Please do not call TF, or my arse will be in a sling."*

Sue laughed, "Please don't worry, I'll call Carter, he is the best one to deal with a matter such as this, and I bet he'll be out like a flash. He has total respect for you, but this will need his calm attitude." The phone went dead.

Sue called Lloydie, apologising for the early alarm call, she quickly went through the story. Lloydie said, *"I'll be on my way."*

Sue's next call was to Carter. After, explaining word for word, that which Mr Chambers, had mentioned. He said, "Get Charlie, and we'll be on our way."

Penny was disturbed by the call saying, "Please Carter not again?" He replied, "Sorry, but an old friend is in trouble, and needs my help." Penny said. "Get a shower, and I'll ready some clothes for you."

By the time that Carter was ready, the intercom sounded, Penny said, "Pull the door Charlie, Carter is ready, and he'll see you downstairs, he's your keeper of secrets ha, ha… Many congratulations."

Carter didn't say a thing he just got into the car, and Charlie sped off towards the Royal. He looked over towards Charlie, "Well, when were you going to tell me, Sir."

Charlie burst out laughing, "Well, it's like this, you were out on your feet, so I thought I'd tell you today." Carter looked at him, "Promotion to DI, does that mean I'm going to lose you?" Charlie just looked straight ahead, "Over my dead body."

Carter said, "But, seriously Charlie, they won't let a DI who is needed in the intelligence gathering for the needs of the APD (Armed protection detail), to drive me about."

Charlie replied, "Well, guv they think you are important to warrant your own protection detail, should I

159

ever reach the dizzy heights of an Assistant Commander, you can bloody drive yourself around." Both men burst out laughing.

Chapter Fifty Two

It didn't take them long to reach the Royal, with it being early morning, Charlie, sped along displaying only the blue lights.

The mortuary is located at the back of the hospital for easy access. Charlie parked in one of the many empty parking bays. Carter recognised Sue's car and that of Lloydie's.

On arrival the usual format is to press the bell for admittance, but on this occasion the door was ajar. Carter and Charlie both walked along the cold corridor leading towards Gordon Chamber's office.

The office has glass on all four sides. On the side that overlooks the PM room Mr Chamber's usually keeps the curtains drawn. On seeing Carter, Gordon Chamber's stood up, he smiled, "Sorry for the disturbance, but what the hell am I going to do?"

Carter looked at him and smiled, "What you've done at my time of need." He looked at Lloydie, "Can you pass the drinking cups around whilst Mr Chamber's gets the bottle out."

"I feel a chill in the air, and a wee dram will warm the cockles of our hearts, plus help us to calm down." At that particular moment he looked at Gordon Chamber's.

Carter said, "Gordon, I don't see why we don't treat this matter as in the same way as a normal burglary."

He looked at Lloydie, when you have finished your dram will you have a quick whizz around the place, we know there is CCTV before you look through that, I suggest that we call Ian out to give you a hand, check the car park for tyre marks, these people have a habit of doing a 'formula one' type exit, they may have left some tread."

"Lloydie, before you ring Ian, and hopefully give him some sort of *BS* about the need for the *'call out'* make sure for Christ, sake that Wendy, does not get a sniff of it." Lloydie answered, "Yes guv."

As Lloydie went out of the office to make his call for the place had form for a poor mobile reception.

Carter said, "I haven't used any reason for Lloydie to be out of the office, as you all know I'd trust him with my life."

He continued, "Technically Charlie is only attached to the 'MCU' so that means that this matter is controlled by only myself. Charlie knows that he would be the last person that I'd drop in the shit. He looked at Charlie, "Feel free to leave" He didn't move a muscle.

Carter said, "It doesn't take rocket science to see where we're going with this, before I say anything else. Gordon, are the fridges, and in particular the fridges that our friends were in, all have card holder on the outside of the draws, or do we still rely on name tags tied to their big toe?"

Gordon Chambers looked at Carter, "Both I'm afraid, but I have their names, if known, with a job number, for the ones unidentified. And I log their position in their respective draws and fridges."

He said, "So Gordon, for someone to break in to steal the cadavers, they must know this system." Gordon chamber's sighed, Oh! Carter are you telling me that this is an inside job? That one of my staff may have been got at." There was silence in the room.

Carter looked at him, "Gordon please look around has anything been moved? Is there anything missing? I can see for myself that your office door hasn't been forced, my two officers will return with their findings."

Now, re your CCTV I trust it is the state of the art, and not some Laurel and Hardy outfit?"

He said, "Carter, I assure you it can record a gnat on your jacket when walking in, or out of my establishment." Carter said, "Is a new tape put in every day/night, or can the tape record 7 days etc."

Carter again looking at Gordon Chambers, now we both know that the entrance used by myself and my team, is not the only way into your establishment. There has to be access for the hospital porter's, who may bring bodies of victim's passed away on the hospital wards. I trust there is CCTV on this area?"

"There is also a need for undertakers to collect bodies on behalf of families, for the preparation of funerals. According to the correct paper work, so yet again there is no perfect form of security."

At that very moment Ian and Lloydie returned to the office, reporting that there are no signs of a forced *'break in'* That CCTV tapes are being removed for further scrutiny?

He became very serious, Carter said, "Now Gordon sometime quite early in this very morning, there will be a need for you to inform your employers. *The Home Office.*

Carter looked at him, my dear friend; I don't see why you can't report this matter, as a *'break in'* that a head count revealed some eight bodies are missing or stolen, that you yourself as our Pathologist reported the matter to the police."

As you well know Gordon, we are all responsible for our own teams, and departments in this particular case, there is a slither of thread running through all of this, that connects A to B and C to D and so on, and so forth. All of which leads back to the bloody HGV.

Carter looked at them all, "In my opinion, someone believes that if you remove all the bodies, then the authorities will have no evidence to proceed with. Rather like the proverbial Ostrich, who buries his head in the sand?"

Before the morning staff turned up for work, Gordon gave Ian, the tape covering from 6pm through to 6am this very morning, which covers the alarm activation, which in turn covers the *'break in'*

Carter looked at Gordon, "We will scrutinise every inch of the tape in an effort to identify the offenders. In the meantime perhaps you could draw up a list of suspects from your own department. Which may help."

He continued, "We may find that there was a time delay before the alarm activation, allowing the offender's time to get into the fridge area, to identify the victims, then to remove the bodies."

Gordon Chambers stood up and shook hands with Carter saying, "Carter you are a good friend, and an important ally in all of this, but I now need to call 'The home office' were the shit will truly hit the fan."

Chapter Fifty Three

On their way back to Derby Lane, Carter made a quick call to Gordon Chamber's, the phone answered on the second ring. Carter said, "Gordon, you do realise that I will have to inform TF?" He replied, *"Of course Carter, it can't happen any other way."* He closed the call.

On entering the general office both men signed on duty, Carter noticed that Sue, Ian and Lloydie had all signed in. He called out, "My office please."

Carter looked at them all, "Now we've sat and tried to limit damage control in this matter, but we as police officers, although concerned as to what has happened, must realise that we are coming at this in two ways?"

"The first, a reported, *'break in'* at the mortuary, in which we have tried to console Gordon Chamber's. But at the end of the day, his reporting this fact to the Home Office, will resonate throughout the ivory towers of power, and will need our support in dealing with this situation. His worry is all administration."

"The second, a major shit storm for us, our ongoing enquiry into all of this, as I previously stated, it's all connected. When I tell TF you will hear the sound of the fall out at the, *'Pier Head'* It's as if we have come a full circle."

"We all know that enquiries to date clearly reveal that we have *'jack shit'* in all of this. We have only scratched the surface; yes, we have Parsons, and his two friends, as simple foot soldiers. We also have Ford, and Rotherham, except the later was only used as a means of helping Parsons, which directly led to the death of, Silversmith."

He continued, I feel for using a top draw Barrister, to act as council to a tear arse like Parsons, means that the bosses at the top were worried as to the extent of his knowledge."

"At the moment, that's it all in a nutshell? Now, time is getting on, and the rest of the team will be signing on duty.

So, I need work schedules drawn up."

"There are the tapes from the mortuary to be studied for the relevant time, and any information gleamed. I also want the Liverpool City Council CCTV traffic tapes obtained two hours before and two hours after the alarm activation."

"While we're at it, let's get CCTV tapes from the Mersey Tunnel police."

"Should we identify a vehicle outside of the mortuary, we may find it could have come through the tunnel, at some time which will give us more evidence of it's origin."

"Now be off with you."

When they had all left, Sue could not help but admire her boss, as whilst he put on such a compassionate and understanding nature with Gordon Chambers, of which was very genuine, for the respect they held for each other. He must have been working out how to press forward with the rest of us.

On his own Carter, looked at his watch it was 7.30am he thought better do it now, than dwell on it, it all needed to be sorted.

Tony Frost answered his phone on the second ring. "Frost" "Sir, it's Carter, are you sitting down. Well, is it that bad?"

Carter said, "Sir, Sue Ford, received a call from Gordon Chambers, her phone number was acquired via the night duty Inspector, in the control room. Frost said, *"We'll talk about that later, now what's the bloody matter?"*

"Well Sir, the reason for the call emanated from Gordon Chambers..." Frost interrupted, *"What the fuck! What on earth's the matter?"* Carter said, "Sir, with respect will you let me tell you? He grunted, *"Get on with it."*

Carter told TF about the situation, in the most succinct way. There was a gasp, followed by a long silence, after which he shouted, *"Carter get your arse down to my office forth with."* Carter said, "Can I get a coffee, as I was

166

called out at 4.30am, and not a sip has passed my mouth."
He shouted, *"No, you'll get all the bloody coffee you want here."*

Carter walked into the general office, were he was met by Eric. He looked at Charlie, "I'm wanted at TF's office now, can I meet you at the car downstairs, I'll only be a minute.

Carter signed out and walked over to Eric's desk, he knew that the news had filtered through. Eric said, "What on earth are you going to do son?" Carter replied, "I wish at this very moment that you were my DS, and I your sprog."

Eric said, "Boss you have a driver, and car waiting to speed you off to TF's office, now en route ask the question, 'why me' The question is self-answered, now be off with you."

Chapter Fifty four

Carter stood in the lift, as it came to the designated floor. The doors opened, Carter immediately noticed that, Jane hadn't arrived for work as yet. But he couldn't help recognising the frame of TF leaning against her office desk.

Both Carter and Charlie walked over to him. He looked at them, "Gentlemen please follow me." He walked toward the door of his office, whilst Charlie went and sat on a chair by Jane's desk."

Tony Frost looking at Charlie, "Where do you think you are going to DI Watkins?" Charlie, with a sheepish look to his face said...But before he had chance to say something Tony Frost interrupted, "DI Watkins, you may not have read Chief Cons orders, but you have been transferred from, The Armed Protection department, to the MCU, so get your arse in here."

When all sat down Tony Frost, looked at Carter, "Well" After ten minutes there was a knock on his office door, he shouted, "Come in" Jane was stood in the door way, looking at the three men. He said, "All is well Jane, could we have three coffees?" She turned and left.

Tony Frost, with a sheepish smile to his face, "When I leave at the end of the day, I leave the office door open, if found closed at this time of the day, it would cause some concern for Jane. But never mind let's await our coffees."

After Jane had left, leaving the tray of hot drinks on his desk, she smiled and left.

He looked at Carter, "Again, well?"

Carter sat up, "Sir as already stated the mortuary was broken into, and the bodies taken. Now, although not investigated as yet, I feel that the offenders may have entered the mortuary, allowing time to remove the bodies, as you must appreciate the removal of eight body's takes time?"

"Now, not all the draws in the fridges had name cards

on them. Gordon Chambers stated that he had a list of some of the other victims, identified by a number only, and no name."

I feel that it's an inside job, as this list must have been stolen out of Mr Chamber's office. It is the only way the offenders could identify, and take the correct bodies."

"Only when the bodies had been identified, and taken, after being loaded up, in what I feel must have been a Transit type van after leaving, it was then that the alarm was activated. Carter said, "Giving a false time line."

"We have the time that the main mortuary was secured, and the time that the alarm was activated, but I feel that they must have known the approximate time needed to load the van, and for them not to do anything until they had gone."

Tony Frost looked at Carter, "So what are your plans?" Sir, we are recovering CCTV footage of the front of the mortuary, as they may not know of a hidden camera located at the junction of Moss Street, and Pembroke Place. I've instructed for CCTV footage from Traffic Cameras located in that area, and about the city."

I feel that if we identify a possible vehicle, then we may be able to track it about the City."

Tony Frost asked, "How is Gordon Chambers taking all of this? He must realise that you'll be all over this like a rash to find his mole." Carter stopped and turning as if suddenly thinking of something, he said, "Gordon Chambers, will want to be in on the hunt also."

Carter looked at Tony Frost, "Sir, what do you think the, Home Office will make of this, it's not after all a case of poor security, or his department failing to meet the high standards of security, befitting such a location. After all said and done, there is no one more committed."

Lastly, Tony Frost coughed, and cleared his throat, "Carter what are your thoughts regarding the press in all of this? He burst out laughing, "I only detect sir, and you're the politician." He got up to leave, TF said, "Well young man, I want a full report in say twelve hours, how do you like those potatoes."

Both Carter and Charlie got up to leave, Charlie said, "I'll see you downstairs guv." He said his goodbyes to Tony Frost and left. When Carter left he stood outside of TF's office looking at Jane, knowing he'd have to run the gauntlet.

Jane looked at him, "Well Carter, you look as if you've been up all night, just imagine if we were to have the same opportunity, I'm afraid you'd be in no fit state for work."

He turned with a broad smile on his face, "Well Jane, it's a pity that you'd never find out, as I'm always full of stamina, what are things like in your household?" The usual smile quickly left her face followed by, "Carter if you'd only show me, and burst out laughing.

At that very moment her intercom activated on her desk, "Jane for Christ, sake will you leave him alone, and get back to work." Her face was crimson, she mouthed, 'Carter help me'

He took off laughing as he went for the lift. All he could hear was Jane saying, "I'll get you Carter." He replied, "Yeah, yeah, yeah, in your dreams."

Jane replied, "You bet, you have no idea carter" and started to laugh.

Chapter Fifty five

After arriving back at Derby Lane, and signing back in he said, "Eric will you locate, Sue, Ian and Lloydie, will you ask them to come to my office?" But before that could you arrange for a decent mug of coffee, I'd hate to be married to the bosses secretary, Jane. Her coffee is crap."

"In fact I'd hate to be married to her full stop."

In his office one of the young girls brought him a decent mug of coffee, after she left there was a knock on the door, he shouted "Come in" Eric walked in, "Well how did it go? Did you manage to control the beast?" Carter laughed at him. "You realise it was all down to you."

There was a knock at the door, Eric opened it, and in walked Sue, Ian, and Lloydie. Carter looked at Eric, "Will you please ask DI Watkins to join us." Eric smiled, "Yes guv."

After he had left within five minutes there was a knock on his door, he shouted, "Come in" And in walked Charlie. Carter looked at the others, "Lady and gentlemen, I'd like to introduce to you our latest acquisition DI Charlie Watkins. It will be in Chief Cons order later today; although TF mentioned it to me this morning."

He thought that I could not be driven around by a DI from the APD, so he has attached Charlie to the MCU, although as my specific APD, plus a valid member of the team." They all clapped as they welcomed him to the team.

Carter said, "How are things going?" Sue smiled, "We are running CCTV from the hidden camera covering the entrance to the mortuary. Should we find anything of significance? We will then use the description of the vehicle to try and identify it through the City, via their transport cameras."

Sue continued, "We have members of the team going through staff details, given to us via Mr Chamber's, he feels if we don't make a personal show at his office, then he can keep matters under wraps. The victims are not looked in on for medical and forensic details that horse has bolted."

"If we find any red flags showing dealing with the staff, we will look in on them, we are as we speak looking into bank accounts, Mr Chamber's has stressed that the Home Office has stated no stone...."

Carter said, "Great" He then looked at Charlie, "This side of the coin will take patients; I suggest that you shadow Ian, for if I put you under Lloydie's wing, he may have to attend at the mortuary and it will only raise eyebrows if the staff notice two officers."

"While I'm at it, Ian, can you arrange for Mr Chamber's to attend at my office at his earliest convenience. I just want a chat. It won't be as suspicious if I attended at his office."

Ian looked at Carter, "Will do guv." He also said, "Have you has any nosey phone calls from Wendy re the reason for the call out, he said, "No guv." Carter sighed, "Thank God for that."

Ian broke down laughing, "Guv that's not to say she won't try to carry out water boarding on me to get at the truth." They all fell about laughing.

There was a knock on his door he shouted, "Come in" It was Peter standing there with a big grin on his face, "Guv would you care to come and see some of the CCTV tape from the hidden camera at the mortuary." Carter replied, "Would I, you bet your sweet life I would."

They all followed him to the conference room where Phil had set up a video player, and screen. With the gismo in his hand he pressed the button, and the screen illuminated.

The picture was grainy at first, and then it cleared, it was pitch black with only a street light to illuminate the picture. He noticed the time showed 3.30am when a dark coloured van pulled up outside of the mortuary.

Four men all dressed in black, wearing black balaclavas, exited from the vehicle. One walked up to the front door, he took out what appeared to be a key card. He swiped the security card reader, and opened the doors to the mortuary. On entering they closed the doors behind them.

Carter said, "Please let's see the reg of the vehicle when you bastards leave. The next thing that happened, the doors suddenly opened.

Working in pairs they each carried out what appeared to be black body bags, with what could only be, or look like a body in each. They made four repeated journeys, until they had retrieved their haul.

Three members of the gang got back into the vehicle, the vehicle was driven off and in seconds it returned facing, Moss Street.

The fourth figure closed the doors to the mortuary, he'd have set the alarm for the building, with the alarm panel inside of the corridor, for he gently pushed the doors open, he then ran jumping into the vehicle as it drove off. Within seconds the alarm activated.

There on the screen for all to see was the reg of the vehicle, Peter made a note of it, and did a vehicle check with the force control room, as all thought it was a Joey.

They all shouted, "Shit" It was Carter who said, "Did anyone notice the small white sticker on the back of the vehicle?" Philip quickly rewound the tape, and there for all to see was a white sticker on the rear bumper of the vehicle.

Carter said, "Peter, Philip please take the tape to the forensic lab, and ask the techs guys, to concentrate on the sticker, and enlarge it, so as we can make out what it says, ASAP." Peter replied, "Yes guv."

Chapter Fifty Six

Peter and Philip took a copy of the CCTV tape to the forensics team, for the bumper sticker to be enlarged for possible identification. The vehicle's progress was caught on the system used by the, Liverpool Council traffic control room on their CCTV system, following the object vehicle out of the City, towards Edge Lane.

Members of the team in two unmarked police vehicles followed the vehicle at a discreet distance.

While that was going on Carter, and his senior officers, who had been on duty from the early hours, sat down and enjoyed a hearty breakfast, in the canteen during which he received a call from Eric.

Eric said, "Sorry to disturb you Carter, thought you'd like to know the vehicle has come to a halt." Carter said, "Were, were, and are we standing off it?" Eric replied yes guv; it's come to a halt at the rear of the old 'Hormby' toy factory, in Binns Road. It would seem there are a lot of unknown warehouses. As the vehicle entered one of the warehouses the roller shutter doors closed behind it."

Carter said, "Thanks Eric we'll be up shortly, I have my gang as you know, will you get team members together who are not engaged on other enquiries."

Whilst he continued with his breakfast he called TF telling him the news. He also informed him that observations would remain on the vehicle, and that they are at present awaiting the information re the bumper sticker?

After his breakfast, Carter returned to his office, on arrival he was met by Eric, who from behind his back he took an A4 size photo, when handed to Carter he realised it was a blown up size picture of the bumper sticker on the rear bumper of the Transit van.

He entered his office followed by Eric. Carter went and sat behind his desk, and looked down at the photo. Displayed on the photograph was the easily read advert for a car and van hire company.

It showed 'Prindle car/van hire' Shaw Street, Liverpool, 0151-709-4351.

Carter looking at Eric, said, "My friend could I trouble you to ask for my senior team members to attend at my office in fifteen minutes." Eric said, "Will do boss, I will lay on hot drinks for you all." Carter looked at him through tired eyes, "Thanks Eric." Eric said, "Let's make it twenty minutes so you could get your head down." Carter looked at him, "Why! Are my team having a kip?" Eric looking at him saying, "Why should I worry" He smiled and walked out.

After Eric had left his office he telephoned Penny. He heard her quiet voice, *"Hello Carter I hope all is well?* He said, "Would it be rude of me to suggest that I'd love to kiss you all over."

Her voice came back saying, *"Steady on buster, let's see what condition you're in when you get home? Now thinking about a certain subject matter, is not the best of ways to stand up and address your team, what would they think if their boss had to hold a file in front of him whilst dealing with your present enquiry."* He heard a raw of laughter come from down the phone.

Penny said, *"Carter why don't you wait and see what there is for tea? When you roll in, I say when?"* It was said in such a way that Carter realised that Penny, was aware of the situation.

As he replaced the phone there was a knock at the door, and he called, "Come in" His team of senior officers was followed by a young lady carry a tray of hot drinks. He looked at them, "Please sit."

When they were all sat down, and the young lady had left, he held up a photo of the enlarged bumper sticker, he said, "When finished could one of you take the photo and put it on one of the white boards, in the boardroom."

He then said, "Do we still have the warehouse under surveillance? Sue replied, "Yes guv" He replied, "Right let's get on, we may have a problem, the photo although it informs us of the name of the hire company, we all know that the reg is a Joey."

"The men involved, although they hired the vehicle, for their despicable task, they may have thought that if they change the reg, the likely hood being is that the vehicle may not be known as a hire vehicle."

"What the idiots didn't realise, that there was a sticker on the bumper. I don't think they even checked the vehicle that closely."

He continued, "Under normal circumstances, we'd send officers to check on who had hired the vehicle, our problem is, 'When was the vehicle hired?' 'Should we sniff around you never know they may have an insider in the hire company, giving us away to the offenders."

"Now, we need to check if there are any red flags thrown up from the mortuary staff themselves. Let's also make a decision as to what may be happening in that bloody warehouse, it rather reminds me of the Carla Davenport case."

He looked at Sue, "If this warehouse is being used, what for? For at present we know not what? Our easiest process would be for the teams keeping obsie's, to take photos of their comings and goings?"

He continued, "I want Parsons, Jackson, and Collins to be brought to Derby Lane, I want pressure to be put on them, pressure from a great height, I feel that we have treated them with kid gloves, where we should be scaring the shit out of them?"

He stood up, and walked over to a white board, stood in the corner of his office. He then took up a large piece of paper, and attached it to the board.

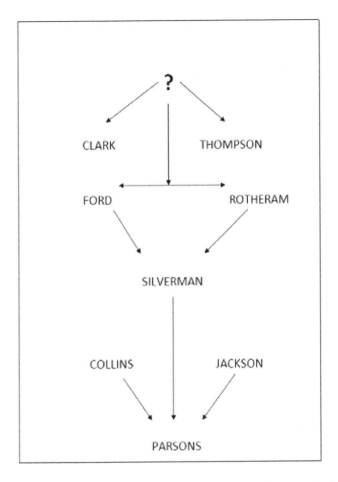

Everyone in his office looked at it seeing the attached: diagram.

He then looked at Lloydie, "Jim, whilst all this is in the air, figuratively speaking, draw a few men from the team, and go through the mobile phone statements, belonging to, Ford, and Rotherham."

"There has to be ties between them, someone must have realised that Ford, a City centre bookie, could be a catalyst, for he must deal with some high end gamblers, he may have been present when the subject arose, or received a phone call when the subject arose, *'Bernie, we need a good brief'* Ford, may have mentioned Rotherham, knowing full well his employment?"

"He may have stated that he had a customer, who just happened to be a Clerk of Chambers in the City. *'They'* Carter suddenly shouted. You know it pisses me off having to say *'They'* must have told him, Ford deal with it, *'Get a good brief '*

"Unfortunately, with Rotherham giving Silverman the case, the idiots mustn't have realised that we, wouldn't have sniffed a rat with the likes of Parsons, getting the likes of Silversmith to represent him. All this is hanging in the air I know. I believe that Ford knew that Rotherham worked for a firm of Barristers. As Rotherham held a betting account, and for that, the bookies must have some sort of financial evidence, His job, salary, etc."

Sue interrupted, "Ford knew that Rotherham was into him for ten grand, although not a great deal of money as Rotherham, had a good income, but? Knowing his slate could be wiped clean, as payment for such a task, he must have jumped at the chance."

Carter looked at Sue and smiled, "Yes, that's correct." He then looked at Ian, "Also take some of the team, go to Fords betting shop, seal it up, and check all of the incoming calls, the date line starting from just before, or after us recovering those terrible victims in the HGV trailer."

He continued, "We realise that someone must have known of the two witnesses, having escaped, as the number of potential victims diminished from eight to six, hence the reason for the excursion of either, Collins or Jackson, followed up by Pearson, into that hospital room. Now someone gave the fucking orders, who?"

Looking around the room he said, "So let's get to it, in conclusion I need someone to contact Gordon Chambers, and for him to be brought to my office for a chat, either today or tomorrow."

As they all dispersed Sue, remained for a few seconds and looked at Carter, he turned, 'What?' Sue could tell that he was tired, yet, she didn't know how to tell him to go home as we need you fresh, she wasn't about to get her head served up in her lap, she laughed to herself as she walked into the general office.

She looked at Eric, he saw the look on her face, and knew he was about to get a shitty job. Sue fully explained it to him, and was shocked when he told her that he agreed with her, he got up and left, walking out towards Carter's office.

Chapter Fifty Seven

Carter, kicked up a stink as Eric, insisted that he was to go home, explaining all of Sue's thoughts, without mentioning the sauce of his information.

Reluctantly, he agreed and was dropped off by Charlie, at 12.30pm outside of the foyer to his flats. He knew full well that if left, he'd push on until he dropped.

He realised that this ball of shit was still likely to unravel, having no knowledge of what was around the corner. Except his only physical evidence was that of the poor eight souls having been stolen from the mortuary. He clearly needed to know the name of the question mark.

As he entered his flat, as if by magic Penny walked down the hall towards him. Penny said, "So this is the man who wanted to kiss me all over? Carter you look as if you'd be incapable of undressing yourself. She smiled, look why don't you take a shower and let's see how you feel?"

Fifteen minutes later she walked into the bathroom to find Carter, sat on the floor of the shower crying. Penny leaned into the shower switching it off, she knelt down on her knees saying, "Carter what on earth is the matter?"

He looked up at her whilst the water was dripping down his face, and wiped the hair from his face. He gave her a weak smile, "It's just this bloody case. Normally you have a reported incident, which hopefully offers evidence that you can investigate, with physical suspects, fingerprints, and a load of witnesses?"

"In this matter we have eight bodies, which have now been stolen to put us, the police in turmoil. Two of the major players, have been murdered. We are left with three gang soldiers, who lead us to believe they acted on orders, but fail to mention where the said orders emanated?"

Our fourth player, a rather intelligent, Clerk of Chambers, who was asked to supply a defence Barrister, for one of the soldiers who'd been arrested, and in return would have his gambling debt, wiped off the slate. The clerk just mentioned it was as a result of a phone call."

"Our only physical evidence is a gun, and ammunition. This gun was originally used in the killings of 6 young girls fund in the rear of a HGV trailer. It was also used in our honey trap, when recovered from an offender who used it to try and kill the remaining witness. This very gun was used in the slaying of a protection police officer, who tried to protect a witness who was also killed."

He looked at Penny, "I have to say that our two main witnesses, a Barrister called, Silversmith, and a Liverpool bookie called, Ford both involved in some degree, were both been found murdered in very suspicious circumstances."

"After both had been brought into Derby Lane, and interviewed by both Sue, and I, had both been bailed, only to turn up murdered. See, we the police, should have realised that there was someone in the know, with their ear to the ground. Not necessarily in the police, hence why we were interviewed by the IPCC."

Penny was at the meeting with Sam, her boss, in Tony Frost's office, and wanting to help Carter. Sam tried to tell her that Carter was the man to shoulder the load, and that it was impossible not wanting to hold out a helping hand.

Sam later explained to Penny. "The MCU was formed not by Tony Frost, or Carter, but by the Home Office. Initially to be trialled throughout all force areas to deal with major crimes. Tony Frost, picked Carter, to head up the one for Merseyside, he has always held the greatest faith in his man.

Eventually on their return home, Penny suggested that Carter, should have a lay down, and that if undisturbed, will awaken him for tea. He reluctantly agreed, and within seconds was fast asleep.

Much later, well past evening teatime, Penny slid under their duvet, and she herself managed to get into bed without disturbing him.

Carter woke sitting up and stretching out his arm, he

looked at his watch it was 8.30am. He looked over to Penny's side of their bed noticing her missing. He jumped up and only dressed in his under crackers; he walked through into the lounge.

Standing in the kitchen Penny looked at him, "Carter is that the dress of the day, where on earth will you hide your gun? They both burst out laughing. Penny said, "Breakfast will be ready in fifteen minutes, shower and dress, and when a smart man, you can enjoy your meal.

Carter did as he was told, what he didn't know that Eric had been on the phone, suggesting that Carter needn't appear in the office before 10.30am, and that his first appointment has been organised for 11.00am.

When fed, and ready for the forthcoming day, whilst talking to Penny, Carter thanked her for all her concern, and attention.

As they talked the intercom buzzed, Penny said, "Awe that will be Charlie." Carter looked at her, "What? I was about to contact the control room for him to pick me up, it would appear that I have no control over my plans for the day."

Penny said, "Please Carter, go with the flow." In kissing Penny goodbye, he said, "I owe you good style, thanks."

Chapter Fifty Eight

In the car, Charlie looked at his boss, "Well, guv you look much better than you did yesterday?" Carter looked at him, "What's this guv crap? You know the rule when on our own, even now a member of the team. You know it applies to you, "Got it!" He smiled, "Yes, got it."

Charlie just smiled, and drove for the office he looked at Carter, "Your first meeting is with Mr Chamber's, you asked for me to set it up, and with your respect, invite him to your office."

"When I drop you off, I'll leave to collect him." Carter smiled, "Thanks Charlie." He just sat back in his seat, setting out a mental picture of what he needed to do for the rest of the day.

Minutes later whilst still en route to the office he called Penny, it was the shortest of calls, "Thank you again."

He got out of the car in Derby Lane police yard, thanking Charlie as he drove off for Gordon Chamber's. He entered the general office to be met by Eric, who smiled, "Who looks a smart boy?" As Carter signed on duty, he turned to take the usual mug of coffee from Eric.

Carter said, "Thanks Eric, I'll be in my office." As he took hold of his coffee in one hand, Eric also offered him a brown A4 envelope, which he took hold of in his other hand. He looked at Eric in surprise, "Please don't tell me it's my P60." Eric laughed aloud, "It will be me before you Carter."

He placed the edge of the envelope into the corner of his mouth, he opened his office door, he entered, and sat behind his desk, whilst enjoying his coffee, he opened the envelope, and several photographs fell out onto his desk.

He noticed a grainy effect to the photographs it was obvious that they'd been taken at night, as the photos seemed to have gained light from a nearby street light. He immediately recognised the scene. They were of individual men leaving a warehouse.

He rang Eric, "Eric, please tell me that the contents of this envelope, are snaps of possible individuals going in and out of that bloody warehouse?" Eric said, "Correct, they were dropped off for your attention by Ian."

Carter had just replaced the receiver when there was a knock at his door, he said, "Come in" When he looked up, he saw the rather large frame of Gordon Chambers who happened to fill the doorframe.

He said, "Gordon please come in." As he did so, Carter stood up, and walked over, to a nearby filing cabinet.

As the young secretary was about to leave, "Carter said, "You couldn't lay on some hot drinks please, he looked at Gordon, "Tea or coffee?" Gordon Chamber's replied, "Coffee please, white with two sugars." The young lady smiled and left closing the door behind her.

Carter returned to his desk having retrieved a bottle of Scotch with two glasses. He placed them on his desk he opened the Scotch, and poured two nips of Scotch into each glass.

They both enjoyed their nips when there was a knock on the door. Carter shouted, "Come in" The young lady placed the tray on Carter's meeting desk, and left.

As they enjoyed their drinks, plus their second nips, as Carter, was trying to repay Gordon, for all of his courtesy on so many occasions.

Whilst they were talking Carter absent-mindedly pushed some of the photographs around his desk, between drinking his coffee, and the odd nip.

It was whilst he was doing this that Gordon Chambers suddenly shouted in his inevitable voice, "Carter, were on earth did you get those photographs from?" Carter replied, "Why?"

Gordon Chamber's, suddenly placed one of his large hands on top of Carter's, "That one, where is it from?" Carter looking at him again said, "Why, Gordon?"

As Carter moved his hand, Gordon Chamber's gently picked up the particular photograph, "This one."

Carter said, "It was taken by one of my team, who were

keeping obsie's on a certain warehouse, a warehouse, were the vehicle that was used to steal the victims from your mortuary disappeared into, why?"

Gordon looked at him with utter revulsion on his face, "This man is, Angus Clark, a onetime surgeon, who was struck off the GMC for what was believed to be misuse of drugs, and alcohol."

He continued, "The story goes that due to his habit, he was found slumped at his desk, and in no state to deal with his operation list. The aftermath resulted in him losing his home, wife, and family."

Carter sat back, "Gordon do you think we have our surgeon who is capable of removing the healthy organs from victims, and for them to be sold on to unscrupulous benefactors."

Carter picked up his phone and rang Eric, "Eric, will you please send one of the team in.?" He continued, "I need to have these photos enlarged for display on the whiteboards in the conference room." He replaced the phone.

Before the photos were collected, Gordon Chambers, shouted as he picked up another photograph, "That's, Paul Thompson, mortuary assistant, he must have been got at, letting them in."

Carter picked up his phone and called Tony Frost, "Any chance of you attending the conference room in two hours?" He replied, *"Yes"* And replaced the phone.

Chapter Fifty Nine

Two hours later Carter, accompanied by Gordon Chamber's, walked into the conference room. The whole room came to attention. Carter said, "Please sit."

Gordon Chamber's joined both Carter, and Sue at the top of the room. He noticed Tony Frost, and Wendy Field, from many other meetings, but failed to recognise both Sam, and, Penny.

Carter stood and introduced Gordon Chamber's to Sam, and Penny informing him that they were both important components of his team. He gave Gordon the telescopic pointing stick, he said, "The floor is all yours, Gordon."

All of the team smirked, for they immediately recognised the, James Robinson Justice type voice, which always seemed to pre seed the man. He looked around the room and blurted out, "Ladies and Gentlemen, I am your Home Office Pathologist, and as you all know, I seem to work hand in glove with your very competent boss, ADC Carter."

"Now this very day I was invited for a chat with your boss, on arrival I was showed to his office, and whilst we enjoyed our hot drinks, I noticed that your boss whilst we chatted absent-mindedly pushed a couple of photographs around his desk."

He raised his voice even louder, and pointed the telescopic stick to one of the enlarged photographs. "Ladies and Gentlemen, this photograph clearly shows a man, and I use the word advisedly, is no other than a struck off Surgeon, Angus Clark."

He immediately heard a shuffle of feet, he realised how all of Carter's team had come to attention, and were on the same page.

He continued, "Whilst I was in your bosses office, I also recognised the photograph of, Paul Thompson, one of my very own mortuary assistant's, which I now realise allowed personnel access afterhours, to my mortuary.

Carter stood up and thanked Gordon Chamber's for his great help in this case, he said, "Gordon, you must realise that time is of the essence, could I suggest that you go with one of my young officer's to give a statement of identity, on both men."

He smiled, "Yes of course." Carter in summing up said, "Gordon I will be deciding on a raid on this bloody warehouse, could I ask that you join us, as in this case your medical prowess will be of the greatest importance, to help in the much forensic work I believe will greet us." He smiled as DC Julie Willkie, came over to assist in showing him to an interview room.

After Gordon had left, Tony Frost, walked over to Carter, he smiled, "You lucky...Bas" but he was unable to finish as his eyes suddenly fell on Sam, and Penny. He smiled, "But you get the gist of my thoughts." Carter smiled, "Yes sir."

Carter looked at Sue, "Would you ask Jim, and Ian to remain, together with Wendy, Sam, and Penny."

He continued, "Now I've asked Eric, to draw up the details for a warrant, to enable us to carry out our raid, this very night, I say night, as I feel that it would be the correct time to hit them."

"Now our latest intelligence informs us that Clark, and Thompson returned to the warehouse earlier. DC Willkie, who at present is busy taking a statement from the pathologist, she will also ask him to remain behind so he can join the raid."

Carter looked at Sam, "Professor Watson, I know we have just been given a key into this matter, may I ask you for your thoughts?" Smiling, she looked up in the direction of Jim, although a frequent speaker to students in the University, Sam always felt safe knowing that Jim was there in support.

"Well, Carter I feel that whilst you have Parson's, Collins, and Jackson, I know that you, and your team realise that they are low on the criminal food chain."

"I feel that if you manage to trap and arrest, both Clark,

and Thompson you may feel that you have two men that may point you in the right direction in finding the man at the top, we both know that people are making vast amounts of money from all of this dreadful mess?"

Carter said, "Well what sort of man, or woman, do you feel that we are dealing with, one that shows signs of a psychopathic nature?" Sam looked at Carter, and members of his senior officers, "We have dealt with so many cases involving persons of this ilk."

Sam looked at Penny, "Miss Wilkinson, what are your thoughts on this matter?" Penny stood up, and quickly fought off a blush starting to creep up her face.

Penny sneaked a quick look at Carter, who had begun to smile. "Well, I feel that the people organising all of this, are in it purely for the money, although we can see a *'Fagan type'* character in all of this. I find that it's not done for any such sexual deviance, that the victims are a means to an end. "

"You have at least twelve people involved, who are assisting, or doing their bidding. He, she, or them, at this point, it is difficult in the use of a particular gender, had ordered the deaths of Ford, and Wilkinson for fear of the authorities gleaming information which may bring down the organisation, and team."

"Mr Chamber's identified two characters, in photographs obtained from a recent intelligence operation. Both men have assisted the perpetrators, in their various fields."

"Thompson, to assist in the recovery of evidence from the mortuary, their thoughts being, gets rid of any ties to, or of non-helpful cadavers."

"Clark, on the other hand, is their main protagonist enabling the farming of organs from suitable victims, to enable there sale for vast amounts of money."

"The powers that be realise that whilst they supply his needs of drugs, and or alcohol, he'll always be at their beck and call."

"Both men if detained may well assist the enquiry, they

may point the way in the right direction, in the pursuit of the organiser in all of this."

Penny sat down to a round of applause, and smiles from both Sam, and Carter.

Carter stood and looking in the direction of Sam, and Penny he said, "I must ask you both to leave as we now have to plan a police operation, to get our heads around all of this, thanks' for all your help." Both ladies stood and left.

Chapter Sixty

After matters had settled down, Carter took out his mobile phone, and called Tony Frost. He told him of his recent information in relation to the case, that he may have the identities of two men, not of our usual criminal fraternity, but may lead us further up the chain.

Carter walked up and down the conference room fully apprising TF of the fact, that they may have the surgeon responsible for the organ harvesting. He went on to explain his needs.

He explained that he wanted to execute an early morning warrant, as early as 5.30am in the morning.

He continued explaining his needs in arresting this man Clark. "Clark is a defrocked medical surgeon, who was struck off for his misuse of drugs, and alcohol. The photographs clearly show his coming and going, in and out of the bloody warehouse."

"Sir, it is very obvious for their need of a surgeon, and that fired up with his needs, he will continue, devoid of any, *'Hippocratic Oath'* I feel if we get hold of him, due to us not being generous with his needs he may well flip over on his boss, or bosses."

"Now with respect, Sir, this is what I need. He stopped his pacing and related his needs. I want DCS Ford, DI Lloyd, and DI Baxter to select five armed officers, to form three teams to set out from Derby Lane, at about 5.00am in the morning."

"If matters are quiet, armed with a warrant we will force our way into the property. I want, 'The Air Support Unit' to take up a position, to maintain a video surveillance, passing information through to the force control room."

"I want armed response officers around the building, ably assisted by other personnel armed to the teeth, the dog section with their, 'Land sharks' I also want our usual officer with the battering ram, as there is a Judas gate to the property. He cried yes, I know it's for luck."

There was a pause for several minutes as Carter nodded. He looked at Sue. Nodding, "Yep, we are good to go."

Sue, who looked worried said, "What did you have to give in support, your arse?" Carter said, "My, my DCS Ford, that is rather personal. A raw of laughter burst out in the whole of the room.

As it all settled he said, "I'll ask Eric, to run off copies of the photographs that clearly show Clerk, and Thompson going in and out. In order we may hand them out to assist in identifications."

As he went to leave, the whole team stood up, he looked around, "Now what the hell have I forgotten, and they all laughed saying, "See you in the morning guv?"

He laughed to himself as he walked out headed towards the general office. On arrival he received a mug of coffee. He sat and talked with Eric. He said, "I've got loads of photo for the teams tomorrow, plus one of the team has come back with your warrant."

Carter said, "I'm off home, but will be back tomorrow to assist with the operation." Before Carter could finish, Eric said, "No arguments, I'll be in as well, you may need us, now be off with you, Charlie will be waiting."

Charlie dropped Carter off saying, "See you at about 4.00am, I won't press the intercom in case Penny, is still in bed." He smiled as he drove off.

Carter had hardly put his key in the flat door when it was suddenly pulled open, to reveal Penny, stood stark naked. He said, "Well Miss Wilkinson, what would you have done if I'd had Charlie with me?"

Penny burst out laughing, her face was beetroot red in colour, and "Well I'd have just grabbed one of your coats off the hall stand, now seeing as he isn't, get your arse in the shower.

He ran into their bedroom trying to undress as he went. Eventually he turned on the shower and as they both waited for the water temp to increase, they both kissed

191

passionately.

When the water had reached the correct temp, they both walked in, putting on their sponge gloves, and liberally poured liquid soap onto them. They then both started to bathe each other with the soapy suds.

Carter quickly realised he was more than ready, Penny looking down said, "My Carter, the decks look cleared, and ready for action."

He smothered her in a giant bath sheet, and carried her to their bed. He gently laid her down, and opened the towel to reveal her firm body.

After their love making, they both fell back with delight, resonated from their bodies. Due to work commitments it failed to lessen their total excitement. Carter looked down, and started to remove the end of the towel from Pennies mouth, used as a muffle, as Penny never trusted herself, with her vocal control.

Carter made a phone call, and ordered a take away curry, with all the works. As after successful lovemaking one always felt hungry, as they were. They both sat in towelling dressing gowns, and consumed their very enjoyable meal.

Chapter Sixty One

Carter and his team were all present at 4.15 am. He had been told that all the other components were ready, and waiting in the McDonalds car park, off Edge Lane.

Sue, Ian, and Lloydie were sat talking with their three teams. All had checked their firearms. Peter was with Sue, acting as her number two. Philip was acting the same with Ian. Julie was acting the same with Lloydie.

At 4.30am they, "All moved down to the police yard were three black coloured seated transit vans stood waiting. Sue said, "Peter you take care of the warrant?" He replied, "Yes boss, and other members of the team have a sworn warrant for Thompson, and his address."

Carter had spoken with the duty Inspector of the armed response team. He also contacted the Inspector of the dog section, whilst he received a message from the duty Inspector in the control room. He relayed a message from The Air Support Unit, that they were scrambled having taken up a position in the area.

Carter also in the police yard stood talking with Charlie, "It's 5.00am, he got on his force radio set to channel 5 he said, "Carter to all patrols, please make sure that you are all wearing your Kevlar body armour?" A chorus of voices returned, "Yes guv." Also I know I have to say it, "No blue lights or horns."

He then said, "Right let's get this over and done with." Prior to getting into his vehicle he invited Gordon Chamber's to join them. Carter said, "Gordon, sorry I can't offer you a nip." He burst out laughing.

Carter spoke to the observation team, they replied, "All is quiet guv, there have been no leavers."

At 5.15am with the sound of the force helicopter, they all took their place outside of the warehouse. An officer dressed in black, wearing a black balaclava, overalls, with the trousers tucked into his boots, with black head protection, and visor walked up to the Judas gate.

He stood with about ten other officers standing behind him, and in their ear pieces they heard, "Go, go, go."

With a loud bang the Judas gate came off its hinges, officers shouted, "Armed police stay where you are." The two dog handlers followed with their charges that yet again turned into the most ferocious animals.

In all the mayhem there was a noise that no one wanted to hear, the discharge of a fire arm. It was an automatic weapon that fired in quick succession, 'bang, bang' it happened twice in quick retort, but from two different directions, towards the officers.

Carter with his teams were quick to answer as they ran in with fire arms drawn, again giving the typical warning. Again there was the sound of automatic gun fire, 'bang, bang.' On this occasion it was followed by the sound of screams, as two uniform police officer's fell to the floor.

Again they heard "Armed police stand down." Carter heard the sound of gun fire, and then there was silence.

Carter looked to his right where he saw two teams of paramedics attending, the two police officers laying on the floor.

His team were busily searching the premises, all dressed in their forensic suits. Sue had handed Carter, and Charlie a suit each. They dressed in seconds. One of the teams took 8 men to a wall at the side of the warehouse, were they were told, "Stand with your hands against the wall, whilst we search you."

There was a scream from a make shift room, Sue, had walked through a plastic draped curtained area, where she found three operation type tables. Carter rushed in thinking that she may be in trouble, only to find her standing between two of the tables.

On the tables were three bodies covered with white plastic sheets, he saw that she was okay, only that her face was drained of all colour, he looked at her, she pulled back one of the sheets to reveal the body of a young girl, with her body gutted, similar to that of a post mortem victim.

Behind Carter was Gordon Chamber's he said, "My

God, what have these animals done, but yet it was obvious as someone had obviously used the victims to harvest body organs, carrying out a series of blatant butchery.

Peter said, "What's that noise?" Gordon Chambers said, "It sounds like some sort of refrigeration system." Philip who had come across a cupboard, with the door open said, "Does anyone know what these are?" As he said it he took hold of a blue coloured plastic box.

They had lids that were held in place by a handle, that when lifted to carry, it seemed to secure the box. Carter together with Gordon Chamber's walked over to where he was standing, for Philip was standing in front of a large cupboard.

The boxes were packed on top of each other, with several spilled out onto the floor, within the plastic cordoned off area.

Gordon Chamber's with a look of utter disgust on his face said, "Just prior to being removed from the donor, or in this case victims such as these. Each organ, is flushed free of blood, with a specially prepared ice-cold preservation solution, that contains electrolytes and nutrients."

Mr Chambers continued, "These organ boxes were strategically intact to maintain the integrity of the organ being transplanted. Under normal circumstances the boxes are sterile, able to be sealed, to prevent it being opened without authority. There should be sufficient melting iced water available for the securing of the organ. And lastly sufficient plastic cable ties, ensuring that the organ is delivered to the recipient."

"Now that is how it should be done, but I fear this picture fills me with utter revulsion."

Carter walked over to Gordon, and placed an arm around his shoulder. "Gordon we both deal in murder, psychopathic killers, serial killings, and umpteen other killers, but yet here we are dealing with managed killing for material gain."

Gordon Chambers said looking around at Carter, "You

are both a good colleague, and friend, "But, you must get SOCO down here immediately, before any evidence may have been spoilt. These bastards on hearing of our attack, may have done so, possibly knowing what was coming."

Lloydie looked at Carter, and smiled as he said down his radio, "Bring in SOCO to report to Mr Chamber's, and send for the mortuary team to deal with the recovered bodies."

Chapter Sixty Two

Whilst all this was all going on, Carter looked at Gordon Chamber's, "Gordon, will you please join me as I'm about to ask you to take part in an identification parade."

Gordon turned and smiled he said, "Lead on." Both men walked over were a collection of prisoners were being held. Carter looked at Alex and nodded. Alex said, "All of you turn around, with that the group of men turned.

Carter said, "Mr Chamber's, I'd like you to identify the two men we are looking for, please take your time."

Gordon Chamber's taking his time walked along the line, without any pictorial evidence he identified the two men, he said, "This man is Angus Clark, the onetime surgeon. He pointed to a second, and this man is Paul Thompson, a technician with, The Liverpool Royal Infirmary mortuary."

Alex walked over and officially cautioned both men, he then placed them in handcuffs and lead them away to a nearby waiting police van. They were taken away, and transported to Derby Lane.

While Carter was talking with Gordon Chamber's, Warren Allis, one of the SOCO managers walked over, "Gentlemen would you both like to follow me. Carter walked over followed by, Gordon Chamber's.

"Well Warren what can we do for you?" In a soft voice he said, "Well, on top of everything else I'd like to show you the contents of one of the metal containers. All three came to a halt were several of the SOCO team were busy working.

Carter and Gordon stood looking into the container, both stood frozen to the ground. For there in front of them they both saw that the container had been fitted out as a makeshift, mortuary.

Gordon Chamber's whispered, "Hence the generator noise?" For, laid on the shelves, were the shapes of bodies, all in see through plastic covers? By this time they noticed that Sue, Lloydie, and Ian, had come over to join them.

Gordon Chamber's without taking his eyes from the terrible sight said, "How many?" Warren turned and said, "We haven't actually counted as yet." Gordon Chamber's suddenly shouted in his usual voice level, "Why not?" Carter looked at him, "Steady on Gordon, we are all under immense pressure, this is a bloody mess, and it will take some time to sort out, I'm afraid there will be a lot of work for you, and your team."

He continued, "Let's get a hot drink." Gordon shouted, "Hot drink! Hot drink! Christ Carter, I thought you more than most would want to push on in all of this. After all said and done, they may after all only be a result of the failed care system, but they are some person's daughter, or son."

He turned, and stormed off in the direction of a mobile chuck wagon, offering hot drinks to the police officers, busy in the enquiry.

Charlie said, "Guv he doesn't mean it, he is obviously very upset that a onetime respected colleague had turned into a monster, to be at their beck and call, of the person who stood to gain in all of this?"

"Guv let me get you a hot drink, and bring it over to you. Ian and, Lloydie walked over, but it was Phil, who took their orders, together with Peter, they brought over the tray of drinks.

Carter pulled over a chair and sat; he took a sip of his coffee and spat it out, "Whoever is responsible for making this should be locked up." They all burst out laughing. He pulled out his mobile and called, Tony Frost.

Chapter Sixty Three

His call was answered on the second ring, he immediately answered, knowing what to expect, in a low voice he said, *"Frost."*

Carter gave him chapter and verse in relation to the raid, he told him that Clark and Thompson, had been identified by Gordon Chamber's, and arrested. Both men have been taken to Derby Lane. The remaining 6 men followed later.

He continued, "We have recovered eleven bodies, three were found by DCS Ford, in a makeshift operation theatre, where the three victims had been opened, like the cavernous bodies in a post mortem, with all of their organs removed, including their eyes."

TF said, *"Oh! Carer, what utter conditions you must all be working in, do you need any extra help?"* Carter paused, "No sir, it is best that we contain it in the team."

On completion of the call Tony Frost said, *"How are the injured officers?"* Carter said, "They're off to the Royal, it would appear that the wounds are in their upper shoulders, were there is no protection, I'll let you know."

He then said, *"What can I say Carter, you and your team have plumbed the depth of utter depravity yet again, but your teams dealing with yet another horrendous mess, clearly respond to your leadership."*

"I realise it was due to an opportune moment, as most fateful matters predict. Please offer my sincere congratulations to the members of your team and hope that with some further enquiries we may get the bastard in charge."

"Now, in conclusion, three things...The first Wendy fields, and the matter of the press. Two, please make it up with Gordon Chamber's, after all said and done he is our Home Office Pathologist, and third, there is a team commendation in the pipeline. Leave it with me I'll see the Chief." Carter could hear him laughing, *"Now play well*

Carter."

As Carter closed the call, and whilst he was putting his phone away, he felt a rather large hand on his shoulder. "Carter, will you ever forgive my rather childish rant. It was not totally uncalled for; it's just what we came across."

Carter said, "Gordon, why don't you return with me to Derby Lane, and we can talk over a tot. "There is still a lot of work to be done, mainly to the cadavers, which is now a crime scene, and your domain."

Back in Derby Lane, Carter invited Gordon Chamber's into his office. They were just enjoying a nip when there was a knock on his office door. Carter said, "Come in"

The door pushed open and they both saw Sue, standing in the doorway. Sue smiling said, "Gentlemen, could I invite you to come to the conference room, there are some items of interest for you to inspect?"

As they entered the room, the team looked up, and in respect stood up. Carter slowly walked over to one of the tables. He pointed, "What are these? Julie said, "Guv we executed a warrant on Thompson's house, here are some of the items we found in a binder.

He noticed a key code on a lanyard. Gordon Chambers said, "That's the key code that the duty mortuary technician holds whilst *'on call'*. Thompson was not *'on call'* on the night of the burglary."

Gordon Chamber's said, "I can supply you with a copy of the *'on call'* duty roster..." Julie interrupted saying, "It's alright Mr Chambers, and we found a copy of the roster amongst all his papers."

Julie looked at Carter, "Guv is it alright to ask Mr Chamber's for a statement of identification?" Carter smiled, "Certainly, Julie I see no problem, in fact Mr Chamber's, may be our guest for a while."

Carter noticed some dark clothing folded up on another table he ambled over, "What are these?" Julie said, "Guv we also found these items in a box under his bed. Julie explained, "You will see black trousers, a black jumper,

200

with black shoes, and a black balaclava."

"I think when he was arrested, and brought in, he was wearing other items of clothing?" Carter looked at Sue, laughing he said, "We'll make a detective of her yet?" Other members of the team joined in the laughter.

Carter looked at Gordon, "Can I place you in the trust of Sue, whilst I go and make a quick phone call."

Chapter Sixty Four

Gordon Chamber's looked in the direction of Sue whilst he walked away; Gordon had a questioned look on his face. Sue said, "He is off to make a quick phone call to Penny, his partner, informing her that all went well."

Gordon looked at Sue, "The loss of Helen, and the children nearly killed him, in fact it would in most men, but I know your boss is one of the good men, deserving of a second chance."

He noticed the look in Sue's eyes it was a look of utter pride. Gordon said, "I know you all love the man, but do you remember when he was given the job, and our first case in, Stanley Park."

Smiling he said, "I'll never forget it, I thought why in God's name did the man pick such a career, for he was so obviously hesitating; not happy to stand too close, it would seem that he'd picked the wrong career, that death was an integral part, and parcel of a career CID officer's life."

Sue looked at Gordon, "Mr Chamber's, although very important, that aspect of the job, he has learnt to steel himself on such occasions, but it's his overall leadership that he excels in, as you must have witnessed."

Gordon Chamber's said, "Yes he has it in spades, you know I've never heard him tell any of the team off?" Sue said, "Why, he leaves us to do our jobs." Laughing she said, "He leaves that up to Eric."

Sue looked at Gordon, "Mr Chamber's I have noticed that you have such respect for the man, that you never insist on him getting close in the most morbid of jobs?" Gordon just smiled, "Yes officer, I'll come quietly." They both burst out laughing, as did her team colleagues.

The next thing he returned to the conference room rubbing his hands together, "Right where are we up to?"

Sue looked at Carter, "Guv Julie or Niki are about to take a statement from Mr Chamber's, over his original identification of Angus Clark, and Paul Thompson, as two of the main protagonists in this matter. He will no doubt issue a statement re the situation in the Binns Road, warehouse."

In relation to all the other men arrested from that site, including Clark, and Thompson, are being detained to enable us to make further enquiries."

Carter said, "Sue I want you to set up a meeting for 9.30am in the morning. Please ask Eric to assist as I want, TF, Wendy Field, Sam Watson, Mr Chamber's and of course all senior officers of the team. Let's hold it in the conference room."

He looked at Gordon chamber's, Gordon I know it's short notice, but could you go to the mortuary, I'll lend you Jim Lloyd, but I must have an overall picture of the situation."

"I'm going to talk with TF with regard of the press, as such a situation has a habit of getting out, *'Chinese whispers'* Carter stood up he looked at his watch, it's lunchtime, looking at Gordon Chamber's he said, "Will it give you enough time? Sorry to rush you." He smiled, "I'll have a go."

As he left the room he turned, "Lunch on me, please ask one of Eric's young lady to take the orders, English, Chinese, or Indian, but please let's have overall agreement, as I don't want to make a meal out of it."

Laughing he walked out of the room heading towards his office. On arrival he was met by Eric holding a mug of coffee, "I heard your laughter as you passed the general office."

"How are you?" Carter said, "Will you stop playing mother." Eric said, "You've a habit of attacking things at 100mph, let me get hold of Charlie to take you home, to rest before tomorrow."

Carter laughed, "Sorry mother, but I've just ordered lunch, and you are all included, now go I need to talk with TF." Eric smiled as he left, but knew of his enthusiasm, it's what always rubbed off on the team, but had a habit of burning himself out.

Chapter Sixty Five

After lunch, Eric was as good as his word and Charlie dropped Carter off. He looked at his boss, "Is there anything that I can be doing?" Carter answered, "Yes, will you get a small team to concentrate on the prisoners. I need them checked out with MerCro, for we need to know who we are dealing with."

Charlie smiled, "See you in the morning guv bright and early." And he drove off.

Carter walked into the lounge he made sure he was alone, as at this juncture, all he wanted to do was to undo the top button of his shirt, and loosen his tie. But before all that he walked into the kitchen and took out of the fridge two cans of beer, he then went back into the lounge, and relaxed in the large armchair.

The next thing he was aware off was a faint kiss on his cheek he sat bolt upright asking the time. Penny took hold of his hand saying, "It's a shower for you my lad, alone mores the pity. And then off to bed with you, you're done in, no arguments."

Penny ushered Carter to the shower, she then pulled the duvet over him, and as usual he was asleep before she had left the room.

In the lounge Penny wondered if the team could do without him for a day, but not wanting to cause a war, the thought went completely out of her head, as quickly as it had entered. She burst out laughing; just concentrate on tea my girl.

Penny decided that if Carter did awaken say about tea time, he may only fancy something light. A wicked thought entered her head, No! No! Girl, get rid of those naughty thoughts.

At about 11.30pm Penny entered their bedroom to get ready for bed. She lightly slipped out of her clothes, and dressed in one of Carter's T shirts she lifted her side of their duvet, and slid into bed.

As Penny rested her head on her pillow, she was able to listen to Carter's light breathing it was steady, and controlled. It was whilst she took up the position close to where Carter laid, that she could feel the damp on the fitted sheet.

Penny gently turned, and started to pass one of her hands along the sheet on which he lay, she pulled it away, unable to believe that he could lie in so much damp. She ever so gently moved her hand over his body, it was drenched. Penny got up out of bed, and walked to the bathroom.

She returned with a large bath sheet, without disturbing Carter, she softly pulled back the duvet, and lightly passed the towel over him.

Getting back into bed Penny thought that he must have experienced some sort of night tremor set on by the pressure of work, plus the level of the particular case in question.

The following morning Carter looked down on the bath sheet, it had dried from the warmth of his body. He noticed that Penny was up, so he tied the towel around him, and walked through to the kitchen.

He stood for several seconds whilst he coughed saying, "Any idea? What's with the towel, please say I've not taken to wrapping myself up in a towel whilst in bed?"

Penny laughed, "No of course you haven't Carter, and it's just that when I came to bed you'd pushed the duvet down? Perhaps you may have been warm, so not wishing to disturb you I covered you with the towel."

He turned saying, "Oh!" as he walked off for his shower, to prepare for work. He came through later as he put on his jacket, covering his gun, and shoulder holster.

Penny walked over, she placed one of her hands on either side of his face, "Yes, I know you'll get a hot drink in the office." She kissed him gently on his lips. "Please take care see you this evening."

Carter smiled at her, turned and left. As he walked to meet up with Charlie, who was patiently waiting by the

car, he laughed to himself, wondering who the better liar
was.

Chapter Sixty Six

It was 8.30am when Carter and Charlie, both walked into the general office to book on duty.

They both noticed a hive of activity, Eric had things organised as usual, he looked at Carter, and "The Girls have seen to the room, it's all set up with the white boards as requested."

Eric said, "It's all senior officers including sergeants? If so there is more than enough work for the other darlings to be getting on with."

Carter burst out laughing, as he took his morning coffee from him and then walked through to his office, Charlie remained with Eric.

Carter on entering his office sat to call Penny, the phone was answered in her usual quiet voice, *"Well you got to work then."* Carter said, "I think I need to explain something to you about last night."

"I knew that towel was supplied courtesy of you. I'm very grateful, and feel that I need to explain, that on occasions, I've been known to sweat like mad. It's a form of night tremors."

Penny in a soft voice said, *"Carter it's a rather alarming experience on the first occasion, I presume it won't be the first or the last, for it's obviously a matter 'A' typical of you, when under stress."*

"All is well, I've stripped the bed, everything's in the wash, as I'm now about to leave for work, I'll see you later, I love you," and the phone went dead.

When Penny arrived at her office she was met by Sam, who was preparing to leave for Derby Lane. Sam said, "Penny fancy a trip out, I've been invited to a meeting with the big boys." Penny burst out laughing.

She looked at Sam, "Can I ask you a question, are there occasions when, Jim suffers night tremors, and breaks out in the sweats?" Sam said, "Yes, at first I tried to pretend by covering him over with a dry towel, but quickly realised that you've got an 'elephant' in the room, that needs addressing."

"Now it's my way of knowing if his work is getting him stressed, he won't admit it, but I turn to, stripping the bed etc, I would think it's very prevalent with Carter, as he is carrying the hole caboodle."

Chapter Sixty Seven

At Derby Lane, Carter was in a brief meeting with Sue, when there was a knock on his door. He shouted, "Come in" They both looked up to see Eric, with a broad smile on his face, "All the usual suspects have arrived."

Carter stood smiling, "We'll let battle commence." He thanked Eric, and they left for the conference room. As they passed the general office, Eric peeled off to open the door.

Carter again smiling said, "And where do you think you're going? Get in line; I feel you may have something to contribute, with the preparation of all the court paper work."

As Carter, Sue, and Eric entered the room, Carters junior officers went to stand, he glanced at them, and they all smiled, and sat down. Sue and Eric took up their seats. Carter walked to the front of the room he stood looking out at all present.

He smiled as he noticed Penny sat together with Sam. "Ladies and gentlemen you will have seen all the matters displayed on the white boards. The most important one is that portrays the layout of our gang in question. The only name missing is the name that should replace the question mark."

Carter looked in the direction of Gordon, and smiled, I would like to call on Mr Gordon Chamber's, our Home Office Pathologist."

Gordon Chamber's burst out in his usual outburst. "Well, I have to say that we have an abundance of bodies, we have 7 young ladies from the dock location, and yesterday's raid brought the total of victim's bodies up to 16 victims."

"Three of yesterday's victims were found in a temporary type mortuary, by DCS Sue Ford. In a post mortem type state, having been totally stripped of their vital organs,"

"In case you don't already know 7 victims, plus a police officer, were stolen in a raid carried out on the City mortuary, and brought to that terrible warehouse. We also found another type of mortuary, were we found five victims swathed in bed sheets."

"When inspected we found all of the five bodies showed that they had been exposed, as we established that all five had been sown up in the most hideous of ways."

"Now in conclusion ably assisted by DI Jim Lloyd, we have carried out a quick check up on the bodies, for it to enable me to give a result of our examinations."

"Apart from the six victims found on the docks all of which resulting in gunshot wounds to their heads, one victim was shot in the hospital, together with the police officer, with the same calibre hand gun."

"We also found eight bodies which were missing vital organs. Three of which we found had just only been performed, for I hate to say they were fresh."

"Blood and tox samples have been taken, as yet although we found needle marks on each body, we have no idea how they had been killed, as there are no signs of any trauma wounds on the victims.

"We found in a metal container, plastic boxes used for the transporting of organs, I have to say there were quite a lot, and not just a few, so this puts into perception the turnover in relation to the money being made."

He sat down somewhat dejected.

Carter stood and looked in the direction of Sue. "I now call upon my deputy to inform us of the situation in relation of the prisoners."

Sue looked out on her audience. We have arrested 6 men prior to the raid on the warehouse, although we lost two by suspicious circumstances, after being bailed from Derby Road."

"On the recent raid to the warehouse, we arrested 8 other men, two of whom we found to be very important."

"All the prisoners will be interviewed, we have checked them out on MerCro and most are known to us.

Sue looked at her audience, "You will all realise how important it is to detect the, *'Question mark'* at the top of the pile, the main drive in all of this."

"In conclusion I have to report two officers were injured during the raid, both officers, received gunshot wounds unfortunately, in the exact part of their bodies, not protected by their Kevlar jackets. Both were taken to the Royal for medical attention."

When Sue had sat down, Carter looked at Tony frost. He stood up, and went to the front of the room.

He looked directly at Gordon Chamber's, "Mr Chamber's whilst I thank you for your quickly managed reports, I have to say that your work deals directly with death, the appearance of something to the mind or eye."

We as police officers, specifically those that make it to the CID, know that during their service there will be a time when they may be asked to deal with grubby, seedy, and grotty cases."

"Yet the officers you all see in front of you find it a day to day occurrence and for those who know them, that they do it with total professionalism."

"It is therefore my great honour to award, a Chief Constables commendation to not only the team, but all the officers, and clerical staff contained in there."

Carter and all of his present officers just remained very stoic, due mainly to this present case.

Tony Frost said, "Right, where do we go in this, from the press aspect?" He looked in the direction of, Wendy Field.

Wendy said, "Two matters are very important one, do we tell the truth, and blow all of this case out of the water, or two, do we say; 'As a result of information obtained, officers attended...'

Tony Frost sat down with a frown on his face. He

looked at Carter, "What do you think?" Carter replied, "I believe we leave it with Wendy, after all the lady knows her job, and is an integral part of the team."

"I will get Eric, to send her all our reports. Wendy could then type up a press release, which we can both read, before it goes to press."

Tony Frost looked at Sam, "Could you please give us your thinking on all of this? Please in layman's language."

Sam stood up Carter, knew what was coming, as he saw her take a sly look at Lloydie, which seemed to calm her."

"Well, as I told you before, you are dealing with a psychopathic *'Fagan type'* character, which rewards his assembled helpers with money of drugs, or both. He turns the organs taken from your collection of bodies, into vast amounts of money."

"Mr Chamber's is an expert in this field, who is fully aware of what full body components are worth? Although they are more likely to be sold singly, perhaps in one's, and two's at a time."

"You protagonist employ's a struck off surgeon, who in receipt of payment in kind, either drugs, or alcohol or both. He will most probably have a network of unscrupulous men, and women to assist in the supply of victims."

"The good thing about your surgeon, he will have a readymade set up of clients, with patients, prepared to pay the earth for suitable organs ready for transplant, rather than wait for the NHS."

This *'Fagan type'* realises that there are plenty of victims, who all initially were, or are lured by the chance of fame. Which is utter BS, but we know that blood tests are taken, again BS."

"The candidates are told they are needed should they go abroad to work, from the tests, he can blood type their blood, finding victims with good to better blood results."

"In conclusion I feel that the toxin tests will show some sort of drug was used, which led to their deaths, a perfect miss use of the unfortunate cannon fodder, supplied by the care system of today. These victims will not be missed."

Tony Frost after thanking Sam, just got up, and walked out.

Eric said, "We have eats for one and all that are interested."

Chapter Sixty Eight

After Sam, Wendy, Penny and Gordon had left; Carter invited the remaining officers to relax, and to try to enjoy the free buffet. They all smirked, but all realised that there wasn't such a thing as a free lunch.

He looked out on all of them, "Right we need to return to the investigation. I mean to break it up into several parts."

"I want to continue with investigations at that bloody warehouse, you needn't take warrants, as it's continued enquiries after the fact. Completion of the major raid, the original warrant will suffice."

"I want Clark, and Thompson to be brought up from the cells. Sue and I will see to Clark. I'd like Lloydie and Peter, to interview Thompson, He looked at Lloydie you have a good working knowledge of the mortuary."

"I'd like Ian and Phil, to both return to the warehouse, get hold of matters that need to be bagged and tagged, they will be needed as exhibits, you don't need me, to tell you what to do."

"Charlie I'd like you to pick Julie, Gill, and Alex to go down to the cells and check on all the other prisoners, please check them out with MerCro, and see what we have."

He looked at them all, "The mess we have is like trying to pull an egg out of an omelette, impossible, yet we like impossible."

"Now, when you have finished with the nose bags, I'm going to ask Eric to call up Clark, and Thompson. I want us to finish for about 6ish, there is another day tomorrow."

Carter looked at Sue, "Could I ask you to call the duty Bridewell Doctor, to examine, Clark. I need to have an update on his health." Sue stood up and smiled saying "Will do guv."

He suddenly jumped up, "I want all your thoughts, I'm thinking of suggesting that we leave all this, and pick it all up in the morning." He waited, cupping his ear with his hand, as if to hear any such suggestions."

Looking at them all, "What do you all think?" A smothered voice replied, "Does the Pope Wear funny hats?" Carter shouted, "I heard that, Peter, your act needs a little more work." They all burst out laughing.

Whilst he walked back to his office he said, "Sue will you make sure no one walks off, I'm about to contact the CPS putting my suggestion to them." After ten minutes he shouted through the open door to his office, "See you all in the morning."

As he walked through to the general office to book off duty, he looked at Eric, "Before you leave will you make sure that all know of the early dart." He replied, "Yes guv."

After Charlie had dropped Carter off at his flat, he shouted, "See you in the morning guv." And swiftly drove off.

Carter realised he had arrived home before Penny. He took off his jacket, shoulder holster, and gun. He then slackened his tie, walked through to the kitchen for a beer, and sitting in the armchair, he tried to relax.

After a couple of hours, and several beers later, he then heard the key in the door. Penny walked into the lounge, and with an urgent voice she spluttered, "Carter what a wonderful surprise!" Then she said, "You are alright?"

He burst out laughing, "Yes, I decided that we all deserved an early dart, and that we in particular, needed to catch up on matters that may have slipped over the last couple of days."

Penny looked at him, "Oh! Sir, what on earth are you trying to say? I'm only a sweet innocent young maiden, and could not possibly know what you mean."

Carter stood up he walked over and took hold of her hand, "Walk this way, she looked at him, "If I walked that way I wouldn't need the talcum powder, boom, boom."

After their totally exotic shower, he gently manoeuvred Penny, to bed. They made love very quickly, with genuine passion still there. Not much was said, but the joy was there so strongly. Afterwards, she fell asleep very quickly and he lay there listening to her gentle breathing, unable to sleep himself, and finally slipped out of bed, he pulled on his shorts and walked through to the lounge.

He didn't need to switch on a light because there was enough light drifting in from the lamp on the estate. He went through to the kitchen and made himself a cup of coffee.

Carter returned to the lounge, sitting in one of the easy armchairs, he began to think of the coming day, and the series of the coming interviews. Eventually tiredness began to envelope him. He stood up and returned to bed.

Chapter Sixty Nine

The following morning Carter was gently awoken by a very tender kiss on his mouth. On opening his eyes he found Penny looking down on him saying, "I can clearly recommend sex as an important aid to the ABC, or 5-2 diet."

Carter said, "Penny what on earth are you going on about?" Penny continued, "Well, after our exotic shower, and our all-embracing fore play, and sex. We both fell asleep, or at least I did, without having our evening meal."

After they had both stopped laughing, Penny exhaled a gentle breath, "My, my, it's such a pity that we couldn't spend our day as a duvet day?"

He gently moved up onto one of his elbows, he lowered his head kissing her firmly on the lips, after several seconds he pulled away, "I know, it would be so easy to continue from where we left off, from last night."

"But I need to get up." He laughed out loud, "To shower alone, you see I need to concentrate, on my day ahead, if I relent, I'll be drained."

Penny got up and very slowly walked towards the bathroom, he quickly looked at her firm body, and he then closed both eyes saying, "Do you need the loo?"

The next thing he felt a pillow hit him squarely in his face. "He said what the hell?"

Penny in an exasperated voice shouted, "Carter?"

He got up out of bed, and walked towards her, her eyes happened to glance down saying, "Oh! Carter, I see you're pleased to see me."

Running into the bathroom, and locking the door he shouted, "No I just need the loo."

He heard Penny huffing, and puffing, and visualized her kicking the pillow, all around the bedroom.

After his use of the loo, he then took a quick shower, and shave. He opened the door walking towards her, wrapped in a towel, and using a second towel to dry his hair.

Penny snorting rushed passed him to use the bathroom, slamming the door. He said, "Darling I see you failed to lay out my clothes, Penny shouted, "Carter, just leave it."

Laughing he dressed and walked into the kitchen to make himself a mug of coffee, for he thought if he'd left it up to Penny she'd pour it over him.

After fifteen minutes he heard the intercom buzz. He said, "Charlie, I'm on my way out, and I'll see you in a minute."

The bedroom door opened, and he saw Penny standing in her white towelling dressing gown. He smiled, "I'm just off." She covered her head with a towel, and walked into the kitchen.

She heard, "See you later," As he closed the door, leaving for the office.

Chapter Seventy

Carter entered the office saying his usual good mornings to all present. He signed on duty. After which taking his usual mug of coffee from Eric, he went and sat next to him.

They chatted briefly, Carter said, "Eric at what age do men learn how to come to terms with women's ways, and senses of humour?" He burst out laughing, whilst the young secretary's just sniggered, "Right! What have you gone and done?" Carter replied, "What set out as a joke, quickly turned into WW3."

Eric looked at him, "Carter I'm a lot older than you, and I still haven't learnt, but what I do know is, "It's better to slide on a yard of bull shit, than a mile of gravel." All the office fell about laughing.

Carter stood, as he reached for his coffee Eric winked, "I'll give you 10 minutes before we start to bring up the prisoners, you may wish to make a call!!?"

He smiled as he left for his office, on entering his, he sat and whilst he enjoyed his coffee, he thought on what Eric had just said, and picked up the phone. It was answered on the second ring, yet there was nothing.

Carter repeatedly said, "Penny are you there?" Eventually a voice said, *"Well, have you telephoned to apologise for your crass, inane behaviour?"*

"Or when you get home, do I have to smack your legs, and bottom... No! Carter... And whilst trying to control her laughter she said, *"No, Carter, that would be right up your street, wouldn't it, just."*

After they had both controlled themselves Carter said, "I haven't much time, I love you, and he replaced the receiver. Within seconds there was a knock on his door, he said, "Come In?"

Sue said, "Morning Carter, and are you out of the *'dog house'* He burst out laughing, "Who do you think wear's the trousers in our house?" Sue burst out laughing, "Yea,

yea, yea I bet?"

As they both entered the general office smiling Carter said, "What do you call an alligator in a vest?" Laughing he replied, 'An investigator' "So please, let's go and investigate."

Carter looked at Eric, can you round up Ian, Lloydie, Charlie, Peter, Philip, Julie, and Gill to attend at my office ASAP.

He walked out with Sue, on arrival at his office he said, "It's just a quick chat before we start."

When everyone were present he produced a diagram similar to the last one, except they now noticed, Clark, and Thompson, had been included.

Ladies and Gentlemen, you will all notice that we now have Clark and Thompson, which I've squeezed in where I see their place in the hierarchy. You can see that they are immediately down from our question mark, still un-named at the top?"

"We need all to take notice of it, as not only will we stand more of a chance of naming 'Mr Big' with the likes of Clark, and Thompson? We may find that one of the lowly soldiers may give him up?"

Chapter Seventy One

Carter and Sue entered interview room one. Opening the door the uniformed officer stood to attention. Carter smiled, "Officer could I ask that you take up station outside of the room. He replied, "Sir" and on leaving closed the door behind him.

They both sat opposite a very dejected excuse of a man. Carter said, "Well, you must be Clark, I of course mean, Angus Clark, to give you your full name." He just nodded.

Carter said, "Clark when you were arrested, you were duly cautioned, and for the purposes of this interview you are still under caution.

Carter said, "Clark have you been seen by the Bridewell Surgeon, he again nodded.

Sue went to sort out the tape recorder as she did so, Carter reached and gently taking hold of her arm stopped her, and looking at her he just smiled.

"Clark, I'm Assistant Commander Carter, and this is my deputy, Detective Chief Superintendent Susan Ford."

"Now before we go through the usual protocol, under caution. I want you to get a grip of yourself, sit up, and try to take stock of your situation, or the mess that you presently find yourself in."

"Now I believe that you are a known drug addict, and alcoholic?" Without any trace of reaction to his face he said, "You forgot to mention a onetime Surgeon."

Carter suddenly banged the palm of his hand onto the top of the table. Clark and Sue nearly jumped out of here skin, together with the officer. He opened the door, Carter turned, "It's alright officer all is under control. He said, "Sir" and closed the door.

Carter looked at Clark, "It would seem that I now have your attention?" Clark nodded his head.

Carter looked him straight in his eyes, "I don't want you to piss me around, and I want to know how the hell you ended up, like this?"

With a smirk on Clark's face he said, "Well, it started about 6 years ago, but became more frequent over the last 4 years. I was married with a beautiful wife, three children, and a large detached house on the Wirral. My wife, and I each had brand new BMW's, I had the lot."

I started at medical school, became a Doctor making my way up the slippery medical pole, until I became a Consultant. Now people deal with pressure in so many different ways. In the beginning I had the love of a good woman, cars, holidays, and hobbies etc."

"That's how and when it all started to unravel. Oh! At first my wife, was very loving and supportive. There was a lot of kudos, married to a Medical Consultant, until she started to get bored with me, and my work load, and she turned to charitable works, and the Charity circuit. I never saw her; she never showed me any fucking charity."

"There was always this charity, or that charity, the rounds of dinner parties, and black tie job's. On top of this, I was expected to turn up with her on my arm, and yet. I had a full operation list on the following morning, together with a packed outpatient clinic."

"I started to take uppers, and downers, alcohol and I then progressed to cocaine." He looked at Carter, "Satisfied? This was my fucking life, when do I get the Red fucking book, and meet, Michael Terence Aspel, OBE.

He slumped back in his chair.

Carter looking at him, smiled, "Angus we're not here to pontificate. I, we truly need your help? How did you manage your getting involved in all of this? Who picked you; you just didn't crop up, or fall from the sky?" With a sick look on to his face he said, "Yes, Carter I know, so fuck you, in fact fuck the lot of you." He leaned back and folded his arms.

Carter stood up, "Well Mr Angus Clark, we as police officers can use the 'F' word, I'm a seasoned police officer, and you don't fucking scare me or my deputy, in fact it's you who should be scared of me, as I'm about to recommend that we reduce your methadone medication."

He shouted. "You can't fucking do that." Carter said, "Can't I, Oh! Mr Clark, there is a lot that you don't know about me."

"For instance, not only can I have your methadone reduced, I can make sure that you'll be late, and miss your medically prescribed medication. He looked at Clark, "That's your first mistake. He looked at Sue, let's get a cuppa."

As they went to stand he shouted, "Wait?"

Carter looked at him, he was sweating profusely. "Yes?" Clark said, "You don't know who you are dealing with, this man just isn't your usual business man, he has his fingers in several pies, both here, and abroad, in Europe."

"If I give him up to you, I want protection. He has people in place they seem to be able to bring people into this country like turning a tap, on or off, in other words, *'people trafficking, as well as the harvesting of organs.'* They're not the usual monkeys that you have downstairs, those just follow orders."

"The people that you are seeking are criminal gangs who without fear of detection, will act as directed by their boss."

Carter looked at him, "Well, Mr Clark we seem to have reached an impasse. On the one hand you give up the name of your boss, and for me to guarantee your constant medication of methadone, and of course your protection."

After several minutes he looked at Clark, "Well?" But looking at Clark he continued, "Clark before we go any further, I will obviously need legal permission before we may proceed."

"So whilst I see to my end of our bargain, may I suggest that we have a break, perhaps a cup of tea? How are you feeling, do you need a methadone fix?" He replied, "Shortly."

Carter and Sue stood up we'll leave and be back in about half an hour or so."

Under escort, Clark was to be taken downstairs to the cells, but before he left, smiling he said, 'Ainsworth, Sir Malcolm Arnold Ainsworth' the very man."

Carter froze to the spot, "What! Do you mean, Sir Malcolm Arnold Ainsworth, the chairman of the Ainsworth Empire?" Clark nodded, "The very man."

Chapter Seventy Two

Carter whilst en route to his office, he looked at Sue, "Do you believe him?" Sue said, "Guv you have been in charge of the MCU since I was a DS, and you were a DI and then promoted to DCI, and now AC, you haven't been wrong yet."

"I realise you must be on your way to call TF and the CPS, but before you do, can I suggest a scrum down with the other members of the interviewing teams to compare notes."

In the conference room together with Eric, he told them all what Clark had eventually told him." They all looked on with open mouths...

Lloydie said, "Well, Thompson would only talk about the nicking of the bodies from the mortuary, and how it was done, but only after being promised protection."

Lloydie said laughing, "At first I laughed at him. He tried to explain the protocol for the afterhours 'on call', security details?"

"But, when I mentioned that I as a serving police officer, with the MCU and one who had worked closely with Mr Chamber's. I informed him that I knew all the out of hours codes etc."

Lloydie continued, "But when I mentioned, why on earth would they needed the eight bodies, knowing that all had been examined, he failed to reply."

He looked at Carter, "Guv when pushed, I got the opinion that there was a reason? Was it to get rid of all the evidence? Did it take the pressure off the three prisoners, Pearson, Jackson, and Collins?"

Carter said, "Well I'm off to have a chat with TF to give him the potential name of the 'Mr Big' as he left he suddenly turned. "Ian, Phil, how was your time in the warehouse?"

Ian said, "Guv there is so much information, I think we'd need a van. The place was sealed after all the bodies had been removed, so working closely with SOCO; we found the following items."

"The three theatre tables used for the work carried out on all good positive victims, endeavouring to remove their organs, the transportation boxes, used to deliver the organs, the metal shipping container for the storage of bodies, the supply of liquid oxygen, and all smaller items retained of which we bagged and tagged. Carter thanked them all and walked off.

The phone was answered on the second ring, *'Frost'* "Sir it's Carter, are you sat down?" He made his usual sarcastic reply, *"Of course I'm bloody sat down."*

Carter continued, telling him of the interview so far, when he came to the part of, Sir Malcolm Arnold Ainsworth, he suddenly heard, *"What the fuck are you going on about?"*

He again proceeded in telling him exactly what Clark had said.

Tony Frost interrupted, *"Well do you trust him?"* Carter said, "Well you know the deal he wants, I suggest that you come to Derby Lane, and bring the head of the CPS with you, and, or even the Chief Con."

Tony Frost said, *"Carter what on earth are you saying?"* Carter took in a deep breath, "With respect sir, I want you all present, for I'm not putting my head on the block, because if this all goes belly up, I'll be up the road." The phone went dead.

Carter returned to the conference room, not one of his team had left. He entered smiling, "What?"

Eric was the first to speak, "I know I'm only a civvy, so I can speak out without fear of police discipline, so what the fuck happened." Carter told them his entire resume of his chat with TF. He also told them of their intended meeting tomorrow.

As Carter left to book off duty, he turned. "Eric could I trouble you to make out place names on white card, for the following names to be placed on tables facing the audience; The Chief Constable, Commander Frost, The

CPS, Wendy Field, Sam Watson, Penny Wilkinson, and 'Uncle Tom Cobley' an all, an all."

He burst out laughing, "And please don't be late, Charlie are you ready. "Charlie coughed in amazement, "Yes guv."

Chapter Seventy Three

On his way home Carter, called Penny. He knew what to expect, but he was only in the market for a chat, he hoped that Penny would understand.

When he had finished he said, "Okay Charles, you look fit to burst, what you want to know?"

After Carter explained his conversation with TF, that if as a result of information gained, they, or he was going to arrest a, Knight of The Realm.

He wanted assurances that he wasn't going to feel a draft around his arse, because he would receive a right royal shafting, if it all went south.

Charlie said, "Guv what on earth would you do if you got shafted, as I know all of the team would submit transfers. So whom would they get to run the MCU?"

Carter burst out laughing, "Charlie I'd never want that to happen, I would never expect anyone other than me to fall on their sword."

With that, he found himself at home, and looking over at Charlie he said, "Good night Charlie" He suddenly stopped in his tracks, looking over at Charlie he said, "Sorry, I think when this ball of shit blows, I may need to keep my head down, and as you're my APO, so will you." Charlie just laughed, and left.

Carter walked into the foyer of his flat, he looked at the doorman, "Evening George, how are you?" "Well Sir." He looked at the APO "How are you, Simon?" Standing up he said, "All is correct Sir." Carter smiling walked off towards his flat.

Putting the key in the door, he shouted, "Is there anyone home?" A voice replied, "Well, at this time of night, all good people are normally tucked up in bed?"

He burst out laughing, "Your voice sounds as if you are talking from the lounge?" Penny replied laughing out loud, "Who said that I was *good people*'

Carter threw off his raincoat, jacket and he kicked off

his shoes, whilst walking through into the lounge, to be greeted by Penny. She was clasping a large glass of red wine in one hand, and a can of Lager in the other.

He stood laughing, "How long have you been standing like that waiting for me to come home? No, wait don't tell me you asked either, George or Simon, to give you the nod when I entered either, the car park, or foyer."

Penny, rather sheepishly said, "Moi?"

"Carter took the beer and thanked her with a kiss. Penny said, "I suppose you haven't eaten?" He said, "No Penny, correct I'm so wired up, the last thing I need is food."

He continued, "Penny you'll get a call from Sam, in the morning to join her in a meeting being held at Derby Lane. I'm giving you the heads up it's very important." She looked at Carter, "What on earth is the matter?" He told her warts and all, after which she, looked at the glass of wine in her hand, and took a long swig.

Penny walked over to him, and sitting next to him on the settee, she looked at him. "Carter, two things spring to mind, One, this case is so far out there, have you thought of the worst scenario, which could well effect your career, and Two, he, your target, must think he is totally bomb proof."

Looking at him she said, "Christ, Carter, how on earth are you going to handle it?" He replied, "Well! The only way I can the truth! As you know the truth is where you find it, and in my case it's information gained from my informant, Angus Clark."

Later that evening after another couple of drinks, they both agreed that one of their exotic showers would go down a treat, knowing what would follow.

The following morning whilst Carter showered alone, as per his request, he heard Penny's mobile burst into life.

Penny walked into the bathroom whilst he was towelling off, she looked at him, "And so it begins, that was Sam, it would seem that I'm invited to the top table."

As Carter left for the office he kissed Penny goodbye,

"See you later, and I don't want any stick from you." They both burst out laughing.

Chapter Seventy Four

Charlie was silent as he drove Carter to the office. Carter put in a call to Eric. "Morning Eric and how are things?"

Eric said, "Well it all looks like a wedding, top table setting, but I'm having trouble with the brides name?" Carter had put the phone on speaker, so all three burst out laughing.

Carter said, "Fuck it, it's only a job" and the phone went dead.

On arrival at Derby Lane, Carter walked into the general office with a broad smile on his face, for he thought that if any other way, the team would pick up on it.

After booking on duty, he went and sat next to Eric, Eric handed him his usual mug of black coffee. He looked at him, "How are things?" Eric replied, "Do you want to come through to the conference room..."

Carter pressed a hand on his arm. "Old friend, when have I ever had to check up on your organisational skills, let's enjoy this moment before the bosses arrive."

Carter rose from his seat and walked out of the office he turned, "Eric I'll be in my office." Eric smiled, "All correct guv."

Carter sat in his office, whilst waiting for the arrival of the top brass. He was pensive, and began to think of all that had gone on before. He could not help thinking of the loss of his wife, Helen, and the twins, Rad, Laura, and all of his many near misses. He was getting rather remorse, when there was a load rap on his door, he said, "Come in"

The door opened and he saw TF, and the Chief Constable, stood slightly behind him to his left. He immediately stood to attention, "Sir" Tony Frost said, "Relax Carter, perhaps you could lead us down to the conference room?"

On the way down the Chief Constable said, "Well Carter, this is rather different. You see the God's can come down from their Ivory Towers?" And he let out a loud laugh.

Carter stood to one side as he opened the door. There was a loud shuffle of feet, as present police officers came to attention. The Chief said, "Please relax. Both he and TF walked over to their acknowledged seats.

Tony Frost looked at Carter, "The floor is yours."

Carter stood up, "Prior to me speaking can I just say that this floor has been sealed until the end of this meeting. The atmosphere was palpable, he took a deep breath.

"My team and I have been chasing our tails it's very obvious that we needed to get ahead of such matters, but unfortunately no chance, until now."

"After painstaking enquiries made by the team, we seemed to come to a halt, we needed to get someone to inform on the people carrying out these horrendous, and unspeakable crimes. All carried out in the interest of money."

"I would like to give you a quick overview of these issues. Victims were gained by people acting as model agents. They were told that blood samples would be needed, as successful applicants may be needed to travel abroad."

"The blood samples were taken not wishing to go into great detail it would seem that the ones with the best blood, were drugged, and killed."

"Their organs were removed to be sold to recipients, with love ones who could not wait for the NHS system. In fact whilst there are people in such positions who can afford the price tags, they are willing to circumnavigate the system."

"Now as a result of information gained we raided a warehouse in Binns Road off Edge Lane. It was there that we caught a struck off surgeon by the name of, Clark. We also detained a man called Thompson, who worked in the mortuary, and assisted in the robbery of the eight former bodies."

"Myself and Detective Chief Superintendent Ford

interviewed, Clark." At that point Carter took out a silver coloured recorder, placing it on the desk in front of him. He looked at Commander Frost, and the Chief Constable.

Carter said, "Clark has given ample reasons for his demise, unable to complete his contract with the health authority, due to him being a drug addict, and alcoholic, two reasons for him being struck off, The Medical Register."

The Bridewell Surgeon examined Clark, passing him fit for interrogation.

Carter switched on the recorder, and commenced the recording of their interview.

On completion, Mr Patterson, head of the CPS said, "Assistant Commander Carter, was Clark cautioned prior to your interview?" Clark said, "Yes, but what I would say, it is obvious that it wasn't an interview that followed the usual protocol."

"The reason being, I knew Clark, would not say a word if he knew it was an official interview that can be picked up at the commencement of our chat."

He continued, "The information divulged in our interview namely the name of, Sir Malcolm Arnold Ainsworth. That Clark would only give up Ainsworth, if he was promised protection."

"I think that Clark felt that although Ainsworth, a pillar of the community, if he thought someone had implicated him in this mess, that if arrested, facing possible conviction, he still had friends to draw upon."

"Whilst we are all amazed at the mention of his name, Ainsworth, is not your Eton, or Harrow type pupil, he came up the hard way, built his empire, but could not resist this most profitable of return on outlay."

"I feel that Clark, if granted his wish, has a lot more information on Ainsworth for us."

"It would appear that, most if not all of the victims are from the care system, and unfortunately not be missed."

"The reason for our meeting is to discuss the way forward, and I want it on record, that decisions taken here today, does not leave one person's head, or his teams on the block."

Carter completely drained sat down. As he did he felt a gentle touch on his sleeve from, Sue."

The Chief Constable stood up, he looked at Tony Frost, "Commander Frost could I ask that together with Deputy Commander Carter, Detective Chief Superintendent Susan Ford, and Mr Patterson, we go to the Deputy Commander Carter's office. Whilst we do so, could I ask that our guests are served refreshment's."

Chapter Seventy Five

When they were all gathered in Carter's office, one of the secretaries served refreshments.

The Chief Constable sat in one of the empty chairs, and beckoned that Carter should sit at his desk, whilst the rest took chairs around the meeting table.

The Chief Constable stood, and took off his tunic to get comfortable he said, "Well, this is a fine mess, Ainsworth, is no fool, and we should be very aware of that."

"If approached he would get himself legally represented up to the hilt." He looked at Mr Patterson, "Well Richard, what are your thoughts?" He looked at the Chief Constable, "Your right, it's up to Carter to get the evidence that will allow us to proceed."

Carter looked at them all, "Look this isn't the Met, were cases like this are ten a penny, the proverbial MP caught with his pants down, or a business man dipping into the pension fund, misappropriating millions of pounds?"

"No, this is one that has fallen on our doorstep, we all know that evidence given by a person of a less reputable nature, may be found to be suspect, the defence will have a field day, particularly in cross examination, knowing that some sort of deal was made. But the jury will have a lot to play in this matter."

"We are also batting on a poor wicket, knowing that the defence will know that Clark is a heroin addict, and an alcoholic."

The Chief Constable looked at Patterson, "Well, Richard, what do you think?" Patterson said, "Well, all of the above will be mentioned to the jury on the day of the trial, which is the normal format. In our case we need to be airtight."

Carter said, "Well at present I'm going to interview Clark under caution, to be recorded on the official tape. But the lever I need is a promise of protection. I have a group of criminal psychologists to advise us in these matters."

In a rather sarcastic manner Carter said, "We'd all love to deal with cases were evidence of identification is over flowing, enabling the police to have air tight arrests, and a smooth passages through the courts.

"But we don't, I've dealt with difficult cases before, it's just a case of finding the right key to open things up, and a CPS willing to support us."

Sue thought ops! But he was right as she could see what they were thinking she thought they'd wash their hands of the matter. Carter would find his head on the block.

Tony Frost said, "We seem to be kicking this all around, he turned to Richard Patterson, what you think? Is there anything that you could give Carter, so that he can open up Clark?"

Patterson said, "We could offer a potential deal on sentence, but we need to prove did he commit the murder, of the victims, in order to gain their organs. That is a capable offence, which carries life, no excuses."

"If he removes the organs, giving them to a third party, that is theft, and whilst acting with others is conspiracy. The sentence is up to the judge. One would have to realise the extent of these matters."

"I believe he is a means to an end, and as such did not go out to commit murder, but that his skills were called upon for the removal of the organs. I could well suppose that the main protagonists maintained him in drugs, and alcohol."

"If convicted on the lower charges, depending on volume, he could be charged with say three counts of theft, and leave the remainder on the books. He could be located in a less arduous prison. Perhaps eventually being relocated to an open prison? The beauty of this is, the whys and the wherefores'' of the prison is up to, us!"

"The sentencing is the Judges domain, so if we are looking at misappropriation of body parts, '*theft*' as long as it's not proven that Clark, took place in their murder's that is one sentence, if murder, then you might as well throw the key away."

Carter looked at them, "I myself do not think he took part in the murdering of the victims in the rear of the HGV. But believe he took part in the removal of organs, we can at least prove three victims, and enquiries are still being made."

The Chief Constable stood up; he buttoned his tunic and turned. "This is a ball of shit, make no mistake. How do we keep a lid on thing's?" Tony Frost replied, "Matters will be kept tight at this end, you have no worries in that regard. I will go through to the others, and discuss the various issues." The Chief said his goodbyes and left.

Chapter Seventy Six

Back in the conference room, Tony Frost, Mr Patterson, Carter, and Sue regained their places. Tony Frost relayed verbatim, the conversation that had taken place in there, sub meeting that had been held in Carter's office.

On completion he looked at Wendy Field, the force *'press officer'* "Wendy, you realise the importance on keeping a lid on all of this. I will serve discipline papers on any person found to have released information, by means of any sort of leak. That applies to any police, or civilian personnel."

He then looked at Sam, "Professor Watson, we'd like to draw on your vast knowledge, and advice?" Sam stood, and although more relaxed in their company, so different from the first time that Lloydie, had brought her to talk to Carter, and his team.

Sam smiled on seeing Lloydie, realizing how at ease she always felt knowing he was sat there in the audience.

Taking a drink of water and replacing the glass, Sam began. "This of course is only my opinion in relation to these facts. You all know if you were to get three experts in a room to discuss, a matter they will of course come up with three different interpretations, on the same subject."

After the laughter that circled around the room died down, Sam looked at Lloydie, and smiled.

"Ladies and gentlemen, the global trade in illegal kidneys, hearts, lungs etc is booming. I give one example, people in need of a kidney transplant are reported to have paid up to £128,000 in countries such as China, India and Pakistan, were the practice of selling kidneys and organs is illegal."

"In many countries, this all comes with great financial and medical risks. Performing a legitimate transplant is an incredibly complex procedure involving scrupulous medical tests, and a range of measures to prevent infection and organ rejection."

"Kidneys for sale; poor Iranians compete to sell their organs. In the only country where the organ trade is legal, the streets near hospitals have been turned into the equivalent of, *'Kidney eBay.'* Potential donor's leave their phone number scratched on the hospital walls."

"There are notices, 'Kidney for sale,' reads one ad, carrying the donor's blood type, o+, and a mobile number, with a note emphasising 'Urgent', insinuating that the donor is prepared to consider discounts."

"Another similar ad reads; 'Attention', attention, a healthy kidney for sale, o+. Many are hand written, though some typed ads, to make them look better. 24 year old, kidney for sale 'Tested healthy.' The price is 20m Iranian Rials which equates to £7,500 for a child's operation the kidney price 12m Rials."

In Great Britain, more than 10,000 people are in need of some sort of organ transplant that could save or improve their life. It is truly upsetting of these, 1,000 will die while they wait, as presently there are not enough organs to go around."

"In the past we or I have looked upon clues that mean that you were dealing with psychopathic murderers, most being driven by a need. Different agencies are poles apart when dealing with such matters."

"Detectives your offenders are not *'serial killers,'* such as we have discussed in the past. You have evidence of between 8 to 16 victims. But your killers are killing to order, although in such a surrealistic way."

"The protagonists are driven by a *'need'* they have found a niche in this dreadful market, which results in a short fall in the NHS. Were patients who are in need of organ transplants, are placed on a donor register due to the lack of donors."

"The leading figures, have come to realise this, and are by their criminal activities, for filling this *'need'* for those that can afford their prices.

"The name, Sir Malcolm Arnold Ainsworth, has been mentioned, whilst your governor interviewed the prisoner

Clark, I understand that many of your colleagues, including your very own Chief Constable, who feels that we need to handle matters with kid gloves."

"I understand that you have a formidable witness, but he comes with baggage. Although he was a onetime brilliant surgeon, he has contacts. His reputation is somewhat tarnished, because of his drug and alcoholic addiction."

"DC Carter, together with DCS Ford will shortly be going in to deal with Clark. I realise he may be wanting a deal, but your colleagues have to get Clark, to nail down Arnold, if pressed Clark, must give bona fide evidence, of Ainsworth's part in all of this."

"I realise that Ainsworth, is synonymous with his fashion empire, and may appear bomb proof. But I've heard rumours that he has a cash flow problem, with his various companies. Due to *'on line shopping'*, his high street outlets are showing a stark decline in business."

"I have heard speculation that he has, or is dipping into the company's pension plan, and could well realise that this is a fundamental way of digging himself out of this hole."

"Therefore I see that through others he has used Clark, to surgically remove, and supply body parts, such as kidneys, hearts, lungs and corneas, harvested for the persons in need, with the necessary funds, willing to purchase privately for their love ones. Ainsworth and his cohorts process the organs, delivering them to their required source."

On completion Sam received a round of applause, from the personnel in the room without being asked.

Chapter Seventy Seven

On completion of the meeting, junior officers left to return to their many duties.

Carter walked up to Sam who was talking with Lloydie, he said, "Jim, could I have a quick word with Sam, before she leaves for work." Sam turned, "Of course Carter, Lloydie sees enough of me at home."

Carter gave Sam a peck on her cheek, he then said, "Thanks Sam, the day Tony Frost, organised a meeting, for me to attend your office, for possible help in the 'Letter serial killer' you have now become a great asset to our team. Best day in our lives."

Sam looked at Carter saying, "Well it was far better for me, when you sent Lloydie, to show me yet another letter." They both burst out laughing.

Carter rather seriously looked at her, "How is Penny doing? I realise that she was employed by the University as your deputy prior to our meeting. I noticed Penny as a result of going into 'Toms' for lunch."

"But it was as a result of you saying that you knew me, and it resulted in our meeting, again at your dinner party, do I smell a rat?"

Sam laughing said, "Carter how many breadcrumbs, does one have to leave, I thought you are the detective?" Carter said, "Serious Sam is she coping with me, and the job?"

"Sam again laughing said, "She loves your bones, and somehow manages to cope. Now please excuse me but I have to get back." He looked at his watch it was 4 o'clock; he called to Sue, "I'm thinking that Clark, can wait until tomorrow?" Carter detected a smile of relief on her face.

He turned and left for his office, as he entered he saw Penny sat in his chair with her feet on his desks. He closed his door and started to walk towards his desk."

Penny with a wicked look on her face, "Carter, has your desk been officially christened?" He smiled, and

240

lifted her from his chair. He then sat down to relax. Penny turned, and whilst she leaned on the edge of his desk, she raised her legs, and placed a leg on each arm.

Penny was wearing a white blouse, and black skirt, she wore black hold up stockings, and black sheer panties, with black high heel shoes. As Carter looked at her, she noticed that it was having the desired effect.

"Well Carter, is there anything that has taken you fancy. And has your desk been christened?" He said, "Well madam, I can assure you that your tactic's are working, but I regret to say that I'm unable to imbibe in such matters, as I'm unable to secure my office door, and if I did what impression would that give."

Penny reluctantly got down and suddenly said, "Well Carter, we'll see if you have the same thinking when you get home?" Laughing she picked up her coat kissed him gently on the lips, and left.

It seemed a matter of seconds when Carter heard Penny's voice, "High Sue, how are things." He heard her laughing, as her voice diminished as she walked away along the corridor.

As Sue entered she said, "Carter are you alright?" Carter coughed, "Um, err, err, I'm fine why?" Sue replied, "You look rather flushed," He said, "No, I'm fine, and what can I do for you?"

Sue said, "Wendy is outside wanting to see you." Carter repeatedly kept saying, "Please bring her in, again, and again." He was gesticulating with his hands. Sue thinking Carter, what on earth has been happening in your office, smiling to herself she thought whatever it was, you lucky dog.

Wendy walked into his office, she looked at both Carter and Sue, and "Do you both have a minute? As we need to discuss this whole subject of mass murder, for the sole purpose of body parts. Tony Frost made his point of view quite clear."

"As I run the large PR department, plus there are others who may not be on your team, yet have access, or

241

knowledge of these matters, I'm not going to take the fucking blame, if they blab, for the longer we sit on it, the worse it will be."

Carter said, "Wendy, I agree with you, in fact he did irk me as he implied that information may leak from members of my team, I won't have it."

Wendy looked at them both, "It's bloody typical, TF and the boss, light the blue touch paper, and leaves us with the potential fallout. What the bloody hell do they want me to do, Carter?"

Wendy continued, "Should you with all the necessary evidence go out to arrest Ainsworth, 'Bang' and we all, not them, get covered in shit." Carter smiled, "Remember my quote in the past about umbrellas." Wendy hissed, "Yes, they come in handy to stop the shit falling on you in a crisis."

She continued, "Carter I'm serious, this man Ainsworth, is a bloody icon, full of charities, and such shit, he's a well-known philanthropist 'What'

Carter said, "Well! Are there no known bent ones, you must know the saying... *'Money begets money'* "Should Sam, be remotely correct, and he is found to be medalling, from a financial point of view."

"Just say for a minute, his bank, or other institutions have knocked him back, he has even raided the company's pension fund. He sees his properties, and large yachts which are moored in the likes of Monte Carlo, going belly up, what do people do in that regard?"

Wendy interrupted, "People like Ainsworth, have no gratitude, or respect for their staff, they are a means to an end, and the loss of their pensions, has no effect on the likes of him, if caught with his hand in the cookie jar, he would riddle, and try to get out of it by him paying back the bare minimum."

"But I think the Knighthood, means more to him than anything. Plus to Ainsworth there is the loosing of all that kudos, but what if he could find a way of getting out from under all the shit. It would enable him to get back on an even keel. He suddenly finds the means of a giant cash injection, from say a more unscrupulous benefactor."

"At present I feel that it's only his bankers, and backers that know of his plight. They will keep things tight until the last moment. So as I see it he has more to lose within his circle of love ones, and friends, and that is almost worse than his money problems."

Carter finished as one of the young secretaries brought a tray of drinks, into his office. All three relaxed whilst they enjoyed their drinks. It was Carter who said, "Wendy leave it until tomorrow, let Sue, and I have a crack at Clark."

"I feel that it will be his damming evidence that is likely to have a bearing on Ainsworth we need to get Clark, to open up, to literally inform on all that went on. We know that he is an incredible witness, with a witness like Clark, it's a case of the more shit you can sling, that at least some will always stick."

"Even if Clark is a tainted witness, he may be the one who helps in us lighting the ignition, and together with other possible witnesses we may get home with a conviction."

"Carter said, "I don't know about you two but I'm on my way home." He leant over and kissed both Wendy, and Sue on the cheek. "Thank you both, you know that your input is always respected."

"I did promise Penny that I wouldn't be late." In the general office Eric looked at Carter, "What a day, to think that, Big Chief Sitting Bull has blessed us with a visit." Carter looked at him don't you mean, shat on us all from a great height."

"When on the job, I didn't think the Chief Constable knew that these outside divisions existed." Carter said, "Now, now Mr Morton, see you bright and early in the morning."

As he left he could still hear the laughter coming from out of the office.

Chapter Seventy Eight

Charlie dropped him off saying, "Don't worry guv, the job will still be there in the morning, laughing he said, "See ya," And he drove off.

As Carter placed his key in the door, he opened it to find Penny standing in the hall walking towards him, wearing the same clothes as earlier in the day, she gave him a big kiss, and they both walked through to the lounge.

They both enjoyed a couple of glasses of red wine, over which Carter discussed his overall apprehensions of tomorrow's interview of the witness Clark."

He leaned back on the settee, "Well, you see it's always having prisoners who want to make deals, if that's not bad enough, I have a prisoner who is tainted; he'll be hammered in court. They'll try to say it was all done for the deal, which he is trying to get from the prosecution, frustrating matters by bringing up his drug and alcohol problems."

"Defence council, will try to tear him apart, stating that it's self-evident that he turned 'Queens Evidence to prosper by way of the deal. But if we can get another potential volunteer to turn 'Queens Evidence' it may shore up the case for the prosecution."

On Carter's return from the bathroom he returned to his seat. Penny looked at Carter, "I've prepared lobster salad for tea, it's all prepped, and ready to go, and I have two bottles of white wine in the fridge."

"Now as tea can't be tainted, I thought that we may complete what I was offering you in your office, being a coward, you declined it as you were so worried that we may get caught."

Carter took Penny through to the bedroom and stood her next to the bed. Carter lingered, taking his time whilst he undressed her. As he did so the aroma of, Penny's perfume *'Angel'* permeated up into his nostrils.

He gentle laid her on the bed. They made love, and as before managed to amaze themselves with the level of passion and intensity. Leaning on one elbow and looked down at Penny. "You will tell me if you think that...Penny burst out laughing, "Honestly Carter?"

Carter who had gotten up to start undressing said, "Right who's for a shower?" Penny replied, "Oh! Carter, do we get to do it all again?" Laughing he looked down at himself, "Well, perhaps later tonight." They both roared with laughter as they walked through to the shower. Carter said, "Perhaps a soapy shower will have to suffice, what?"

After their shower they both dressed in sweats, and walking through to the kitchen, they both partook in the sumptuous meal, with the promised white wine.

Chapter Seventy Nine

Charlie arrived on time, heralding his arrival by the intercom to their flat.

Penny pressed the button allowing him access into the flats. Penny, of course announced that Carter would be down in a minute.

When ready to meet the rigors of the day, Carter turned, and as he kissed Penny goodbye he smiled. "We could never have given it justice if we performed on my office desk, plus I think the noise would have given it away."

As he left, and about to pass into the hall Penny shouted, "One day Carter, one day." As he entered the car, Charlie could not but help notice the grin on Carter's face. Charlie said, "Is everything alright Carter, as he thought that they had all been under pressure over the last couple of weeks, and neither had shown elation in any way.

Carter turned, "Just wonderful Charlie, God is in his heaven, and all is well with the world." Charlie said, "Guv Keep that in mind as you enter, the interview to commence battle with, Clark."

There was a roar of laughter from them both, Carter had also picked up on the fact that their journeys to, and from the office had been lack lustre affairs. Carter wondered if it was caused by Charlie's, transfer to the team.

For as an APO, he was under someone else's jurisdiction, and not Carter's, this seemed to change their outlook, for he was now a DI with the MCU.

On arrival at Derby Lane, Carter took hold of Charlie's arm as he was about to egress from the vehicle. Carter said, "Charlie have you got a minute?" Charlie said, "Why of course guv."

Carter looked at him, "I realise that over the last couple of weeks there has been an enormous amount of pressure on the team, in relation to our present case. I have to say that it has manifested itself on everyone,"

"I feel that that has had a distinct effect on our relationship, I have felt for a long time that our cordial banter has somewhat dried up. Now this of course could be that I had you transferred to the team from the AP unit."

"I of course thought that it would suite both our needs. It would give me an extra DI, putting you on a more established duty roster. Were as being attached, as my APO, it would put you on a permanent standby duty, like an *'on call'* duty system."

"Now being the guv that I am, I want all of my team to be happy? If this is not working out I can have you returned to the AP unit, no questions asked. I now feel that my security threat has been downgraded to *'slight'* as we are not dealing with psychopaths, what do you say?"

Charlie thought for a while, "True the threats have diminished, and I personally feel that you can drive yourself around. Now this is no BS, I have never worked for a better governor before, a man that derives so much respect from his team, and gives his team so much respect."

"Now I thought that I'd love to work under a governor such as you. But there is a great deal of difference working in your team on a day to day basis, from say my old job as your APO."

"The work of an APO is so different, and as such I'd like to return to my post, but only on the understanding that any red flags, and or suspicions of any kind either to you or Penny, I'll be back."

Carter smiled "Well I'll put the request back to your outfit to TF, putting it along the lines that we have discussed, so will you please come up to the general office, whilst I do the very same. Charlie smiled, "Will do guv."

When in the general office and signing on duty Carter looked at Eric, "Could you and Sue join me in my office and bring your drinks through with you."

All three sat down, Carter explained fully the

conversation that had taken place between him, and Charlie, and that he was about to put the request through with TF.

Sue looked at him, "Carter, Charlie is here for a specific reason, with respect I think that you should have run it passed TF before you had your heart to heart with Charlie."

Eric looked at Carter, "No use looking at me like that, I agree with Sue. I know the time will come when you will put your ticket in, and retire, as previously mentioned that date is a while off."

"I know that Sue is feeding on all the scraps of experience that she can draw upon, whilst you are in command, so why on many occasions do you think that members of the criminal fraternity have tried to eliminate you? No Carter leave things how they are, TF sill go fucking spare if you were to think of asking."

Carter said, "Alright, alright, when you both leave for the general office send Charlie through. What I'm going to recommend is that he is back as my APO, and not involved with the team, but to attend certain meetings, as he has to know what is going on."

Both Eric and Sue smiled as they left. Eric said, "Sue, do you know the difference between, common sense, and intelligence?" Carter shouted, "I heard that."

Minutes later Charlie, presented himself in Carter's office, Carter looked up at him, "Well Charlie it's as we were, I had a chat with my two senior members of the team, and they both thought I was nuts."

"So as from now on you will remain, attached as my APO, I will explain? You haven't mentioned our chat to anyone have you?" Charlie gave an emphatic, "No."

Chapter Eighty

After their chat, Carter entered the general office, followed by Charlie, who sat talking to one of the secretaries, having been offered a mug of coffee.

Carter looking at Sue and Eric, he coughed, and then coughed again, they all looked around, one of the young secretaries stood, "I'm so sorry guv, I'll only be a minute." Eric stood saying, "It's okay, Mandy, I've got this, I think that the guv is capable of pouring his own."

As Carter walked towards the coffee percolator, Eric cut him off at the pass, and, poured him his coffee. They both smiled at each other.

After a couple of minutes, Carter who had sat next to Eric, looked over at Sue, "Well DCI Ford, are you ready to begin the affray?" Sue stood up, "If I'm not ready now, I never will."

As they both began to leave the office Eric said, "Clark is in interview room one."

On opening the door, the uniform officer stood to attention. Carter smiled, "As you were." The officer smiled, Sir" And left the room.

Carter and Sue sat in the vacant seats, Carter said, "Well Clark, you look a lot better than you did the other day, I can tell you must be receiving your doses of methadone?" Clark smiled.

Carter looked at him saying, "Clark, when we last had our chat, you were in a bit of a state. So today, DCS Ford and myself are again here to interview you, pick up on the various points you mentioned. You do realise that like on our previous interview, you are still under caution."

He looked over at then, "Yes believe it or not, I'm ready." Carter said, "Well let's get on with it."

Sue leaned over and did the honours they all heard the traditional bleep of the tape."

Carter said, "Clark, I need your permission to search your address, if not I will have a warrant sworn, and your property will then be searched. Clark said, "The keys to the front door of my house are in my property held downstairs. I live at, 46, Lisburn Lane, Tuebrook, Liverpool 13. I have no doubt you will find the obvious accoutrements befitting a person of my standing.

Carter took out his phone, and called Peter giving him the heads up, explaining fully what Clark had said.

On completion he said looking at Clark, any objection if I call you by your Christian name, Clark smiled, "Well, what page in the interrogation study book is this bull shit on. I don't mind for Christ sake, let's get down to the nitty-gritty and let's get on with it."

Carter said, "Right, Angus, in our last interview you wanted a deal, I explained fully what constitutes a deal. I told you that it's a question of give, and take, you'd have to give us something, and in return depending on the validity of your information, I'd take it to the CPS. So, what do you have to offer?"

"Clark before you answer, "I have to ask you did you ever commit any of the murders on these victims?" He replied, "Definitely not, I was always called in when they were ready for me. However much I was under the influence of my two problems, I never killed anyone."

Carter said, "Well what is the total amount of corpses did you work on?" Clark looking very sheepish said, "About ten."

There was a silence for about a couple of minutes, after which Carter coughed. "Clark what do you have to offer. Clark leaning back in his chair smiled, he folded his arms against his chest, he then lent forward, he placed both folded elbows on the desk top, still folded, and looking up at them, again smiled and said, *"The lot."*

Carter looked at Sue, with a smile on his face. "Well, Angus, what do you mean by *"The lot"* without a change to his demur, he said, "How about, Ainsworth, in all his glory? Ainsworth is in the shit, all of his businesses are about to fail, he is desperate, and in need of cash, to sure up all of his holdings."

"He has been in constant meetings with his property landlords, suggesting would they accept interim payments on each of his premises, until he gets himself straight. So you see his present cash flow is in trouble, he needs cash, but the banks won't help him."

Sue looking at Carter saw it was self-evident that he had been given the potential key to the case, and the effect that it was beginning to have on him. Carter said, "What do you say to us taking a break, it will allow me to chat with the CPS, and allow you, any methadone that you may be due. Clark nodded his head.

Sue attended to the recording machine, when stopped she got up, and opening the interview room door she said, "Officer will you please return the prisoner downstairs, and see to any methadone that he might be due." He replied, "Yes boss."

Out in the corridor after Clark had gone down stairs, he looked at Sue, and moving towards her he placed a peck on her cheek. She looked at her, "Guv what do you think?" Carter said, let's get a drink for ourselves, I think we deserve one, after which I'll call, Simon Patterson, to talk things over."

In his office both Sue and Carter sat to enjoy a well-earned mug of coffee. Whilst they were there Carter rang TF the phone was answered on the second ring.

Carter told him the extent of their interview with Clark. He then went on to tell him that he was about to call the CPS to see what they say. TF said, *"Carter make sure you have dotted the 'I's' and crossed the 'T's' I realise you've had experience with situations and cases such as these, after your dealings with the last two very important cases."*

He said, *"Look, ring Patterson and tell him of the situation, and then ring me back and we can discuss the matter."* Carter agreed and replaced the phone.

Sue after finishing her coffee stood up, and looking at Carter said, "Ring me when you're ready." He smiled as she left.

Carter's next call was to Simon Patterson. When answered, Carter told him of the deal he wished to offer Clark. Simon Patterson said, "Were all the interviews and subsequent conversations with this man, Clark recorded?" Carter replied, "Yes, it was as a result of information received, that we served a warrant on a warehouse in Binns Road, Liverpool."

"Clark was subsequently arrested, it was during his interview that he wanted to do a deal, and I told him it depended on what he had to offer. Through the course of the second interview, again under caution, Clark said, "I can give you Ainsworth, and his team."

Simon Patterson said, "My reply to Clark would be due to the amount of his involvement, did he ever commit murder in all of this." Carter continued, "No it would seem he was only called upon when they had attained the poor victims."

Simon Patterson said, "If he wished to turn Queens Evidence, I know that you are fully aware of what that entails, emphasising that he would receive a custodial sentence, for his part in all of this."

"That the Judge would warn the Jury as to him having been hooked on alcohol and drugs, lastly that the defence would press as to why he had turned on his co-defendants and what was he after."

With that Patterson said, "Good luck Carter speak later." And he replaced his phone.

Half an hour later Carter who had sat with all his thoughts he suddenly stood up "Fuck it" And he left his office, and walked down to Sue's office. He knocked and entered, He saw Sue, Peter, and Phil looking at papers on her desk. He said, "What's all of this?" The three of them looked up with smiles like Cheshire cat's.

Sue said, "Guv the result of the warrant served on Clark's place." Carter said, "What have we got?" Sue said, "Look at this? She handed him a letter, on looking at it he smiled as he noticed, Ainsworth's company letter heading? It was very apparent from the contents of the letter that it gave evidence of contact between the two men."

Carter looked at Sue, "I know you may need others to deal with all this lot, get bodies as I need to have a resume of the information. Bring in SOCO and let's see if we can have finger print evidence? It will help when we come to arrest Ainsworth, and his team." He congratulated them and left.

Chapter Eighty One

He returned to his office, on sitting at his desk he picked up the phone and called Penny, she replied almost immediately, *"Hello you, how are things going?"* He replied, "How would you like to come down here, and help to christen this bloody desk?" He burst out laughing.

Penny, laughed out loud, *"Sorry sunshine, you only get one chance, you blew it, that subject is now closed."* Carter in a quiet voice said, "Actually I'm in need of some, TLC I've had a mare of a day."

Penny, on getting to know Carter, had quickly come to realise that there is an invisible line one treads, on one side of it, you could laugh and joke. But the idea is to quickly recognise what mood he was in. *"Well, Carter let's see what I can call upon when you get home?"*

Carter after his call went along to collect Sue; they had asked Eric to arrange for Clark, to come up to the interview room. The duty officer opened the door and smiled saying, "All is correct" They both entered the room and the officer closed the door behind them.

Carter said, "Clark you must realise that you are still under caution?" he answered, "Yes" He continued, "You mentioned that you were called upon to deal with the process of the retrieval of the viable body parts?" He replied, "It was my task to open the victims with the required blood group, to enable me to identify healthy organs."

"I would remove all viable organs, and flush them in ice cold preservative solution. This starts the process of preserving the stolen organs. All organs except kidneys are stored using simple hypothermia, in other words they're just kept cold in a preservative solution."

"Members of your team whilst searching the warehouse would have found several medical machines. That would continuously pumps preservation solution through them this machine is called a pulsatile perfusion device.

"Well, Angus how many corpse have you worked on?" What seemed an indeterminate amount of time? Clark took a deep breath, and looking very sheepish said, "About 10, but I assure you that I tried at all time to treat them with the utmost respect."

Carter said, "We have medical teams looking into these matters, and the form of transport for the organs, you Clark will write a list of the receiving Doctors, and hospitals." Clark nodded.

"Yes, this is something I'm willing to do. Ainsworth and his team saw this as a means to his monetary problem. He was producing with my help, the organs to order, knowing that they were being sold on for unscrupulous amounts of money."

Carter said, "The CPS will want you to be charged with, *'Conspiracy to murder, and 'Theft of body parts.* For turning 'Queens Evidence' you must answer the charges. If you were to plead guilty, to the lesser charge of theft, you will no doubt receive a custodial sentence. All of your individual offences will be dealt with, and whatever your sentence, they will run concurrently."

"The Judge will of course warn the Jury, as he must do under these circumstances. He must warn them of your criminal record to date. The defence of course will want to know what you received for turning Queens Evidence."

Carter looked at Clark, he could see that he wasn't very happy, yet he knew that Clark, must have realised that the other way would be disastrous. "Do you understand what I have just said?" Clark replied, "Yes, it's what I deserve."

Carter said, "Clark you will be taken downstairs and be formally cautioned and charged with these charges. I will make an order that you will be refused bail, and I will ask the CPS, to have you placed in HMP Risley until produced to the Magistrates court."

Clark said, "I understand."

Carter said, "This brings our interview to a close, you will of course receive visits from my officers to take an official statement from you."

Sue leaned over and did the honours when stopping the machine. When stopped Carter said, "Angus, I will ask for you to be kept in solitary confinement if you so wish, I would agree, as this would be the safest place for you."

Clark said, "Do you think they'd try to silence me, Carter replied, "Well, we lost a solicitor, and friend by the name of Silverman, and another possible witness called Ford. We are about to arrest a *'Sir'* what do you think?"

Clark was removed, before he left the room he asked, "Would it be possible to receive a selection of books I have kept in my house, would it be at all likely to receive a few?

"As I could go nuts locked up, looking at the, the, four walls, with nothing to read except the profanity of sexual poems, and other such literature written upon them."

Carter and Sue burst out laughing, Sue said our problem is, no prisoner should have any property whilst on remand, but I'll see what we can do, how about the racing times? Clark said, "Better than nothing, do you accept bets?"

Carter and Sue saw Clark taken away. They both walked back towards the general office. They entered telling Eric and Charlie, how it all went. Carter looked at Sue, "Can you please arrange for a scrum down, for tomorrow morning. I'm going to call TF to invite him, could you also invite, Wendy Field, as I'm now off home."

Sue replied, "Yes guv." She looked at her watch, "Glory be it's seven o'clock, Eric, why are you still here?" He said, "Well, you may have needed things, so if you're all off, I'll join you."

Chapter Eighty Two

Charlie waited down in the yard for Carter, on his arrival they both got in the car and left for Carter's address.

Whilst en route he made a call to Tony Frost, he used the call to bring him up to date with their interview on the defendant Clark. He also invited him to join both him, and the team tomorrow, at Derby Lane.

Carter on completion of the call said, "Sir, I have only invited you, as If I was to invite the CC (*Chief Constable*) as you know we will be discussing the political implications of, Sir Malcolm Arnold Ainsworth's, potential arrest. I wish to discuss this in a police mode, and not a political one."

Tony Frost said, "*See you in the morning Carter,* and the phone went dead."

On Carter's arrival at his home address, he looked at Charlie, he smiled, "Well, Charlie how are they hanging?" Charlie smiled, "Guv, all is well see you in the morning, he smiled and drove away.

Carter entered his block, saying evening to the duty, APO and duty doorman. He continued in towards his ground floor flat.

He opened the door with his key, he was met in the hall by Penny, who took hold of his hand, and walked him into their spare bedroom. On entering he noticed that Penny had cleared her desk top that she used for her computer, when working from home.

Penny walked over towards the desk; it was at that point, that Carter noticed that Penny was wearing the same outfit that she had used the other day, when he had knocked back her gesture in his office.

Penny pulled up a chair and gestured for him to sit down. As Carter sat, Penny sat on the edge of her desk, and lifted up her legs placing one, on each of the arms.

Carter quickly realised that Penny was serious and not play acting. He looked up and began to move his hands up her legs, at the top he realised that she was only wearing hold up stockings; Penny having leaned forward, placed her lips on Carter's, with her tongue darting in and out of him mouth.

Carter began to kiss Penny's neck, and could smell the aroma of her perfume, *'Angel'* together with her worm body smells.

Penny began to un-buckle his trouser belt, and began to loosen his trousers; she then slid her hand down under his shorts, "Well, a result."

She began to manoeuvre her bottom to the edge of the desk. Within a matter of seconds, Carter entered Penny, and as he did she let out a whimper. He began to gyrate, and with each thrust her whimper got louder, and louder.

As Carter held her close to him, Penny looked at him saying, "For Christ sake Carter I hope you are ready I can't wait much longer, I've been thinking of this all day, with that they both began to feel an electrifying shudder pass between their bodies.

Penny wrapped her legs around his waist and squeezed, it pulled Carter into her. She kept tightening, and releasing her grip again, and again, each time she squealed in delight.

Eventually she released her grip and pulled him down on top of her, it was then that he noticed that she was crying. Carter placed his arms about her, holding her tight. Some minutes later he kissed her on the mouth saying, "My God Penny, it seems to get better each time."

Penny looked at him with tears in his eyes; she kissed him with a passion. Carter looked down at Penny, "Do you really think we could have christened my desk in the same mode?"

Carter realised that Penny, had offered with such a tender act of love, that she herself by her actions, had undertaken so much TLC In an effort to dispel the events of the day.

She clasped Carter's hand, "Why, don't we just take a quick shower, and then relax, and enjoy a quiet tea in front of the telly."

Chapter Eighty Three

The following morning Carter heard the inter-com he walked down their hall, and picking up the hand set he said, "Charlie I'm ready, see you in five minutes."

Penny walking on her tippy toes had quietly walked up behind him. Penny put her arms around his waist saying, "Five minutes, I thought it would take at least ten to kiss, and fondle me through my dressing gown before you left for work?"

Carter said, "Madam, I'm a senior line officer in the Merseyside Constabulary, I cannot walk out of my apartment, having to fold my raincoat in such a position in front of me, now kiss me goodbye, and I'll call you later."

Penny said, "Spoil sport," and made the sound of a chicken, they both kissed each other passionately, and he left.

In the car Charlie saw that Carter was smiling, he said, "Morning Carter, is all well?" Carter said smiling, "Kindly mind your own business." Charlie with a sly grin to his face said, "It's like that boss?"

At Derby Lane, he went up to the office and signed on duty. Eric handed him his usual mug of coffee. As he did so he said, "All are present even TF."

Carter entered the conference room, and his team came to attention, he said, "As you were."

He went and stood at the top of the room looking out on the team. Tony Frost, Wendy Field, Charlie, and Eric, were sat next to Sue, on his right. Ian and Lloydie were sat on his left.

He stood for several seconds as if gathering himself, he coughed and began.

"Ladies and gentlemen we are about to embark on one of our most infamous of cases."

As he said it he turned one of the whiteboards to reveal the inevitable pyramid; "The difference between the first and second pyramids, each failed to replace the question

260

mark with a name."

"Well, that matter has been dealt with, for the name at the top of this management pyramid, is no other than, Sir Malcolm Arnold Ainsworth." The atmosphere in the room was culpable.

Carter picked up from a nearby table, a telescopic pointer, with a small red beam. He looked at the pyramid diagram; pointing the tiny light, he illuminated names. "You will all know the names of the offenders, plus the names of the victims murdered, when released on bail."

"I feel that there are other people involved, as I'm sure there is a name that is missing from this organization. Who instructed Parsons, to return to the hospital against his will, for the express use in cleaning up the mess?"

"This person could work directly under Ainsworth, and although as yet we have no proof, or possible trace of him. I feel for failing to tidy matters up, we may well find him murdered; his body may well be somewhere, and in these circles, he will not be reported as your usual NFH *(Missing from home)*

Chapter Eighty Four

There was a knock on the conference room door. Carter shouted, "Come in" The door opened, and a red faced detective stood in the door way. Carter said, "Well, you'd better come in and take a seat."

After a couple of minutes Carter turned, and looking at him he said, "Were have you been the meeting was scheduled to begin at 9.15am it's now 10.15am.

The red faced officer nervously looked at the assembled group of personnel, and started to spit it out...Tony Frost interrupted, well son were where you?" The young officer replied, "I stopped to answer the phone in the general office, after you'd all had left." Tony Frost said, "That's a poor excuse."

Carter looked at the officer, "You do realise that, excuses are like armpits, everyone has one, and they all stink." There was a roar of laughter in the room.

He continued, "Son, when you're the last man leaving an office, and the phone rings...?" Interrupting him was a loud harmonic sound from the team shouting, "Never, never ever answer the phone for the calls are always ball ache'rs, and you being the last to leave, have to deal with it."

Carter smiling said, "What was it?" The young detective said, "A man whilst walking with his daughter, and their family dog, noticed the dog became suspicious of a mound in, The Recreation ground, by Acanthus road. His dog wouldn't leave it alone. He left his daughter there, as he was suspicious of the mound. He left her and drove to, Derby Lane to report it, hence the call."

"I decided to go downstairs and talk to the man; I came up to the conference room to tell you."

Carter smiled, "Well done son." Carter looked at Lloydie, take the young man with you, call Mr Chambers, and all, we'll be along later." As they left Carter said looking at the young man, "What's your name he said,

"DC Paul Jones, guv."

The room was disturbed by the shuffling of chairs as Lloydie, and a few of the team left, together with the sprog.

Carter said, "Coincidences are too good to be true? So let's wait and see."

He turned to the remainder of the meeting. He again pointed to the diagram. "Our main problem is that from information received, we are now in a position to name the top man in all of this, who is Ainsworth, as he said it he pointed to the pointer, to identify the name."

"You will all know that during the raid on that awful warehouse, one of the detainees was a person of interest called, Angus Clark, as he said it, he pointed to the name."

"This information has been collaborated by Mr Chambers, who has identified Clark, and Thompson, from photos taken by the obsie's team, showing them both coming, and going from outside of the warehouse, he pointed out Thompson on the diagram."

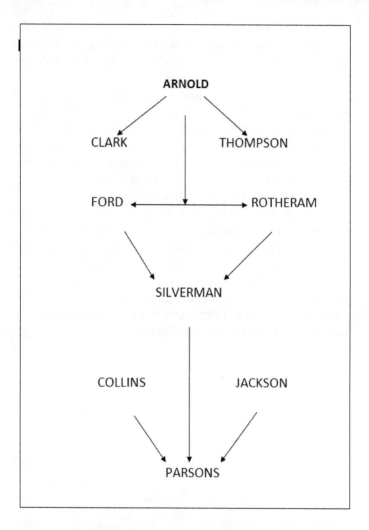

"Paul Thompson worked in the mortuary, and Gordon Chambers knew of Clark, as a onetime surgeon, who had since been struck off."

Our interview with Clark, he revealed that after a bumpy start, and in the course of time he began to open up. He revealed that the top man in all of this is no other than, Sir Malcolm Arnold Ainsworth."

"He is the chairman of *'Ainsworth holdings'* He is the

owner of several large department stores, such as *'Ingram's' 'Beautiful Girl' 'Woman's World', and 'Lillian's Linens'* to say but a few."

"Clark can supply evidence that Ainsworth, is in some serious financial trouble. It would appear that he has exhausted his line of credit with the banks, and other financial institutions."

"Clark is aware that Ainsworth had been dipping into, *'Employees pensions'* Ainsworth has the usual trappings of properties around Europe, with the usual yachts, and fast cars. He also has a beautiful wife, all of which need maintaining."

"Now it is believed that Ainsworth has had undertaken secret meetings with his creditors, namely the landlords of his many stores in which he has asked to be given time to sort himself out. At this point there is a tight lid on matters, but for how long no one knows?"

"Let's remember that to a man like Ainsworth the kudos of the Knighthood is uttermost on his list, to lose it would be unimaginable."

"So what do we have, he is truly in the financial shit. So whilst having drinks with a friend of a friend, he meets a group of say men of a less scrupulous natures, who could offer him a get out of *'jail'* card.

"As you all know Clark was struck off for his use of drugs and alcohol. So I feel that the gangsters realised that with Clark in their pocket, and Ainsworth's need for cash *'tout sweet'* that a plan was hatched."

"I have no need to go into the great details in all of this suffice to say, there was a great deal of money to be made.

Chapter Eighty Five

Carter looked out at the team he smiled; "Now we have a huge amount of work in front on us. He looked at Sue, DCS Ford, will you please organise and supervise the work pattern."

"What information was recovered from Clark's house? We need to match evidence between him and Ainsworth. Will you also get together all personnel arrested from the warehouse, they need to be interviewed, and again a need to get associated evidence, which may include Ainsworth."

"Now I'll leave Ian, Peter, and Philip and the rest of the team to assist you. I'm going to have a chat with Sue, Wendy, and Commander Frost, for our next step forward, after which I'm off to Acanthus Road."

Later in his office he sat with Sue, Wendy Field, and Tony Frost he arranged for drinks, and after the young lady had left he looked at TF and said, "Sir how are you going to sell it to the Chief?"

He looked at Wendy, "Normally we release a low action press release, but how on earth do we fudge a subject such as this?" He looked at the three of them, "Perhaps you could both go away and formulate a plan? Now I'm off to see what is happening in the, Recreation ground, near Acanthus Road."

Carter walked into the general office, he looked at Charlie, and "We're off on our travels to Acanthus Road, re the suspicious circs. Carter signed out after which he looked at Eric and winked, "Could you please keep a roving eye on what's going on." And they both left.

In the car he got on the radio, asking for the duty Inspector in the information room, for an update on the situation. He received the reply, *"Ch. to Assistant Commander Carter, all crime scene personnel are in position, your team have taken control along with SOCO, Ch. Out."* With blues and twos, they sped off.

On their arrival Carter noticed that metal rods had been

placed around the scene, bound together with the traditional blue and white tape, "Do not pass – police crime scene.

On leaving the car they both put on their forensic coveralls, and both joined Lloydie. He looked up and seeing Carter he said, "Hello guv, we seemed to have fielded a body?"

Gordon Chamber's looking rather flushed, for his forensic suit, always seemed uncomfortable, due partly to the tight fit, due to his mass. Bellowed, "There you are Carter, I have news for you?" As Carter walked over he noticed the metal trays lay as a forensic pathway, which always meant one thing? As they lead up to the edge of the scene.

Gordon Chambers, who with a reddened face was on his knees, examining what Carter, could clearly make out to be a partly covered body. The pathologist, working with a small brush in one hand, gently removed soil from around the face of what was now clearly a male body.

Carter looked into were Gordon Chambers was working, "Have you a TOD?" As Carter said it, he noticed Lloydie, had turned to DC Jones, who had a vacant look to his face, and whispered, 'Time of Death'

Mr Chamber's replied, "Well as stated he wasn't killed here. "One can clearly see that rigor mortise has left the body. Liver, and rectal temperatures, refer he has been dead sometime."

"He was undoubtedly transported here from somewhere else, preferable, a location, with considerable amounts of dirt, and cement deposits.

"Whilst Mr Chamber's was talking, Carter was fascinated in how he, slowly, and gently worked, lightly removing the covering material to reveal the body. He first began to lift the top of the material to one side, which undoubtedly loosened the soil he then removed the lower part, revealing the full body.

Gordon Chambers flustered looked up, "Carter as you can see you're perpetrators wrapped the John Doe, in some sort of cloth, or blanket, being in a possible hurry; they failed to bury him completely, thus relying on the soil, and sod's to hide him."

"But you can... Chamber's stopped in mid-sentence, "One, if standing closer, and not on the other side of the field, can clearly see...Carter moved nearer. "When I removed the attempted covering, it revealed that our victim was shot twice in the head." He then reached down and shouted, "Aha" He lifted up the victim's right arm, and then his left for all to see.

"You will notice scuff marks to both of his wrists, as if he may have been handcuffed, whilst he was detained. Oh, yes he was definitely killed elsewhere?"

"I will know a lot more when I get him home, after the PM?" Carter looked at Lloydie, who smiled, "Yes guv, will deal with it perhaps the sprog may enjoy the event." Carter just smiled.

Gordon Chambers looked at Carter, "Now, Carter do you remember when a certain young detective, one not so very far from where we are standing, who use to view bodies..." Carter interrupted him, he coughed, "Now is not the time."

There was a stifle of laughter from all that were present, "Now Gordon, let's leave well alone." He replied, "Would one wish to join us at *'Rose cottage' (The name used for the mortuary)* Carter coughed, and went off to find Charlie.

Whilst en route back to Derby Lane, he called TF after putting him in the picture he explained that he'd call him back on receipt of the PM result. After the call he sat with the phone still held in his hand, waving it backwards, and forwards. Looking at Charlie he said, "The man has no manners."

Charlie looked over at Carter, "Boss when you become our next Commander of CID, you can break the mould. For, although you both served as CID officers, you are definitely not cut from the same cloth."

Throwing his head back laughing relentlessly, Carter

looked over at Charlie, and with tears in his eyes, that when his laughter subsided he said, "Charlie, please tell me you are joking? "Charlie hesitated and said, "Why, not? It's not that farfetched."

"When I was promoted to DI, and made head of the MCU, Carter continued, "It was rather like Caesar's speech, the one about, 'Friends, Romans, countrymen' were, Mark Anthony, and co all stabbed him with daggers. Carter, looking at Charlie, well, could you imagine what it would be like if I was offered TF's job. They'd all be bloody axes."

They both burst out laughing, when stopped Carter said, "No Charlie I'll see my timeout in the MCU."

Chapter Eighty Six

Back in his office Carter picked up his phone and dialled Penny, it went straight to her answer phone. He pressed the middle of his phone down with the hand set and dialled his home landline number. It was answered immediately, *"Hello Carter, long day?* He replied, "Yes and getting longer by the minute."

"Just letting you know that I'm going to be late, I mean late, late in case tea spoils." Penny said, *"Err, I love you Carter."* And she immediately hung up the phone. He was left staring at the handset.

Just then there was a knock on his door, he shouted, "Come In" He looked up to see Sue standing on the thresh hold of his office with a smile on her face. "Please tell me that you've not been talking with Charlie?"

Sue said, "Why on earth did you say that?" Carter said, "Okay fine." Sue said, "Could you please come through to the conference room. He stood up and with sleeves rolled up and his tie slackened, and followed her down to the room.

On entering, he saw several members of his team busy working on items spread out on large tables, in a very active and energetic way.

He walked slowly around the room, looking down on the vast amount of items. He turned looking at Sue, "You seem to be very busy?" Sue smiled, "Well, you asked for us to recover any evidence that may tie Clark, with Ainsworth."

"This is the sum total of items not just from Clark's house, but other items collected from the homes of, Jackson, Collins, Parsons, and the other scum that were arrested in that awful warehouse." On completion Sue sat looking at Carter.

Carter said, "Mr Chamber's mentioned that this latest victim was held somewhere, for there are scuff marks to his wrists, possible signs that he was held, secured by some sort of metal type manacles, or handcuffs. I want a team down to the warehouse to pull it apart."

The door to the conference room opened, and Eric stood in the doorway. They both looked up at him. He said, "I've Gordon Chambers on the phone in the general office, you'll both want to hear what he has to say."

Carter thanked him, and said, "Eric could I trouble you to put it through to my office." Eric smiled, and turned away.

He picked up the phone in his office, "Gordon, good evening, to what do I owe the pleasure, what do you have?" He replied, "It would be better if you could come down." Carter said, "We're on our way."

On arrival at the mortuary, Charlie parked up into one of the vacant car parking bays, all three officers walked up to the front door of the building. Sue pressed the intercom and gave the usual announcement. They entered, and walked along the cold corridor towards, Gordon Chamber's office.

Memories flooded back, of the time that Carter had made the same walk to identify Helen, and the children. He felt a cold shiver.

Carter could see Gordon Chambers chatting with Lloydie and DC Jones, who had a certain paler to his face, for which sprog's seem to generate on their first visit to the establishment.

Entering the office, both Lloydie and Jones went to stand up, Carter said, "How you were." The pathologist with his booming voice said, "Come in Carter, we were just about to abide in the unusual. *'What'!'* " Smiling, he noticed the tower of plastic cups, and the bottle of Scotch, displayed and ready for action. Carter said, "Why not it's been one of those days."

Carter looking at DC Jones, said, "Well how did it go?" Remembering his first PM at which DS Morton (Eric) his boss said, "If you're going to faint, make sure you fall away from the table." Those words were frequently stated in Carter's early days as a DC.

Jones looking at Carter said, "I'm fine sir." Carter smiling said, "Right! Jonesy, could I trouble you to fetch some chairs from the other office, with a weak smile he said, "Yes guv."

While he was out Carter looked at Lloydie, "Well! How was he?" Gordon Chambers interrupted him replying, "He did far better than you did?" And they all burst out laughing.

Whilst they all nursed their drinks, Gordon Chambers opened a plastic evidence bag and deposited the contents onto a nearby table. He said, "Carter this was the blanket used to wrap around our John Doe."

Carter stood up and as he fondled the blanket he said, "Is there anything in particular that I'm looking for?" Lloydie stood up and looking at Jonesy said, "Show the boss"

Standing he manoeuvred the blanket until he found on one of the corners a silk label with the words embroidered on it...Lillian's Linens Whitney's woollen blanket below and on the bottom right hand corner of the label, the words; Double size blanket 90x180.

Carter looked at Sue, she smiled, "Guv it's one of Ainsworth's products? It's from the bed linen shop he owns." Gordon Chambers had replenished their drinks.

Carter sat back, "Well it definitely 'puts us in the ball park, but it's purely circumstantial evidence, yet it points us in the right direction.

Gordon Chamber's said, "We've also recovered soil samples from both the blanket and on the clothes and wrists of the victim, I've sent them to the forensic lab, for comparison with the floor of that warehouse."

He continued, I retrieved two 9mm bullets from the victim, gunshot residue was found from, and around the wounds, again the victim was shot at close range, I've also sent them for comparison with the bullets retrieved from our other victims."

Chapter Eighty Seven

Gordon Chambers said, "Carter, Sue, will you please join me, I need to show you the body of our John Doe." Sue clearly heard a low, "Oh shit" from the direction of, Carter.

The post mortem room had the inevitable effect on Carter he noticed all the medical and technical equipment on the trolley's, placed at the back of the room, a cold shiver spread through his body...

"They both observed signs of a single body laid on one of the three tables, covered with a white rubber sheet. The overhead lights illuminated the immediate scene....ending short of the walls giving the air of darkness.

They took up a position on either side of the table; Gordon Chamber's walked over, and pulled back the sheet to reveal the alabaster coloured closed eyed face of the victim.

He pulled the sheet further down as far as the victims waist, revealing the tell-tale signs of the 'Y' shape wound initiated with the commencement of the PM. Gordon Chamber's pointed out the two gunshot wounds, he then lent forward, and gently pulling up the victims arms, one after the other, pointing at the skin discoloration caused by the vicious injuries.

He pointed to, and explained the dark coloured bruises around each of his wrists. "The tender area of skin discolouration is caused by blood leaking from blood vessels damaged by his detention. The probable cause being that the victim was detained by rusty type manacles, and or chains, which left the marks and bruises around the victim's wrists."

Carter sighed, and looking at Gordon, he said, "Did you find any further evidence from your PM on our victim?" Gordon replied, "No Carter, all was in order, no signs of drug misuse, or any other issues. Bloods and fluids have been passed to the forensic labs for the various tests."

He suddenly stopped talking, "Carter there is this." He lifted the victim's left hand and offered it to Carter. Full of uncertainty, Carter took hold of it; he looked down noticing the ring on the victims *'ring finger'* and it clearly revealed a gold coloured signet ring. Carter said, "Yes, I think we noticed it earlier, Gordon."

Examining the ring, he noticed on the top flat surface of the victim's property that three initials had been engraved in a scroll style, CMP, after a couple of minutes, Carter gently placed his arm next to his body, on the table.

Gordon said, "Carter the reason why it's still on the victim's finger is due to the fact that we cannot remove it, you will notice that the victim's fingers have swelled, and we'd need the use of a small power circular saw, or cutters."

Carter said, "Let's please leave it to when he is identified, and claimed. You can suggest removal of the ring, via your idea."

On leaving the mortuary Carter, and Sue got into the car, and Charlie headed back to Derby Lane. En route Carter turned to Sue, sat in the back. "Sue, can you please arrange for Collins, Jackson and Parsons to be produced at Derby Lane, I want them all interviewed in an effort to try to identify this victim, perhaps the three initials on the ring may help?" Sue replied "Yes boss."

"I also want officers at that bloody warehouse, and if needed, to do a fingertip search of the floor. We need to find the site, or where the victim was detained, and murdered?"

On their return to Derby Lane, Sue signed back in, and left for the boardroom. Carter realised that it being so late, that she'd make notes for the morrow.

Carter after signing back in, realised that Eric and his staff had left, he looked down at his watch it was 1.30pm he said under his breath, "Shit, it may well be deaf and dumb supper...Looking at Charlie he said, "Sorry Charlie, will you please race me home."

Carter thanked him, he said, "Charlie, please offer my

apologies." Charlie laughed, and drove off.

Entering their flat, Carter tip toed along the hall, in the kitchen he saw a note leant against a convenient vase. *'Carter if you return home before 10.30, 11.30, 12.30pm you may be lucky, love Pen xxx.*

He pulled it up and smiled, he took off his coat, jacket, and his holster, carrying his pistol and holster he again crept towards their bedroom. He noticed the duvet mound in their bed. He placed the weapon and holster into the safe he turned and started to undress.

When down to his skidies, he gently lifted the duvet and slid into bed, he turned to get comfortable when a tired voice mumbled, "What do you think you're doing?"

He turned to face her. Penny smiled, "Good evening Carter, welcome home." She snuggled up to him. "Carter you're freezing, where the hell have you been?" He said, "Well, the day started well, and went downhill fast."

"After a meeting in the conference room, I received a message from Gordon Chamber's to take a call in my office. The reason for the call was to invite me, and Sue, to his mortuary."

"The purpose of which was to view the body recovered from a nearby park. The body revealed three major facts; one, two gunshot wounds to his head, two, scuff mark wounds to each of his wrists, and three, the blanket in which he had been wrapped in, it had a silk label depicting the name of the shop it was sold in. This shop happens to be one owned by, Ainsworth's organisation?"

Penny suddenly sat up, "Great news Carter you have the bastard." He looked at her, "Sorry Pen, but it's all circumstantial evidence, but it does put us nearer to him, and his team."

Chapter Eighty Eight

The following morning after a hot shower Carter shaved and dressed. He walked out into the lounge to be met by Penny. "Was it another late night?" Carter smiled, "I think today, I'll play the bosses card, and leave early for a change."

Carter gave Penny a lingering kiss, and left to meet Charlie who was waiting outside for him. Charlie was leaning against the car, with his arms folded against his chest. He looked at his boss saying, "Get in Carter we're off to that bloody warehouse, Ian's team has matters to show you.

As they left Charlie put on the blues, leaving off the sirens until he had cleared the immediate neighbourhood. On Sefton Park Road, he switched on the sirens, as it was the rush hour, and he needed to cut through the traffic.

They made their way along Lodge Lane, Tunnel Road, crossing over Smithdown Road, into Durning Road, and then turning right onto Edge Lane. Carter always felt safe with Charlie's driving, having trained as an advanced driver, and armed pursuit driver.

On arrival at Binns Road, Charlie brought the car to a halt, close to where a large white canvas had been fitted over the front of the warehouse. They both noticed that personnel dressed in white forensic overalls, and masks were darting in and out like bees.

Carter immediately saw Sue walking over carrying a white forensic suit, for him. He dressed and walked away towards the canvas, as they walked Carter turned, noticing Charlie was dressing in his suit. Carter said, "Try and drive faster next time, I thought you were rather slow." As he walked away Carter burst out laughing.

Before he entered the property he looked at Sue, "Good job miss, well done for getting all this organised in such short notice." Sue just smiled, and continued to walk along side of him.

As they approached the white canvas screen a uniform officer took their details, after which he lifted the canvas sheet. Both Carter and Sue thanked him and walked in.

They both were flabbergasted, with Carter saying, "Bloody hell, when I said, rip the place apart..." He stopped talking in mid-sentence...

They both looked around, and noticed that at one side of the building, SOCO and their technicians, had placed a large sheet of plastic on the floor, and laid the lengths of wood stripped from off the walls. On receipt of each plank they made a direct examination.

Carter approached Warren Atkins, the SOCO manager. "Warren, you all look busy? What is your main aim with the wood?" He replied, "Well, Carter there may be blood splatter, and there can be small micro dots."

"You will notice Carter, that we are spraying each plank of wood with. 'Luminal' and then move a light source over the wood, as you well know, it highlights the areas, unseen by the human eye."

He continued, "We are working in several areas, in an effort to detect blood on other surfaces, plus we are taking soil samples from around the place." Carter thanked him and his team and moved over to where Ian was standing.

Carter looked at him, "DI Baxter, you look rather puzzled, what's causing my special boy's upset? You know that I worry about you." At that point all the team burst out laughing. They all noticed his crimson face.

"Do you have a problem?" Ian looked at him, "Guv, yes I've been thinking, have you noticed, that when you enter the warehouse, you immediately see that there is a long worktop that runs several yards along the left hand wall, with hooks, that they most probably used for tools."

Carter said, "Yes I see it?"

Ian continued, "Well if you follow the worktop to the end, it joins a wall that sticks out some eight feet, that continues for about fifteen yards, ending in an office that recedes further into the warehouse wall."

Carter again said, "Yes I see it?"

By this time Sue was looking at Ian she said, "What if it was a false wall? Whilst talking they both walked over to the area, Ian started to knock on the wall, getting a hollow sound.

Sue frowned, "Why erect an extension out into the floor some eight feet by fifteen yards for nothing, was it just to follow the design of the office?"

By this time the other team members began to show interest, and began to wonder over.

Whilst they were both surmising this issue, they heard a shout from Carter, "That is why?" They both walked over to were Carter was standing in the office.

Carter said, "We didn't realise that the office door opened inwards, when you look behind the door one can see a smaller door? He had tried to open it but it was locked.

He turned to one of the team, "Alex, will you please get hold of a bar to enable us to force this door." He turned, and replied, "Yes guv."

Chapter Eighty Nine

Alex returned some minutes later, armed with a metal jemmy bar. He stood opposite the door, he turned and Carter shouted, "Police" get away from the door." He waved members of the team to stand back, whilst he took the bar from Alex.

He walked up to the door, and placing the iron bar in the door frame he forced the door open. The door swung open the smell was awful, Carter pulled his face mask up covering up his mouth. Other team members stepped back, voicing their impression of the smell coming from that awful room.

Carter shouted, "Get SOCO here with their camera's, inside he noticed a rusty metal pipe, which he thought acted as a conduit protecting a potential light wire which reached from the roof to a commercial type light switch, on the left wall.

"The light illuminated the hell hole. He turned to Sue with a pale face, "Sue it's similar to the rear of the lorry in Bootle." She walked up to him and looked in.

Again they noticed a dirty urine stained mattress, and the usual bucket in the corner. As Carter walked in he saw metal rings with chains hanging from them, at the end of the chains he noticed metal manacles.

He also noticed blood stains on the mattress, and beamed when he saw two empty bullet shells, he shouted, "Eureka eureka, "Sue, the poor victim was murdered here, and I bet my pension, taken to the Recreation Ground to be buried."

He looked at Lloydie, "Could you organise for Gordon Chamber's to attend to this place, with his team. I want him to try and recover any evidence that can put our victim here before being killed and taken elsewhere." He replied, "Yes guv."

He called, "Could I ask someone to organise hot drinks, and we will then regroup at Derby Lane." He then looked at Sue, "I'm going to see TF, in the meantime could I trouble you, and Ian to have a go at Jackson, Collins, and Parsons, and I need our victim identified." She smiled, "Yes guv."

"We know he had a signet ring on his finger, with the initials CMP see if that ignites their thought processes."

He left the room looking for Charlie. After his sexual boxing match with Jane, he was told to get his lovely arse down here straight away. "Charlie, we're off to HQ, I need to talk with TF."

As he walked out of the lift, Jane's head looked up, "Ah Carter, gorgeous as ever." Laughing she looked at Charlie, "Will you hold the fort while I take your boss into a spare office, to show him a few moves?"

Carter looked at her, with a smile on his face, he said, "Jane, one of these days I'm going to put you over my knee and slap your bottom." He was fully aware what she'd say, but all he heard was Jane, spluttering, "Carter?"

He and Charlie both laughed aloud, and walking over to TF's office, he knocked on his door to await his reply. "Come in"

Carter and Charlie both entered. He beckoned them to take a seat, he looked at Carter, "Well, what's so important?" Carter looked at him, "Well boss, I need the green light to arrest Ainsworth." Not realising at that precise moment, TF was taking a mouth full of coffee. He blew it all over his front, and shouted, "Carter?"

He stood up, and walked over to a door in his office, he opened it to reveal a wash basin, together with a mirror fixed on the back of it. "Carter, just look at the fucking state of me, I'm a mess."

He returned to his desk and picking up the phone he shouted, "Jane, do I have a clean shirt?" Minute later there was a knock on his door. He bellowed, "Come in Jane." She entered carrying a cellophane bag, with a beautifully laundered and ironed shirt, as if newly purchased.

Jane said, "Boss what on earth happened?" With a

crimson look on his face he said, "Ask him," Looking at Carter. She handed the shirt to TF and smiling at Carter left the office.

While he was changing he looked at Carter so what on earth were you about to say, he smiled, "Can I interest either of you a drink?" Minutes later Jane entered with two coffees on a tray. She offered the first to Charlie, and then deliberately leaning over she smiled, and whispered, "Anything you fancy Carter?"

Unfortunately Charlie overheard her question, and like TF spluttered his coffee from his mouth, and nose, but unlike TF it missed his clothes, but it landed over TF's desk.

TF said, "What on earth is happening?" Jane walked back and with a tissue wiped the desk top. Jane, looked at Carter and whispered, "Is there anything I can wipe for you, and with a smile on her face, she left the office.

Chapter Ninety

TF looked at them both, "Well, can we please get down to business? Now, what the bloody hell did you want?"

Carter was about to say when his phone activated, he opened up his phone, "Yes." On completion of the call, he looked at TF saying, "We have more evidence that may implicate Ainsworth, we've found a partial receipt for a MOT carried out on the same HGV found on the docks, with the six bodies in the trailer."

Closing the call, Carter explained the contents, he looked at TF and said, "I want to arrest Ainsworth, matters are gaining speed. Ainsworth must realise that we have Clark, and others. I personally feel that's the reason for this present murder."

At this moment Ainsworth realises that Clark has disappeared, so his supply of organs has dried up. If he is out of circulation, how would they progress? Without him they have nothing. So before he takes flight, we must act."

He continued, "Boss I need to instigate an, *'All points warning'* to all, Airports and docks."

Tony frost said, "The both of you go and get a coffee, I'll get Jane to call you when I have the *'get go'* see you shortly." They both left.

Jane realised that there were times when she could joke with Carter, but she also knew when matters were serious, and that Carter wasn't in the mood. Jane busily prepared coffees whilst Carter phoned Sue.

"Sue, will you together with Ian, and Lloydie arrange warrants for Ainsworth's home, and business addresses. I also want, *'All points warning'* for Ainsworth, should he try to abscond. As we know that he has the where with all. Please contact our friends in HM Customs, let them have the necessary paper work."

"Will you please arrange for armed undercover officers, and please get them rigged out in *'Ghillie'* snipers camouflage suits, I want them dropped off tonight to hide around his home in the countryside. I also want teams in cars, in and around his home, to discreetly follow should he try to leave."

"I want him corked up, like a fart in a bottle; if he should fart, I don't want to hear it." Sue replied, "Guv I understand leave it with us." He thanked her and closed the call.

Whilst Jane, was busy making their coffees, Charlie sat, and tried to reassure him. As Jane was stood in the nearby kitchen, Charlie said, "Guv, I know it's your head on the block, but you have a wealth of evidence on the bastard, remember the *'idiom'* "Let the chips fall where they will."

Jane returned with their coffees, she took them from the tray, and smiling offered each their coffees. As Carter thanked her, she looked at him.

"Carter there is no one thought more of by some of the bosses on this floor, and may I say that includes The Chief. But the one that has the greatest regard is no other than the one you refer to as, TF."

As she turned to leave, she looked over her shoulder. "I mean it, as you know I hear everything?" Jane smiled as she returned to her desk.

Chapter Ninety One

Carter looked at his watch it was ten thirty, he said, "Charlie, how bloody long does it take to get the "Get go?"

He had no longer finished the sentence, when the phone rang out on Jane's desk. All three looked at the phone simultaneously. She answered, "Yes sir."

Jane looked at them both, "Carter, will you move that lovely arse, good luck, it makes my day." They both burst out laughing.

He opened the door and walked in. Tony Frost looked at him, "You've got the green light, now please bugger off." Carter smiled, and as he turned to leave, TF said, "Just bugger off, and close the door after yourself." Carter without turning said, "Yes boss."

In the outer office he looked at Jane, "And when do you leave for home?" Jane laughing said, "Why, Carter are you offering." Jane said, "No I'm here while he is, just in case the wheel falls off."

In the car as they soared off to Derby Lane, Carter excitedly called Eric, "Eric will you arrange for all non-operational team members to be in the conference room ASAP." He thanked him and closed the call.

In the conference room Carter stood in front of all the assembled officers. "We have been given the green light, anticipating this we've had people in place watching Ainsworth."

"I want you all to be prepared and ready to go, so please no drinking, it's continuous *'on duty'* until I say." There was a chorus, "Yes guv."

He looked at Sue, DCS Ford, "Will you please ensure that all officers are armed, and in the event that Ainsworth tries anything, we'll be ready." Sue replied, "Yes guv" As Carter left for his own office he looked back, do we have that warehouse covered?" Sue smiled.

En route to his office he walked into the general office,

Eric looked up, "Yes of course boss, just try to stop me."

Carter took hold of his coffee. And sitting next to him, he took a sip, and looking at Eric again he was about to say something...Eric interrupted, "Guv all is under control, Sue and the team have it, go home, I'll tell the duty officer in the control room. If anything breaks you'll be the first to know."

Carter after his coffee placed it on a tray and said, "Well I feel redundant, I'm off home..." He called "Charlie"

He left Charlie, waving him goodbye, he turned and walked towards the entrance hall of his flat. Saying his usual greetings with the APO and the duty doorman he walked off towards his flat. He suddenly stopped dead...

He took out his phone and dialled Penny, it was answered immediately. *"Hello Carter, please tell me that you're on your way home?"* He replied, "Yes, see you shortly." He put the key in the door and walked in, Penny, was sat in an armchair shouted, "Cater, what a wonderful surprise,"

When she stood up his eyes widened in amazement, for Penny was dressed in only a French Maids apron, and nothing else. Penny said, "I was meant to be in the hall awaiting your arrival." He said, "Well Mademoiselle, Ton home est. a la maison." They both fell about laughing.

Carter took hold of her in a tender hug, "I suppose it would be useless to ask, *'What's for tea?'* as fried stuff is off the menu, due to your apparent apparel." With a sad face he looked at her, "Hey Ho! It will have to be a salad."

Penny looked up at him, "Well! I definitely know what *'is'* on the menu... And cooking plays no part in it. Will you please go through to the bathroom and take up the position."

As he walked through he turned saying, "Do I have to?" "Well, Carter I have spent all day thinking about you, for every hour that passed you've been in my thoughts every second, now please for everything you hold sacred, get in the shower and... At that very moment his pager activated.

Penny screamed. "Christ, Carter."

Chapter Ninety Two

Charlie was waiting outside his flat block entrance, together with two, 'Traffic Motor Cyclists.' As he got in the car they set off, blues and two' blurring.

Carter turned to Charlie, "Well" He smiled, "Emigration, and Special Branch officers detained Ainsworth trying to leave via the private passenger gate, at Speke airport."

"He had a 'Gulfstream G650 jet' fuelled and ready to go. DI Walton asked to see his passport, you know the usual operational procedure, and recognised his face and particulars from our, *'All ports warning.'* Congratulations boss they have detained him awaiting your arrival."

Carter rang Sue, he could detect the excitement in her voice, *"Carter, Carter, we've got him, we eventually got, Parsons, Collins and Thompson to flip over on him, and together with, Clarks evidence he's going down."*

He interrupted her, "Sue, Sue, please will you grab the necessary arrest warrant, we're on our way to arrest him..." He could hear the excitement rise even higher, "We'll pick you up outside of Derby Lane nick say in ten." He closed the call'

Sue looked at her phone somewhat perplexed, "Eric." "Yes, I know be off with you, for whilst she had the conversation with Eric, she could hear the blues and two's getting nearer. None the less, making sure that all was in order she went and waited outside the police station.

From the direction of St Oswald Street, Sue could see the approaching blue lights, plus the sirens. The first motor cyclist continued towards the corner of Prescot road. Charlie pulled into the edge of the pavement, Sue jumped into the back of the car, before she could say hello they were off.

Charlie and one of the traffic motor cyclists, completed a 'u' turn, and raced off back to the junction of Prescot Road and St Oswald Street. The second motor cyclist had stopped the traffic.

All three vehicles then raced along Prescot Road towards Queens Drive. They then turned right on the Drive, and raced south towards the airport. The two motor cycle escorts played leap frog all the way to the airport, holding the traffic up at all the major junctions.

It seemed like seconds when together with their escort, they arrived at the private departure, and arrival building at "The John Lennon airport" Speke. Carter looked at his watch, "Not bad 12 minutes, from Derby Lane." As he got out of the car he walked over and thanked both traffic officers.

Knowing that they were on the landside of the airport, although they could hear the jet engines of the private plane idling, awaiting it's passengers. Charlie opened the door and Carter, and Sue both walked in.

In reception they saw two smartly dressed men one of the men walked over and offered Carter his ID. "Deputy Commander Carter, I'm DI Walton, and this is my partner DS Murphy, we are both attached to, 'Special branch.' "

Carter said, "This is DCS Susan Ford, and this is my protection officer, Charlie Watkins, Walton was about to speak, when Carter held up his hand, "Would it be possible for hot drinks for our two, Traffic officers?"

DS Murphy said, "Can I interest you all in hot drinks, before you meet Ainsworth?"

After their drinks DI Walton said, "Could I ask you to follow me to the custody suit, it's in the next building." He led the way out and they passed the waiting 'Gulfstream jet' with it's airstair down awaiting the arrival of the intended passenger, or passenger's.

As they passed it Walton said, "Yours for a mere $65 million dollars, it was then that Carter suddenly noticed that the livery of the jet, in large blue letters was, "Ainsworth Corporation" He suddenly turned, someone please get me a photo of that." And he pointed to the jet.

They entered what had the appearance of a modern type police station. A uniform sergeant stood behind a reception desk, Walton did all the introductions whilst Sue walked over and handed the sergeant the arrest warrant.

It was as easy as that, a door opened and a smartly dressed man, who Carter immediately recognised as Ainsworth. The uniform sergeant said, "Ainsworth please face these officers."

Sue walked forward and said, "Ainsworth, I'm Detective Chief Superintendent Susan Ford, of The Major Crime Unit, based at Derby Lane police station."

"I'm in possession of an arrest warrant in your name, Sue gave him the full caution, and on completion he made no reaction. Sue said, "The defendant made 'no reply.' Ainsworth, you will now be taken to Derby Lane police station, where you will be detained."

Tomorrow you will be produced and interviewed still under caution, by my senior officer, Assistant Commander Carter, and myself." Sue turned to the duty sergeant, do you have his possessions?"

The sergeant produced a large vanilla envelope. The sergeant said, "When arrested he had in his possession, a watch, gents gold coloured, gents leather wallet, brown coloured containing, £300 in cash, and 1000 in EU Euro's, and credit cards, his UK, passport and £6 in small change."

Sue checked all the items, signed for them and replaced them in the envelope. Charlie went over, and as a precaution searched him, on completion, Carter thanked Walton, for his hospitality. Ainsworth was taken outside and placed in the car with Sue in the front next to Charlie, and Carter sat in the back next to the prisoner.

Their return journey was just as quick, but on this occasion they had the extra protection by the force helicopter.

On arrival at Derby Lane, Carter thanked the two traffic officers. Sue and Charlie attended to Ainsworth. Carter said, "I'm off to the general office to sign in, and contact TF see you both in a minute."

On entering the general office he got the shock of his life for there was Eric sat working. As Carter signed back in he turned and looked at Eric, "Kath will have my life, you do realise that it's 1.30am in the bloody morning."

Eric looked up and smiled, "I do my best work at times like these, there is very little traffic pounding through in their size 12's?" As he said it he offered Carter a coffee." Carter smiling said, "We also have officers with delicate feet."

The door immediately opened and Sue smiling said, "He has been tucked up in bed with his teddy, and hot milk ready for the...well let's say in a couple of hours." They all burst out laughing."

After his coffee Carter yawned, "I'm off see you in the morning..."

Chapter Ninety Three

Charlie dropped Carter off, and drove away.

Carter entered his building walking up to the front door to his flat, put his key in the lock, opened the door and gently walked up the hall. In the lounge he stripped off placing his clothes neatly folded onto the settee.

As he was about to turn a voice from the rear aid, "And what do you think you're doing? Should you not be doing that in the bedroom, I think that is where one prepares for bed..."

Carter turned saying, "Op's! As he jokingly placed his holstered pistol over his private parts, and began to walk towards the bedroom. Penny stood to one side of the bedroom door, and singled with her arm pointing towards their bed.

He placed his gun in the safe at the bottom of their wardrobe floor. Locked it, and walked over to their bed.

As he was about to near the bed, Penny suddenly took hold of his hand and steered him towards the bathroom and shower. As they both stood under the powerful sport shower she looked up at him.

"Carter I don't know if you noticed that before you were called out, I mentioned that I'd been thinking of you all day, and was more than ready for you, on hearing your pager, I screamed, "Christ Carter."

"Will you please believe me that it was a sheer reaction to the situation, and I was pumped up, and ready for action?"

"Now can I run out the guns, and get ready for action." Carter looked at Penny. "Were on earth does, 'Nelson, and Captain Hornblower' come into such matters?"

Under the heavy gushing water, the two burst out laughing. Carter, took hold of the two hand sponges and began to soap Penny down. She began to turn in slow circles allowing Carter total access to her body, from head to toe.

On completion Penny, took the both sponges from Carter, and began to pay reciprocal attention to him. Whilst working with equal enthusiasm, she gently whispered in his ear. "Darling, have you ever thought that there is more surface to cover whilst carrying out the same procedure, between the bodies of women, and men, I often wonder where the difference lay?"

At that specific moment, with both sponges she caressed his penis whispering "Ha! There it is."

After drying each other, they both walked to their bed, and jumped under the duvet. Carter lay on Penny and began to kiss her all over her body.

He began to slip under the duvet, and kissed the inside of both her legs, from her toes up to her thigh's , were she gently opened her legs, and began pleasuring her in a most wonderful way.

It was during this time that she, and her body was about to explode, to diminish any sounds of delight she decided to stuff the end of the duvet in her mouth to stop her screaming.

On completion of her delight, Penny whispered in his ear, "Carter please relax, and let me be in control." With that, she slid her hand under his shorts where she gently took hold of him. He felt the whole of his body react with the effect of her gentle and rhythmic act.

Ceasing she manoeuvred and climbed on top of him, as Carter entered her she let out a soft cry of delight. It happened as if it was the most natural of acts.

Penny started to gyrate backwards and forwards, while her knees where either side of him, giving out noises of pleasure. Penny looked down at Carter saying, "For God's sake Carter, I hope you are ready I can't wait much longer." With that they both began to feel an electrifying shudder pass between their bodies.

When Penny fell on top of him, he noticed that she was crying. He gently passed his arms around her and held her tight. Some minutes later she covered his mouth with a kiss after which Penny said, "Carter, it's always so good."

They both failed to notice that the cloak of sleep had descended upon them, and they both fell fast asleep in each other's arms. The following morning he leaned over and kissed her on the lip's, as he got up and walked to the bathroom. Penny, who suddenly sat up in bed bolstered up by her pillows behind her head said, "Carter how the hell can you walk, after all that we did?"

He laughed out loud, "It's a man thing, because I'm fit." Penny laughing aloud said, "Well, I know that Carter, but that's not up for discussion."

Chapter Ninety Four

Carter had wondered around his office in a time honoured way, in which he used, to get his mind on the forthcoming events. He eventually returned to his desk. He sat at his desk with the remains of his inevitable mug of coffee, presented by his friend, and mentor, Eric.

As Carter sat nursing his cold mug of coffee, his thoughts of last night's remarkable events immediately reminded Carter of his times with Helen. His incredible memories, which formed an indelible pattern in his mind, filled him with guilt.

What Carter was realising, that in his mind Helen's dominance was beginning to waver, and that Penny was now the dominant thoughts in his mind. Carter had fought with this for months, but realised it was a natural procedure.

He seemed to be asking for forgiveness, for allowing himself to seek a replacement in his life. He stood up and thought, Carter, Penny although not Helen, will in some way allow you to relax, and seek comfort in her love.

Carter had tears in his eyes that began to break down his cheeks, he shivered. It was then that there was a knock on his door. Before his usual shout of *'Come in'* He quickly wiped his face with the back of his hand.

He shouted, "Come in" Looking up he saw Sue, smiling with a thick file under her arm. Carter are you ready?" "Yes, let's get on with it." They both left and called into the general office.

It was whilst they were stood talking with Eric, that Ainsworth was brought up from the cells, and walked passed on his was to interview room, 'One' together with his uniformed escort.

"Well, don't you stand for a Knight of the Realm?" Carter said it laughing as he picked up his own file ready for the interview. Eric said, "Should we have doffed our caps, and the ladies curtseyed?" He continued, "No bloody chance."

Eric wished them both, good luck as they left for the interview room. Outside of interview room one, Carter opened the door and the officer came to attention. Carter said, "Okay son, as you were." The officer stood to one side.

Both Carter and Sue sat down in front of Ainsworth. He was dressed in an immaculate suit, white shirt, and brown slip on loafers.

Whilst Sue readied her papers she leaned over to carry out the usual procedure with the tape. She took out two new tapes and placed them in the recording machine, there was a short customary bleep from the machine.

On completion Carter said, "This interview is being carried out at 9.30am on, Monday 7th January 2008, at Derby Lane Police Station, present, Deputy Commander Carter, and Woman Detective Chief Superintendent Susan Ford, both officers of, 'The Major crime Unit.' And the accused, Malcolm Arnold Ainsworth, who it would appear, is not legally represented.

The next minute Ainsworth shouted, "You've forgotten my title, Sir." Carter looked at Sue and laughed. He immediately looked at Ainsworth, "Your title for the purposes of this matter is void. More importantly Ainsworth do you have a Solicitor?" He replied, "Yes. The QC, Mr Andrew Benson, I telephoned him he is on his way."

At that very moment there was knock on the door, Sue stood up and opened it, to be greeted by a uniformed officer together with a very smart gentleman, carrying a briefcase. He walked in saying, "Deputy Commander, I do hope you were not proceeding without my client's rights?" Carter lent forward and switched off the tape.

He looked at the very smart looking gentleman, "Why, Mr Benson, of course not. I asked your client about legal representation, he stated that you were on your way. Before your entrance I was going to inform your client that we would stop the interview, and tape until you arrive. He was about to be returned to the cells."

The Barrister, went and sat next to his client, Carter looked at him, "May we proceed?" He replied, "Yes."

Carter lent forward and re-started the tape saying, "For the purposes of the tape we will restart the interview as the accused Barrister has now arrived."

After the short bleep Carter looked at Benson, "Mr Benson you are a Barrister and QC, and currently have rooms with Messrs, Harris, Gordon and Jones, and that you are here to represent the accused, Ainsworth?"

Before Carter continued, he looked over at Sue, and could see the utter look of shock on her face. Within seconds he noticed a cynical smile.

Carter could see that Benson was about to say something... Carter cut in. "I have already told your client that he will not be referred to as 'Sir' for the duration of this interview, you may wish, or request a change, that is for the courts to decide."

Carter continued, "Ainsworth could you please state for the purposes of the tape, what you were doing when arrested by officers, from Special branch, on duty at Speke Airport, whilst trying to leave the country, last night?"

Benson said, "What?" Carter interrupted, "Why, Mr Benson it would seem that you are totally unaware that an, 'arrest warrant' had been sworn out on your client. Now I would not wish to harm your client's rights in not having prepared representation."

Carter lent forwards saying, "Interview terminated at 12.15pm on Monday 7th January 2008." He stopped the tape.

Carter looked at both men, in the interest of fairness Ainsworth, you have the right to full representation, and given the opportunity to discuss matters with, your represented counsel."

Benson seemed to recover from his shock and nodded his head. Carter said, "Shall we say three hours? Should you need longer it can be arranged, but I wish to point out that your client when charged, will not be allowed bail, for the most obvious of reasons."

He continued, "You have the offer of interviewing your client here in the interview room, or downstairs in the cells. Up here you will both be permitted the hospitality needed."

Benson lent back in his chair and thanked him saying, "Yes, Carter your repartition precedes you." Carter said, "There will be an officer on duty outside of this room, you realise all you need to do is ask for hot, or cold drinks. All toilet breaks made by your client will be under escort."

Both Carter and Sue got up turned and left.

Chapter Ninety Five

Carter left Sue, in the general office and took his mug of coffee through to his office. He sat and picked up the phone, and called Penny. The call was answered on the second ring.

"Carter, well, how are things?" Laughing Penny continued and whispering said, *"Last night was truly wonderful, I feel it shows we are on a level playing field with no matters that may distract us?"*

He said, "Penny, it's that very reason that I'm calling. I thought that I'd take this opportunity in telling you that, I love you. That our love has grown over the last year or so, and that I'm willing to commit whole heartily to our endeavours."

Before she had time to say anything, Carter continued, "I've realised that it is love that I'm thinking, and feel so good about it."

Penny eventually said, *"Why, Carter it has been my feelings from day one. It would be fair to say that we both come with a history. I've always hoped that eventually our love for each other would blossom. Last night was my way of showing you how much I loved you. Now if you are a good boy, I may show you some more moves. "And she burst out laughing.*

Carter smiled inwardly, and said, "Penny, I do love you. Please do not think this is a cop out, but I have to go." She replied, *"Go, Carter go, I'll see you later at home."* The phone went dead.

He got up and walked down to the general office, he looked in at Eric, "Well, any special requests, drinks, food etc?" Eric replied, "No not a thing."

He sat next to Eric, and picked up his phone, and dialled TF. *"Frost"* "Sir it's just to bring you up to date. Ainsworth is at present with his legal rep, the Barrister, Mr Andrew Benson, QC he continued."

"Guess the name of his chambers, he waited?" *"Who,*

or whom, said Frost?" Carter said, "Messrs, Harris, Gordon and Jones...The same chambers that Silverman, and Rotherham worked for." Tony Frost said... *"Carter, Christ."*

"By the way, Wendy Field has released a press release, an over view of this business, but none of the awful details, they can come later, so when you go in to see Ainsworth, tell him. I'm about to get Jane to fax it over for your attention." TF closed the call.

Carter and Sue walked down to the interview room the duty officer opened the door. They both thanked him and walked in.

Both Ainsworth and Benson looked up as one. Carter said, "Well, I think your time is up...

Carter said, "Ainsworth you do realise that you are still under caution." He just nodded.

As the tape started Carter said, "Ainsworth, I have to say that officers from this unit are about to search your home address, under a necessary search warrant." Carter then took out a document from a file.

"Ainsworth, I'm about to hand you a copy of a press release, about to be released to the broad sheets. It fully explains your arrest and the reason for it." The blood seemed to drain from his face, it was obvious that he was about to faint.

Sue stood up and opening the door asked the officer to bring a drink of water, seconds later it was handed to him.

Carter cleared his throat. "Ainsworth there is a common thread that runs throughout all of this. I do hope you don't think you were arrested for trying to leave the country? You will quickly notice that it is certainly more than just a simple case of avoidance."

Ainsworth fell backwards in his seat, and again nearly fainted. Carter said, "This edition is just a background of your business practices, over the next couple of days, editions will report that you and a team of criminals have carried out the most detestable actions."

Carter opened a file and laid out several photographs of

victims. "Ainsworth, these are the tip of the Ice berg." He went on to explain, "For the purposes of the tape, Deputy Commander Carter has laid out a series of 6 photographs marked DCC1 to DCC6 in front of the accused.

Ainsworth pushed them away saying, "Why are you showing me these I'm a businessman not a murderer, please take them away."

Carter looked over towards Andrew Benson, and could see the utter look of distain in his face.

Carter continued, "Ainsworth you will be given access to your Barrister, as and when required. But I have to tell you that it will always be at Derby Lane police station, you will both be afforded the use of an interview room."

"In the meantime I suggest that we re-group here tomorrow at 9.30am, at which time I will continue with our investigation. The duty officer will escort you Ainsworth, back to your cell, later this afternoon you will be taken to 'Risley Remand Centre.'"

He continued, "Mr Benson you may wish to attend there to take further instructions, at which, as you know you'll need to obtain a visitors pass. Or my colleague and I can continue the investigation there, will you please let me know before you leave."

Carter leaned over saying, "Interview terminated at 4.30pm on Monday 7th January 2008.

When the tape bleeped, Andrew Benson said, "Deputy Commander Carter, I trust you have more substantial evidence than just some photographs, which shows no proof of my client's involvement."

Carter looked at him, "I see that you waited until I had stopped the tape and the official interview to mention this information. Why, Mr Benson I can re-start the interview, and continue producing more incriminating evidence about you client."

"Err, Deputy Commander, I just thought..." Carter interrupted, "Mr Benson I was just thinking about you client, not wishing for you to state he was tired etc, so let's meet again in the morning, good bye."

On leaving and in ear shot of both Ainsworth and Benson, Carter said, "Please take Ainsworth back to the cell's, and please escort Mr Benson off the premises." The officer with a crisp reply said, "Yes sir."

Carter and Sue went into the general office, and both had a welcomed cup of coffee. Eric looked at Carter, "Is all well guv?" Carter replied, "Oh Yes." Sue, interrupting said, "The smooth bastard tried, *'off tape'* to accuse the guv of having no evidence?" Eric smiled, "Well I never!" They all burst out laughing.

Carter said to Sue, "Will you see how the search went of the family pile, try should there be anything of an incriminating nature have information for us for tomorrow, "I'm off home."

Chapter Ninety Six

Charlie dropped Carter off at 'Keswick Mansions' he was greeted by the duty doorman Ashley, and the duty ASO Wills. He said "Hello" to both men, and walked through to the door of his ground floor flat.

Putting his key in the door he shouted, "Your man is home, home from the sea, you do know the second thing a sailor does, when he arrives home, he waited a couple of seconds, 'No' He puts down his bag?"

Walking through from the lounge, with a broad grin to her face, Penny said,   "Oh! What can a lady say except, Sir; you must have a lot to catch up on."

After their intimate antics, they showered then both dressed in sweats, walked through to the lounge. Penny said, "Carter, are you hungry?" He replied with a massive grin to his face, "Starving?"

After tea they both went into the lounge and relaxed in front of the television, during brief lapses of concentration to the present programme, Carter explained how his day had gone.

When they both thought it was time for bed, they both lay like spoons, it was so natural, with Carter showing comfort to Penny with his large arm about her waist, he didn't have to force her to relax, and she just melted into him.

He leaned over and kissed her goodnight, giving her a little love nip to the skin on her shoulder, she just purred in delight. Seconds later they both fell into a deep sleep.

The following morning, Penny pretended to still be asleep, for she knew that Carter needed to be where he was with his thoughts of the day, knowing full well that he had a heavy day in front of him.

Whilst Carter was in the shower Penny quickly arose from their bed, and rapidly laid out Carters fresh clothes on their bed, ready for him to dress.

He eventually walked through into the kitchen, were

Penny offered a cup of coffee that she knew he'd never finish, yet it had become a habit. As he placed the mug down after a couple of sips, Penny walked over and gave him a hug.

Penny took a step back, "Carter no holster?" "No, thought it was a bit of over kill, and Charlie is armed enough for the both of us Carter said." As quickly as he said it, he knew it to be the wrong thing to have said.

Penny said, "Has Tony Frost, given the stand down over the carrying of fire arms?" Carter looked down to the floor, "No" Penny said, "Carter get back into that bedroom and put on your holster, and firearm. You more than most know all of the risks."

It only took a couple of minutes, he returned to where she was standing, and stood arms raised. Penny walked over, "Now that's better, it's taken me years to find a good one, now be off with you and kill all the monsters."

He kissed her goodbye, and whispered, *"Am I a good one?* Perhaps tonight you can show me" And they both burst out laughing as he left.

Chapter Ninety Seven

On arrival at Derby Lane, Carter went into the general office and signed on duty. He turned and went and sat next to Eric, to collect his habitual mug of coffee. It was ever just so, always the one he enjoyed the most.

Whilst they sat talking the office door opened and in walked Sue, he noticed that she was carrying several evidence bags filled with clothes and papers. He smiled, "Have we been shopping on our way to work?" Sue replied, "As if? No guv it's some items collected from the Ainsworth's mansion."

He immediately sat up and paid attention, whilst they enjoyed their coffee's Sue went through the items. "The bag marked DIB 1. (DI Baxter 1)Contains a man's two piece suit, Ainsworth's wife mentioned it belonged to her husband, it would appear there are matters of interest on it, namely what appears to be soil stains."

"The bag marked DIB 2. Contains a man's shirt and a gent's handkerchief, Ainsworth's wife identified both belonging to him. Both with blood stains on them."

"The bag marked DIB 3. Contains a pair of men's black shoes, Ainsworth's wife identified they belonging to her husband. The shoes had soil compacted in the soul of the shoes."

Sue looked at Carter, "The items were recovered as a result of the search warrant. All the objects were found in a large dumpster bin, in the back of the property. His wife genuinely thought the items were being thrown out. Statement duly completed. Now the important thing is all the things have been forwarded to forensics, with an ASAP tag marked on them."

Sue smiled at both Carter, and Eric. "You both know of the saying, *'Always keep the best till last'* Carter shouted, "What! What! If you don't tell me, you'll be on point duty at the entrance to the Mersey tunnel?"

Eric burst out laughing, as he knew back in the day it

was a terrible eight hour duty, with the horrendous amount of traffic.

Sue was crying with laughter, suddenly produced the fourth bag that she had kept close to her body, marked DIB 4. When lifted the temperature in the office suddenly reduced, she said, "A 9mm revolver..." Carter suddenly interrupted her, "Christ Sue, please tell me it's, it's." Sue continued "Carter, we need to have it examined, it's being done as we speak."

Sue looked at Carter. "Guv Lloydie has contacted me, fingerprints taken from the body found in the Recreation ground, with the initials CMP on a ring belong to one, Colin Mitchell Proby, who has form."

She continued, "Gordon Chambers has sent blood samples taken from his body, for comparison with the blood found on the shirt, and handkerchief found in the dumpster bin. He has also sent bullet, and shell casings for comparison, both marked DIJL 1 and 2 Carter leant back in his chair please remind me to give them both a kiss when I see them."

He suddenly stood up, "Right, we need to get in touch with Ainsworth's QC, Andrew Benson, and put off our intended interview for to-day. Will someone please call him or the clerk of chambers, to cancel the meeting?"

"Now, when that has all been seen to, Sue, you and I are both going to the forensic labs at Chorley, to await the results."

Sue returned from her office saying, "All done! Off we go." Carter turned to Eric, he looked up, "Yes u know, now bigger off." In the police yard they found Charlie waiting, leant against the car arms folded.

They all left for Chorley, and the forensic labs. There was some urgency in the matter, so Charlie, drove with the blues and twos activated. On arrival at the labs, Carter looked at Charlie, "Not bad, you seem to be getting the hang of things."

All there burst out laughing as they walked into reception. The young lady on duty looked up smiling.

When, all three when under control, showed their Id's to the duty receptionist, who smiled, then placed the 'sign in book' on the counter.

On completion he said, "Would it be possible to go through to the labs? The young lady smiled, "Why, of course, sir, it's on the first floor, the lift is over there pointing to the large silver doors on the right."

Carter thanked her, and they all walked over to the lift. Pressing *'the call'* button the doors opened immediately. The location panel illuminated with all floors, Charlie pressed the lighted glass square with the figure one in it.

The doors opened, and as they left the lift, they were met by a large clear glass wall. On the other side of the glass they saw forensic officers, like worker bees, with intricate equipment, busily carrying out different types of examinations.

One of the officers came from behind the glass wall. She smiled, "Can I help you?" They all produced their Id's, and it was Carter who informed her why they were there.

The young lady still smiling said, "Oh yes, please follow me. As they walked via the tables, they peered, showing interest at the officers at work. At the end of the room they were introduced to a man called, Dr Julian Evans, senior forensic officer.

Carter introduced himself, together with Sue, and Charlie. Dr Evans said, "Are you here, re the, Ainsworth case resulting from items recovered during a search of his property."

Carter nodded, Dr Evans said, "I have passed the items to three of my team, specialist officers, who meticulously search suspect items? I'll take you over to meet them?"

He took them over to a large flat table, were they found a man's two piece suit lain out on a large piece of plain white paper, on the table. A young officer was busily brushing the material were minute items fell onto the paper.

The officer looked at both Carter and Sue, "Don't look

so worried we can detect the most minuscule items of matter, and compare them with the control sample given to us by SOCO officers."

"I'll have any results for you later to-day. She smiled at both of them, "Please try and relax."

They were then taken through to another room with again another large table. On this table a man's white shirt and handkerchief was spread out. Another young officer was spraying the shirt and handkerchief with a versatile chemical called Luminal, as she sprayed the garments they noticed a striking blue glow given off from the materials.

The young officer smiled at them both, she said, "Can I trouble you to put on these goggles, which shows a striking blue glow, when mixed with an appropriate oxidizing agent. We use Luminal to detect trace amounts of blood, left at a crime scene it reacts with iron found in haemoglobin."

Chapter Ninety Eight

It was whilst on their return to Derby Lane that Carters phone activated, he opened the call saying "Carter" A quiet voice said, *"Deputy Commander it's, Julian Evans, just thought you'd like to know, results have come through, and I'm pleased to say that you have a winning hand, so to speak. 'All positive'*

He closed his eyes, "Are you sure?" Julian Evens said, *"Yes, our reports are on their way, together with statements made by the various forensic officers."* As Carter was about to thank him, Evans closed the call.

Carter leaned back in his seat and screamed, "Yes, yes, yes we've got the bastard." He then related the call to both Sue, and Charlie. The journey home to Derby Lane was as if they were soaring through space, cutting through the masses like a speeding bullet.

It was whilst they journeyed home that Carter phoned TF and related the facts given to him by, Julian Evans. Tony Frost said, *"Well congratulations Carter, your interrogation of Ainsworth, will be a doddle. Let's speak later?"* And he closed the call.

Carter turned to Sue, "I think we could all do with a 'do' to let our hair down, now how long has it been?" Sue turned to Charlie, "When we get home..." Carter interrupted, "Look Sue, I'm not trying to embarrass you with knowing it would have been when Helen was alive?"

He continued, "Penny is my life now, so let's find a place that can fit us all in? Can I ask you to arrange matters get either Alex or Gill, let's get to it?"

Sue smiled, "Okay guv, leave it with me, I'll pick a Saturday night, perhaps the northern crime squad will cover, I'll involve Eric."

Carter said, "So be it. While on the subject, can we make arrangements to interview Ainsworth, please set it up with his brief?"

On arrival at Derby Lane, Carter entered the general

office, Eric looking up smiled, "Well how did things go?" Carter smiled, "We seem to have a full set, 'Aces, and kings'" Eric, looked over to one of the young secretaries. "Carol could you make a coffee for the boss?" Carol smiled, and prepared the coffee. For it was only, one teaspoon of coffee in his mug, filled with boiling water.

Carter sat talking with Eric, telling him of the results made by the forensic officers, at Chorley. Whilst in full conversation with Eric, the young secretary placed the prepared coffee on the edge of Eric's desk. "Thank you" Carter said, as he looked up at her.

Chapter Ninety Nine

The following morning Carter enjoyed a solo shower, Penny realised that he needed to get his head together, for the approaching interview with his prisoner, Ainsworth.

On arrival at Derby Lane, he signed on duty, after which he went and sat next to Eric. As he sat down, one of the young secretaries produced his 'start of the day' mug of coffee.

Whilst Carter was engrossed in conversation, Sue walked in and stood holding two major files, and four plastic evidence bags filled with the necessary exhibits. He burst out laughing, "Are you looking for the first tee?"

He immediately stood up, walking over to assist her with all the items, and exhibits, Sue gave Carter the exhibits, whilst she stood holding the files. Eric wished them both 'good luck' as they turned to leave the office, heading for the interview room.

A uniform officer was stood on duty outside of the interview room. The officer stood to one side whilst he opened the door for them both. Carter thanked him, and they both entered.

Ainsworth and his QC were both sat talking on the other side of the table. As the door opened they both stopped and looked up at them both.

On entering the room Carter, placed he exhibits bags to his left on the floor whilst Sue put the two files on the table. Sue and Carter both sat down opposite. Carter turned to the both, "Ainsworth you realise that you are still under caution?" He just nodded his head.

Sue took out two tapes and placed each into the recording machine, after the machine bleeped, Sue stated all the introductions, and all four sat facing each other.

Carter said, "Ainsworth, I wish to show you several items." He leaned down and pulled up one of the evidence bag's which contained a pair of men's shoes. He opened the bag and took out one of the black handmade shoes, inside of the shoe was a sign saying, 'Bespoke shoes' made by, *'James Taylor & Son'* Taylormadeshoes.co.uk.

Looking at Ainsworth Carter said, "I do hope that you're not superstitious? placing it on the desk. He continued, "Ainsworth, do you recognise this shoe?"

Ainsworth looked at Andrew Benson, his QC Benson, looked at Ainsworth, shaking his head from side to side, Ainsworth looking down said, "No comment"

Carter took hold of the shoe saying, "Ainsworth please take hold of the shoe, and have a good look at it." Ainsworth still looking down, and again turned to his QC, again Benson waved his head from side to side, and Ainsworth said, "No comment."

Before Carter was about to speak, Sue interrupted, "Ainsworth, you do realise that by not looking the interviewer in the eyes when being questioned, gives the impression that you are portraying issues of guilt?"

Again looking down he said, "No comment."

Carter put the shoe back in the evidence bag. He then produced a gents white shirt and handkerchief, marked DIB2. He had deliberately folded the shirt to hide all the blood stains.

Carter said, "Ainsworth, do you recognise this shirt, and handkerchief, you will notice that the shirt is hand made by 'Van Heusen' of 'Savile Row' London. You will also notice the monogram, MAA, sewn neatly on the top left hand chest pocket of the shirt.

Again looking down Ainsworth said, "No comment."

Carter placed the bag back on the floor, he then picked up another bag, marked DIB3. He said, "Ainsworth do you recognise the gent's two piece suit, made by Aquascutum of Savile Row, London. Ainsworth looked down and said, "No comment."

Carter took the bag off the table, he leaned down and picked up yet another evidence bag, he placed it on the desk in front of Ainsworth. Ainsworth looked down and saw a photograph inside of the plastic bag.

Carter said, "For the purposes of the tape, Deputy

Commander Carter, is now

Showing; the prisoner a photograph of a man's hand, marked DCC1, on the little finger, it showed a signet ring, with the initials CMP. Do you recognise this ring? have you ever seen this ring before?"

Ainsworth still looking down said, "No Comment."

Carter removed the evidence bag placing it down on the floor, he then picked up yet another bag marked DIB4, He deliberately dropped the bag and contents from about two inches, it hit the table top, the sound of the contact with the desk, suddenly made Ainsworth and his QC jump.

Carter said, "Ainsworth do you recognise this 9mm revolver?" Ainsworth looking down, his face suddenly drained of blood. He suddenly pushed the bag away and for the first time for several hours he suddenly shouted, "Why are you showing me this, I've told you I'm not a killer."

Carter suddenly said, "Well, I think this is an appropriate time for a break, I'm sure that both sides would enjoy a coffee, tea, and a sandwich?"

Ainsworth and his QC both nodded, saying "Yes please."

Sue leaned over, interview terminated, giving the time, day, and date. On completion she looked at Ainsworth, "You realise that you are still under caution, you will now be escorted to the Bridewell down stairs for some lunch."

Ainsworth just nodded, but his QC thanked her. Sue opened the door and the duty officer entered the office and escorted Ainsworth away.

Chapter One Hundred

Carter spent a quiet lunch in his office, for afterwards he was to see one of his young DC's called, Simon West he was one of the latest officers to gain a position on the team.

There was a knock on the door, he shouted, "Come in" The door opened and there stood a very smart officer. Carter said, "Simon please come in." They both shook hands, Carter said, "Simon please take a seat." He replied, "No guv I'm good."

Carter looked up at him, "How are you finding things? I realise that we do matters a bit different to division." Simon smiled, "Yes guv." He said to him, "Simon please take a seat, for you standing has command of the situation, and I feel that we should be speaking on level terms."

Simon pulled out one of the chairs to the left of the conference table and sat. Carter smiled, "Well how are you fitting in?" He replied, "Thanks guv, all is well."

Carter said, "Simon, a wise man once said, do not keep secrets from a man who makes a living selling human lie detectors. He immediately saw Simons shoulders sag, in fact his whole body began to slump.

Carter leaned over and picked up the phone, "Eric could I please have my usual." He looked at Simon, and raised up his chin, Simon smiled, "Coffee white with two sugars please guv." He said, "Eric did you hear that? "Yes guv came the reply they're on their way." Moments later their drinks arrived, he thanked the young secretary who looking at Simon, smiled on leaving.

He said, "Look Simon, I have a strict rule, for the conference room, and even stricter in here, what is said in either place, stays in that place. I make just one rule; I demand, and expect total loyalty, both to me, and your colleagues."

Simon shuffled in his chair, Carter said, "Let's have it son." Simon bowed his head, "Guv I'm a recovering alcoholic, I've been dry for four years, and once a week I need to attend my *AA* meetings, and I'm running out of ideas and excuses for getting off for an hour, I do put in the time, like the others, and if on an operation, I ring my *sponsor,* with my regrets."

Carter burst out laughing, "Oh Simon, is that all, I thought you had been caught with your fingers in the till." He stood up and standing in front of him said, "Stand up son." Simon did as he was told. Carter placed his arms about him saying, "I realise it can be difficult on our job, because of promotional do's, engagements, babies. And me when I demand to let our hair down etc?"

Carter explained that he had read a leaflet about recovering alcoholics, "I read a wonderful quote, *'Do not attend do's, family or work, known as a wet place, trying to prove to yourself that you can handle the temptation, because like barbers, you will eventually get a haircut.'"*

He said, "Simon, we have your back. I suggest at this evenings scrum down you tell the team, no big speeches, just stand and tell them all. You will have mine, and the teams respect, and help, and cover if needed."

He remained standing and as he left he said, "Thanks guv that's a big load off my mind." Carter said, "You do realise you will be pestered to be the official driver from now on." Simon laughed out loud as he walked off.

Chapter One Hundred and One

Carter and Sue both walked down the corridor towards the interview room. Sue looked at him, "Did you meet with DC West?" Carter replied, "Well prey madam, what's the reason for the formality? Yes I did talk with Simon, all is sorted."

On arrival at the interview room, the usual uniform officer smiled as he opened the door, they both thanked him. They both sat down opposite, Ainsworth, and his QC Mr Andrew Benson.

Whilst Sue was sorting out the tape, she looked at Carter, and after the usual machine bleep he said, "Ainsworth you realise that you are still under caution." He again just nodded.

He said, "Ainsworth have you ever heard of Binns Road off Edge Lane?" Ainsworth replied, "What on earth are you going on about?" Carter said, "Never mind, it may well crop up later."

Carter began, "Prior to our break, Ainsworth I showed you several items of property in their various evidence bags, when asked do you recognise the different pieces of evidence you replied, "No comment" to most of the assorted things until I produced the bag containing the 9mm pistol, to which you suddenly shouted, "I've told you I'm not a killer."

He continued, "I also produced a photograph of a man's hand with a signet ring on the little finger with the initials CMP engraved on it and yet again you replied, "No comment."

Carter sitting back in his chair said, "Well, Ainsworth I have to say that all the items of property except, that of the photograph of the ring, were found as a result of a search warrant served on your property, on the Wirral. So what do you have to say, please, please do not say "No comment?"

Ainsworth, jumped up banging the desk and shouted,

"You bastard Carter, you and your men planted them." With that the uniform officer opened the door saying, "Guv" Carter still sitting smiled up at him, "Yes Jack, it's just Ainsworth letting off a bit of steam." He closed the door.

Carter looking at both men, Ainsworth red faced and flustered, whilst, Andrew Benson, was trying to calm him down. "Well, has normal service resumed Carter said, or do you wish a bit of time to get your act together?"

Ainsworth's QC replied, "No we are fine."

He said, "So let's press on, I'll put your mind at rest Ainsworth, I, and my men do not plant evidence, for on so many occasions idiot criminals like your good self, leave them in such stupid places."

"Now in your case, officers found these items in, and around your house. Mainly in the dumpster at the rear of the property, in fact your wife, lovely Pauline, was amazed as she had thought you were giving them to charity."

"All accept the pistol of course, which was, found and recovered in your study." Carter sat back to await any form of comment, it didn't come. Ainsworth just stared aimlessly at him.

Carter looked back at him, "Ainsworth have you ever heard of a small town called Chorley?" Ainsworth shouted, "Of course I have." Carter said, "Do you know what is there?" As he said it, he noticed Andrew Benson's face fall.

"Well, that is where the, *North West Forensic Laboratory* can be found. Now do you know which way this conversation is going?" Both Carter and Sue looked at Ainsworth, whose face had such a stoic look to it.

Carter said, "Well, all the evidence collected from your home, as a result of the search warrant, were sent to the forensic laboratory. I have to say all the objects, have returned positive."

"When correlated; appear to prove convincingly, your two piece suit has particles of soil found in a warehouse, off Binns Road, which is off Edge Lane, now do you realise why I asked you if you knew this location? Your reply was, *"What are you going on about?"*

"The white shirt and handkerchief, that I showed you had traces of blood on both of them, blood that we recovered from a body of a man found in, The recreation park, off Acanthus Road."

"The man has been identified as: Colin Mitchell Proby, does that ring a bell? Remember the photograph of the hand that I showed you with the signet ring on the little finger, with the initials CMP?"

"Remember me showing you a pair of your shoes found during the search, they also have particles of soil, the same soil as in the warehouse' off Binns Road."

Carter looked at him, "Now for the 9mm pistol found in your study, we can match bullets fired from that weapon, with bullets recovered from nine victims, one of which was a police officer?"

He looked at Ainsworth, "You will now be escorted downstairs to the Bridewell, were DCS Ford will recite the charge of, being in possession of a stolen pistol, and ammunition, contrary to the theft act 1986 section?"

He continued, "Your QC will explain to you that this is just a *'holding charge'* you will appear on Monday morning, in The Liverpool City Magistrates Court, for a plea. We the police will ask that they refuse bail and that the court retains your passports, as you are a *'flight risk'*

When Sue had finished with the conclusion of the interview, switching off the tape he looked at Ainsworth who was crying. He said, "You are nothing but scum." He stood up and left.

He sat next to Eric in the general office, "These jobs just fly themselves." And they both burst out laughing. Whilst he enjoyed his coffee, Sue walked in she walked over to him bending over and kissed him on his cheek. As she left the office with her coffee, she said, "Eric they should use that interview by the guv, for the C.I.D training course?" and left.

Eric said, "Now why don't you get yourself home, no

one would dare to argue." Carter walked over to the daily diary, and signed off duty, as he did so he heard Eric calling Charlie.

On his way home Carter called TF, the call was answered by Jane, who went into some sexual fantasy. Carter said, "Jane you do realise that this call is on *speaker,* and Charlie is listening?" Jane in a low voice said, "Oh! Carter, two men at once, that is my ultimate fantasy." She burst out laughing.

As she did so a voice said, "Frost" Suddenly it was down to earth with a bang!!

Chapter One Hundred and Two

Carter said, "Afternoon sir, just thought I'd give you an update on the Ainsworth case?" He told him of the interview, and the fact he is up before the Magistrates court on Monday for a plea.

Frost said, "Well how do you think it will go?" Carter said, "Not guilty all over it, sir. I would like to ask if you could use your influence with the CPS, to get the legal people to assist in this matter, as it's an enormous case."

"We have about 8 to 10 defendants, and a humungous amount of statements, and evidence." "Okay Carter, leave it with me." And the phone went dead.

It was about 5.30pm when he eventually got home. He was met by Penny, who entered the hall on hearing his key in the door. Penny reached up to him landing a sumptuous kiss on his mouth.

Carter said, "Well now, I must try to get home early, more often." He stood back saying, "Now lookie here, you look rather gorgeous, and I can smell the aroma of your favourite perfume, Angel permeating the air, have you anything planned?"

"Yes, Carter go and take a quick shower, and change. I've laid out fresh clothes for you; I'm treating us both to a sumptuous meal, as it seems an absolute age since we last went out."

When ready, they both left their flat, acknowledging the APO officer, and the duty doorman, who opened the door; thanking him they entered the awaiting taxi. Penny said, "Smith's restaurant please, Hardman street."

Alighting from the taxi; they both entered the restaurant, the hostess approached them, taking Penny's coat. They were then showed to their awaiting table.

Carter said, "Penny you look beautiful. I realise that due to the pressure of work, I've paid little or scant attention to you, it's very remiss on me, and you try very hard to detect my mood when I come home. If all my officers had wives, or partners who tried as hard, I'd always have a well-balanced team."

He leaned over and kissed her on her cheek, he said, "Will you take that as a deposit, the balance will be paid in full, I assure you when we get home."

They both shared in a sumptuous meal, after which they settled the bill, and thanked their gracious hostess, and left to getting into their awaiting taxi.

On arrival home, they both entered the lounge Carter went into the kitchen, returning with a bottle of red wine, and two glasses, placing the bottle on their splendid ornate coffee table.

When both relaxed and settled on the settee, Carter opened the wine, pouring it into their two beautiful crystal cut wine goblets. They both made the most delicate of touches, for their goblets to ring out. Mutually saying, 'Cheers'

After two glasses of wine, Carter stood up taking Penny by her hand, and escorted her through to their bedroom standing her next to their bed. Carter lingered taking his time as he began to undress her. They made love, and as before as on so many occasions managed to amaze themselves with their level of passion and intensity.

The following morning was Saturday; they awoke as usual and went into the bathroom for one of their exhilarating, exotic type showers, all of which ended with great delight.

They both spent a leisurely breakfast, after which Carter turned to Penny, "I hope you don't mind, but I need to spend some time on the case, making sure all is ready for Monday?"

Penny stood up, and as she collected some of the breakfast dishes, and whilst she walked towards the kitchen, bent over kissing him on his head saying, "If that's the price one has to pay to get you home early, allowing us to have a splendid evening? So be it."

Carter got up and walked through to his makeshift study. He called Sue, apologising for disturbing her week-end. They spoke for half an hour, both going over any pit falls for the appearance of Ainsworth in the Mag's on Monday.

They both knew from all their vast amount of experience, that for the first appearance, all that was needed was a resume of the case. If his plea is *'guilty'* which they both thought was impossible, and then he will be remanded in custody for an appearance in the big house.

They both chatted, if *'not guilty'* the team will be inundated with evidential statements, recovered exhibits from all the warrants served. They would need to gain all the statement of collaboration from Pearson, Collins Jackson, and Clark.

He continued we will need to gather all of the forensic statements, and exhibits, in other words all of the bloody prosecution case. Carter said, "I contacted TF on the way home on Friday, I highlighted all the variables, asking if he could call on his influence for assistance from the CPS.

Carter ended by asking Sue for a full team scrum down on Monday for 8.30am as he felt that we all need to be aware of what is in front of us, that this matter could be bigger than the *'Davenport case'* At the time, we thought, that was a monster.

Chapter One Hundred and Three

Carter kissed Penny goodbye, and left for work. He got in the waiting car, with Charlie, and they then sped off.

The drive to work was spent in idle chit chat. On arrival at Derby Lane prior to getting out of the car, Carter invited Charlie, to the scrum down, he said, "Charlie please get involved there will be plenty for you to assist with."

They both entered the general office to sign on duty Carter, took the habitual mug of coffee from Eric. He sat next to him whilst they awaited the rush from the team.

Eric looked at Carter, "Why are you sitting here next to me whilst the team are already waiting for you in the conference room?" Carter looked at him in utter surprise. "What time did they come in?" Eric said, "Does it matter guv, they are here." Carter looked at him, "Well smart arse, come and join us."

All three of them walked into the conference room, and was met with the usual pushing and bumping of furniture, as they all stood to attention. Carter shouted, "As you were."

Charlie peeled off and went to the rear of the room, Eric went and sat at the top left of the room, close to where Sue was about to sit down. Carter walked to the front, and took station looking out on the team.

"Well how many of you will be going home to deaf and dumb meals to night, having to have got up, and left early enough for this date, unable to do the school run etc?" There was a raw of laughter, it settled and Carter looked out at them.

"DCS Ford and I are leaving for court this morning, depending on the result; we could all be met with a ball of shit. All officers who worked on the *'Davenport case'* who knew of the amount of work we put into it, well this could blister into one several times bigger."

"Now I know I don't need to say this, but DI's Lloyd and Baxter together with the SD's will formulate groups to deal with all the statements, and exhibits."

He looked at his watch he then looked at Sue, "It's time we left."

At that precise moment there was the shuffle of a chair, when they all looked round they saw that, DC Simon West had stood up. He looked at Carter and then at the team.

"Before we all get very busy, I'd just like to say that I'm a recovering alcoholic, he then quickly sat down. After a couple of seconds, an anonymous voice from the back of the room said, "Can we have you as our chauffeur?" The whole team burst out laughing, and whilst looking in Simon's direction, they all stood up and applauded?

Lloydie remained standing after the team had sat down, he said, "Right let's get to it." Carter and Sue both left for court.

Sue clutching her papers, and reports sat in the back of the car whilst en route to court. She leaned forward saying, "Well what do you think of that?" Carter replied, "I expected no less. It was true police gallows humour."

On arrival at court they were both met by Mr Simon Patterson, head of the CPS, with a throng of his staff. The main waiting area and corridors leading to the various courts were packed to the rafters.

At the same time Carter saw Wendy Field, the police press officer making her way through the heavy throng towards him. He said to her, "Well who let the cat out of the bag?" Wendy smiled, "Carter, please do not aim to tell me that an officer..." He interrupted her, "Yes, I know *the walls all have ears*." They both burst out laughing.

Carter heard a coughing noise, "DC Carter, are we ready?" Carter replied, "Mr Patterson, for all court procedures in this case, such as addressing the court about this matter should the Magistrates wish to be addressed by the officer in charge, please address WDCS Ford."

He could see Sue standing nearly pole axed. Carter raised his chin towards Simon Patterson. After regaining her composure Sue said, "Ready when you are sir."

They all walked over to court number 1, the

Stipendiary Magistrates court. On arrival the prosecuting Solicitor looked at Sue. "With a case of this magnitude, it will be put before the *'Stipe'* I may have to call you to the stand, so that you, the arresting officer, can tell, The Stipendiary magistrate, what had been suspected, and how you came to arrest Ainsworth?"

Chapter One Hundred and Four

The prosecutor stood up in the packed court. He handed the Magistrates Clerk a copy of the resume. After he had read it he said, "Right let's have the defendant brought into court." Ainsworth entered flanked by two prison officers.

The Clerk continued. "For the purposes of this initial hearing, you will formally be arraigned, and a note made of your reply. You will then be committed to The Crown Court for trial, or sentence."

The clerk then asked him his name and date of birth." He answered, "Sir Malcolm Arnold Ainsworth, 12.01.1964. He then read out the charges. He then said, "How do you plead, guilty, or not guilty?" He replied, "Not Guilty."

The prosecutor stood up. "Sir, I have the Senior Officer in charge of this case present in court, and should you wish, with your permission I would ask that she addressed the court?" The Magistrate nodded.

The prosecutor stood up and looking at Sue, said, "Officer." Sue stood, and walked over to the witness box, took the oath, and very succinctly addressed both the Magistrate and the court, giving a full resume and background of the events leading to the arrest of the defendant, after which there was total silence.

The prosecutor stood up, "Your Worship, due to the severity of this case, I ask that the defendant, who is a known flight risk, should surrender his passport, and that he be remanded in custody, to enable further enquiries to be made."

The Magistrate said looking at Ainsworth, "You will be remanded in custody until a suitable date is made for your attendance at, The Crown Court, take him away."

Whilst travelling back to Derby Lane, Charlie was at the wheel. Carter handed Sue his phone. "Sue why don't you ring TF and tell him what happened. By the way, you have all the making of a great guv." Sue blushed as she dialled the number. Carter said, "Sue, put it on speaker."

Sue heard a voice, *"Is that the sexiest boss in all of the force? By the way my husband is out of town to- night, if you come over I'll endeavour to make the earth move for you."* Sue said, "Jane sorry to disappoint, but it's DCS Susan Ford." Jane said, *"Op's shit, sorry I thought it was...*Sue interrupted, "Yes I know Jane, but he is rather busy…"

All three burst out laughing, Charlie gave Carter a sly look, as Sue said, "Jane, could you please put me through to the boss?" A quiet voice said, *"Just putting you through."*

A gruff voice said, *"Frost"* Sue explained, the whole of the events from the court hearing, explaining that Ainsworth, had pleaded not guilty, and that she and the guv are returning to Derby Lane, to start the evidential process.

Sue ended by saying that Ainsworth is to be remanded in custody, passport withheld as he is a known flight risk. Tony Frost replied, *"Keep me informed Ford,* and closed the call.

Chapter One Hundred and Five

On arrival back at Derby Lane they all got out of the car making their way up to the General office. They all signed, *'back from court,'* in the duty book. Carter went and sat next to Eric, who organised coffee's all round.

On completion Carter left for his office leaving Sue to bring Eric up to date with the court details.

In his office the first thing Carter did was to call Penny. "Hi Penny, all went well, he pleaded, 'not guilty', the mad fool, he must think he can squirm from under all of this. The court has confiscated his passport."

"Well our love making last night seems to have had no effect on your performance in work, Penny asked." "Well Penny, experience and dedicated officers take such matters in their stride." They both burst out laughing.

"Well, Carter will that mean you may be home early again tonight, Penny said, in a low sexy voice?"

Carter said, "Now, now madam, 'Give someone an inch and they'll take a country mile.' Getting back to business, I'm sorry but it could be a long one."

"Carter, please don't worry for I'll be here waiting patiently, whatever the time. Love you always," Penny closed the call."

After the call he smiled and left for the conference room, he entered saying, "How you were." He walked over and stood next to Sue, who had been busily writing names on the large white board.

He stood back and looked at Sue. "Well, guv, on this board we have prepared a list of the runners and riders, the defendants who we can call upon to help with the prosecution, should Ainsworth stick to his guilty plea."

"Lloydie is busily writing down the list of exhibits, and the names of the SOCO officers, together with evidence from Mr Chambers, all of whom will prepare statements of evidence again to assist with the prosecution.

Sue continued, "Baxie..." Carter interrupted, "Who, the

hell is 'Baxie'?" Sue and all the team burst out laughing, "Well guv we needed a name for DI Baxter, while we're all together here is this room, when matters are far less formal?" He smiled, "I wonder what they call us?"

Sue said, "That's simple..." "I'm called, Boss, and you're called Guv." Carter said, "What! What about when we're not here, I do believe they will have names, but let's leave it at that." The team let out a collective sigh.

Baxie, who gave the impression that he, was showing no interest, suddenly burst out laughing, as he continued to write down all the remaining miscellaneous subject matters.

Carter looked at Sue, "Could you arrange a prison visit, I wish to speak with Ainsworth there are a few matters that I'd like to put to rest." He then turned and as he left he said, "I'm off home, see you all tomorrow." There was a chorus of, "Bye guv."

He got into his car and drove off for home. Whilst driving he started to make mental notes of important topics, knowing that he was going to see, Arnold.

Carter had done this on many occasions it was his way of relaxing. If one had a blank piece of paper what would you mentally record?

He began listing the names of all the defendants who had asked for deals, and who were prepared to give evidence against him. He continued with the science evidence from SOCO, and Mr Gordon Chambers.

On arrival home, if asked what he had seen, and his idea of the volume of traffic, a guilty mist seemed to descend over him, for his mind had been truly elsewhere.

He parked up, and as he was about to leave his car, his mobile phone went off. He opened it and saw it was Charlie, he suddenly realised that whilst being totally so singly minded, had realised that he had driven home without his faithful APO, Charlie.

Before Charlie could say anything Carter said, "Charlie I'm so, I've driven home on automatic pilot, in fact I didn't realise that I'm in my own car. I haven't driven in ages." He heard a sigh from Charlie, "I'll pick you up in the morning, good night guv."

Carter felt terrible, as it would be Charlies head on the block, should have anything transpired.

He entered their flat and immediately Penny said, "Carter what on earth has happened you look as if you've seen a ghost?"

Carter related the circumstances if the situation to Penny who immediately hugged him saying, "Carter!"

Chapter One Hundred and Six

The following morning Carter met Charlie, who was stood leaning against his car. They both got in and Charlie drove off. He looked at Charlie saying, "I'm sorry it was bloody stupid of me, but I just didn't think."

Charlie looked at Carter, "One doesn't get to your rank without thinking? Your mind is constantly thinking..." Carter looked at him saying "Charlie, I've said I'm sorry, can we just drop it?" Charlie said, "TF knows." Carter shouted, "For fuck sake who told him?" Charlie smiled, "Gotcha." And burst out laughing.

Carter said, "Yes, yes very funny." He burst out laughing himself, for he knew how much he had upset Charlie, by his stupid actions. Carter thought best to let it go, whilst his thoughts turned to their prison visit.

Charlie looked at him, "Guv we are picking up Sue, and then heading on to 'Risley remand centre' to see, Ainsworth." Carter rang Eric, after their usual pleasantries, he asked Eric to ask Sue to bring a pad, with the file.

Whilst travelling to Risley, Carter made a list to assist with his interview of the prisoner. At the prison gatehouse, they all produced their ID's and Sue produced the visitors pass's for all three.

Ainsworth was produced and brought to the visitor's area. Whilst all three sat at a table, they all noticed that Ainsworth, was dressed in the usual prisoner's uniform.

Carter looked up at him, "I see it's not your usual Armani two piece, but it will do." The guard sat him down; he looked up at the guard, "Would it be possible to remove the cuffs? The officer was about to say something when Carter said, "Please."

Whilst still standing, Ainsworth looked at Carter with an expression of utter distaste. Carter looked up at him, "Malcolm, before you drill into me with those eyes of yours, please be reminded that you are still under caution, and it's your fault alone for the reason that you are in here." Pointing, he gestured for him to sit on the other side of the table.

Sue produced a tape recorder and placed two fresh tapes into it, she then stated the names of all present, with the time day and date.

Carter commenced the interview, looking at Ainsworth, he said, "Every man is born as many men…But dies as one!! Ainsworth you are dead in the water, why the *'not guilty plea'* you must realise that we have a heap of evidence, from your so called colleagues, and SOCO evidence."

Ainsworth stared at Carter with a glare in his eyes saying, "Deputy Commander Carter that is your title? My reasons for being here are temporary I assure you, my 'not guilty' plea arises from me being black mailed."

Carter looked at Sue, knowing full well that the look of utter shock on her face must have mirrored his.

Carter leaned back in his chair with the fingers of his hands clasped behind his head. He stated, "Well Ainsworth, we are all ears,"

Ainsworth looked at him you people have no idea of matters of such high finance?" Carter smiled, "Well please explain, as your idea seems to have landed you in this situation that you find yourself in."

Unperturbed Ainsworth began to explain his business model, setting out all of his retail department stores, his merchandising methods, and the amount of staff employed.

Carter looked at him, "Was it not that very staff pension account that you raided in an effort to remain out of debt, in the support of your lavish lifestyle?"

Ainsworth replied, "It was the sudden downward fall in my sales, and I needed a cash infusion for which the banks, and other financial institutes refused to bail me out."

Continuing he said, "It was one night that I was out having drinks with friends, when I was approached by a man who mentioned that he knew about my problems. He suggested that we set up a meeting."

Ainsworth stated, "I do not wish to go into great detail, save to say that I was given a substantial loan, but again due to business problems I was unable to make the re-payments as per the condition of the loan."

"I was collected one night, or should I say abducted whilst I was leaving my office. I was bungled into the back of a car and taken to a lock-up. It was there that it was put to me that should I renege on the loan, my wife, children would not be out of reach."

"The man speaking was in the dark, so please do not ask me if I could identify him. He also spoke by using a speech synthesizer?"

Carter said, "Well what did he say?" Ainsworth said, "He knew of my association with Clark the surgeon, who knew Thompson. It was put to me that my way out could be to suggest to Clark, organ removals."

Ainsworth continued, "He mentioned there was a black market demand, as waiting on the NHS is fraught due to the list of patients needing transplants, and the poor response of willing donors. He stated transplanting and sales, with monies received would help to pay off his debt."

Chapter One Hundred and Seven

On completion of their interview Ainsworth was removed back to the custody area of the prison, and the main population.

On their return to Derby Lane, Carter looked at Sue, "Well what do you make of that?" Sue looked at him "Well guv, I think we put him up in front of a jury, and back it up with all our witnesses, and exhibits, and see how it goes."

"Or we have a meeting with Ainsworth, and his Barrister informing them both of what we have, hoping that he may change his plea."

Carter with a serious look on his face said, "There is a third option, we put Ainsworth up before a Magistrate, remove the remand in custody on the grounds of personal problems with his family, still retaining his passport."

Sue said forgetting his rank and title, Christ Carter, what on earth are you up to?" Even Charlie, looked over at him with a surprised look on his face. Carter said, "When we arrive at Derby Lane, I want the three of us to go up to my office, we can hit the book later, just remember the time of our return."

On arrival, Eric was aware of their return, but with them going straight into Carters office he realised there may be a problem, but decided to sit tight.

Sat in his office Carter looked at them both, "Please let me pass something by you. The third option…What if we devise a plan that when Ainsworth is released, we have him under round the clock surveillance, hoping that it entices this man and his team out in the open."

We put phone taps on all his phones both mobile, and landline. Under the surveillance we include; his wife, and children. I want a team in his grounds dressed in snipers Ghillie camouflage suits" Carter sat back with his hands behind his head, waiting their overwhelming verbal assault on him.

Both Sue and Charlie looked flabbergasted, after a couple of seconds Sue said, I suppose TF knows nothing about all of this?" Carter smiled, "It only developed in my head on our way back to the nick."

He said, "I know it's out there." As he spoke he spread his arms open, signifying how he intends to give credence to his plan. He said, "I know we are pushing the envelope to breaking point."

"Now Sue I want you to get hold of, Ian and Lloydie, this is hush hush, the four of you are to work on a feasibility study, use team members only please use bullet point headings. I wish you to put the amount of personnel next to a heading, but only numbers circled in red."

"Sue this matter in the planning stage is to be held in your office only, I'll give you a week, and we need our heads around this before Ainsworth is next in court."

"Now let's go and sign back in at the time we returned, I hope no one has signed out whilst we have been chatting, and coffee's all round, what?"

On entering the general office Carter asked Eric if one of his young secretaries could oblige?" Charlie and Sue took their coffees with them when they left for Sue's office.

Carter sat next to Eric and whilst he drank his coffee he asked, "Eric could you ask one of your young ladies to contact Tony Frost office and see if he could squeeze an appointment this afternoon." He stood up and took his coffee with him through to his office.

He sat and called Penny. *"Hi Carter what a lovely surprise, how are things?"* "Well I think I'm about to let the fox out into the hen house!" Penny said, *"What on earth have you done now?"* Carter gave her a brief resume of his plan.

Penny said, *"Carter! Have you gone completely mad, I do hope you have a plan for your career after the police?"* She laughed out loud. *"Only you Carter could come up with such an idea."* Carter heard a loud laugh down the phone, as it went dead.

There was a knock on his office door, he shouted, "Come in" The door opened, and he saw Eric standing there. He said, "How about 2.30pm, Carter looked at him, knowing he couldn't ever fool him." He said, "Can I tell you all about it later?" He smiled, "When you are ready boss. Charlie will be waiting downstairs."

Chapter One Hundred and Eight

Carter stepped out of the lift, followed by Charlie, only to be greeted by Jane, Tony Frost's secretary. Carter knew that he'd have to withstand her sexual rants. "Hello Carter, what a pity you're not alone, you could whisper sweet nothings in my ear." Jane burst out laughing.

The next thing they heard was the intercom, and Tony Frost's growl, "Put him down Jane." Jane looked at Carter, "Why is it that I have so little time…?"

Carter leaving Charlie with Jane walked into Tony Frost's office. TF said, "Sit, and tell me what you want." Carter could feel a blush covering his face. Carter told him about their visit to seeing Ainsworth, but not all. He said, "As you know boss, Ainsworth is pleading 'not guilty' what I'd like is your permission to invite Ainsworth, and his QC into Derby Lane,

Tony Frost said, "Why on earth would you want do that?" Carter replied, "To lay out the prosecution's intention in bullet point form, hoping that it may sway him to change his plea."

Frost said, "Carter I'm no fool, what is behind all of this? You know we never show our hand to the defence. Knowing you, could there be a *'but'*?" Carter looked him straight in the eyes, boss it will take a week to set up Ainsworth's visit, if all fails I have a backup plan? The plan will be on paper, and presented to you for a decision."

Frost sat back in his chair, with his hands behind his head he laughed saying, "Carter, I love you son, it's a joy being your boss, all on the top floor love receiving notice of a potential operation, can you not lay out your intentions?"

Carter looked at his boss, "The road to hell is paved with good intentions…Please give me my head over this, as it's only hypothetical at this stage." Frost burst out laughing, "Carter I know it all starts like little acorns, which grow into bloody gigantic trees. Go Carter, I'll leave you to organise the plan, plans cost nothing."

He left his office with the sweat rolling down his back, only to be met by Jane. He walked over to her and kissed her, she fell back in her chair.

Carter thought, *'could that be the way to shut her up'* as he entered the lift he heard, "Carter get back here you coward…" It was followed by a burst of laughter. Charlie looked at him, "You do realise she is gorgeous?" Carter replied, "Charlie she is TF's secretary, you should never shit on your own door step."

Back at Derby Lane, they both signed back in, Carter said, Charlie will you go and find Sue, for you both to come to my office." In his office prior to Sue's arrival he rang Eric. Eric answered, "Boss." "Could I trouble you to come to my flat after work?" "I need to have a chat." The line went dead.

He had no sooner replaced the receiver when there was a knock at his door, He shouted, "Come in" He looked up to see both Sue and Charlie. He said, "Please sit."

Carter succinctly laid out his conversation with TF, they both realised that Carter was determined to deal with this most revolting case in any way possible. He looked at both of them. "As you both know it's Friday, the start of the week-end. Let us take this matter up on Monday?"

He looked at Sue, "Sue will you get Ian or Lloydie, to deal with the production of Ainsworth and his QC. It must be kept in the family, I'll deal with the interview, with either Ian or Lloydie, and it will leave you and Charlie, to make a start on the plan."

Sue looked at Carter with a panic look in her eyes. He looked at Charlie, "Can I ask you to give us five minutes?" He replied, "Yes guv of course."

After he left, Carter looked at Sue. "I realise I've given you a near impossible project, but please realise that it's because I have total faith in you. And when you take over from me, it may well be a recurring issue, and you will need to make such decisions. *'Never no innocents again'* I only hope you'll have a second in command as competent, as I have in you."

They both stood up and without warning Sue walked over to Carter, and kissed him on the cheek saying, "Thanks Carter." He said, "My, my, Miss Ford, and they both burst out laughing.

Chapter One Hundred and Nine

Charlie dropped Carter off at about 6.30pm; he entered their flat and received a very warm welcome from Penny. He stood back and looking at Penny he said, "I hope you don't mind but I've invited Eric, round for a chat."

She looked at him, "Why Carter that's fine. Do you wish me to make myself scarce?" Carter burst out laughing, "No Penny, but I need to speak to him on a confidential matter." She said, "Carter, I've brought work home with me, so I can disappear into the study for a couple of hours? Do you want me to make extra for tea?" Carter said, "Well we can offer."

Eric phoned Carter, "How about 7.30pm?" Carter said, "Will you call for tea?" Eric declined, "I'll have eaten thanks."

At 7.30pm on the dot the intercom buzzed, Carter said, "Is that you Eric? He said, "Yes." "Then pull the door." Seconds later the bell to the flat rang out. Carter opened the door. He smiled, "Hello boss come in,"

Penny greeted him, and then subtly left for the study, Eric looked after as she left. "Carter how important is this?" Carter put a discreet arm on his back, and steered him into the lounge.

They both sat down, Carter offered a coffee, and he replied, "No thanks." Carter said, "Well" and then started to explain the situation, both aspects of it, after half an hour, Eric sat back with a look of utter shock on his face.

Carter said, "Eric you know you are a trusted friend and ex-boss who I respect more than anyone else, and I feel so concerned that I didn't invite you in on this project from the beginning."

Eric looked at him smiling, "Carter, you policeman, me civilian. We both know there is a line that I as an ex policeman cannot cross, and I'm no longer privy to your inner sanctum, yet at times you include me in a consultative post when required, for that I'm truly grateful."

Carter looked at Eric, "Well what do you think?" He looked at his prodigy. I see you have two courses of action. One, the one which involves Ainsworth and his brief, you can try bull shitting, laying it on with a trowel, informing them that you have more than enough to put him away for life, and more."

The second, I feel will take an inordinate amount of both man power and specialist IT personnel, and equipment. Do you not feel that Ainsworth is clutching at straws? Imagine the supposed perpetrators mentioned by Ainsworth are real, and not a figment of his imagination? Are you thinking he may use it to sway a Judge, or jury. He must be aware of all the prosecution evidence amassed by you, and the team. He will fail?"

Both men shook hands as Eric left. He looked at Carter, "You will find an answer, but please do not put yourself up as a target."

Over the course of the week-end, although Carter tried to give the impression that he was relaxed, Penny knew his mind was elsewhere.

On the Monday morning, Carter was usually positive whilst leaving for the office, but Penny got the decided impression that he was in no rush to leave.

Looking at him, she said, "Carter what on earth is the matter, you normally leave out of here on the rush, you seem loathed to leave? I feel somewhat guilty, as if I'm forcing you out, but Charlie is waiting."

Carter took a deep breath, "Sod it what's the worst they can do, sack me?" With concern on her face Penny said, "Carter what on earths the matter?" He gave her the abridged version, he explained the position he was placing Sue in, and what if he messed things up."

Penny gently walked over to him and placing a hand on either side of his face, looked him straight in the eyes. "Carter I have always thought a problem shared is a problem halved; your team of which the total is equal to all it's parts."

In the past they have proven on many occasions to act as one, you have placed more than once, your total faith in them. Now go, and sort it all out."

Chapter One Hundred and Ten

Carter gave Penny a kiss goodbye and headed for the office. Outside he found Charlie leaning, arms folded against his car. He said, "Guv I thought you weren't coming in to work?" Carter said, "Just needed to sort something out?"

Whilst they were travelling to Derby Lane, Carter telephoned Eric, "Could you ask Sue to see me in my office?" On completion of the call he turned to Charlie, and that means you as well." The rest of the journey was spent in silence.

After Carter had signed on duty he smiled at Eric, took his prepared coffee, and left for his office, followed by Charlie.

In his office he looked at them both sat on either side of his meeting table. "I apologise for my action on Friday, I sudden have put the pressure on you both, together with perhaps, Ian and Jim. The possible logistics in the preparation of the imaginary plan is something that as a team, we must deal with it all together."

"Can we have a full scrum down in the conference room, ASAP?" Sue smiling said, "Leave it with me guv, I'll let you know when all gathered."

They both left his office leaving Carter with *'The black dog'* lying at his feet; he was deep in thought when there was a sudden knock on his door. He shouted, 'come in' Sue stood in the door way smiling, "All present and correct guv."

He stood up, "Right let's get at it." They both walked in silence to the conference room, as he opened the door he shouted, "As you were." He entered the room and took up his place at the front of the team.

He coughed and said, "On Friday morning, DCS Ford, and myself went to see Ainsworth, in Risley. It was my intention to try and per sway Ainsworth, to change his plea from not guilty to guilty. It was then that Ainsworth mentioned that he was being black mailed."

He laid out such a preposterous storey, that it almost seemed credible. Now me for my sins wanted to keep it between my senior officers. Over the week-end I had a chat with two very close friends, the information given to them came back with the same answer, *'Go to your team for help in the matter'*"

"I'm ashamed to say that I wanted to preclude you because of the recoil if it all back fired, trying to protect you from all the shit it may put on your files. I'm an officer at the near end of my career…" He was interrupted.

A voice from the back of the room shouted, "How dare you guv." Another voice shouted, "When do we start?" Carter stated, "You all realise that if this all goes belly up, our only employment will be selling deckchairs on the Titanic."

A female voice shouted form the back of the room, "I bags to being held by Leonardo DiCaprio, an uproar rebounded around the room, he looked to his left to see Sue, Charlie, Ian and Jim, crying with laughter, he'd never felt so more proud of his team. He just sat back laughing.

After it all calmed down he said, "Right, I want DI Baxter, to contact Andrew Benson QC via his chambers, and explain that we wish to hold an interview with his client, Ainsworth, at Derby Lane."

He continued, "Coordinating with Benson QC will allow us set a suitable date to produce Ainsworth."

Carter looked out on the team, "I would like to know if anyone knows the name of a good IT expert? I realise that if I picked up the phone and rang the force IT department, they would send me an IT geek. What I need is an expert with police experience, who can keep his mouth shut."

Carter left and went to the general office, he sat next to Eric. Over a cup of coffee, he said, "Well, I've set the wheels in motion."

Chapter One Hundred and Eleven

Over the next couple of days whilst it would seem that all the stars were beginning to align, Carter sent for Sue, when in his office he told her to take a seat. Looking at her he said, "Should Ainsworth, and his brief fail to be bowled over with all the prosecution evidence, then we'll have to go to plan 'B'

"That being possible, we'll have to appeal to Benson, his QC suggesting that if his client wishes to play the black mail card, then we'll need proof of all calls received on either his mobile, or land line phones, presumable before he was locked up. I want the IT geek to trace all calls prior to him going into Risley on remand."

He continued, "I want a warrant to place a tap upon his land line, and mobile phones. I would think a man like hive will have at least several mobile phones, I want it as tight as a drum."

"Lastly, I want to talk with Andrew Benson QC alone, to explain it would be in his clients best interest that I go to the CPS, suggesting that we produce Ainsworth back before the court to lift off the 'no bale' restrictions, on the grounds of immense domestic and personal matters.

The meeting was arranged; Sue and Carter met with Ainsworth, and his QC. Carter looked at Ainsworth stating that he was still under caution. Sue put the two new tapes into the machine and when the machines buzzed she recorded the time day and date, and all who were present.

Before Carter had time to say anything, Andrew Benson said, "Assistant Commander Carter my client has something to say to you. He looked at Ainsworth and nodded. Carter looked at Sue, and Sue saw a look of scepticism on his face.

Ainsworth let out a low cough, and taking in a sharp breath began. "You are both hoping that if you paraded out all the relevant evidence in relation to the case, I'd fold, changing my plea, on talking with my legal representative,

I see a no win situation in all of this, it's not as if I'll get a reduced sentence for the change of plea, so right I agree, will change the plea to guilty, so let's move on."

He shuffled in his chair and staring intently at both Carter, and Sue he began, "The black mail is very relevant, these bastards know that they are willing to attack my home, and my family in an effort to regain some, if not all the monies owed."

"They must believe that I know if I don't pay up, then they will endeavour to pass on all the appropriate information that they think they have on me, of course to you the police."

Carter looked over at the two men, "Okay then, what we need is for you, Ainsworth to be produced in court, in order to ask the Magistrates; that due to the severity of your domestic and personal problems, which will be well documented in all the press, we hope that the villains knowing you've been given say 4 days to sort matters out, it will be over that time frame that they will make their move."

Carter returned from court, Ainsworth, who had been kept at Derby Lane, was produced back into the interview room with his brief. Together with Sue who had turned on the tape. "You've been given 4 day to sort things out."

With a stoic look on his face Carter said, "This had better not be a ploy for you to instigate a run away, we have your passport, although men like you may have several others…" Ainsworth interrupted, "Carter, I want this sorted, if this all gets fucked up, it is my family at risk." He fell back in silence.

Carter looked at him saying, "Wendy Field, the Merseyside police press officer, with obvious intent slipped a copy of the bail application resume to all the relevant news hounds, especially the crime reporter for the Liverpool Echo. The matter had also drawn the attention of the local BBC and ITV, evening news teams, so we can expect full coverage. It will be nigh impossible to miss the information."

Chapter One Hundred and Twelve

It was slowly heading towards the third day of Ainsworth's compassionate bail restriction. Carter was walking around the general office like a caged lion. Eric knew better than to interrupt him, but knew the only possible ploy was the coffee suggestion.

Eric looked up from his work he eyed up Carter, and decided to take the bull by the horns. "Enough guv let's have a cup of coffee." Carter looked at him and decided to plonk himself down next to Eric. One of the young secretaries duly obliged and presented two coffees.

He looked at Eric, "You must realise what is riding on all of this, and I must have in excess of 30 officers or more from some of the most elite specialised departments, sat twiddling their thumbs waiting for these bastards to break cover. What on earth will I do if it goes tit's up?"

Eric looked at his young staff, "Will you please give us five minutes, and the young secretaries duly obliged. Eric looked at Carter with a look that in the past had been known to bring some of the hardest villains to book.

"Carter, since you lost Helen and the children you seem to have lost your nerve. When placed in a situation like this, it could be the psychological effect that has had a mental and emotional state on you mind and thinking."

"Carter in matters such as this none of us can be sure, it would seem that you, or we are all running from, or to something at times in our lives no matter your speed, but the truth Carter always seems to run that bit faster." Carter looked at Eric, and with a smile on his face said, "Well thank you Dr Spock."

"Now look here Carter, as you know we go far back, and it's you that I have to thank for giving me the opportunity to work as part of this specialist team."

"We must have worked on the taking down of some of the biggest teams of criminals known to the force, since the formation of the MCU, and you have taken risks in order of catching the perpetrators, so why don't you park your arse and enjoy your coffee, it will all work out fine."

Eric had no sooner stopped speaking, when the phone on his desk rang out. He lent forward and picked up the headset, and in a calm voice said, "MCU Eric Morton speaking." With a smile on his face he said, "Will do sir." He replaced the handset and with a casual effect he said, "Guv Will you please call the duty Inspector in the control room."

Carter ran through to his office, he picked up his phone and dialled the number he took a deep breath, "DC Carter can I speak to the duty Inspector?"

"Sir, we have just received a call from DCS Ford, can you call her at your earliest?" Carter replied, "Yes will do, and thank you."

Carter then called Sue, she replied immediately, *"Guv the bastards have called, they seem to have left it to the last minute, realising that Ainsworth is being returned to Risley in the morning."*

"Their message we recorded, was very succinct. 'I want £500 grand in various denominations, and sequential numbers, no tracking devices, or colour dyes which explodes when opening the bags, if we find any such devices then after your return to Risley, we'll attack your property and family, and I assure you we will carry out the threat.'

The message continued, 'You Ainsworth, and I mean you alone, will drive over to Liverpool, take the new tunnel, head for Queens Drive heading south, at the large round about in Allerton, turn left along Menlove Avenue, then along Hillfoot Road, turning left at ASDA; continue along Hillfoot Road, follow the signs for the M53 prior to the motor way you will see a RSPCA centre, opposite is a HGV lorry park, for drivers who have reached their driving limit, drive in and we'll be watching you, you must be there no later than 5.30pm'

Carter looked at his watch it was 11.30am he said, "Sue, I want you back over here, leave APO's with

347

Ainsworth, and his family, all undercover officers to remain in the grounds of the property. See you soon." And he closed the call.

He left his office and walked through into the general office with a deliberate difference to his gait. He stopped in the middle of the room, he looked at Eric, "Can you please try and get me a large blow up shot of the Higher Road, and Bailey's Lane, Halewood. I need it to show the RSPCA site, and the lay-bye opposite, where HGV drivers park up when their driving time is up."

He invited Sue, to sit, and began to explain his plan. "We have up to 5.30pm, as you know the villains want their cash, so we need to get our fingers out and get started with a possible plan.

Chapter One Hundred and Thirteen

Carter had called a full team meeting for 1.00pm in the conference room. He walked in the room followed by Sue. There was the usual shuffle of chairs to which Carter said, "As you were."

He looked out over the faces of his team; he could see that they were more than ready for action. He said, "I do hope you've all got pens and paper, for like the TV programme, 'Hello' Allo! Because I'll say this only once." There was a raw of laughter, quickly followed by a controlled silence.

He turned and walked over to the blown up picture showing the area of Halewood were the villains have suggested that the drop should be made. He said, "You will all notice that the potential lay-bye being the suggested location for the drop off point for the money is on the inwards bound A562."

"For the villains to have any access to the motor way system, technically they'll have to drive up to the round a bout at the junction of Higher Road, Bailey's Lane this will give access to the outbound A562 which will give a clear run at the A5300 which of course connects with the M62 East bound, and away."

On the other side of the City there were a similar logistics meeting taking place, they were clearly the group who stood most to gain should their operation be a success.

On arrival at a private office off White Chapel, the five men arrived to be met by a sixth man who was already waiting. They entered the well-appointed office on the vacant floor to find a large table situated in the middle of the room, with six chairs around it.

He said please sit, "I've picked you five, Kenny Gary, Mike, Jack and Eddie, your all top draw operatives, willing to take a risk. You all know each other and must realise that if caught we're looking at 18yrs plus in the nick."

So I want you all at your best, the police aren't stupid, they will have all sorts of monitoring equipment, which I intend to block."

"On a more important matter, you will all receive £81.000, my share will be £91.000 as I have had to lay out £10.000 for sundries, now if you all agree then let's get on with it. Does anyone have a problem with that? There was a total silence."

"Right, Kenny and Gary, you'll both operate the two HGV's I'm providing, I know you are both qualified drivers?" They both grunted and nodded. "Micky you will deal with comm's, for that is your field. Finally, Jack and Eddie, you will both cause havoc, setting off flash bang devices, and smoke bombs in the area of operation." They both smiled.

"I've purchased a jamming device to cover a radius of up to 1 mile. This will have an adverse effect on the police radio network that will also include the police helicopter. That's you Mickie. I've purchased some smoke bombs, and thunder flashes. That's you two Jack, and Eddie." As he was speaking he walked over to a large plan on the wall. They could see that he had drawn a circle with the help of a protractor.

He pointed to the plan. "All police vehicles operating in this area will find their communications will be useless. "My plan is to block off Higher Road, one of the HGV's will be parked up in Old Hutte Lane, when Ainsworth goes past the first HGV will block the road, I don't care if you cause carnage, you just drive out. The second will be waiting in Bailey's Lane, by the round a bout, when the first HGV moves into place, the second after Ainsworth's vehicle has passed, will shoot out blocking off Baily's Lane."

"Now Ainsworth will be driving a black 4x4 with a personalised plate A1, if he keeps to time he will be driving past at about 5.28pm this evening. Now it's a cert that he will be followed by a plain cloths police vehicle or vehicles."

"Both HGV drivers prior to leaving for the car park, make sure you put on your supplied breathing masks, smash the window with a tyre leaver, and throw in a thunder flash, and smoke bomb, in a such vehicles, this will cause complete disorientation."

"You will then jump in Ainsworth's car and tell him were to drive to. One will stay with Ainsworth, putting plastic tie wraps on his wrists and ankles. All others will assist in the setting off of the devices, me included to create the biggest distraction going, I want the loudest nose, and the place filled with smoke."

"In case the police have personnel hidden in the scrub by the railway line, or behind the hedge by the dog's home, sling some of the flask bangs in that direction, and of course the smoke bombs."

"I feel that with all the commotion going on, it will only be natural for any police mobiles, covering our escape route for the motorway to drive over to lend assistance. Under the enormous cloud of smoke we will make good our escape. It is important no screeching of wheels, as the tyre skid marks can be traced."

"Prior to our getaway we must decide what to do with Ainsworth, as long as we wear our gloves, overalls, balaclavas, and sunglasses he will have no chance of identifying us, we of course could leave him with a nasty bump on his head."

Kenny said, "I realise if we kill him he can say nothing, and if caught it's, '*life*,' but look what the bastard organised, it was only for the money. He hoped he could carry on supporting his wealthy lifestyle."

"I say knock the bastard out, I'd far rather be arrested for '*Conspiracy to commit aggravated assault, than murder,*'"

Voices broke out in agreement, and Mr Blue said, "So it's agreed we knock him out and push him out of the car whilst we make good our escape."

Chapter One Hundred and Fourteen

Carter and Sue had decided that after running through the plan of action, in dealing with the extortionists, and their instructions. Whilst they both sat in Carters office, she had noticed that he was repeatedly checking his watch.

Sue said, "Guv you've left it all in good hands…" When there was a sudden knock on his door. He shouted, "Come in." His office door was opened and they both saw Eric, filling the door frame, with a sheer look of total panic to his face.

Carter shouted, "What, what on earth is the matter?" Eric walked into his office, "Guv, the wheel has truly fallen off, and I've just received a call from the duty Inspector of the force control room, the 999 emergency systems is in meltdown."

With a sudden pale look to his face Carter said, "What on earths the matter?" Eric said, "Calls are coming in from civilians in the area of Higher Road, and Bailey's Drive, Halewood. It would seem that two HGV vehicles have suddenly collided, blocking off the two roads."

"The two drivers, all dressed in black overalls, balaclavas, and what seemed like breathing apparatus and face protectors, jumped from their cabs, and running to a following vehicle '*one of ours*,' smashed the window, and threw into the vehicle devices that seemed to explode, with a very loud bang, together with a second device, that when exploded it caused an immense amount of smoke."

Carter shouted, "Are we just getting to fucking know about this now?" Eric in a low voice said, "It would seem that all our com's are down, even 'India 99' call sign (Force helicopter) is grounded." Carter shouted, "That means we are blind, how the hell are we meant to follow these bastards?"

He stood up and walking to his office door shouted, "Charlie" he must have recognised the inference in Carters voice, because he came on the run. He then looked at Sue,

"You should be armed." As he spoke he took out his firearm from a safe in his office, and began to slip the shoulder holster and firearm on.

Eventually all three began to run down to the police yard below. Charlie jumped behind the staring wheel, whilst Carter, entered the front passenger seat, and Sue sat in the back.

Charlie pressed the horns, and the blues and two's, whilst at a devastating speed, the vehicle left for Halewood. As they screamed around a left hand bend close to a service station, all three quickly saw the devastation of all the smoke, with both Peter and Philip sat on the pavement trying to catch their breath.

Paramedics were in attendance, but all Carter could see was the large HGV that had blocked the road in front of them. He looked at Sue, and Charlie, does this not remind you of anything?"

Sue, who was stood close by said, "Yes, the stroke that Hughes, pulled on us in the City when he effectively blocked off the cross road, which stopped our surveillance, on the kids who did the drug run to Glasgow."

Both complaining at the paramedics, Peter and Philip, were reluctantly placed in the rear of the waiting ambulance. Carter walked over, and before the doors were closed, he noticed that bandages were being wrapped around their heads.

He said, "No use me asking how you both are? As it was something that we had all experienced before, now please be good boys and I'll call to see you both at the?" He looked at the paramedics, as if wishing for conformation. One replied, "The Royal sir." He closed the door and slapped the door twice as it sped off, with sirens, and lights prefiguring there way.

Carter turned he looked at Sue, and Charlie saying, "Let's go and see what awaits us on the other side of this mess." They couldn't drive so they quickly walked around the HGV. It was there that they realised that Bailey's Lane had also been closed off.

353

Whilst they walked towards the supposed drop of point, Sue's phone activated, she said, "Ford" It was Eric he said, *"SOCO and all the troops have been activated, the force helicopter has been scrambled."* Sue replied, "Eric, please do not feel bad of me, but can anyone tell us what we are fucking looking for?"

She continued, "It would seem all coms were jammed, and unless we have an independent witness with a possible number plate of the vehicle that they got away in we are truly in the shit." Eric, in a quiet voice said, *"I realise you are worrying for Carter, as I don't remember him running it passed TF."* Sue said, "No he didn't, he decided to do it under his own steam." Eric replied, *"Oh shit."*

Carter received a call, it was Penny. *"Carter where are you alright? Are you anywhere near this mess in Halewood?"*

He stupidly said, "Why?" She replied, "It's all over the Northern News, they are clearly showing what appears to be the aftermath of a staged high jacking. They are mentioning how two men smashed the windows in a vehicle and threw in what appears to be a flash bang and smoke bomb."

They then both ran and jumped into a vehicle on the far side of the lorry, and drove off." Carter said, "Why Penny, you seem to know fucking more than I do, see you later, and he closed the call.

The second call was by far the worst. He said, "Carter." Tony Frost roared, *"Carter, what the fuck is happening?"* He explained fully to the best of his ability what had taken place. Carter said, "I'm truly sorry boss, I realise it's all over the evening news."

Carter looked over to Sue, who he realised knew that it was TF that he must be talking to; he looked at her shrugged his shoulders, and continued with the call.

"Boss, it's all gone tits up, and it's my fault for trying to pull this stroke without telling you." Tony Frost in a quiet voice said, *"Carter have you forgotten that you told me about this last week telling me that the black mailers were running out of time, before Ainsworth's return to Risley."*

Carter said, "Boss, you know what happens when the shit hit's the fan? It covers us all." Frosts gruff voice said, *"Carter you tried, if it had come off and you'd caught the bastards, you'd be the hero, now for once you will have to dig yourself out of a hole, now keep me in the loop, and don't forget Wendy Fields."* The phone went dead.

Chapter One Hundred and Fifteen

Carter, Sue, and Charlie walked passed the HGV that blocked the road, and came across the remnants of his team tasked with surveillance duties. Six members of the team were receiving medical treatment from a group of paramedics.

Lloydie and Ian walked over both wiping their eyes, whilst quickly followed by a paramedic insisting they return to the ambulance for continued treatment or face A and E.

Carter said, "I'll come over and see you both, now please go and receive treatment to your eyes, although you both may feel fine. It's essential, as I do not want two DI's in my team with white sticks."

When they were both back at the ambulance, both Sue and Carter, walked across to see them. Whilst receiving treatment, both men were subjected to eye washes in an effort to eradicate the effects of the flash, and the smoke bombs.

Lloydie was the first to speak, "Guv we took up positions as requested, but the bastards just hurled their devices to either side of the road repeatedly, making sure they covered along the fencing by the dogs home, and similarly into the undergrowth to the rear of the lay-by. They may be ex forces as judging by their reactions, they knew exactly the positions that we were likely to take up."

On the occasion, Lloydie temporarily took hold of the paramedics arm holding him off. Carter was distressed to see all the redness, and potential damage all around his and the rest of the teams eyes. "Would you not be better off going to the Royal, your eyes look terrible?"

Ian said, "I thing you may be right guv, the burning in my eyes is getting worse." Carter said, "I know you'd all continue, wishing to remain at the crime scene, please leave it to SOCO. There's no if or buts about it, your eyes are essential, therefore an executive decision, ladies and gentlemen take yourselves off to A and E."

As they were led away Sue, said, "I'll be down to see you all later, take care. By the way do all your relatives know of your dilemmas?" They all said, "Yes boss."

Whilst the ambulances sped off with lights, and siren sounding, Carter and Sue, walked over to the remainder of the unhurt members of the team. Julia and Gill, gave a very succinct report to both of their senior officers.

Carter said, "It would seem that someone has the knack of anticipating our every move, it's painfully obvious that they've seem to have thought of everything."

At that very minute Carter's phone activated. "Carter" *"Sir, it's the duty Inspector in the control room, a black 4x4 has been reported abandoned close to the junction of the A5300 and were it crosses with Netherley Road the B5178. The vehicle is on the A5300 but in the scrub area on the side of the road. India 99 who are in attendance hovering overhead, have noticed what appear to be a body close to the vehicle."*

He thanked the duty Inspector, asking for SOCO to be tasked to the location. He said, *"They're on their way."* In the meantime he had not realised but somehow Charlie had managed to get his car around the road block.

He looked at Julia, Peter, Philip and Gill, "Guys can I ask that you deal with this mess, liaise with Traffic and get the road opened." They all looked at Carter, "Yes guv, see you later."

Carter and Sue, sped off with Charlie at the wheel, they made the location in a matter of minutes, carving through the evening traffic with the help of the blues and two's.

On arrival the officer with the traditional clipboard, who had his head looking towards the board was heard to say, "Could I please have your names it's a formality I know." Charlie was heard to say, "Oh shit!" Carter took a look at him, "Simmons, wake up." He looked up from his board the blood seemed to run from his face. Carter heard a very loud, "Sorry sir" As he walked on with a smiled on his face.

The three of them realised that either the air support team, or the control room Inspector had summonsed the medic's. Sue noticed they were all in attendance. Carter quickly identified the person incapacitated was, Ainsworth, but was he alive?

Walking towards the medic's Carter shouted, "Please leave him a couple of minutes longer, it will not affect him in any way." He then turned and shouted, "I need a SOCO officer over here immediately. The officer will take photographs, prior to the removal of the plastic tie wraps, as we may recover vital evidence."

All came to a halt as the officer walked over, and she knelt down and began the task. He heard Ainsworth shout, "Carter trust you to deny me medical aid." He replied, "Oh shut up your alive aren't you, now behave yourself."

Prior to the tie wraps being bagged, they were placed on a piece of white paper and photographed next to a scale rule. They were then placed in an evidence bags and sealed, another officer working on the car shouted, "Guv Do you have a minute?" Carter and Sue leaving Ainsworth in the capable hands of the medic's walked over to the SOCO officer.

The officer stood up, "Look what I found, he held up a piece of material in his gloved hand, Carter and Sue, had also put on plastic gloves. Carter took the piece of material which measured approximately, eight inches by four inches.

On close scrutiny of the evidence he noticed that the material was a black piece of heavy duty denim, with parallel stitching in the corner, looking at Sue she said, "It looks like it's been a piece of jacket or trouser pocket of sorts?"

Prior to the officer placing it in an evidence bag, he took photographs, with a scale rule next to it.

Under police guard, Ainsworth was taken to Fazakerley Hospital, lower Lane. Carter looked at Sue. "Sue would you mind following up on the team members, at the Royal, whilst Charlie takes me to follow up on Ainsworth?" Sue smiled, "I'll ask Julia to come and pick me up, and I can check on the two HGV vehicles."

Chapter One Hundred and Sixteen

Charlie eventually dropped Carter off at approximately 10.30pm, when outside of his flat realising the time... Charlie smiled, "Good luck guv, will it be a deaf and dumb meal?" He started to laugh, "See you tomorrow guv." Carter quickly thought, *'Smiling to himself cheeky sod'* as he drove off.

As he passed the door man he said, "Evening Jay, how are things?" hearing Jays reply, "Fine Mr Carter..."

He opened the door to their flat, and as he did so he saw Penny, with an anxious look on her face. Penny seemed to exhale with a big sigh, "Carter at last, I was beginning to give up all hope, both you by name only, and your team have been all over the national and local news, it would seem that Ainsworth is still a newsworthy item."

After a hug and lingering kiss from Penny, together with a glass of red wine, Carter slowly began to unwind. Whilst Penny began to rustle up a meal, he then realised that he had gone all day without so much as a morsel of food.

He looked on with crest fallen eyes as Penny went about her work; she burst out laughing, "Carter you haven't taken your eyes off me, you are like some faithful dog waiting to be fed?" Carter burst out laughing, "Pen if you put it in a bowl on the floor I'd eat from it, I'm starved."

Over his busily scratched together meal of mostly leftovers re heated which Carter, demolished with a complete look of satisfaction, he sat back and said, "My word Pen that hit the spot, it was lovely."

Over a second glass of wine and a coffee, Carter told Penny, what had taken place, and that Tony Frost, was protecting his arse. Carter yarned. "It's bed for you my lad Penny said." Carter complained setting out an argument that it would be far better for them to make love prior to sleeping.

Penny said, "Okay Carter you get into bed, I've bought some sexy underwear I'd like to show you, I'll just nip into the bathroom to get changed." Penny looked through the gap in the bathroom door, wondering if she gave it ten minutes he may be a sleep, looking at him under the duvet…

She walked from out of the bathroom in one of Carters T shirt Penny said to herself, *'This will have to do Carter, as she laughed under her breath…* She pulled back her side the duvet and slid under. His breathing was shallow and soft, looking over at him she kissed him on his forehead, turned over and fell fast asleep.

The following morning Carter woke, feeling Penny's side of the bed finding it vacant; he got up and walked through to the lounge. He was yarning as he combed his fingers through his hair. He knew that nothing took place last night, yet he said, "Well sweet cheeks, and how was that for you?"

Penny turned to face him giving him the full view of the T shirt, which clearly showed the girls pressing on the front of the material…

Carter smiled to himself... on the way to the bathroom, to prepare for work.

Chapter One Hundred and Seventeen

Carter and Charlie simultaneously entered the general office walking over to sign on duty, Carter greeting all present whilst relieving Eric of the usual mug of black coffee, smiling whilst he thanked him.

Leaving for his office he turned, "Eric, will you please ask Sue to come through, when she comes in." He paused, "And you Charlie, please."

He was sat debating should he ring Penny, realising that matters had been left in the air prior to leaving for work, whilst having this conversation with himself there was a knock on his door, he shouted, "Come in."

The door opened and both Sue and Charlie walked in, each sitting in one of the chairs around his meeting table. Looking at them both he said, "What is the situation with both Ainsworth, and the team members injured by the flash bangs, and smoke bomb devices?"

Sue replied with a smile on her face, "As you are in no doubt, all officers, after receiving treatment, at the *Royal*... have booked on duty this morning. Although none are the worse for wear, they all looked as if they'd been crying all night." Carter had a smile of total respect for them all.

As Carter was about to ask for an update on Ainsworth, his phone rang, picking it up he said, "Yes Carter." The voice on the other end on the line said without a pause, or inflection *"Morning, DS Phillips of the number one reginal crime squad, my officers together with traffic 'wooden tops' have..."*

That was as far as the caller got... for both Sue, and Charlie could see a look of utter disgust showing on his face. "Caller, I presume that the extension dialled, is that of *'Assistant Commander Carter'* Plus I said *'Yes Carter'* so whilst addressing a senior officer it's polite to commence the conversation 'Sir' or 'guv' for respect of rank. Plus never, ever, refer to your uniform colleagues in the same sentence when addressing me as 'wooden tops.'

There was a long pause then the caller said, *"Sorry Sir…*Carter again interrupted, "Now what do you want?" *"Sir, Members of my section together with traffic officers have stopped a vehicle on the M62 heading east, towards Manchester, for speeding, possibly heading for the M6 for Birmingham?"*

""We happened to be close by in an unmarked vehicle, and per chance thought of your details which had been circulated."

"We pulled in behind the traffic vehicle. I told the officers who we were. On searching the vehicle, apart from the four men, we also found two bags with a significant amount of money in them, together with flash bang devices, and smoke bomb's canisters hidden within the vehicle, all items mentioned in your circulation."

Carter with a smile on his face shouted, "Well DS Phillips, you have totally exonerated yourself of your earlier misgivings, and now you have my undivided attention."

"Now will you please excuse me whilst I put the phone on speaker? I happen to be with my deputy, DCS Sue Ford, together with my APO, DI Charlie Watson."

DS Phillips said, *"Why of course sir."* Carter looked at both Sue and Charlie, with a broad smile on his face he said, "Please continue, DS Phillips where do you have the prisoners?" Phillips replied, *"St Helens divisional HQ on Garswood Street sir."*

Still excited Carter said, "DS Phillips, I'll be sending officers to collect the prisoners, and the recovered property, I will organise for their vehicle to be collected and taken to the forensic garage for examination."

Phillips said, *"Sir, We will be waiting their arrival."* Carter thanked him and closed the call.

He still could not hide his excitement he banged his desk with a clenched fist scaring the life out of Sue and Charlie, "Officers from the *'No1 reginal crime squad'* have come across a vehicle with four up, stopped on the M62 for speeding, it was stopped by traffic officers from the *'North West Traffic group.'*

"A search of the vehicle revealed all the necessary evidence in relation to the Ainsworth case, what do you think of those potatoes?"

When Carter looked at them both, they both looked dumbfounded. Within seconds they both recovered, and became equally as excited. He suggested that they go to the conference room and pass on the information... Prior to leaving, Carter gently took hold of Sue, "Pick an eight man team, in four cars, let's have one prisoner to one car, so there is no collusion.

In the conference room Sue, made the announcement, the room irrupted into total chaos. Sue raised her arms, and the team quickly redeemed their composure.

Minutes later Sue found Carter. "All has been organised...I've also asked young DC Alex Wilson to liaise with SOCO, with the assisting of the vehicle recovery, and escorting it to the forensic garage." Carter looked at Sue, "All we have to do is wait?"

Carter took himself back to his office, and rang Penny... "Sorry Penny but it looks as if it's going to be a long one, so please don't wait up." Penny said, *"Well in that case I'll leave something out for you as I know you wouldn't stop for eats. And please do wake me up..."* He detected a lightness to her voice, as she replaced the phone.

Carter's next call was to Tony Frost. The phone was answered immediately, *"Frost"* "Sir it's Carter, just to put you in the picture. "Traffic officers stopped a vehicle for speeding on the M62. Whilst the officers were dealing with the vehicle, officers from the No1 Reginal Crime Squad, noticed the car and got a gut feeling, and DS Phillips thought about out circulation for being on the lookout etc."

Carter continued, "Members of the team are en route to St Helens police station to collect the men, the ransom money, smoke bombs, and the flash bang devices used at the ambush of Ainsworth."

Tony Frost said, *"Well Carter If I was you I'd do the bloody lottery this week because yet again you fly by the seat of your pants and it comes off, the Chief will be delighted hearing another one of your exploits, but I'll leave out the fact that it was all done without all due authority?"* He again roared with laughter as he replaced the phone.

Chapter One Hundred and Eighteen

On arrival at St Helens Ian police station Lloydie, walked through the automatic glass doors, with strips of blue plastic signage, with police in large letters. He walked over to the counter and produced his ID.

Lloydie said, "I'm DI Jim Lloyd of the, *'Major Crime Unit,'* to collect the prisoners, together with the recovered property. Jim handed over the prepared warrants, and the necessary paper work.

The duty sergeant said, "DS Phillips has asked me that on your arrival, for you all to go up to the CID office on the 1st floor." He pointed to a nearby glass door which led to some stairs. Lloydie thanked him and led off towards the door following the sign for the CID office.

After spending a half an hour with DS Phillips, the duty sergeant telephoned saying, *'That the prisoners were good to go...'*

Lloydie smiling thanked Tom Phillips personally stating that his brilliant actions had saved his bosses arse, they both burst out laughing, and he then asked him to forward his statement of evidence, for his attention at Derby Lane...

Lloydie had asked for a motor cycle escort back to Derby Lane as they didn't want to stop for no one. Outside the backdoor of the police station all was arranged. Each prisoner was handcuffed to a member of the team, and placed in the back of each vehicle. When ready they began their journey back to the office.

The traffic motorcyclist's did their revolving escort, the lead officer, stopped the traffic at the first major junction, whilst his colleague roared off to the next junction and so on, it was quite the adrenalin rush, as the drivers of the CID vehicles were at full speed, needing full concentration.

Ian Baxter was left in the office, with Eric to prepare for their return. Whilst Carter who was busily dealing with reports, and targets in relation to his team. The phone rang it was Eric inviting him to come through for sandwiches and coffee. Carter who was starving after replacing the phone left his office on the double, in the general office were Sue, Charlie, Ian, and Eric enjoying their snacks.

Half an hour later it was painfully obvious what with the noise of their claxons, and the vibrant reflections of all the blue lights which were reflecting on their office window, that their colleagues had returned.

Jim on arrival thanked the two motorcycle traffic officers inviting them both to the canteen for coffees and light refreshments on him they both thanked him but had to decline his offer as they had to return to their traffic group.

Sue was waiting in the charge office as the prisoners were presented, led in by Lloydie and his team. Sue turned to the Bridewell sergeant, as she related the circumstances of their arrest. "The offenders will be charged with Conspiracy in the abduction of Ainsworth, theft, and blackmail, when formally charged. She continued, "Sergeant there may well be additional charges in this matter,   as investigations are still continuing."

Whilst the prisoners were being booked in, fingerprinted, and their DNA taken, Sue returned to the general office, casting an eye around looking for Carter.

She looked at Eric, "Is he in his office?" Eric nodded, "Yes, knowing by his body language, it would seem he needed some privacy." Sue thought for a while, "Eric will you contact Wendy Field for me, he just nodded.

In his office Carter was looking at the phone, *'Carter would it be possible for you to slip home for a minute?* Carter agreed and was leaving for the general office to sign out.

Chapter One Hundred and Nineteen

The journey was in silence as Charlie drove Carter to his flat. On arrival Carter looked at Charlie, "Will you please wait, as I don't see this taking long?" Charlie just smiled as he walked towards his flat entrance.

He smiled at the doorman as he walked to his ground floor flat. On entering he met Penny in the lounge, sat on one of the armchairs. On seeing Carter she immediately stood up and walked over to him kissing him on his cheek.

Alarm bells immediately sounded in his head. "Penny what is the problem?" She looked at Carter, "Can I get you a coffee?" He replied, "No thanks Pen, just tell me what the matter is?"

He noticed that she became rather sheepish, Carter I feel terrible about this but I've been head hunted by the head of the criminal Psychology department at Cambridge University, offering me a chair.

Before could say anything else Carter said, "An offer you can't resist?" Penny replied, "Well, I could always say 'No'" Carter replied, "Don't be so bloody supercilious. I'm off back to the office, I'll be late. Will know your decision when I return home to the flat, you'll be either here, or gone." He turned and walked out.

All he could hear from Penny was, "But Carter." He carried on walking.

Outside he re-joined Charlie, who could clearly see he was in a temper and thought better of asking, *'Is everything alright guv'* Carter buckled up and with his chin pointed suggesting that they just drive, Charlie started to head towards the office, Carter just barked, "No, Riverside Drive, please Charlie.

On arrival Charlie pulled into one of the small car parking areas. He looked at Charlie, "It's here were I escape to when I have problems over a particular case, or team matters."

"Do you mind if I leave you for a while I have some

thinking to do?" "No guv." Charlie replied, "Help yourself. Carter smiled as he got out of the car, whilst he pulled up the collar of his coat against the stiff breeze, and he was off.

He pushed his hands deep in his coat pockets and began his know walk along the front, and again he could hear the rattling of the metal riggings slapping against all the yacht's masts in unison.

The more serious of matters came flooding back of him thinking he was waving to an APO, who was acting as a duty surveillance officer.

When in fact no one knew where he had gone, not realising that he was waving at a serial killer who had followed him, unbeknown to him, being the very man he was after. It caused such a shit storm when it was realised that he had left for his walk without his firearm, phone, or emergency bleep. He returned to a party being held in the Grafton, to be confronted by Eric, who pointed out the panic he had caused.

He returned to the subject at hand, all about Penny's job offer. Yet again his life was in turmoil. Carter suddenly decided that if Penny was gone, he'd call Tony Frost in the morning and put in his 'ticket.' He had known all along that the team were in good hands, with Sue at the helm...

He felt it was time she should take the load on her shoulder, and that would never happen if he remained, time to cut the umbilical cord. He nodded his head up and down realising all seemed very clear to him. He quickened his pace back to Charlie...

Back at the office, Carter signed back in. Eric offered him a cup of coffee. Eric looking at Carter said, "Guv you have a face like a farmer's arse, where have you been." All in the office burst out laughing, including Carter, but they all knew it was only Eric who get away with such a comment. He smiled at Eric, "Just thinking guv." He smiled at Eric as he left for his office, taking his coffee with him.

When in his office he placed his coffee down onto his desk. He then sat in his comfortable office chair staring down at his phone. He eventually picked up the handset and punched in Helens parent's number. The phone was answered in seconds by Diane, his ex-mother in law. "Hello" He said, "Diane it's Carter, in an excited voice he heard her say, "Martin, it's Carter, them both being Helen, his wife's parents.

Martin said, "Hello Carter how on earth are you?" Carter said "I'm fine thanks, if things plan out how I expect them to, could you stand a visitor?" He could hear an excitement in Martins voice, who he must have whispered to Diane, "He wants to come and see us." He could hear Diane shout, "He needs no permission." Carter laughed to himself.

He said, "Martin, it may not be for the odd week-end, I want to rent one of your cottages, but it must be on a business footing, and I mean it." He heard Martin say, "Yes, yes, yes Carter, please don't talk stupid, just tell us when, and we'll be ready." Carter replied, "It could be in a months' time?"

Martin said "When you're ready son." And the phone went dead. He had no sooner put the phone down when there was a knock on his office door, he shouted "Come in" He looked up to see Eric stood in the doorway carrying two mugs of coffee.

He walked in and took a seat around the meeting table whilst he handed Carter his mug of coffee. "He looked at Carter, "Charlie happened to mention you asked him to take you to, Riverside Drive, now we all know it's somewhere you go to when you have a problem. So what's up son?"

Carter knew that of all people, Eric was the only one he could trust with his problem…He mentioned to Eric about the conversation he'd just had with Penny.

During their coffee's and conversations, Carter eventually said, "Eric could you cover for me, I know Sue will have all matters under control, will you send Charlie through, and then putting me *off duty* via my phone call?"

Eric stood up, and as he walked towards the office door he turned, "I do hope all is well, you will find her in the flat as usual." Minutes later Charlie came through, he smiled, "Where to guv?" "Will you just run me home…?"

Chapter One Hundred and Twenty

On arrival he thanked Charlie saying, "See you in the morning Charlie?" As he got out of the car setting off towards his flat entrance with a certain amount of trepidation…

Carter walked into his flat, and for a moment thought all seemed well except there was no sign of Penny. He walked into their bedroom and it was only when he opened her wardrobe when he immediately realised she was gone. For the cupboard was bare. Walking into the bathroom he realised that all of her shower preparations were also gone.

Walking into the lounge his eyes fell upon a white envelope, propped against a Wedgewood figure, with his name on the front. He walked into the kitchen taking out a beer from the fridge he, with a heavy heart he walked back into the lounge…

He picked up the envelope; he then sat in one of the comfortable armchairs. He opened his beer took a sip, and then opened the inevitable harbinger of bad news…

Opening the envelope he immediately saw the beautiful handwriting of Penny…

Dearest Carter,

You must have realised by opening this note the decision that I've taken, I can only think the hammer blow it must be. The matter that concerns me is way I have handled this matter, just asking you to come home to hit you with my news.

I've spent years in academia, having played second fiddle to numerous heads of departments. Of which my recent one being your good friend Sam, at The John Moore's University. I have sat spending several hours talking with her on receipt of my recent news.

Our conversations were in two categories; One, the academic elevation of my career to a post in one of the most prestigious Universities in the country and Two, our relationship. Sam, being a very loyal friend, mentioned she would refrain from telling Lloydie, of my decision. Holding off until you choose to tell folks?

Now Carter it would be very remiss of me if I don't mention about our relationship over the last four years. I thoroughly enjoyed both our domestic bliss, and a truly wonderful personal life. That aspect of our situation, I will never, ever experience the levels of eroticism we both shared, you have formed me into a total woman.

Carter there is nothing more I can say, but I'm so sorry.

All my love,
Penny xxx

Carter sat back letting Penny's note fall to the floor. He finished his beer and raided the fridge of another. He took out his mobile phone and contacted his favourite curry shop, asking for his usual order to be delivered to his flat…

Chapter One Hundred and Twenty One

Carter awoke the next morning having, endured about three hours sleep. He tossed and turned, unable to get Penny's goodbye note out of his head. But Carter's mind eventually submitted, and he drifted off to sleep.

The following morning after his lack lustre night's sleep, he got out of bed and went through to the bathroom for his usual shave, and shower. After dressing he made himself a coffee, and sat at the breakfast counter to drink it. It was there that like a bolt of lightning bolt he decided on his plan of action.

Carter, feeling that much better for his decision walked over to where Charlie was waiting; he smiled at Charlie and got into the car. Charlie said, "Where to guv?" Carter replied, "The office of course."

He walked into the general to be met by a chorus of, "Morning guv." He signed on duty and went and sat next to Eric, where he had his second cup of coffee of the day. Carter looked at team member whilst they signed on duty saying, "Good morning one and all."

Whilst he sat at Eric's desk he found a piece of scrap paper. He picked up a pen and discreetly wrote... *'Will you please try to get me an appointment with TF at his earliest.'* After Eric scrutinised the note, Carter screwed up the piece of paper putting it in a nearby paper bin.

Carter continued with his coffee, but could not help seeing the look of sheer concern on Eric's face, when he finished his coffee he got up to walk through to his office in the doorway he turned, Eric, "When Sue comes in will you send her through to my office." He just nodded.

It was ten minutes later when there was a knock on his door. He shouted, "Come in." Sue entered and sat on one of the chairs. She looked at Carter with a smile on her face. "Before you bollock me for being late, I've been to see the prisoner's. The condemned men have each had their hearty breakfasts..."

As they were talking, there was a second knock on his door. Sue got up to open it, and saw Eric with a piece of paper in his hand. Her blood started to race, because it was always the formula, *Eric+ piece paper=Potential case?* He handed it to Carter, who opened it and read, *'TF will see you at 10.30am, and Sam wont's a word?'* He smiled thanks Eric.

He looked at them, "Now be off with you both." Looking at Sue he said, "Can you hold the fort for a couple of hours?" Sue smiled, "Why yes guv, I have plenty to do…"

After they had both left, Carter set about formulating his decision on tendering his resignation. He opened up his computer, and after searching the list of blank forms he clicked on the form '104' the standard *'Discipline form'* used for such things as, holiday requests, but in Carters case, his resignation.

On completion he printed it off, signed it, and placing it in an envelope, that he'd taken out of his desk draw, he then placed it carefully into the inside pocket of his jacket.

On completion he telephoned Sam, she answered it on the second ring he immediately recognised her beautiful American accent. *"Oh! Carter, what on earth can I say? You must realise that Penny is a brilliant criminal psychologist. As you must also realise, she has been my deputy for a number of years, and her only progression in this department and University, is for me to leave, and that I'm very sorry Carter is not for the foreseeable future."*

"Carter I've not even mentioned this to Lloydie, for I see it as your business, to deal with this, when and how you want? But Carter please do not bottle it up, I'm here should you need to talk about it?"

After a slight pause He said, "Well Sam, after this conversation I off to see Tony Frost, to hand him my resignation." Sam cried, *"Carter what on earth are you talking about? You have dealt with matters far worse than this in your life. The loss of Helen and the two children is a matter that would knock most men for six, yet you came through. So why on earth are you taking this course of action, you are the essential part of your team, the team revolves around you. I see you getting over this in time. Although upsetting, it's not worth taking such an action?"*

Carter said, "Sam, you do realise that Frost and Co, asked me to come back to assist Sue, with this present Ainsworth case, although at the beginning it was just the slaughter of eight young girls in the back of a lorry on the docks. But never the less I was asked to come back and assist…"

"As matters seem to be under control, Sue Ford has turned out to be a very capable officer, as my number two. I feel that she now needs to embrace the post as head of the MCU without me leaning over her shoulders.

"With the support of, Lloydie and Ian, again two fine, and very capable officers, I feel all is in good hands. After the initial shock normal service will resume."

"Now Sam, I must love you and leave you as I'm due to see TF shortly."

Sam's voice quivered, *"Carter it has indeed been a privilege, although we first met when you asked advice on that terrible serial killer, John Gainsford responsible for some thirteen deaths, of the people who had such a profound effect on his childhood."*

"You were responsible in my meeting, and falling in love with Lloydie, for which I will always be so very grateful. Thank you Carter." And she replaced the phone.

Carter sat back for a minute whilst all the events of their friendship came flooding back. The most important of which was her considerable help in the dealing with Helen and the children's murder.

He got up and walked to the general office to sign out, as he did he pondered over his next meeting, that being with the TF and the fallout from it.

After signing out he said to Eric, "Will you please, when you next see Charlie, mention that I've just popped out to deal with something personal on my own."

Eric looked at him, as they were alone in the office he

said, "Carter are you sure of this next move? As if you go should I go, as I only came back because you asked me too?"

Carter looked at him, "Eric if what I do this day is accepted, and then no doubt Sue will need all the initial assistance she can call upon, especially from one such as you, now let that be the end of it…for you never know?"

He could hear Eric's raw of laughter as he walked down the corridor.

Chapter One Hundred and Twenty Two

Carter stepped from the lift on the appropriate floor, on leaving, the first person he saw was Jane, Tony Frost's secretary, sat at her desk busily typing. On hearing the ding indicating the arrival of the lift, she looked to see Carter walking towards her.

He knew that he'd have to walk the plank of all her sexual innuendoes. She smiled, "Well Carter don't you look smart, I could eat you all up."

He said to her, "Jane, are you no respecter of rank?" He could see the wicked look in her eyes, she laughed, "Why Carter, the bigger the rank the better, why don't you let me sit on your knee, and let's talk about the biggest thing that turns up?" Jane burst out laughing.

Jane picked it up the phone, and seconds later said, "Darling you can go in." Smiling Carter walked over to the office door, knocked and entered.

Tony Frost looked up from something he was reading, "Why Carter come in and have a seat, is all well with the Ainsworth case?"

He replied, "Yes sir, we have all the offenders, they were nearly caught in the act, but were later detained by a sharp eyed DS Phillips, of the reginal crime squad, who happened to be passing a car that had been stopped by traffic officers."

"Remembering our circulation, he happened to notice 5 men in the car, and his gut instinct took over, and he, together with the traffic detail hit the jackpot."

The men were caught with the ransom money, still intact, remaining blast bombs, and smoke bombs, still in their vehicle, used to cause absolute havoc at the scene. They were hauled to St Helens police station, from where DS Phillips, contacted the office, and we went over to collect them, bringing them back to Derby Lane. The vehicle went off to be forensically searched by SOCO."

"Ainsworth is being returned to Risley, awaiting his

trial at the Crown Court." Tony frost said, "Great work Carter, by both you, and your team as usual, what on earth do you want with me?"

His hand went into his inside jacket pocket were he removed the envelope, and handed it to him. Tony Frost said, "What on earth is this, Carter?" With a stern face he said, "Sir it's my resignation."

Tony Frost stood up, and with both hands placed on his desk he shouted, "You are fucking joking?" He was so loud that Jane walked in, "Sir, is everything alright?" He barked, "No, I need drinks, and coffee's all round, and include yourself, as I may need you to keep matters under control?"

He sat down and minutes later Jane entered the office with the tray of coffees. After handing them round, she went and poured two large Scotches, and after handing them round, and then went and sat down at a nearby table with her own coffee, and scotch.

Tony Frost looked at her, "We have a problem? My best ever detective has only just handed in his resignation. If I accept it how the hell do I tell the chief?" When Carter turned looking over at Jane, he could tell that she was also shocked, on hearing the news.

She quickly gathered her thoughts. "Sir if you accept Carter's resignation not only will you need to tell the chief, but you will have to contact, Wendy Field, (PR secretary on behalf of the force) And of course appoint Carters replacement ASAP for the best continuity."

Carter thought my word Jane you do have a business brain in that head of yours, and it's not just used for sexual fantasy when I come to see the boss.

Tony Frost looked at Carter, "Well who do you think?" He continued, "I see no reason why DCS Sue Ford, should not take over the team?" He looked at Tony Frost, "Well at least Sue will have a thorough knowledge of the team, she is more than capable, and she just doesn't need to have me breathing down her neck."

Tony Frost looked at Jane, "Right book three

appointments in my diary for tomorrow, but await confirmation from me." Jane got up and left the office.

Carter came out of Tony Frost's office after convincing him that he still wished to resign and the reasons for it. He insisted that it was nothing to do with his present environment, but insisted that he was asked to return to assist Sue and the team over the heinous events that had taken place.

He noticed that Jane at her desk seemed upset, she looked up, "Please say he didn't except your resignation?" He smiled down at her, "I'm afraid so." Jane said, "Carter, what on earth am I going to do for my sexual fantasies when you come to see the boss? Do you realis the many times I've undressed you in my, mind and my dreams at night."

Looking at him she said, "Hey ho! You do realise that Mike and I have separated, I'm free, for dinner and afters."

As Carter entered the lift he said, "Well perhaps you can dream of tomorrow?" And burst out laughing.

He returned to the office and signed, '*back in*' whilst he did Eric produced a black coffee. Carter sat next to him and looking at him he fidgeted on his chair. When other team members on entering the office greeted Carter and left, the office was empty except for them both.

Carter explained the extent of their meeting, and that matters will be made official tomorrow. Eric looked at him, "Is it one month, or immediately?" Carter smiled saying, "Eric, it will be made official tomorrow you will get a call from TF's office asking for Sue and I to attend. Wendy Field, will also be there."

"Eric said, "Before the shit hits the fan. May I say it's been an honour to have worked with both as a sprog, and now as my senior officer? Both men shook hands, Carter said, "Eric never a truer word said." He then turned and left for his office.

Chapter One Hundred and Twenty Three

At 9.30am all three arrived at Tony Frost's office. Carter and Sue were both driven there by Charlie. Who, together with Sue pestered Carter about it all the way to HQ? He smiled, "Let's wait and see…"

Outside of his office Carter, Sue and Charlie, were met by Wendy Field, before she could say anything, Jane said, "You may all go in." As they all settled down, Jane came in with a tray of coffees.

Tony Frost looked out from behind his desk, "Well I can't sugar coat this, Deputy Commander Carter has tendered his resignation, his main reason being, that he was asked to come back to assist in the *Ainsworth case,* which has been successfully accomplished, now all offenders are awaiting sentence when listed in the crown Court."

He also feels that so much has happened in his personal life, together with the matters that have affected his health, with the attacks which hospitalised him on so many occasions…

Both Wendy and Sue stared at Carter with their mouths open. Tony Frost said, "DCS Ford, Carter has recommended that you take over the MCU, for which I've endorsed it, recommending my decision to the Chief Constable."

"Ms Field, do we need to release this matter to the *press,* if so will you leak it to the crime reporter of the, Liverpool Echo a couple of hours before the nationals?"

Carter looked at Sue, "DCS Ford may I see you outside for a minute?" Sue got up and joined Carter who led her to an empty office. "Sue I'm sorry to drop this on your toes, but I know you can do it, and you'll even be a lot more proficient without me looking over your shoulders. Plus you'll have the support of a great team. Eric knows of my plans."

On arrival at his flat all three stood at the rear of

Charlie's car. Carter went over to Charlie, he looked at him and was about to speak when Charlie interrupted him... "No guv, you needn't say anything, all is good." He turned and got back into the car.

Sue looked at Carter she walked over to him and gave him a hug, and a kiss on his cheek. She stood back, "Are you coming to tell the team?" He said, "No Sue, "I'll leave that with you, call it your first major task." He continued, "I've left my office in ship order."

All I ask is for you, or Charlie is to run by my flat, tomorrow and collect my uniform and firearm."

Sue looked at him with tears in eyes. "Yes, of course boss..."

She walked over to him and kissed him passionately on the lips. "You do realise that I've loved you from afar, from day one. But I had to make a decision, you were my boss. And where I lost out in love, I've more than profited by my career. But, and it's a big but, I'd have given it all up in a heartbeat." She turned and left.

Later that day Carter, telephoned, Diane and Martin Sinclair, "Alright if I come through tomorrow...?"

CPSIA information can be obtained
at www.ICGtesting.com
Printed in the USA
BVHW030839060719
PP10083500001B/1/P

9 781789 555608